FAIRYTALE
CHRISTMAS

LIZ FIELDING
CHRISTINE FLYNN
JENNIFER FAYE

MILLS &
BOON

First Published in Great Britain 2017
By Mills & Boon, an imprint of HarperCollins*Publishers*
1 London Bridge Street, London, SE1 9GF

FAIRYTALE CHRISTMAS © 2017 Harlequin Books S.A.

Mistletoe and the Lost Stiletto © 2010 Liz Fielding
Her Holiday Prince Charming © 2013 Christine Flynn
A Princess by Christmas © 2014 Jennifer F. Stroka

ISBN: 978-0-263-93175-4

24-1117

MISTLETOE AND THE LOST STILETTO

LIZ FIELDING

Liz Fielding was born with itchy feet. She made it to Zambia before her twenty-first birthday and, gathering her own special hero and a couple of children on the way, lived in Botswana, Kenya and Bahrain – with pauses for sightseeing pretty much everywhere in between. She now lives in the west of England, close to the Regency grandeur of Bath and the ancient mystery of Stonehenge, and these days leaves her pen to do the travelling.

For news of upcoming books visit Liz's website: lizfielding.com

PROLOGUE

Wednesday, 1st December
Appointments for Miss Lucy Bright
09:30 Beauty salon
12:30 Lunch with Marji Hayes, editor, Celebrity
magazine
14:30 Celebrity photoshoot (with my mum!)
16:00 Serafina March, Wedding Designer.
20:00 Dinner at Ritz, guest list attached

Lucy Bright diary entry, 1st December:
Wish I could be at press conference for the unveil-
ing of the Lucy B fashion chain this afternoon but,
according to Rupert's dragon of a secretary, it's for
the financial rather than the gossip pages. Which
put me in my place. I can't even appeal to Rupert
since he won't be flying in until lunchtime. And how
come he gets out of the meeting with the über scary
Serafina March? It's his wedding, too.

Stupid question. He's too busy for 'girl' stuff. He's
been out of the country more than he's been in it for
the last month and at this rate I'll be walking up the
aisle on my own.

The celebration dinner tonight is, as I'm constantly
reminded, my moment in the sun and, obviously,

a morning being pampered, a luscious lunch with the editor of Celebrity *and then a meeting with the wedding designer to the stars meets all the criteria for the fairy tale. I am Lucy Bright. It's my name— Lucy B—that's going to be above the doors of a hundred High Street shops come the spring. So why do I feel as if I'm on the outside looking in?*

RUBBING at the base of her engagement ring with her thumb so that the huge diamond sparkled, Lucy Bright made an effort to shake off the feeling that things weren't quite as fairy tale as media coverage of her romance with Rupert Henshawe would suggest. Determined to shake off the feeling, she logged into Twitter to update her followers on what she'd be doing for the rest of the day.

Morning, tweeps! Off to have the curls flattened. Again. I swear everyone hides when I turn up at the salon! #Cinderella
LucyB, Wed 1 Dec 08:22

Hair straight for the moment. Fab lunch at Ivy. Lots of celebs. Off to meet Mum for photoshoot. Will update blog later. #Cinderella
LucyB, Wed 1 Dec 14:16

PS Don't miss Rupert's Lucy B press launch live on website feed today, tweeps! 4 p.m. It's going to be so exciting. #Cinderella.
LucyB, Wed 1 Dec 14:18

'Is that the time?' Lucy squeaked.

'We are running a little late, miss.' Rupert's chauffeur

held the umbrella aloft as she ran from the photoshoot to the car.

Little was an understatement. The photographer had been relentless in pursuit of the perfect photograph and she had less than twenty minutes to make the meeting with the wedding planner—sorry, make that wedding *designer*—to discuss a theme for the big day. While it was acceptable, even necessary, for the bride to arrive late at her wedding, Serafina March did not allow the same latitude where appointments with her were concerned.

'There's no time to go home for the wedding file, Gordon. We'll have to stop by the office.' Rupert's deadly efficient PA maintained a duplicate in the office. She could borrow that.

CHAPTER ONE

'LIAR!'

The only sound in the room was the clatter of motor drives as tycoon, Rupert—just-call-me-Prince-Charming—Henshawe's press conference was hijacked by his fiancée, Lucy—I-feel-like-Cinderella—Bright as she tugged off her engagement ring and flung it at him.

'Cheat!'

Every lens in the room zoomed in on the bright splash of blood where the huge diamond found its mark on Henshawe's cheek.

The gathered press pack—city newsmen, financial pundits, television news teams—held their collective breath.

They'd been summoned to a full dress press conference by the Henshawe Corporation. Whatever Henshawe did was news. Good news if you were one of his shareholders. Bad news if you happened to be on the receiving end of one of his corporate raids. At least until recently.

The news now was all about how he'd changed. How, having met his 'Cinderella', he had been redeemed by love and was no longer Mr Nasty, but had been transformed into Prince Charming.

Boring.

This was much more like it.

'Why?' Lucy demanded, ignoring the cameras, the

mikes, dangled overhead, pushed towards her face. The larger than life-sized images of herself, wearing her own custom-made originals of the Lucy B fashions, being flashed across a screen. All she could see was the man on the podium. 'Why did you do it?'

Stupid question. It was all there in the file she'd found. The one she was never meant to see. All laid out in black and white.

'Lucy! Darling…' Rupert's voice was deceptively soft as, using the power of the microphone in front of him, he drowned out her demand to know *why her?* 'These are busy people and they've got deadlines to meet. They've come to listen to the plans I've been making, *we've* been making, for the future of the company,' he stressed. 'Not a domestic tiff.'

His smile was tender, all concern for her. It was familiar, reassuring and even now it would be so easy to be sucked in…

'I don't know what's upset you but it's obvious that you're tired. Let Gordon take you home and we'll talk about it later, hmm?'

She had to fight the almost hypnotic softness of his voice. Her own weakness. Her longing for the fairy tale that had overtaken her life, transformed her into a celebrity, to be true.

She had a Lucy B fan page on Facebook, half a million people following her every word on Twitter. She was a modern day Cinderella, whisked from the hearth to a palace, her rags replaced with silken gowns. But Prince Charming's 'bride ball' had been a palace-generated crowd-pleaser, too. There was nothing like a royal wedding to keep the masses happy.

It was exactly the kind of stunt to appeal to some super-smart PR woman with a name to make for herself.

'Talk!' she hurled back as someone obligingly stuck a microphone in front of her, giving her equal voice power. 'I don't want to talk to you, Rupert Henshawe! I never even want to see you again.' She held up the file for him to see. So that he would know that there was no point in denying it. 'I know what you've done. I know *everything!*'

Even as the words left her mouth, Lucy sensed the mood in the room change. No one was looking at the podium now. Or Rupert. She'd stolen his limelight. She'd stormed into this plush hotel, her head exploding with the discovery that her new and exciting life, their engagement, the whole shooting match, was nothing more than a brilliantly executed marketing plan. The focus was now on her as she put an end to a sham smoke-and-mirrors engagement that was as false as his 'new man' change of heart.

Rupert Henshawe had no heart.

But, as the attention of the room shifted to her, it belatedly occurred to Lucy that this might not have been her best move.

In the months following her whirlwind romance with her billionaire boss she had become used to the press, but this was different. Until now she'd been supported every step of the way, whether the interviews had been personal or about her new role as the face, and name, on his re-branded chain of fashion stores.

When she'd gate-crashed this press conference, she hadn't had a thought in her but to confront the man who had so shamelessly used her.

Now the focus point of every lens, every eye in the room, she suddenly felt alone, vulnerable and all she wanted to do was escape. Escape from the lies, the cameras, the microphones. Disappear. But, as she stepped back, attempting to distance herself from Rupert, from everyone, she stumbled over someone's foot.

She put out a hand to stop herself from falling, grabbing at someone's lapel. There was the ominous sound of cloth ripping and, as she turned, instinctively, to apologise, she discovered that her retreat was blocked by a wall of bodies.

And the man whose lapel she was clinging to was now hanging onto her, pulling her towards him, shouting something into her ear as she was jostled, pushed by other newsmen trying to get closer, photographers shouting to attract her attention.

She forgot all about apologising, instead yanking her arm free. Someone tried to grab the file she was carrying. She used it to beat him off, swinging the tote bag she was carrying to clear a space, provoking a blinding series of flashes as the photographers caught the action.

Another hand made a grab for her in the scrum, catching the back of her coat. One of the buttons flew off and she nearly went down again, but the sight of two of Rupert's bodyguards elbowing aside journalists and cameramen alike as they made their way towards her sent a shot of adrenalin surging through her veins.

Until now she'd only seen the gentle side of Rupert Henshawe, had believed that he was truly her Prince Charming. But she was carrying proof of just how ruthless the man could be in pursuit of his ends and he wasn't going to let her leave with that.

Of course they would make it look as if they were rescuing her from the press scrum, but denouncing him in public, on camera, had put her on the other side.

She'd seen his eyes, the truth behind the soft words, the smile, and she knew that he'd do whatever it took to keep her quiet.

Swinging her tote again in an attempt to batter her way through the enclosing wall of bodies, she managed to make a little headway but then someone grabbed her wrist, a camera lens caught her a sharp blow on the temple and, head spinning, she staggered back.

There was a yelp loud enough to be heard over the bedlam as her stiletto heel encountered something soft and yielding.

As the man behind her backed off, swearing creatively, an apology was the furthest thing from her mind. A gap opened up and she didn't hesitate. She dived through it.

Christmas.

'Twas the season to make money.

Nathaniel Hart paused at the brushed stainless steel rail of the department store founded two hundred years earlier by another Nathaniel Hart, looking back down into the swirling mayhem of spend, spend, spend.

It was a scene being replicated in Hastings & Hart stores in major cities throughout the country as money was poured out on those small luxury items that made such easy and portable gifts. Scent, jewellery, silk scarves, all perfectly placed on the ground floor to be within easy reach for the desperate shop-and-run male.

Women, fortunately, were prepared to put real effort into shopping. They thronged the glass escalators that rose into the atrium as if ascending to the sky. An architectural illusion created by light, glass, mirrors.

He knew it was an illusion because he'd created it, just as he knew it to be a cage. One he was trapped inside.

Lucy's shoulder hurt where she'd charged the emergency exit, setting off a barrage of alarms that lent wind to her heels as she raced down the narrow, darkening streets behind the hotel.

She had no idea where she was heading, only that there

were men on her heels, all of them wanting her, all of them with their own agendas. But she was done with being used.

'Aaargh!' She let out a wail of fury as her heel caught and snapped in a grating, bringing her up with a painful jerk. Someone yelled behind her, closing fast, and she paused only long enough to kick her foot free of the grating, leaving the shoe behind, and race on, casting around desperately for a cruising cab. But there was never one when you were desperate!

Idiot, idiot, idiot...

The words hammered in her head in time to the jarring of her feet on the freezing wet pavement as she ran, dot-and-carry-one lopsidedly on one heel.

She'd just made the biggest mistake of her life. Make that the second biggest. She'd made the first when she'd fallen into the fairy tale trap.

In retrospect, she could see that calling her erstwhile Prince Charming a liar and cheat in front of the nation's assembled press pack had not been her brightest move. But what was a girl to do when her magic castle-in-the-air had just turned into one of those blow-up bouncy things they had at kids' parties?

Stop and think?

Stand back, line up her allies before firing her ammunition from a safe distance? Hardly the action of the girl Rupert had proclaimed to love for her spontaneity, her passion.

That was the difference between them.

The woman who'd appeared on the cover of *Celebrity* wasn't some figment of a PR man's imagination. She was real. Capable of feeling not just joy but pain. Which was why she'd leapt in with both feet, puncturing the fake castle with the four-inch heels of her Louboutins, letting out the hot air and bringing it down around her.

Idiot was right but who, having just discovered that she was the victim of the most cynical, manipulative, emotional fraud imaginable, would be thinking *rationally?*

As for allies, there was no one she could turn to. The press had already bought everyone who'd known her since she was a baby—anyone who had a photograph or a story to tell. Every moment of her life was now public property and what they didn't know they'd made up.

And Rupert owned the rest.

All those people who had fawned over her, pretended to be her friend, there wasn't one she could trust or be sure was genuine rather than someone on his PR company's payroll.

As for her mother...

She had no one and, run as hard as she might, nowhere to go. Her legs were buckling beneath her, lungs straining as she headed instinctively for the sparkle of Christmas lights and crowds of shoppers in which to lose herself, but she couldn't stop.

In moments her pursuers would be on her and she didn't need the dropping temperature, the huge white flakes that had begun to swirl from a leaden sky, to send a shiver up her spine. Then, as she rounded a corner seeking the safety of the crowds of Christmas shoppers, she saw the soaring asymmetrical glass pyramid of Hastings & Hart lighting up the winter gloom like a beacon.

She'd been in the store just the day before on a mission from Rupert to choose luscious Christmas gifts for his staff. Giving the gossip mag photographers who followed her everywhere their photo opportunities. It was all there in the files.

The plan to keep her fully occupied. Too busy to think.

The store seemed to mock her now and yet inside were nine warm and welcoming floors, each offering a hundred places to hide. Within its walls she would be off the street, safe for a while, and she flew across the street, dodging through the snarled-up traffic, heading towards the main entrance, slithering to a halt as she saw the doorman guarding the entrance.

Only yesterday he'd tipped his top hat to her in deference to her chauffeur-driven status.

He wouldn't be so impressed by her arrival today but, dishevelled and limping, he would certainly remember her and, pulling her coat tidily around her and shouldering her bag, she teetered precariously on her bare toe as she slowed down to saunter past him, doing her best to look as if she was out for a little shopping.

'You'll find footwear on the ground floor, ma'am,' he said, face absolutely straight, as he opened the door. And tipped his hat.

Scanning the ground floor from his bird's-eye view, Nat's attention was caught by two burly men in dark suits who'd paused in the entrance. They were looking about them, but not in the baffled, slightly desperate way of men trying to decide what gift would make their Christmas a memorable one.

Men didn't shop in pairs and he could tell at a glance that these two weren't here to pick out scents for the women in their life.

He'd seen the type often enough to recognise them as either close protection officers or bodyguards.

The doorman, well used to welcoming anyone from a royal to a pop star, would have alerted the store's security staff to the arrival of a celebrity, but curiosity held him for the moment, interested to see who would follow them through the doors.

No one.

At least no one requiring a bodyguard, just the usual stream of visitors to the store, excited or harassed, who broke around the pair and joined the throng in the main hall.

Frowning now, he remained where he was, watching as the two men exchanged a word, then split up and began to work their way around the glittering counters, eyes everywhere, clearly looking for someone.

Make that a charge who had given her bodyguards the slip.

In the main hall, mobbed in the run-up to Christmas as shoppers desperately tried to tick names off their gift lists and stocked up on exotic, once-a-year luxuries, Lucy had hoped that no one would notice her. That once she was inside the store she'd be safe.

She'd been fooling herself.

She did her best to style it out, but she hadn't fooled the doorman and several people turned to look as she tried—and failed—to keep herself on an even keel. And then looked again, trying to think where they'd seen her before.

The answer was everywhere.

Rupert was *Celebrity* magazine's new best friend and his and her—mostly her—faces had been plastered over it for weeks. Their romance was news and cameras had followed her every move.

Everything she'd done, everywhere she'd been was a story and, as she tried to ease through the crowd, eyes down, she knew she was being stared at.

Then, from somewhere at the bottom of her bag, her phone began to belt out her *I'm In Love With a Wonderful Guy* ringtone.

Could anything be any less appropriate?

Or loud.

She might as well put a great big sign over her head, lit up and flashing 'Dumb blonde here!'

Hampered by the file, she hunted for the wretched thing but, by the time she'd dug it out of the bottom of the bag, it had gone to voicemail. Not for the first time.

There had been half a dozen missed calls while she'd been making her escape and, as she looked at it, it beeped at her, warning that she now had a text, adding to her sense of being hunted.

She had to get off the ground floor and out of sight— now—and, giving up on the attempt to look casual, she kicked off her remaining shoe—after all, if she was four inches shorter she'd be less noticeable—and stuffed it, along with the file, in her bag.

As far as she could recall, the nearest powder room was on the third floor. If she made that without being discovered, she could hole up there for a while, lock herself in a cubicle and think. Something she should have done before barging into that press conference.

Avoiding the glass lifts and escalators—her red coat was too bright, too noticeable and the people following her had been close enough, smart enough to have figured out where she'd gone to earth—she hurried towards the stairs.

It was a good plan. The only problem with it was that by the time she'd reached the first floor she had a stitch in her side, her legs felt like jelly and her head was swimming from the crack on the temple.

For a moment she bent double as she tried to ease the pain.

'Are you all right?' A sweet lady was looking at her with concern.

'Fine,' she lied. 'Just a stitch.' But the minute the woman was out of sight she slithered behind a floor-to-ceiling arrangement of silver and white snowflakes that had been constructed in the corner where the stairs turned. Safely out of sight, she sank down onto the floor and used her free hand to massage her ankles, which were aching from the strain. She pulled a face as she saw the state of her foot. Her shredded tights. But there was nothing she could do about that now.

Instead, she leaned back against the wall to catch her breath, regarding the state-of-the-art all-singing, all-dancing phone that had so quickly become a part of her new life with uncertainty.

It held all her contacts, appointments. She dictated her thoughts into it. Her private diary. The elation, the disbelief, the occasional doubt. And it was her connection to a world that seemed endlessly fascinated by her.

Her Facebook page, the YouTube videos, her Twitter account.

Rupert's PR people hadn't been happy when they'd discovered that she'd signed up to Twitter all by herself. Actually, it had been her hairdresser who'd told her that she was being tweeted about and showed her how to set up her own account while waiting for her highlights to take.

That had been the first warning that she wasn't supposed to have a mind of her own, but keep to the script.

Once they'd realised how well it was working, though, they'd encouraged her to tweet her every thought, every action, using the Cinderella hashtag, to her hundreds of thousands of followers. Keep them up to date with her transformation from Cinderella into Rupert's fairy tale princess.

Innocently selling the illusion. Doing their dirty work for them.

But it was a two-way thing.

Right now her in-box was filling up with messages from followers who had watched the web feed, seen the ruckus and, despite everything, she smiled as she read them.

@LucyB Nice bag work, Cinders! What's occurring? #Cinderella
WelshWitch, [+] Wed 1 Dec 16:08

*@LucyB What's the b*****d done, sweetie? #Cinderella*
jenpb, [+] Wed 1 Dec 16:09

@LucyB DM me a contact number. You're going to need help. #Cinderella
prguru, [+] Wed 1 Dec 16:12

Too true, she thought, the smile fading. But not from 'prguru', aka Mr Public Relations, the man famous for selling grubby secrets to grubby newspapers and gossip mags. It didn't matter to him if you were a model in rehab, a politician having an affair with his PA or the victim of some terrible tragedy. He'd sell your story for hard cash and turn you into a celebrity overnight.

Nor any of the other public relations types lining up to jump in and feed off her story. As if she'd trust anyone in the PR business ever again.

She wasn't sure how long the phone would function— Rupert would surely pull the plug the minute he thought of it—so she quickly thumbed in a message to her followers while she had the chance.

And maybe she should update her diary, too. Just in case

anything happened to her. Something else her hairdresser had clued her up on. That she could set up a private web document, record her thoughts on her phone and then send it to be stored on her own private Internet space.

'Think of it as your pension, princess,' he'd said.

She'd thought him cynical, but she had started keeping a diary, mostly because there were some things she hadn't been able to confide to anyone else.

Diary update: *Day hit the skids after the photoshoot when I realised I'd forgotten the wedding file and went to the office to borrow R's copy. His dragon of a personal assistant had gone with him to the Lucy B press launch and her assistant is on holiday so there was a temp holding the fort or I would never have been handed the key to his private filing cabinet.*

I had my hand on the wedding file when I spotted the one next to it. The one labelled 'The Cinderella Project'.

Well, of course I opened it. Wouldn't you?

Now meeting with wedding planner off. Celebration off. Dinner at Ritz most definitely off. As for wedding... Off, off, off.

Time to Tweet the good news.

Thanks for concern, tweeps. Fairy tale fractured—kissed prince, got frog. HEA cancelled. End of story.
#Cinderella
LucyB, [+] Wed 1 Dec 16:41

The phone belted out the ghastly ringtone again just as she clicked 'send' and made her jump nearly out of her skin. It was a sharp reminder of the need to keep her head down and she switched it to silent, unable to cut herself off entirely.

There had to be someone she could ring. Someone she could trust. But not from here.

This was no haven.

She had to move before someone spotted her, but first she had to do something to change her appearance.

She'd felt so utterly Christmassy when she'd set off in her bright red coat that morning. Utterly full of the joys of a season that had never before felt so exciting, so full of promise.

Now she felt as conspicuous as Santa in a snowdrift.

She would have liked to abandon it. Abandon everything. Strip off, change back into who she was. Her real self, not this manufactured 'princess'.

Easier said than done.

This morning she'd had everything a woman could possibly want. This afternoon she had nothing in the world except what she stood up in and it was going to be freezing tonight.

But she could manage without the coat for now and, easing it off in the cramped space, she folded it inside out so that only the black lining showed. Better, although she could have done with a hat to cover her head.

She didn't even have a scarf. Why would she? Until half an hour ago she was being chauffeured everywhere, an umbrella held over her head at the slightest suggestion of anything damp descending from the sky whenever she stepped onto a pavement. Cosseted. Precious.

Very precious. A lot of time and money had been invested in her. And Rupert—not the fantasy figure of her dreams, but the real one—would expect, demand a profit for all that effort, cost.

Legs still a little shaky, she shouldered her bag, tucked

her coat over her arm and, still clutching her phone in her hand, peered cautiously around the display.

No sign of any big scary men, or journalists, hunting her down, just shoppers preoccupied with what to wear at a Christmas party or buying gifts for their loved ones. Taking a deep breath and doing her best to look as if it was the most normal thing in the world, she eased herself back into the flow.

It took all her nerve to take one ladylike step after the other, matching her pace to those around her and trying to look as if walking barefoot through the poshest store in London in December was absolutely normal, when what she really wanted to do was take off, race up the stairs two at a time and get out of sight.

She kept her eyes straight ahead instead of looking about her to check for anything suspicious, doing absolutely nothing that might draw attention to herself.

Nat called down to his head of security to brief him on the fact that they might have a 'situation'; something to keep an eye on. That done, he continued his afternoon walk through the store, conscientiously looking in on each department before heading for the stairs to the next floor.

Even at the height of the Christmas buying frenzy the H&H reputation for perfection had to be maintained. He might not want to be here, but no one would ever be able to accuse him of letting standards slip and he was alert for anything that jarred on the eye, anything out of place.

Why, for instance, had the woman ahead of him taken off her coat? Was the store too warm? It was essential that shoppers had both hands free, but it was a delicate balancing act keeping the store comfortable for both staff and customers who were dressed for outdoors.

Not that he was complaining about the view.

She had pale blonde hair cut in soft, corn silk layers that seemed to float around her head, stirring a thousand memories. Despite the fact that they were in the middle of the busiest shopping season of the year, he wanted to slow the world down, call out her name so that she'd turn to him with an unguarded smile...

He slammed the door on the thought but, even while his brain was urging him to pass her, move on, the rest of him refused to listen, hanging back so that he could hold on to the illusion for a moment longer.

Foolish.

She was nothing like the fragile woman whose memory she'd evoked. On the contrary, the black cashmere sweater-dress she was wearing clung enticingly to a figure that curved rather more than was fashionable. No snow queen, this. Inches shorter, she was an altogether earthier armful. Not the kind of woman you worshipped from afar, but the kind built for long, dark winter nights in front of an open fire.

Then, as his gaze followed the pleasing curve of her hip to the hem of her short skirt and he found himself enjoying the fact that her legs lived up to the rest of the package, he realised that she wasn't wearing any shoes.

She might have taken them off for a moment's relief. It wouldn't be the first time he'd seen a woman walking barefoot through the store carrying shoes that were pinching after a hard day's shopping. But she wasn't laden with glossy carriers. The only bag she was carrying was a soft leather tote clutched close to her side beneath the coat, heavy, but with the weight of a protruding file rather than parcels, gift-wrapped by his staff.

But what really jarred, jolting him out of the firelight fantasy, was the fact that one foot of the ultra-fine black tights she was wearing had all but disintegrated. That her slender ankles had been splashed with dirt thrown up from the wet pavements.

As if sensing him staring, she turned, still moving, and almost in slow motion he saw her foot miss the step and she flung out her arm, grabbing for him as she stumbled backwards.

He caught her before she hit the stairs and for a moment they seemed to hang there, suspended above them, his hand beneath her as she peered up at him with startled kitten eyes, her arm flung around his neck.

His head filled with the jarringly familiar scent of warm skin overlaid with some subtle, expensive perfume that jumped to his senses, intensified colour, sound, touch…the softness of the cashmere, the curve of her back, her weight against his palm as he supported her, kissing close to full, soft lips, slightly parted as she caught her breath.

His world was reduced to the pounding of his heart, her breath against his cheek, her gold-green eyes peering up at him over a voluptuous cowl collar that was sliding, seductively, off one shoulder.

She smelled like a summer garden, of apples and spice and, as he held her, a rare, forgotten warmth rippled through him.

CHAPTER TWO

LUCY was drowning in raw sensation. Lying in the arms of a total stranger, drowning in the quicksilver heat of his eyes, his touch, parting her lips to gasp in air, struggling to breathe as she went under for the third time.

What was she thinking? What was she doing?

For a moment her brain, its buffer overloaded with more information, more emotion, more of just about everything than a body was built to handle, had backed up, was refusing to compute.

On some distant level she knew she had to move, run, but here, now, only the most primitive sensations were getting through. Touch, warmth, confusion...

'The bedroom department is on the fifth floor,' someone said with a chuckle as she passed and Nat felt, rather than saw the sudden realisation hit her.

The sheer madness of it. But her reaction was not the same dazed feeling that had him staring at her like an idiot. Not even an embarrassed laugh.

Instead she emitted a little squeak of alarm and squirmed away from him, using her hands and feet to scrabble backwards up the steps before she got far enough away to turn, push herself to her feet and run.

'No!'

It wasn't a command, it was the cry of a man bereft.

'Stop!'

But the urgency of his words spurred her on, giving her feet wings as she bolted, dodging through slower moving shoppers, taking the stairs two at a time, fear driving her escape.

Leaving him shaking, frozen to the spot while visitors to the store flowed around him. Not surprise, or pleasure, or even amusement at an unexpectedly close encounter with a stranger. Raw fear that dredged up the memory of another woman who'd run from his arms. Who, just for a moment, he'd forgotten.

Fear, and the bruise darkening her temple.

Someone tutted irritably at him for blocking the stairs and he forced himself to move, pick up the shoe that had tumbled, unnoticed, from her bag.

He turned it in his hand.

It bore an expensive high-end designer label at odds with the damp edge around the platform sole, splashes of pavement dirt on the slender and very high stiletto heel. This was not a shoe for walking in the rain. It had been made to ride in limousines, walk along red carpets, to be worn by the consort of a very rich man. The kind who employed bodyguards.

Could she be the one the two men on the ground floor were seeking? That might explain her fear, because she hadn't run from his touch. On the contrary, she'd been equally lost, wrapped up in a sizzling moment of discovery until a crass comment had jolted her back to reality.

He didn't know who she was or why they were looking for her, only that she was afraid, running perhaps for her life, and the last thing he wanted was to draw more attention to her. No one hunted a frightened woman in his store, not even him, and he clamped down on the swamping need to race after her, reassure her, know her.

Not that there was any need to hunt.

If she was looking for a hiding place, common sense suggested that she was heading for the nearest Ladies cloakroom, looking for somewhere to clean up, hide out for a while.

But why?

His jaw tightened as he continued up the stairs with rather more speed, fighting to hold back the memories of another frightened woman. Vowing to himself that, whoever she was, she'd find sanctuary within his walls. That history wouldn't repeat itself.

He'd ask one of the senior floor managers to check on her, return her shoe, offer whatever assistance she felt appropriate. A new pair of tights with the compliments of the store. A discreet exit. A car, if necessary, to take her wherever she needed to go.

But his hand was shaking as he called Security again, wanting to know where the two men were now.

Before he could speak, he was practically knocked off his feet by one of them, racing up the stairs, heedless of the safety of the women and children in his way, running through, rather than around them, scattering bags, toys.

His first reaction was to go after him, toss him bodily out of the store, but a child was crying and he had no choice but to stop and ensure that no one was hurt, pick up scattered belongings and summon one of his staff to offer the courtesy of afternoon tea in the Garden Restaurant. Deal with the complaints before they were voiced. It was a point of honour that no one left Hastings & Hart unhappy.

But, all the time he was doing that, the questions were pounding at his brain.

Whose bodyguards? Who was her husband, lover? More to the point, who was she?

And why was she so scared?

While her face—what had been visible over the big, enveloping collar—had seemed vaguely familiar, she wasn't some instantly recognizable celebrity or minor royal. If she had been, her bodyguards wouldn't have wasted time scouring the store for her but would have gone straight to his security staff to enlist their help using CCTV. Keeping it low-key. No drama.

There was something very wrong about this and, moving with considerably more urgency now, he ordered Security to find and remove the two men from the store. He didn't care who they worked for, or who they'd lost, they had worn out their welcome.

'Hold the lift!' Lucy, trembling more now than when she'd run from the press conference, heart pounding beyond anything she'd ever experienced, sprinted for the closing doors. 'Thanks,' she gasped as someone held them and she dived in, squeezing into a corner, her back to the door where she wouldn't be instantly visible when they opened again. Her brain working logically on one level, while everything else was saying, no… Go back…

'Doors closing. Going down…'

She snapped out of the mental dream state in which she was floating above the stairs, her whole world contained in a stranger's eyes.

Nooooo! Up, up…

The recorded announcement listed the departments as, despairing, she was carried back down to the ground floor. *'Perfumery, accessories, leather goods, stationery. Ground floor. Doors opening.'*

As the doors slid open, she risked a glance, then froze as she caught sight of one of Rupert's bodyguards scanning the surge of passengers making a beeline for the exit.

She pressed herself back into the corner of the lift,

keeping her head down, drawing a curious glance from a child who looked up at her as the lift rapidly filled. Holding her breath until the doors finally closed, aware that it wasn't just the people she recognized who would be searching for her.

She'd got used to the front page—she'd been booked for a photoshoot this afternoon just to show off her new haircut, for heaven's sake—but this was different.

She'd announced to the world that she had the goods on Rupert Henshawe and it wouldn't be just the gossip magazines who'd want to know where she was.

Within hours there would be a press-orchestrated man-hunt. It was probably already underway. And there was the risk that any minute now someone was going to say Excuse me, but aren't you, Lucy B?

It had happened before when she'd been shopping and the result tended to be mayhem. It was as if everyone wanted to touch her, capture a little of the magic.

Rupert's marketing men had got that right, but it was the last thing she wanted now so she kept her head tucked well down, desperate not to catch anyone's eye.

Not all eyes were over five feet from the ground, however, and she found herself being scrutinised by the little girl, who continued to stare at her as the recorded announcement said, *'Going down... Sporting goods, gardening and recreation, electrical. And...'* there was a pause. *'...The North Pole...'*

The rest was drowned out by whoops of excitement.

'Are you going to see Santa?' the child asked her as the doors closed.

Santa?

Well, that explained why the North Pole had been relocated to a department store basement.

'We're going on a sleigh ride to see him at the North Pole,' she confided.

'Well, golly… What a treat.'

Right now a sleigh ride to the North Pole was exactly what she could do with. She'd planned to clean herself up, certain she'd be safe for a while in the Ladies. She didn't know what had made her look back. Just a feeling, a prickle on the back of her neck…

The man following her hadn't been a bodyguard. She knew them all and that wasn't a face she would have forgotten.

Eyes grey as granite, with just a spark of silver to lighten an overall sense of darkness; a reflection from the store's silver and white decorations, no doubt. That moment of magic was all in her imagination. It had to be. Whoever he was, he'd oozed the kind of power and arrogance she'd come to associate with Rupert's most intimate circle.

He was a power broker, the kind of man who took orders rather than giving them. She'd learned to recognise the type. Mostly they ignored her and she was happy about that, but there had been an intensity in his look as he'd caught her, held her, that had turned her bones to putty. And not with fear.

A déjà vu moment if ever there was one, the difference being that whatever Rupert had been feeling on the day he'd picked her up, dusted her off, all concern and charm, her heart rate hadn't gone through the roof. The air hadn't crackled, sizzled, fried her brains. He'd taken his time, wooed her so gently, so…so damn *sweetly* that she'd fallen for every scummy lie. Hook, link and sinker.

She'd thought he was the genuine article, a real Prince Charming, when the truth was he hadn't actually fancied her enough to jump her bones.

The grey-eyed stranger, on the other hand, had made

her forget everything with a look. It was as if his touch had fired up some deep, untapped sexual charge and she felt her skin flush with heat from head to toe at the memory, the promise of the kiss that she'd been waiting for all her life. The real thing.

Maybe.

She shivered. Shook her head. She'd been drawn into a web of lies and deceit and she would never be able to trust anyone ever again. Never be able to take anyone at face value.

Mortified as she'd been at being discovered as good as kissing a total stranger on the stairs, that remark had jolted her back to reality. Common sense and self-preservation had kicked in and she'd run because there were some mistakes a smart woman didn't make twice.

Some she didn't make once.

She'd thought the Ladies room would provide a safe haven but, even as she'd bolted, she'd realised her mistake. It would be obvious to anyone with half a brain cell that was where she'd take cover and in the nick of time she'd seen the trap. That it was a dead end with only one exit.

It was several hours until the store closed, but Rupert was a patient man. He'd wait, call up female reinforcements to keep an eye on her until she had no choice but to emerge.

He had enough of them.

All those women in his office who'd collaborated with him in the make-believe.

What she needed was somewhere to hide, a bolt-hole where no one would ever think of looking for her while she considered her options. Easier said than done.

All she possessed in the world was what she currently wore. She'd been too shocked to plan anything. To even think of going back to the little apartment at the top of

Rupert's London house. Packing the gorgeous wardrobe that was all part of the fantasy. Always supposing she'd got out with a suitcase.

No doubt someone would have delayed her while the alarm was ráised and Rupert was warned that the game was up.

And she'd bet the farm that the platinum credit cards Rupert had showered on her would go *uh-uh* if she attempted to use them.

Or maybe not. Could he use them to track her movements? Or was that just something they did in TV thrillers?

Either way, they were useless. Not that she wanted anything from him. Right now she wished she could rip off the clothes she was wearing and toss them in the nearest bin.

Since she was trying not to draw attention to herself, that probably wasn't her best option.

Not that she'd done such a good job of keeping a low profile, she thought, still aware of the tingling imprint of a stranger's kiss.

'Do you think there'll be room on the sleigh for me?' she asked the little girl.

She lifted her shoulders in a don't-know shrug, then said, 'Do you believe in Santa Claus?'

Tough question. Right now, she was having trouble believing that the sky was blue.

'My big sister said there's no such person,' she added, then stuck her thumb in her mouth, clearly afraid that it might be true.

Okay, not that tough.

In her years working in the day-care nursery, she'd come across this one plenty of times. Big sisters could be the pits, although right now she wished she had one. A really cynical, know-it-all big sister who would have ripped away the rose-tinted spectacles, shattered her naivety, said, *Prince Charming? Are you kidding? What are the odds?*

She wasn't about to let that happen for this little girl, though. Not yet.

'Your sister only told you that because she thinks that if you don't write to Santa she'll get more presents.'

The thumb popped out. 'Really?'

Before she could reply, the lift came to a halt and the doors opened, sending her heart racing up into her mouth. Under cover of the mothers, dads, children pouring out, she risked a glance.

There were no dark-eyed men lying in wait for her, only more parents with hyped-up children, clutching gifts from Santa, waiting in a magical snowy landscape to be whisked back up to the real world. Which was where she'd go if she didn't make a move and get out of the lift. And that was not an appealing place right now.

Nowhere near as attractive as the North Pole, which the finger-post sticking out at an angle from a designer snowdrift suggested was somewhere to her right. As if to confirm that fact, an ornate sleigh was waiting in a glittering ice cave, ready to whisk the children away.

They stampeded towards it, climbing aboard while their mothers dealt with the more mundane matter of checking in with the elf in charge of the departure gate. Trips to the North Pole did not, after all, come cheap.

She barely hesitated.

She could do with a little magic herself right now and Santa's Grotto had to be just about the last place anyone would think of looking for her.

As she stood in the queue she nervously checked her phone—it was as good a way to keep her head down as any.

There were half a dozen texts, voicemail messages and the twittersphere had apparently gone mad. *WelshWitch* had started it with—

Where is Cinderella? What have you done to her? Tell the truth, Your Frogginess! RT@LucyB Kissed prince, got frog. #Cinderella
WelshWitch, [+] Wed 1 Dec 17:01

It had already been replied to by dozens of people. Rupert was going to be furious, but since this—unlike all her other social media stuff set up by his PR team—was her personal account, there wasn't a thing His Frogginess could do about it. At least not while she managed to stay out of his way.

What he might do if he caught up with her was something else. She shivered involuntarily as she continued to scroll through the tweets.

There was another one from Jen.

@LucyB If you need a bolt-hole, DM me. #Cinderella
jenpb, [+] Wed 1 Dec 17:03

In a moment of weakness she almost did send her a direct message. But then she came to her senses and shut the phone.

That was what was so horrible about this. It wasn't just Rupert she couldn't trust.

She'd chatted daily on Twitter. She had nearly half a million 'followers', an army of fans on Facebook, all apparently fascinated by her story, her amazing new life. But who were they really?

Jen had seemed like a genuine friend, one of a few

people who, like WelshWitch, she constantly tweeted with, but suppose she was just another of Rupert's people? Someone the PR company had delegated to stay close. Be her 'friend', guide her tweets, distract her if necessary, steer her away from anything controversial? She was well aware that not everyone in the Twittersphere was who or what they seemed. Logging into her appointments, she scrolled down and, under the crossed-through entry for *Dinner at Ritz*, she added another entry—

Rest of life: up the creek.

And then her thoughts shifted back to the man on the stairs. His face forever imprinted on her memory. The strong jaw, high cheekbones, the sensuous curve of his lower lip…

'Can I help?'

She jumped, looked up to discover that everyone else had moved off and she was being regarded by a young elf.

'Oh…um…one adult to the North Pole, please,' she said, closing her phone and reaching for her purse, wondering belatedly how much it would cost. She didn't have that much cash. With a fistful of credit and charge cards, she hadn't needed it. 'A single will do,' she said. 'I'm in no hurry. I can walk back.'

He grinned appreciatively but said, 'Sorry. This flight has closed.'

'Oh.' It hadn't occurred to her that there wouldn't be any room. 'How long until the next one?'

'Forty minutes, but you have to have a pre-booked ticket to see Santa,' he explained.

'You have to book in advance?' Forty minutes! She

couldn't wait that long. 'Where's the magic in that?' she demanded.

'There's not much magical about dozens of disappointed kids screaming their heads off,' he pointed out.

'True…' She had enough experience with screaming children not to argue. 'Look, I don't actually want to have a one-to-one with the man himself. I just need to get to the North Pole,' she pressed as the doors to the ice cave began to close. 'It's really urgent…'

It occurred to her that she must sound totally crazy. That, shoeless and apparently raving, she was going to be escorted from the premises.

It didn't happen. Apparently, someone who could cite 'elf' as his day job took crazy in his stride because, instead of summoning Security, he said, 'Oh, *right*. I was told to look out for you.'

What…? *Nooooo!*

'You're from Garlands, right? Pam's been going crazy,' he added before the frantic message from her brain to flee could reach her feet. 'She expected you ages ago.'

'Garlands…'

What the heck was that? The department responsible for store decorations? Did a snowflake need straightening? A tree trimming?

Whatever.

She was up for it, just as long as she was out of sight of the lift.

'You've got me,' she said, neither confirming nor denying it. 'So, *now* do I get a ride on the sleigh?'

'Sorry,' he said, grinning. 'The sleigh is for paying customers only. Staff have to put on their snow shoes and walk. Both ways,' he added with relish. Clearly this was a young man who enjoyed his job. 'Don't look so worried.

I'm kidding about the snow shoes.' He looked at her feet and, for a moment, lost the thread.

'It's a long story,' she said.

'Er…right. Well, you're in luck. There's a short cut.' He opened a door, hidden in the side of a snow bank and tucked behind the kind of huge Christmas tree that you only ever saw in story books. Smothered with striped candy canes, toys, beautiful vintage decorations. 'Turn left, ask for Pam Wootton. She'll sort you out.'

'Left…Pam… Got it. Thanks.'

Better and better. She'd be much safer behind the scenes in the staff area.

Forget Pam whatever-her-name-was. She'd keep her head down until closing time and then leave through the staff entrance with everyone else. By then, she might even have worked out where she could go.

'She's not in there, Mr Hart.'

'Are you sure? She hasn't locked herself in one of the cubicles?'

'All checked. That's what took me so long.'

'Well, thanks for looking,' he said, outwardly calm.

'No problem.' She hesitated, then said, 'The lifts are right opposite the stairs. If she got lucky with the timing, she might have doubled straight back down to the ground floor and left the store.'

'It's possible,' Nat agreed, although he doubted it. He had her shoe and no one with a lick of sense would choose to go barefoot from the warmth of the store into the street. She was still in the store; he was certain of it. And, with nine sales floors, she had plenty of places to hide.

In her shoes—or, rather, lack of them—where would he go? What would he do?

If it was serious—and her fear suggested that this wasn't

just some rich woman wanting a little time out—changing her appearance had to be the first priority. Not a problem when she had a store full of clothes and accessories to help her, except that would mean exposing herself while she stood in line to pay for them.

Maybe.

Just how desperate was she?

Desperate enough to grab something from a rail, switch clothes in one of the changing rooms? When they were this busy it wouldn't be that difficult and she could rip out the security tags without a second thought. It wouldn't matter to her if the clothes were damaged, only that they didn't set off the alarms when she walked out of the store.

'I'll put the shoe in Lost Property, shall I?'

'No!' Realising that he'd overreacted, that she was looking at him at little oddly, he said, taking the shoe from her, 'I'll do it. I've already wasted enough of your time. Thanks for your help.'

'No problem, Mr Hart. I'll keep my eyes open.'

He nodded, but doubted she'd see her and, more in hope than expectation of finding some clue, he retraced his steps back down to the first floor, where he stopped to take another look out over the busy ground floor.

As the afternoon had shifted into evening and offices had emptied, it had become even more frantic, but he would have spotted that black dress amid the madness, the pale blonde swish of hair. That was a real giveaway, one that she should cover up as quickly as possible.

She'd need a scarf, he thought. Or a hat. A hat would be better. It would not only cover her hair, but throw a shadow over her face where a scarf would only draw attention to it.

And once she'd changed her appearance she could risk the shoe department. He'd wait there.

As he started down the stairs, he noticed a display slightly out of alignment, stopped to adjust it and saw a lace-trimmed handkerchief lying on the floor.

He bent to pick it up and caught again that faint, subtle scent that hadn't come out of any bottle.

Had she dashed in from the street to take cover, bolted up the stairs, paused here for a moment to catch her breath, get her bearings?

Where was she now?

Famous last thoughts.

The minute Lucy opened the door to the staff area she was leapt upon by a flushed and harassed-looking woman wearing a security badge proclaiming her to be Pam Wootton, Human Resources.

'At last! The agency said you'd be here an hour ago. I'd just about given up hope.'

Agency? Oh, good grief, the elf hadn't been talking about Christmas garlands but the Garland Agency. The suppliers of the crème de la crème of secretarial staff. She'd had an interview with them when she was looking for a job but she didn't have the kind of experience it took to be a 'Garland Girl'.

There was a certain irony in being mistaken for one now, but she wasn't going to let that stop her from grabbing the opportunity with both hands.

'I'm soooo sorry. The Underground…' She didn't have to say another word. It was the excuse that just gave and gave. 'And it's started to snow,' she threw in for good measure.

'Snow! Oh, great,' Pam said. 'That's all I need. Getting home tonight is going to be a nightmare.' And she pressed her hand to her forehead as if trying to keep her brain in.

'Are you all right?' Lucy asked, forgetting her own worries for a moment. The woman looked flushed and not at all well.

'Ask me again in February,' she replied with a slightly hysterical laugh. 'When the January sales are over.' Then, pulling herself together, 'It's just a bit of a headache. I'll take something for it when I get back to the office. Come on, there's no time to waste. Let's get you changed.'

'Changed?'

'Into your costume,' she said, opening a cupboard and revealing a rail of short green tunics. Then, glancing back at her, 'Didn't they tell you anything…' she looked at her clipboard '…I don't seem to have your name.'

'Lu…' *Noooooo!*

Pam looked up. 'Lou? As in Louise?'

Gulp.

'Yes! Louise.' Whew. Pam was still waiting. 'Louise… Braithwaite.' It was the first name that came into her head.

'And you *have* got a CRB Certificate, Louise?' Pam asked, pen poised to tick boxes, going through the motions.

'A CRB Certificate?'

She sighed. 'You can't work in the grotto without a criminal records check. I did explain the situation to Garlands. If you haven't got one…'

Grotto?

The penny dropped.

Pam had mistaken her for an elf.

Out of the fairy tale frying pan, into the…um…fairy tale fire…

CHAPTER THREE

'DIDN'T Garlands explain?' Pam asked.

'It was a bad connection…' so bad it was non-existent '…I must have missed that bit. But I have been CRB checked,' she said. 'I worked in a day-care nursery before… Well, until recently.'

Oh, boy, Lucy Bright. The ability to look someone in the eye and tell a big fat lie had to be catching. His Frogginess would be proud of her.

Not that she'd lied about having a CRB Certificate. It wasn't under the name Louise Braithwaite, of course, but it was the real deal. She'd had to have one for the day job at the nursery while she'd been studying at night school. She'd worked as a waitress in the local pizza parlour on her free evenings and at the weekends to earn the money to pay for her course.

Much good it had done her.

She'd applied for hundreds of jobs before she'd got an interview for a clerical assistant post at the Henshawe Corporation. The fact that there had been an interview panel for such a junior position had thrown her, but it had been very informal. They'd been incredibly impressed at how hard she'd worked and encouraged her to talk about her ambitions.

She still remembered the stunned silence when she'd

finished telling them passionately that she wanted to prove herself. Make something of herself, be someone. And then they'd applauded her.

When, the following day, they had called her to offer her a job, she'd thought herself the luckiest woman in the world.

'I realise that Garlands know what they're doing, but I still have to ask,' Pam muttered. 'It's been so difficult since the new laws about working with children were introduced. We normally get in drama students at Christmas but not too many of them have had the foresight to get a CRBC. I don't suppose they see themselves doing a Christmas gig as one of Santa's Little Helpers when they get a place at RADA. That's why I called Garlands.'

'They supply elves?' she asked, which got her an odd look.

'They place temporary nannies.'

'Just kidding.' *Whew...*

Pam stared down at her feet. 'What happened to your shoes?'

'I broke a heel in a grating.' The truth, the whole truth and almost nothing but the truth...

'Oh, bad luck.' They shared a moment of silent mourning, then, pressing on, 'You're a bit buxom for an elf,' she said, looking at her doubtfully, 'but beggars can't be choosers. There should be something that fits.' She held one of the tunics up against her, then thrust it at her, piling the rest of the costume on top. 'You've got small feet. These should do.' She put a pair of soft felt bootees on top of the pile and then took a small plastic pouch out of a box and added that to the pile. 'The elf make-up pack. Rouge for your cheeks, a pencil for freckles—you'll find a picture of what's required inside. And there's a pad to remove your nail polish. You can change down here,' she said, leading the way down a short flight of steps. 'Find a spare locker for your clothes and be as quick as you can.'

She opened a door and Lucy found herself confronted on one side by a vast locker room that seemed to stretch to infinity and on the other by a room providing not only loos and basins, but showers, too.

She quickly crammed her coat and bag into an empty locker, stripped off her dress, tossed the shredded tights in a bin. There was no time for a shower so she dunked her feet, one at a time, in a basin of warm water to wash off the street dirt, half expecting Pam to burst in with the real elf at any minute.

She didn't but, until she did, she was grateful for being in the warm and, more importantly, in a very neat disguise.

She dabbed circles of rouge on her cheeks, scattered a few freckles across her nose, then a few more, before removing the nail polish that had been applied at great expense just hours ago. A shame, but clearly elves didn't have bright red nails.

Finally, she donned the costume, tucking her hair out of sight under the pointy felt hat and regarded herself in a handily placed mirror.

It wasn't a good look.

The green and white striped tights made her legs look fat and the tunic was doing her bum no favours. Right now, she didn't care.

Diary update: *The day has gone from bad to surreal. I've been mistaken for an elf. Not an entirely bad thing since I'm off the streets and I've been supplied, free of charge, with a neat disguise. It's just temporary, of course, like the new name. What I'm going to do when Hastings & Hart closes at eight o'clock is my next problem. But with luck I've got three hours*

*breathing space to work on a plan, always assuming
the real elf doesn't turn up in the meantime.*

*Three hours to get my breath back after
a very close encounter with Mr Tall, Dark and
Dangerous.*

Lucy ran her tongue over her lips to cool them, then shook
her head and stuffed her phone and her locker key into the
little leather pouch on her belt before presenting herself
for inspection.

Pam sighed, adjusted the hat so that a little more of her
hair showed. 'You've been a little heavy-handed with the
freckles.' Then, frowning, 'Is that a bruise?'

'It's nothing,' she said. 'Someone caught me with a bag,'
she said.

'The Underground just gets worse... Never mind.' She
took a small camera from her pocket. 'I'll just take a picture
for your ID. Say cheese...'

'Cheese.'

'Great. I'll log you into the system later. Sort you out a
swipe card.'

'Swipe card?'

'It's how we keep track of staff. How we know who is
working, how long they've worked and that they've left
the premises at the end of the day. You'll need it to get out
and, hopefully, get in again tomorrow.'

'Oh, right. Absolutely.'

'Come on. I'll take you to meet Frank Alyson, Deputy
Manager of the toy department and Chief Elf, and then you
can get started.'

She passed her over to a tall lugubrious man wearing
a long green tunic. She sort of sympathised with him. It
couldn't be much fun being a middle-aged man with his

dignity in shreds, but walking around Santa's grotto in a suit and tie would undoubtedly compromise the illusion.

'Louise Braithwaite,' Pam said, her voice fading to nothing as she introduced her. She cleared her throat, gathered herself. 'Be nice to this one. Elves don't grow on trees, you know.'

'Don't they? You surprise me. Most of them appear to have sawdust for brains.' He gave her a look that suggested he had no hopes that she had anything but wood pulp between the ears before turning back to Pam. 'You look ghastly. Go home. You'll be no use to anyone if you're ill.'

'And ho, ho, ho to you, too,' she said as she walked away.

'You could have handled that better,' Lucy said without thinking. She was good at that. Saying the first thing that came into her head. According to her file—the one she wasn't supposed to ever see—it had been her most usable asset. That and her passion. People would, apparently, *"…instantly warm to her enthusiasm, her natural openness and lack of guile…"*

They'd nailed that one.

It was saying the first thing that came into her head without thinking that had got her into this mess in the first place and now Frank was staring at her, clearly unused to criticism. Or maybe he was wondering where he'd seen her before.

'So, what happened to the last elf?' she said to distract him.

'She asked too many questions and I fed her to a troll,' he replied.

Sheesh…

'Anything else you'd like to know?'

She pressed her lips together and shook her head.

'Fast learner,' he replied with satisfaction. 'Keep it up and we'll get on.'

'Great.' She couldn't wait.

'So, Louise Braithwaite, what can you do?'

Do?

Wasn't standing about in a pointy hat and stripy tights enough?

Obviously not. Through a small window in his office, she could see an army of elves busily 'constructing' toys in Santa's workshop. They were dressing teddies and dolls, test-driving remote-controlled cars and encouraging children to join in and help them while they waited their turn to see Santa.

Otherwise known, if you happened to have a cynical turn of mind—and she'd just had a crash course in cynicism from a world master—as try-before-you-buy.

'Have you any experience?'

'Of being an elf?' Was he kidding? 'No,' she admitted quickly, 'but I am used to working with children. They tend to throw up when they get over-excited. Just tell me where the bucket and mop are kept and I'll cope.'

That earned her something that might have been a smile. 'Well, I have to admit that you're less of a fool than the last girl Pam brought me. She couldn't see past her mascara.'

Lucy resisted the urge to bat her expensively dyed eyelashes at him, but it was harder to keep the smile from breaking out. And why not? She was safe.

Without a pre-booked ticket, no one, not even Rupert's bodyguards, would be able to get beyond the entrance. More to the point, they'd realise that she couldn't either and wouldn't even bother. For the moment, at least, she could relax.

And what about grey eyes?

The thought popped, unbidden, into her head. The

thought of those eyes, a mouth that gave her goosebumps just thinking about it.

For heaven's sake, Lu...Louise Braithwaite, get a grip!

What would a man on his own be doing in Santa's grotto? And why would she care? He was the last person on earth she wanted to see.

Not that he'd recognize her dressed like this.

Even if, beneath the rouge and abundant freckles, someone spotted a passing resemblance to the face that had been on the front cover of *Celebrity* magazine a dozen or more times in the last few months, they would dismiss it. Why, after all, would Lucy B, aka Cinderella, be working as an elf in a department store?

'You can start by tidying up, straightening shelves while you find your way around. When you've done that you can take the empty space on the bench, dressing dolls and teddies. You'll have to fit in a break with the rest of the staff.'

'Right. Thanks.'

She stood in the doorway for a moment, taking a look around, familiarising herself with the layout before launching herself into the mix of elves, children and parents.

This was all new to her. Shunted around the care system all her life, she'd never been taken to see 'Santa' when she was a child. Even if she had got lucky, it would never have been like this.

The grotto had been designed to give children the illusion that they were in Santa's North Pole workshop and there was a touch of magic about it that only a high-end designer—and a great deal of money—could have achieved. She didn't know about the kids, but it certainly worked for her.

She was still taking it all in when there was a tug on the

hem of her tunic and she turned to find herself looking at the child from the lift.

'You're not an elf,' she declared loudly. 'I saw you out there—' she pointed dramatically '—in the real world.'

Oh… fairy lights!

Having done her best to restore a little girl's faith in Santa, she'd immediately shattered it.

Maybe that was the message. There are no such things as fairy tales. On the other hand, if she'd had a moment or two of fantasy as a child, she might not have grabbed so desperately for it as an adult.

But this was not about her and, putting her finger to her lips in a quick, 'Shh!' she folded herself up so that she was on the same level as the child. 'What's your name?'

'Dido.'

'Can you keep a secret, Dido?'

The child, thumb stuck firmly back in her mouth, nodded once.

'Well, that's great because this is a really huge secret,' she said. 'You're absolutely right. You did see me in the lift, but the reason I was up there in the real world was because I was on a special mission from Santa.'

She hadn't worked as an assistant in a day-care nursery for years without learning how to spin a story. The pity of it was that she hadn't learned to spot one when it was being spun at her.

'What's a mishun?'

'A very special task. The toughest. I shouldn't be telling you this, but the thing is that Rudolph—'

'Rudolph?' Eyes wide, Dido abandoned the comfort of the thumb.

'Rudolph,' she repeated, 'had run out of his favourite snack. I had to disguise myself as a human, go up to the food hall—'

'Is he here?'

Lucy raised her finger to her lips again and then pointed it towards the ceiling. 'He's up there, on the roof with all the other reindeer,' she whispered. 'As soon as the store closes on Christmas Eve, we're going to load up the sleigh and off they'll go.'

'Really?' she whispered back, eyes like saucers.

'Elf's honour,' she said, crossing her heart.

'Can I see him?'

Oh, good grief... 'He's resting, Dido. Building up his strength. It's a big job delivering presents to all the children in the world.'

'I 'spose...' For a moment her little face sagged with disappointment, then she said, 'Was it a carrot? His favourite snack? We always leave a carrot for Rudolph.'

'Well, carrots are good, obviously,' she said, wondering what the rest of the poor reindeer had to sustain them. 'Great for his eyesight as he flies through the night. Good for children, too.' Good for you was so boring, though. Christmas was about excitement, magic. 'But what Rudolph really loves when it's cold is a handful of chilli-flavoured cashew nuts to warm him up.' She paused. 'They're what make his nose glow.'

'Wow! Really? That is so cool...'

'That's a very special secret,' Lucy warned. 'Between you, me, Rudolph and Santa.'

'So I can't tell Cleo? She's my big sister.'

'The sister who tried to tell you that Santa doesn't exist? I doooon't think so.'

The child giggled.

'Only a very small handful, though. If Rudolph has too many his nose will overheat...'

Stop! Stop it right there, Lucy Bright!

'Dido... It's time to go,' her mother said, rescuing her.

Mouthing a silent *thank you* over her daughter's head. 'Say bye-bye.'

'Bye-bye.' Then she whispered, 'Say hi to Rudolph.'

'I will.' Lucy put her finger to her lip, then said, 'Merry Christmas.'

'Merry Christmas.'

Whew. The magic restored to one little innocent. Clap if you believe in fairies...

Not her.

Not fairies. Not fairy tales.

Lesson learned.

She looked up, saw the Chief Elf watching her from his little window and, as ordered, began picking up toys that had been picked up and dropped, restoring them to the shelves. Holding the hands of children who'd momentarily lost sight of their mothers.

When all was calm and ordered, she hitched herself onto the vacant stool and began buttoning teddies into jackets and trousers. While her fingers moved on automatic, she found herself wondering not about her future, or where she was going to spend the night, but about the man on the stairs. The way he'd caught her, held her for what seemed like minutes rather than seconds.

The broad support on his hand at her back. Dangerously mesmerising grey eyes that had locked into hers, turning her on, lighting her up like the national grid. She could still feel the fizz of it. She'd never understood why men talked about taking a 'cold shower' until now.

'Any trouble evicting the bodyguards?' Nat asked, dropping in at the security office in the basement. It was hopeless hunting through the store, but he might catch a glimpse of her on the bank of screens being fed images from CCTV cameras around the store.

'No, although they were on the phone calling up reinforcements before they were through the door. Whoever replaces them won't be as easy to spot.'

Women. He'd use women, he thought, scanning the screens but she'd gone to earth. Found a hiding place. Or perhaps she really had slipped back out into the dark streets. That should have been his hope; instead, the idea of her out there, alone in the cold and dark, filled him with dread.

'Have you seen them before?' he pressed. 'Any idea who they work for?'

Bryan Matthews, his security chief, frowned, clearly puzzled by his interest, but shook his head, keeping whatever he was thinking to himself.

'They didn't say anything? Offer any explanation?'

'No, they were clam-mouthed professionals. They must have been in a flat panic to have drawn attention to themselves like that. Any idea who they've lost?'

'Maybe. It's possible that she's about this high,' he said, his hand level with his chin. 'Short pale blonde hair, green eyes, wearing a black knitted dress with a big collar.' He looked at the shoe he was still carrying. 'And no shoes.'

'You saw her?'

He'd done more than that. He'd not just seen her, but caught her, held her and she'd filled up his senses like a well after a drought. There had been a connection between them so physical that when she'd run it had felt as if she'd torn away a chunk of his flesh and taken it with her.

'I saw someone who seemed to be in a bit of a state,' he said. 'Pass the word to keep alert for anything out of the ordinary, especially at the store exits. When she does leave I want to be sure it's her decision. Any problem, call me.'

'I'll pass the word.'

He nodded. 'I'll be in my office.'

He glanced once more at the screens, not knowing whether to be relieved or disappointed when he came up empty.

The common sense response would be relief, he reminded himself as he strode through the electrical department, heading for the lift. But this was about more than the smooth running of the store. It was rare for a woman to catch his attention with such immediacy.

Her fear had only sharpened his reaction, taking it beyond simple interest in an attractive woman. A snatched moment that had raised his heart rate, leaving him not just breathless, but exposed, naked, defenceless. The kind of feelings he hated, did everything possible to avoid. But still he wanted to know who she was. What, who, she was running from. Wanted to taste lips that had been close enough to tantalise his memory, send heat spiralling down through his body…

He came to an abrupt halt as he realised that she was there. Right there in front of him. Not just once, but over and over, her face looking out from dozens of silent television screens banked up against the wall. Her hair was longer, her face fuller and she was smiling so that those green eyes sparkled. The heat intensified as he focused on her lips. How close had he come to kissing her?

Close enough to imagine how it would feel, the softness of her lips, how she tasted as her body softened beneath him…

Whoever she was, it seemed that her disappearance was important enough to make the national news.

Or maybe just dramatic enough.

He reached the nearest set and as he brought up the sound the picture switched to a ruckus at a press conference.

'…*scenes of total confusion as she very publicly ended*

her engagement to financier, Rupert Henshawe, accusing him of being a liar and a cheat...'

The camera caught Henshawe's startled face, moving in for a close-up of a trickle of blood that appeared on his cheek, before swinging wildly to catch the green-eyed girl clutching a file against her breast with one hand, while swinging her bag, connecting with the jaw of a man who was trying to hang on to her with the other.

The picture faded to the familiar figure of business tycoon, Rupert Henshawe, making a statement to camera.

'I blame myself. I should have realised that such a change in lifestyle would lead to stress in someone unused to the difficulty of being always in the public eye—'

His phone rang. He ignored it.

'Meeting Lucy was a life-changing moment for me. She's encouraged me to see the world in a new light...'

Lucy. Her name was Lucy.

'...her passionate belief in the fair trade movement has given a new ethical dimension to our fashion chain, which today I'm relaunching under the new name, Lucy B, in her honour...'

That was why she'd looked familiar, he realised as Henshawe paused, apparently struggling to keep back the tears.

He'd seen something in the papers about a romance with some girl who worked in his office—about as likely as Henshawe becoming a planet-hugger, he'd have thought...

'Yes?' he snapped, finally responding to the phone's insistent ring, never taking his eyes from the screen.

'It's Pam Wootton, Nat—'

'...I realise that I have been too wrapped up in all these new initiatives, visiting overseas suppliers, to give her the

support she so desperately needed. To notice how tired she has become, her lack of appetite, her growing dependence on the tranquillisers that were prescribed after the press drove her to move out of the flat she shared with friends—'

Tranquillisers?

Nat felt a cold chill run through him. History repeating itself...

'She needs rest, time to recover, all my best care and, as soon as I have found her, I will ensure—'

'Nat?'

The voice in his ear was so insistent that he realised it wasn't the first time his PA had said his name.

'Sorry, Meg, I was distracted,' he said, still staring at the screen. Then, as the news moved on to another story and he forced himself to concentrate, 'Pam Wootton? What's the matter with her?'

'She's collapsed. She was down in the grotto when it happened and Frank Alyson has called an ambulance, but I thought you'd want to know.'

'I'll be right there.'

'What are you doing?'

Lucy, teddy-dressing on automatic while her brain frantically free-wheeled—desperately trying to forget the man with the grey eyes and concentrate on thinking about where she could go when the store closed—looked up to find a small boy watching her.

'I'm wrapping this teddy up in a warm coat. It's snowing,' she said, glad of a distraction. Short of a park bench, she was out of ideas. 'It will be very cold on Santa's sleigh.'

'Can I help?'

'James, don't be a nuisance,' his mother warned. She

had two smaller girls clutching at her skirts, half scared, half bewitched. Lucy smiled reassuringly.

'He's fine,' she said. 'Do you all want to give me a hand?'

Within minutes she was surrounded by small children dressing teddies, grinning happily as she helped with sleeves and buttons.

How long had it been since she'd done that? Not a posed for the camera smile, the kind that made your face ache, but an honest-to-goodness grin?

She'd been so busy shopping, being interviewed by the gossip magazines, having her photograph taken, that there hadn't been any time to catch her breath, let alone enjoy the crazy roller coaster ride she was on. Or maybe that was the point.

She hadn't wanted time to stop and think because if she had, she would have had to listen to the still small voice whispering away in the back of her mind telling her that it couldn't possibly be real.

Mental note for diary: always listen to still small voice. It knows what it's talking about.

Being here reminded her of how much she'd missed working in the day-care nursery. Missed the children.

'Your turn for a break,' one of the elves said, as it was time for the children to get back on the sleigh, and she began to gather up the bears. 'Through the office, turn left. Coffee, tea, biscuits are on the house. There's a machine with snacks if you need anything else.'

The tea was welcome and although Lucy wasn't hungry she took a biscuit. Who knew when she'd get the chance to eat again? With that thought in mind, she stocked up on chocolate and crisps from the machine.

Rather than get involved in conversation with the other staff, she took a moment to check her phone, although what she was expecting to find, she didn't know. Or rather she did. Dozens of missed calls, all of which she ignored. Texts, too. And hundreds of tweets, all demanding to know the whereabouts of Cinderella.

They couldn't all have been from Rupert's stooges. But how could she tell the real from the phoney? If someone was hoping to entice her into trusting them, they wouldn't be leaping to his defence, would they?

She was considering whether to send a tweet to reassure the good guys that she was safe—at least for now—when something made her look up. The same prickle of aware-ness that had made her look around on the stairs.

And for the same reason.

There, not ten feet away, talking to Frank Alyson, was the man with grey eyes. The man who'd caught her, held her in one hand as easily as if she were a child and who had, for one brief moment, made her forget everything. Where she was, why she was running...

She could still feel the imprint of his hand on her back, the warmth of his breath against her cheek and, as she sucked her lower lip into her mouth to cool it, she almost believed that she could taste him on her tongue.

CHAPTER FOUR

GREY EYES was head to head with the Chief Elf and Lucy scarcely dared breathe as she watched the pair of them.

One look and the game would be up.

It was one thing keeping her identity a secret from people who weren't looking for her, didn't expect to see her, but anyone who knew her, or was looking for her, wouldn't be fooled for a moment by her disguise. And he had to be looking for her. Didn't he?

The thought filled her with a mixture of dread and elation. While her head was afraid, she had to restrain her body from leaning towards him, from shouting *Look! Here I am!*

But, standing back like this so that she could see all of him—the broad shoulders, the long legs—she could also see that he was wearing an identity tag just like the one Pam had been wearing, which meant that he wasn't a customer, someone just passing through.

He worked in the store and if Rupert's bodyguards had elicited help from the management in finding her she was in deep trouble because one thing was obvious. He wasn't junior staff.

His pinstriped suit was the business, his tie, navy with a tiny pattern, was eye-wateringly expensive; she'd bought one like it in the store just yesterday. And, even without the designer gear, he had that unmistakable air of authority.

But if she'd thought he'd seemed intense as he'd held her balanced above the stairs, now he looked positively grim.

'Keep your eyes open, Frank.' His voice was low; he didn't need to raise it to make a point.

As she watched, pinned to the spot, he took a step back, glanced around, his eyes momentarily coming to rest on her. She'd left it too late to move and she lowered her lashes, opting for the if-I-can't-see-you-then-you-can't-see-me scenario. Holding her breath as she waited for the *got you* hand on the shoulder.

Her heart ceased to beat for the second or two that he continued to stare at her, but after a moment she realised that, while he was looking at her, he wasn't actually seeing her. He wasn't even in this room, not in his head, anyway.

Then someone put his head around the corner. 'Whenever you're ready, sir.'

Without a word, he turned and walked away. Which was when she realised that he was gripping something in his hand. A shoe.

Her shoe.

Had it fallen out of her bag when she'd stumbled?

Well, duh… How many red suede peep-toe designer shoes were there lying around Hastings & Hart? How many dumb females whose coach had just turned into a pumpkin were there fleeing up the H&H stairs scattering footwear in their wake?

How many men who could stop your heart with a look?

Stop it!

Enough with the fairy tales.

She was done with fairy tales.

'Wh...who was that?' she asked, as casually as she could, once she'd finally managed to retrieve her heart from her mouth and coax it back into life.

Frank gave her a weary look and she remembered, too late, that he didn't like inquisitive elves.

'That, Miss Mop and Bucket,' he replied, 'was Nathaniel Hart.'

'Hart?' She blinked. 'As in...' She pointed up at the building soaring above them.

'As in Hastings & Hart,' he confirmed.

'No...' Or, to put it another way, *Nooooooo!*

'Are you arguing with me?'

'No!' And she shook her head, to make sure. 'I just hadn't realised there was a real Mr Hart.' It certainly explained the air of authority. If he looked as if he owned the place it was because, well, he did. 'I thought that most of these big stores were owned by big chains.'

'Hastings & Hart is not most stores.'

About to ask if there was a Mr Hastings, or even a Mrs Hart, she thought better of it. She was having a bad enough day without feeling guilty about lusting after some woman's husband.

'Is that all?' Frank asked with a sardonic lift of the brow. 'Or are you prepared to honour us with another teddy-dressing class for the under fives?'

'I'm sorry. It got a bit out of hand,' she said, fairly sure that was sarcasm rather than praise. 'I won't do it again.'

'Oh, please don't let me stop you. You are a hit with the children, if not with their mothers.'

Definitely sarcasm and she had been feeling rather guilty since several of the children had refused point-blank to surrender their bears to the rigours of a freezing sleigh ride and insisted they come home with them in a nice warm taxi. Not that it should worry Frank Alyson. It was all the more profit for Nathaniel Hart, wasn't it? Which was all men like him cared about.

But all the practice she'd had smiling in the last few months stood her in good stead and she gave him one of her best.

He looked somewhat startled, as well he might—she didn't imagine he got too many of those—and, satisfied with the effect, she returned to her stool, where she would be safely out of sight of Mr Nathaniel Hart, unless he borrowed Frank Alyson's Chief Elf robes.

But, while the children kept her busy, her brain was fizzing with questions. Had Grey Eyes been contacted directly by one of Rupert's minions? Asked to organise a discreet search for her? Or even perhaps by Rupert himself? They probably knew one another—billionaires united was a very small club—because he seemed to be taking a personal interest in the search.

He hadn't sounded at all happy when, having belatedly come to her senses, she'd taken off up the stairs, leaving only her shoe behind.

And it would explain why he was carrying it around with him. He assumed that she had the other one tucked away in her bag and, obviously, she would need two of them if she was going to walk out of here.

Tough. He should have kept his mind on the job.

Or maybe not. Even now, her heart flipped at the memory as she absently sucked on an overheated lip.

Having been assured by the paramedics that Pam was suffering from nothing worse than the latest bug that was going around, Nat drove her home and insisted that she stay there until she was fully recovered.

'But how will you cope? There's so much to do and—'

'Pam, we'll manage,' he insisted. 'And the last thing we need at this time of year is an epidemic.'

'Sorry. I know. And no one's indispensable. Petra will manage. Probably.' She rubbed at her temple. 'There was something I was meant to be doing...' He waited, but she sighed and said, 'No, it's gone.'

'Can I get you anything? Tea? Juice?'

'You're a sweet man, Nathaniel Hart,' she croaked. 'You'd make some woman a lovely husband.'

An image of the woman on the stairs, her scent, the softness of her dress, disturbingly real, filled his head...

'I'm just a details man,' he said, blanking it off. 'Go and get into bed. I'll make you a hot drink.'

'You should get back to London before the roads get any worse,' she said. Then, as headlights swept across the window, 'That's Peter home.'

'Closing time, Lou.' The elf sitting on the next stool stood up, eased her back. 'Reality beckons.'

'I'll just finish dressing this bear.'

'You're keen. See you tomorrow.'

It was a casual throwaway line, needing no answer, and Lucy didn't reply. Tomorrow would have to take care of itself; it was tonight that was the problem.

She tucked the teddy into a pair of striped pyjamas and a dressing gown, putting off the moment when she'd have to face a cold world. Because no amount of thinking had provided her with an answer to where she could go. Certainly not the flat she'd shared before she'd met Rupert. That would be the first place anyone would look.

She had a little money in her purse that would cover a night at some cheap B&B. The problem with that was that her face would be all over the evening news and someone was bound to spot her and call it in to one of the tabloids for the tip-off money.

The sensible answer, she knew, would be to contact one of them herself, let them take care of her. They'd stick her in a safe house so that no one else could get to her and they'd pay well for the story she had to tell. That was the reason they'd been grabbing at her, chasing after her. Why Rupert would be equally anxious to keep her away from them.

The problem with going down that route was that there would be no way back to her real life.

Once she'd taken their money she'd be their property. Would never be able to go back to being the person she had been six months ago.

Instead she'd become one of those pathetic Z-list celebrities who were forever doomed to live off their moment of infamy, relying on ever more sleazy stories to keep themselves in the public eye. Because no one would employ her in a nursery or day-care centre ever again.

But this reprieve was temporary. Out of time, she placed the teddy on the shelf and went to the office.

Frank looked up from his desk, where he was inputting figures into a computer. 'Are you still here?'

'Apparently. I was looking for Pam.'

He pulled a face. 'She collapsed not long after you arrived,' he said in an I-told-you-so tone of voice.

'Oh, good grief. I'm so sorry. Is she going to be all right?'

'It's just a bug and an inability to accept that we can manage without her for a day or two. Mr Hart took her home a couple of hours ago. Why did you want her?'

'Well…'

About to explain about the swipe card, it occurred to her that if Pam had collapsed not long after she'd mistaken her for an elf, she might not have had time to do the paperwork. Make her official. Log her in.

'It's nothing that won't wait. Although…'

She couldn't. Could she?

'She didn't mention what time I'm supposed to start tomorrow,' she added, as casually as she could.

'The store opens at ten. If you're honouring us with your presence, you'll need to be in your place, teddy at the ready at one minute to. Is that it?'

'Er…yes. Ten. No problem.'

He nodded. 'Goodnight.' Then, as she reached the door, 'You did a good job, Louise. I hope we'll see you tomorrow.'

'Thanks,' she said. 'Me, too.'

Nat switched on the radio as he drove back through thick swirling snowflakes that were beginning to pile up on the edges of the road. The footpaths were already white.

He'd hoped to catch an update about Henshawe's missing fiancée—ex-fiancée—on the news, but it was all weather warnings and travel news and the bulletins focused on the mounting chaos as commuters tried to get home in weather that hadn't been forecast.

She'd got lucky. But not as lucky as Henshawe. An embarrassing story was going to be buried under tomorrow's headlines about drivers spending the night in their cars, complaints about incompetent weather forecasters and the lack of grit on the roads.

They'd probably be reunited and back on the front cover of some gossip magazine by next week, with whatever indiscretions she was accusing him of long forgotten, he told himself. Forget her.

By the time he returned to the store it was closing. The last few shoppers were being ushered through the doors, the cloakrooms and changing rooms thoroughly checked in a well rehearsed routine to flush out anyone who might harbour ideas of spending the night there.

He parked in the underground garage, removed the shoe from the glove compartment and walked through to the security office.

Bryan looked up as he entered.

'Anything?' he asked.

'Not a sign. She probably slipped out under cover of the crowds. She's certainly not in the store now.'

'No.' He looked at the shoe and, instead of dropping it in the lost property box, held onto it.

'Are you going straight up to the tenth floor?'

He nodded. 'I'll be in the office for a while. You're working late?'

'We're a couple of men down with some bug that's going around.'

'Let me know if it becomes a problem.'

But it wasn't the likelihood of staff shortages at their busiest time of year that was nagging at him as he headed for the lifts. It was something he'd seen, something telling him that, despite all evidence to the contrary, his fugitive hadn't gone anywhere. That she was still here.

It was stupid, he knew.

She'd undoubtedly used the phone she'd been clutching in the hand she'd flung around his neck to call a friend, someone to bring her a change of clothes and whatever else she needed.

He needed to put the incident out of his mind. Forget the impact of her eyes, the flawless skin, long lashes that had been burned into his brain like a photograph in that long moment when he'd held her.

What was it? What was he missing?

He walked through the electrical department, but the

television screens that had been filled with her larger-than-life-size image were all blank now.

Her hair had been darker in that photograph. She'd been wearing less make-up. It was almost like seeing a before and after photograph. The original and the made-over version. Thinner, the image expensively finished, refined, everything except a tiny beauty spot above her lip that could not be airbrushed out of reality...

He stopped.

The beauty spot. That was what he'd seen. He scanned his memory, fast-forwarding through everything he'd seen and done in the hours since that moment on the stairs.

And came skidding to a halt on the elf.

The one who'd been standing so still by the drinks machine while he was talking to Frank. She was the right height, the right shape—filling out the elf costume in a way it hadn't been designed for. And she'd had a beauty spot in exactly the same place as the girl on the stairs.

Coincidence? Maybe, but he spun around and headed into the grotto.

While everyone else raced to change, get away as quickly as possible, Lucy dawdled and it had taken remarkably little time for the locker room to empty.

It was a little eerie being there on her own, the motion-sensitive lights shutting down all around her, leaving her in just a small area of light. And, while she was grateful to be off the streets, in the warm, she wasn't entirely sure what to do next.

Where she would be safe.

While the locker rooms would be free of cameras—she was almost certain they would be free of cameras—there would undoubtedly be a security presence of some sort.

Would it be high-tech gadgetry? Motion sensors, that

sort of thing. Patrols? Or just someone tucked up in an office with a flask of coffee, a pile of sandwiches and a good book while he monitored the store cameras?

At least she would be safe in here for a little while and she could use the time to take the shower she'd longed for. Wash off the whole hideous day. Wash off the last few months and reclaim herself.

And if someone did happen to come in, check that everyone had left, she could surely come up with some believable reason for staying behind to take a shower after work.

A hot date?

Actually, she did have one of those. Well, a date, anyway. Rupert didn't do hot, but neither would he cancel the Lucy B launch dinner at The Ritz just because she'd caused him a little embarrassment. She had no doubt that his PR team had already put some kind of spin on that. Stress. Pre-wedding nerves.

Of course if she turned up in the elf costume—the paparazzi would certainly be on the job tonight—it would wipe the smug smile off all their faces.

For a moment she was sorely tempted but, recalling the scrum at the press conference, she decided to give it a miss.

No. If she needed an excuse for being in the shower so late, she'd stick to the second job story. Everyone needed extra money at Christmas and a waitress—her own particular preference when she'd needed the cash to finance her studies—had to be clean and fresh.

She reclaimed her dress from the locker and then, having folded her costume neatly and left it on the bench, she took a towel from the rack and stepped into one of the stalls.

The water was hot and there were shampoo and soap dispensers. Hastings & Hart staff were very well taken care of, she decided, as she pushed the pump for a dollop of soap. Maybe she should reconsider her career options.

Could being an elf in a department store be considered a career? What did Santa do for the rest of the year? And would she get to meet the boss again?

Cold shower, cold shower!

She squeezed some shampoo. Her hair didn't need washing—she'd spent two hours in the salon having it cut and pampered earlier in the day—but she felt the need to cleanse herself from top to toe, rid herself of the past few months, and she dug in deep with her fingers, washing away the scent of betrayal, rinsing it down the drain.

Then, in no hurry to stop, she reached out to adjust the temperature a touch.

The grotto, Santa's workshop, was deserted. Nat walked through to Frank's office, hoping he might find a staff list, but the man was too well organised to leave such things lying about. Besides, he knew he had to be wrong. It had to be a coincidence. There was no way Lucy could have transformed herself into an elf.

It was ridiculous. He was becoming obsessed, seeing things.

Hearing things...

A deluge of ice water hit Lucy and she let out a shriek that would have woken the dead. She groped blindly for the control which, having spun at the merest touch, was now stuck stubbornly on cold.

She gave one last tug. The control knob came off in her hand and, freezing, she burst out of the shower stall, dripping, naked, eyes closed as she grabbed for the towel.

She wiped her face, took a breath, opened her eyes and discovered that she was not alone.

Nathaniel Hart—the man with his name above the front door—had obviously heard her yell. More of her 'openness and lack of guile', obviously. Not her best move if she wanted to keep below the radar.

She didn't scream, despite the shock. Her mouth opened; her brain was sending all the right signals but nothing was getting past the big thick lump that was blocking her throat.

He took the control from her hand, reached into the shower stall, screwed it deftly back into place and turned off the water, giving her a chance to gather her wits and wrap the towel around her before he closed the door.

Then he helped himself to one, dried his hands and only when he'd tossed it onto the bench behind her did he give her his full attention.

'Making yourself at home, Cinderella?' he enquired after what felt like the longest moment in her life while a slow blush spread from her cheeks and down her neck, heating all points south until it reached her toes.

Cinderella.

He knew...

It took forever to unglue her tongue from the roof of her mouth, making her lips work.

She took a step back, slipped on a floor awash with cold water. Torn between grabbing for safety and hanging onto the towel, she made a grab for the shower door.

No doubt afraid that she'd bring that down on them, Nathaniel Hart reached for her arm, steadying her before the towel had slipped more than an inch.

An inch was way too much. The towel, which when she'd first picked it up had seemed perfectly adequate for decency, now felt like a pocket handkerchief.

'This is the women's locker room,' she finally managed.

As if that was going to make any difference. This was

his store and she was trapped. Not just shoeless this time, but 'less' just about everything except for a teeny, tiny towel that just about covered her from breast to thigh. Not nearly enough when this close to a man who'd sizzled her with a look when she'd been fully dressed.

He was looking now—which dealt with freezing...

'You shouldn't be here,' she said, finally managing to get her voice to work and going for indignant. She failed miserably. She just sounded breathless. She felt breathless...

With good reason.

She was naked, alone and at the mercy of a man who almost certainly meant her no good. But, far from fleeing, his touch was like an electric charge and all her instincts were telling her to forget modesty, let the towel fall and cooperate with whatever he had in mind. One hundred per cent.

Nooooo!

She forced herself to take a step away, put some distance between them, get a grip. Regretting it the minute she did. There was something about his touch that made her feel safe. Made her feel...

'And that's not my name,' she added, cutting off the thought before she lost it entirely.

'No?' He flipped something from his pocket and offered it to her. 'If the shoe fits...'

He was still carrying her shoe?

'What do you think this is?' she demanded, ignoring the shoe. 'A pantomime? I'm all through with the Cinderella thing, Mr Hart.'

'You know who I am?'

'Mr Alyson told me. You're Nathaniel Hart and you own this store.'

'I run it. Not the same thing.'

'Oh.' She wasn't sure why that was better, but somehow

it was. She was totally off billionaire tycoons. 'I just assumed…'

'Most people do.'

'Well, if the name fits,' she said and thought she got the tiniest response. Just a hint of a smile. But maybe she was imagining it. 'What do you want, Mr Hart?'

'Nothing. On the contrary, I'm your fairy godmother.'

She stared at him but said nothing. She was in enough trouble without stating the obvious.

'I know what you're thinking,' he said.

'I promise you, you haven't got a clue.'

'You're thinking where is the frilly skirt? Where are the wings?'

No… Not even close. 'Trust me, it would not be a good look for you. Take my advice, stick with the pin-stripes.'

'Well, I'm glad you take that view.'

The barest suspicion of a smile became a twitch of the lips, curling around her, warm, enticing. Tempting. Heating up bits that it would take a very long cold shower to beat into line and she was very glad indeed that he hadn't got a clue.

'Hastings & Hart takes its role as an equal opportunities employer very seriously,' he assured her.

'We have to take our fairy godmothers wherever we can find them in these enlightened days,' she agreed, firmly resisting the temptation to fling herself into his arms and invite him to make free with his magic wand. Instead, she tightened her lips, keeping them pressed down in a straight line. A smile meant nothing, she told herself. Anyone could smile. It was easy. You just stretched your lips wide…

But he was really good at it. It wasn't just the corner of his mouth doing something that hit all the right buttons. It had reached all the way up to his eyes and the warmth of it reached deep within her, turning her insides liquid.

She clutched the towel a little tighter. 'I guess the real test comes with Santa Claus? Would you employ a woman for that role?' she asked a touch desperately.

The lines carved into his cheeks became deeper, bracketing his mouth. And the silver sparks in his eyes had not been reflections of the Christmas decorations, she realised, but were all his own. It was all there now. Every part of his face was engaged and while it wasn't a pretty smile, it was all the more dangerous for that.

'Not my decision, thank goodness. Human Resources have the responsibility of employing the best person for the job and keeping me on the right side of the law.'

She tutted. 'Passing the buck.'

'There has to be some advantage to go with the name,' he replied, 'but, as far as fairy godmothers go, right now I'm not just your best option, I appear to be the only one.'

'Oh?' she said, putting on a brave front. If she was going down, she refused to be a pushover. 'Why do you think that?'

'Because if there had been anyone you could ask for help you wouldn't be hiding out in Santa's grotto dressed as an elf. You'd have used the phone you were carrying to call them.'

'Who says I'm hiding?' she demanded. 'That I need help.'

'The fact that you're here, prepared to risk getting caught on the premises after closing, speaks for itself.'

She couldn't argue with his logic. He had it, spot on, but she still had the backup excuse. 'I'm just late leaving,' she said. 'I needed a shower before I start my other job.'

He shook his head.

'You're not buying it?'

'Sorry.'

'Oh, well. It was worth a shot.' She managed a shrug

even though her heart was hammering in her mouth. 'So. What happens now?'

'I congratulate you on your ingenuity?' he suggested. 'Ask how you managed to get yourself kitted out with an elf costume so that you could hide out in Santa's grotto?'

'I'm smart?'

'Obviously. But, if you managed it, there are security issues involved.'

'Oh, look, it wasn't anyone's fault,' she said quickly. Clearly the game was up for her, but she couldn't allow anyone else to suffer. 'I was mistaken for a temp who was expected but never turned up and it was too good an opportunity to miss. Pam won't get into trouble, will she? She was desperate. Not just desperate but sick,' she stressed. 'Well, you know that since you took her home.'

'Don't worry about Pam, worry about yourself,' he said, the smile fading.

She shivered. Not from fear. This man was not a bully. He wasn't crowding her, there was no suggestion of the physical threat that had seemed so real in the press conference. Why she'd run.

He was much more dangerous than that.

He could bring her down with a look. As if to prove it, he reached for a dry towel and draped it around her shoulders, assuming that she was cold. His touch tingled through her and she knew that all he had to do was put his hand to her back and she'd put up her hands, surrender without a struggle.

Fortunately, he didn't know that.

'What were you planning to do next?' he asked, not lingering, but taking a step back, putting clear air between them.

'Get dressed?' she suggested.

'And then?' he persisted.

'I thought I might bed down in one of your tents.' There seemed little point in lying about it. 'I noticed them yesterday when I was Christmas shopping. I've never been camping,' she added.

'It's overrated. Especially in the middle of winter.'

'I don't know. I could brew myself some tea on one of those little camp stoves. Fry a few sausages for my supper. I'd leave the money for the food on the till in the food hall.' She clutched the towel a little more tightly against her bosom. 'Maybe have a bit of a sing-song to keep my spirits up,' she added a touch recklessly. 'I did work for three hours for nothing. And I was planning to work tomorrow on the same terms. Bed and breakfast seems a reasonable exchange.'

'More than reasonable,' he agreed. 'Which one did you have your eye on?'

'I'm sorry?'

'Which tent? I can recommend the one-man Himalayan. I'm told that it's absolutely draught-proof.'

'Oh. Right. Well, thanks.'

'I'd strongly advise against the cooking, though. The security staff are based on the same floor and the smoke alarms are extremely sensitive.'

CHAPTER FIVE

Lucy swallowed hard. Was he joking? It was impossible to tell. When he wasn't smiling, Nathaniel Hart could give lessons in how to do a poker face.

'Well, thanks for the tip,' she managed. 'I've got a bag of crisps and a chocolate biscuit that I bought from the machine. They'll keep me going.'

He shook his head and a lick of thick dark hair slid across his forehead.

'That won't do,' he said, combing it back with long fingers. 'Chocolate biscuits and crisps aren't going to provide you with your five-a-day.'

Her five-a-day? She stared him. Unreal. The man was not only conspiring with her to trespass in his department store, but he was concerned that she was eating healthily. Consuming the government's daily recommended five portions of fruit and vegetables...

Or had he already summoned Rupert and was simply amusing himself at her expense while he waited for him to arrive and remove her?

Of course he was. Why was she even wasting time thinking about it?

'Who are you? The food police?' she demanded crossly. At least that was the intent but his hand was still on her arm, his fingers warm against her goosepimply skin and she didn't sound cross. She sounded breathless.

'Hastings & Hart take a close interest in staff welfare. We have a cycle to work scheme—which is why you have the luxury of shower facilities—'

'Luxury!' Finally she got her voice back. But then there wasn't much luxury in an unexpected ice-cold dunk.

'—and subsidised gym membership as well as a healthy options menu in the staff canteen.'

And he'd driven Pam Wootton home when she was taken ill, she reminded herself. That was taking staff welfare very seriously indeed. Not many men in his position would have done that. It suggested that he was unusually kind, thoughtful and, about to tell herself that Rupert would never have done that, it occurred to her that he had. Done exactly that. And, as she'd just discovered, he was neither kind nor thoughtful.

'Impressive, Mr Hart, but I'm only a temp. Temps don't get fringe benefits.'

Not just a temp, but an illicit one at that. He might be a great employer but she had no more reason to trust him than he had to trust her.

'Besides, the crisps are made from potatoes,' she said, playing for time as she tried, desperately, to think what to do next. Pull away from his hand, for a start, obviously. Put some space between them…'And they're cheese and onion flavour.'

There were no windows down here, but even in the basement there had to be a fire escape. Or would Rupert have learned from her last dash for freedom and have those covered before he moved in?

Was that what all the time-wasting was about?

'So potato and onion, that's two of my five,' she added, wishing she'd spent more time thinking about her escape instead of day-dreaming about a dishy stranger while she dressed teddy bears. 'There's the protein from the cheese, too, don't forget.'

Think... *Think!*

'And it's an orange chocolate biscuit.'

'Is that it?' he asked. 'All done?'

'All done,' she admitted. She was out of ideas. Out of excuses. Out of flavourings.

'Nice try—'

There was the smile again. The whole works. Crinkles fanning out from the corners of his eyes, something magical happening to his mouth as the lower lip softened to reveal the merest glimpse of white teeth. And then there were his eyes...

His eyes seemed to suggest that he was as surprised as she was to find he was smiling and, as quickly as it had appeared, it vanished.

And she could breathe again.

'—but no cigar,' he said. 'I'm sorry to be the bearer of bad news but potatoes don't count as a vegetable.'

'They don't?' She made a good fist at surprised.

'Not as one of your five-a-day.'

He didn't look sorry.

'You're telling me I'm going to have to stop counting fries?' she demanded, hoping to make him forget himself again and actually laugh. Get him on her side. 'Well, that's a swizz.'

'And you can forget the flavourings, too.'

'I was afraid that might be stretching it. I did have orange juice with my breakfast,' she assured him, as if determined to prove that she wasn't a complete dietary failure. Playing the fool in an attempt to lull him into believing that she'd bought his act.

'Good start. And since breakfast?'

'I had green beans with my lunch and I'm fairly sure that the fruit in the dessert was the real thing.'

'Apple tart, right?'

'How on earth do you know that?'

'The cinnamon was the giveaway.'

'Cinnamon?' Had he been that close? Mortified, she smothered a groan. Time to put a stop to this. 'What about you, Mr Hart?'

'Nat.'

'Nat?'

'Short for Nathaniel. A bit of a mouthful.'

'But nicer than Nat, which is a small spiteful insect which takes lumps out of you when you're innocently enjoying a sunset.'

'Very nearly,' he agreed, rewarding her with a flicker of a smile that went straight to her blush. And too late she realised her mistake. 'What about me?'

She'd thought she was being clever, keeping him talking, while she scoped out the shower room, hoping to pick up the faint illumination of an emergency exit, but it was hopeless. This was the basement and there was no escape, but she could still let everyone know where she was. What was happening. If only she could convince him that she wasn't going to make a run for it so he'd leave her to get dressed...

She shook her head. 'It doesn't matter. My name is Lucy, by the way. Lucy Bright. But you already know that.'

'I caught the Lucy on the news. Not the Bright. It explains the B in Lucy B.'

News?

That hideous scene had been on the news? Well, of course it had. The unveiling of the new look for his fashion chain, taking it upmarket, providing aspirational clothes for the career-minded woman. Clothes for work and play.

Clothes with a touch of class and a fair trade label was a big story. Providing new jobs both here and in the Third World.

'How d'you do, Lucy Bright?' he said, finally removing his hand from her arm and offering it to her.

She clutched the towel with one hand, placed her other in his, watching as his long fingers and broad palm swallowed up her own small hand. A rush of warmth warned her she was doing the head to toe blush again.

'To be honest, I've had better days, Nathaniel Hart.'

'Maybe I can help. Why don't you get dressed and then we'll go and see what's good in the Food Hall? I'm sure I can find something more enticing than crisps and chocolate for your supper.'

What?

'There is nothing more enticing than crisps and chocolate.'

Healthier, maybe, but right now she was in the market for high carb, high calorie comfort food.

'And we do need to discuss your camping arrangements,' he continued, ignoring the interruption, 'because, even if you manage to evade the security cameras, I'm afraid the cleaners will spot you.'

'They clean inside the tents?'

'That's probably a push of the vacuum too far,' he admitted, 'but they will certainly notice one zipped up from the inside. You don't imagine you're the first person to have that idea, do you?' He didn't wait for her answer. 'Take your time. No rush,' he said, surrendering her arm, leaving a cold spot where his hand had been, using it to take a phone from his pocket as he turned and walked away, finally leaving her to get dressed.

* * *

Appointments...
20:00 Camping out for the night in H&H outdoors
department.
20:30 Or maybe not.

Nat finished his call, then leaned back against the wall opposite the locker room door and waited, closing his eyes in an attempt to block out the image that was indelibly imprinted upon his mind.

Lucy Bright backing naked out of the shower stall, water pouring off her shoulders, back, the deliciously soft curve of her backside. Her determined chin as she'd faced him down despite the hot pink flush that had spread just about everywhere.

Her struggle not to smile, when a smile would, undoubtedly, have been in her best interests.

A drop of water sliding slowly around a curl released from its airy hold, hanging for a moment before it finally fell. Lying for a moment in the hollow above her collarbone before it was joined by another and had gathered sufficient weight to overcome inertia and trickle down between her breasts.

Smooth shoulders lifted in the merest shrug as she adopted a carelessly casual response to the awkwardness of the situation.

Like a swan, all appeared serene on the surface, while her brain had clearly been whirring like the freewheeling cogs of a machine as she tried to engage gear and figure out how to escape him for a second time. Work out her next move.

Or maybe his.

Good question. What exactly *was* he going to do?

Until five minutes ago, he'd thought it was simple. He

would deliver her to friends and walk away. No more, no less complicated than driving Pam home this afternoon.

But it wasn't simple. Simple had become a fantasy from the moment he'd touched her, looked into her green-gold eyes. From the moment he'd glimpsed her luscious curves.

While his head was demanding that he call a cab, dump her in it and send her on her way, do what he could to help without getting involved, his heart—mostly his heart—wasn't having any of it.

That foolish organ demanded that he scoop her up, carry her to his apartment and keep her safe from harm.

Neither was an option.

It was clear that she didn't trust him further than she could throw him, and why would she? In her shoes, he'd be expecting the police to arrive at any minute to remove her from the premises.

What he had to do was keep his head, keep his distance—despite arms aching to wrap her up, keep her safe—but, most important of all, keep her from running.

He had no idea what had caused the row with Rupert Henshawe, or why he'd sent his heavies after her, but he did know that while she was here, under his roof, no harm would come to her. And that, he told himself, was all that mattered.

He looked at the shoe he was still holding, hoping that without it she'd think twice about making a dash for it the first chance she got.

Not so easy with the store closed but she was right, she was smart and, like the involvement issue, he wasn't banking on it.

We?

Lucy caught sight of herself in one of the mirrors and snapped her jaw shut. For a moment there she'd almost succumbed to the fantasy that he might be a good guy.

Perhaps the atmosphere in the grotto was rubbing off on her and, like the little girl in the lift, she wanted to believe.

Had they seen that in her? Rupert's PR people. The longing for something that had always been out of reach. Not the glamour, the clothes, but something deeper. A need for love so desperate that she would be emotionally seduced by the fairy tale of the beast tamed by the innocent.

In other words, a sucker.

Because only an idiot would have fallen for it. She knew she wasn't special. Not tall and elegant or the slightest bit gorgeous. She wasn't an 'It' girl, or a model, or an actress. Nothing like the kind of woman billionaires were usually seen with. Not the kind of woman Rupert had dated in droves—even while remaining determinedly uncommitted—before he'd apparently been bowled over by her innocent charms.

So innocent that he'd insisted on waiting until they were married before they moved their relationship beyond a few kisses.

How many women would have been dumb enough to fall for *that* fairy tale?

Forget the still small voice in the back of her head. The fact that he found it so easy to resist temptation, the fact that she was perfectly happy to go along with it, wasn't panting with frustration, should have sent not just warning bells clanging but klaxons wailing an ear-splitting warning.

It was so obvious, faced with reality, that she was in love with the idea of being in love, the fairy tale, rather than the man. While Rupert...

Well, his motives were clear enough.

He could have paid a celebrity to be the face, the figure

to relaunch his fashion chain, but he wanted a real woman who he would transform with his new 'look'. An ordinary woman.

Apparently she was a breath of fresh air. Real. That was how the PR people had described her in their report. Not a model or a star, but someone who every women in their sales demographic would instantly relate to, aspire to be. Would believe.

So far, so simple. And the rest of it had started as a throwaway line scribbled in the margins of a report.

And she'd fallen for it, believed him, because it had never once occurred to her that it was all a big fat lie. What, for heaven's sake, would be the point of that?

Innocent was right.

The point, of course, was money. A lot of money. Now she knew the truth, she could bring the whole edifice crashing down. It would cost him millions and he wasn't about to let that happen.

She dug out her phone and with shaky fingers she keyed in a tweet while she had a chance.

Lies, lies, lies...

She stopped. There was no signal. Had she been cut off? Or was it just because she was in the deepest part of the basement, surrounded by concrete? She'd had one a couple of hours ago by the coffee machine...

It didn't matter. Whatever the cause, she was, for the moment at least, totally on her own.

Nothing new there. She'd been on her own for most of her life. And if she was trembling by the time she tugged a comb through her damp hair it was with anger rather than fear.

She was absolutely furious with Rupert for lying to

her, with Nathaniel Hart for making her want to believe him, but most of all with herself for being so gullible, so stupid.

Diary update: Everything was going so well. I was safe for the night. All I had to do was keep my head down, stay out of the way of security patrols and I was home dry. Well, wet, actually, because I couldn't resist taking a shower...

Oh, for goodness' sake, she thought, closing the phone. What was the point?

She was up the creek without a paddle and going nowhere. At least not for the moment. Once she was out of the basement all bets were off, but for now the best she could do was get dressed and be ready to take advantage of the slightest opportunity.

She lifted the towel from her shoulders and began vigorously rubbing at her hair. The last thing she needed was pneumonia. In fact... She gave up on the hair and sorted through the pile of discarded elf clothes, picking out the tights, bootees and even the hat, pushing them into the depths of her bag.

The bootees weren't going to be snow-proof, but they would be a lot better than bare feet.

Guilt warred with a sense of triumph as she finished towelling herself off. Triumph won as she stepped into fragile lacy underwear which would do nothing to keep the cold out. She fastened her bra and then reached for her dress.

Her hand met the bare slats of the bench and she turned to look.

Her dress, along with the towel tossed aside by Nathaniel Hart, had slipped to the floor.

She made a wild grab for it but both dress and towel had been lying there quite long enough to soak up water like a sponge and, as she lifted it from the floor, it dripped icy-cold water down her legs.

In desperation she squeezed it. Rolled it up in a dry towel. The towel got wet. The dress did not get noticeably drier.

It was the elf costume or nothing.

She groaned. She might be in a mess but the dress did things to her figure that the elf costume could never hope to achieve. She *knew* what effect the dress had on Nathaniel Hart. Wearing that, she had a chance of distracting him but, while her underwear would have undoubtedly done the job with bells on, she could hardly make her escape in a couple of scraps of lace.

Too late to do any good, she moved to the far end of the bench where it was dry and climbed back into the only warm clothes she possessed. The elf suit. The gorgeous stripy green tights. The tunic that was a little too tight. The neat little belt with the pouch to keep her acorns in. Or whatever it was that elves ate. The flat, floppy around the ankles bootees.

Terrific.

At least she could put on some make-up. And she wasn't talking about freckles.

Five minutes later, lips pink, eyes smudgy, blusher discreetly applied and her damp hair released from the iron grip of hair straighteners and curling ridiculously around her head, she tugged on the tunic and sighed.

This was so not a good look. Her only hope was that some persistent paparazzo would snatch a snap of her leaving the store, being bundled into Rupert's car.

Or did that come under the realms of fantasy, too? There was an underground car park and that was where he'd pick her up, out of sight. Drive her away in a car with blacked-out windows. Or just shoved to the floor out of sight. No need for pretence.

She gathered her coat and bag, scared but determined not to let it show. Then, with her hand on the door, she paused. She still had the file and that gave her an edge. Bargaining power. Removing it from her bag, she stowed it in an empty locker, then looked around for a place to hide the key.

Once that was done, there was nothing more she could do but face the music—or, more accurately, the deliciously elegant Nathaniel Hart.

She gave one more tug on the hem of the tunic, reminding herself that it could be worse—at least she was wearing more than a damp towel. Actually, come to think of it, that might not be…

No. Telling herself to behave, be brave—she had more to worry about than how she looked—she took a deep breath and opened the door.

No poker face this time.

Between the elf costume and her wet hair sticking out at all angles, it was not her finest fashion hour, at least if the eyebrow gymnastics were anything to go by.

Making the most of a bad job, she pasted on a bright smile and gave him a twirl. 'What do you think?' she asked. 'Does my bum look big in this?'

There was a long moment—too long–while he considered the matter and her smile began to wobble. What kind of idiot drew attention to her worst bits?

'What happened to your dress?' he finally asked, avoiding her question.

'Are you referring to the world's most expensive floor cloth?' she responded, giving herself a mental slap for asking a question to which she already knew the answer.

'I don't know. Am I?'

'The dress that some idiot man managed to knock into a freezing puddle with a badly tossed towel?' She didn't wait for him to answer that one. 'You don't think I'd be wearing this if there was any choice, do you?'

'You were happy enough to grab it this afternoon,' he reminded her, 'although I have admit that it is rather—'

She glared at him, daring him to say the word *tight*.

'—green.' He opened the door that led into the electrical department. 'It goes with your eyes,' he added, taking her elbow as he fell in beside her. Not in a frog-marching way. Just a touch, a guiding hand, rather like a gentleman escorting a lady in to dinner in some Jane Austen movie, but she wasn't fooled by that. Or his attempt at gallantry. She knew he was simply keeping contact so that if she decided to make a run for it all he had to do was tighten his grip.

She'd do it, too, at the first chance of escape.

For the moment, however, she forced herself to relax so that she wouldn't telegraph her intentions. She'd already witnessed the lightning speed of his reactions when he'd stopped her from falling on the stairs. Lightning in every sense of the word. That moment while something seemed to fuse between them had been like a lightning strike. For a moment they had both been a little dazed. She wasn't dazed now, though—well, not much—and carrying her kicking and screaming through the store was an entirely different kettle of fish. And if she decided to play hide and seek she might be able to hold out until morning.

Not so easy when the store was empty. There were cameras everywhere. But that worked both ways. His security people, the ones he'd warned her about, would be watching...

She realised that he was looking at her.

'What?' she demanded.

'Nothing. I was just speculating on Frank Alyson's response to the liberties you've taken with your elf costume.' He sounded grave, but a smile was tugging at the corner of his mouth. 'Your belt is a little too tight and your make-up is definitely non-regulation. Where are the rosy cheeks and freckles?' he asked. 'And you must know that you're improperly dressed without your hat.'

Okay, he was teasing and, despite everything, she was sorely tempted to smile. Instead, she reminded herself that they were *his* security people. They would believe whatever he told them and she couldn't deny that she was on the premises illegally.

Cool. She had to play it cool. Wait her chance.

'So…what? He'll feed me to the troll?'

'Troll?' he asked, startled into a grin and set off a whole new wave of sparks flaring through her body.

Maybe she could set off a fire alarm, she thought desperately, doing her best to ignore them. Or there were the cleaners. They would be arriving soon; he'd said so. They had to get in. And get out again.

'It's what he does to underachieving elves,' she replied, deadpan. 'But I'm off duty so I'm afraid you're going to have to live with "improper", at least until my dress dries,' she said, as if her clothing disaster was the only thing on her mind. 'Always supposing it survives the dunking.'

'I'm sorry about the dress. For some reason I didn't notice it.'

Well, no. He'd been too busy not noticing her towel slipping all over the place…

'I'll replace it, of course.'

'It was a one-off. A designer original.'

'Oh. Well, let's hope it dries out.'

'It had better. Everything else I own is packed up in a couple of boxes. Along with my life.'

The life she'd had before she met Rupert Henshawe. It hadn't been very exciting, but it had been real. Honest. Truthful.

Her clothes, including the most expensive suit she'd ever bought, the one she'd bought for her interview at the Henshawe Corporation—she'd been so determined to make a good impression. It had done its job, but of course it hadn't been good enough for Lucy B.

There was an ancient laptop she'd bought second-hand. All the letters were worn off the keys but it had seen her through her business course. A box of books for her college work. A few precious memories from her childhood.

She'd left pretty much everything else behind when the constant presence of the media on the doorstep of the tiny flat she'd shared with two other girls had made it impossible to do even the simplest thing. When even a trip to the corner shop for a bottle of milk had become a media scrum.

Her kettle, radio, her crocks and pots. The bits and pieces she'd accumulated since she'd left the care system.

She was now worse off than she'd ever been. No job, nowhere to live. She was going to have to start again from scratch.

How much did she have left in her old account? Enough for the deposit on a room in a flat share?

There had been a time when she'd have known to the last penny.

'I didn't plan this very well, did I?' she said, trying to keep the panic out of her voice.

'I've no idea what you've done, Lucy.'

Nothing. She hadn't done a thing...

'I missed the start of the news bulletin but you wield a mean handbag.'

'That man grabbed me,' she protested. 'He wouldn't let me go.'

'I wasn't criticising. It must have been terrifying to be caught up in that kind of media mayhem. I didn't catch the wrap up,' he prompted. 'As you're aware, Pam collapsed and I was called away.'

'Is she going to be okay?' Lucy asked.

'Just a seasonal bug. She should have stayed at home, but it tends to get hectic at this time of year.'

She glanced at him. 'You saw me, didn't you? When you were talking to Mr Alyson.'

'I saw the costume,' he said. 'Not you. I was looking for a girl in a very sexy black dress.'

At least he didn't deny that he'd been looking for her.

'It was later,' he added, glancing down at her, 'when I remembered your beauty spot, that I realised it was you.'

'My what?'

'Your beauty spot,' he repeated, pausing, turning to face her. 'Here.'

'That's not…'

Her voice dried as he touched his fingertip to the corner of her lip. He was close, his eyes were dark, slumberous as he looked down at her, and for a moment she thought he was going to kiss her, finish what he'd started on the stairs.

Her heart rate picked up, hammering in her throat; all she could see was his mouth, bracketed by a pair of deep lines and, as his lower lip softened, she finally understood the depth of Rupert's betrayal. Just how shockingly she had been fooled. Because this was how it should be. The entire body engaged, every cell focused on the desire for the touch, the taste of that mouth against hers. Nothing else. And, as a finger of heat spiralled through her, a tiny, urgent gasp escaped her lips.

The sound, barely audible, was enough to shatter the spell. He raised heavy lids, lifting his gaze from her mouth to her eyes and dropped his hand.

'It's j-just a mole,' she said quickly, taking a step back, putting an arm's length between them before straightening her shoulders, lifting her chin. 'Rupert wanted me to have it removed. Just a little bit too warts-and-all ordinary for him, apparently.'

'If Henshawe thinks you're ordinary he needs to get his eyes tested.'

'Does he?' she asked, for a moment distracted by the unexpected compliment. But only for a moment. 'Well, green striped tights do tend to make you stand out from the crowd,' she said in an attempt at carelessness that she was a long way from feeling. And then wished she hadn't as he gave her legs the kind of attention that they could do without at the moment.

'True,' he said, finally dragging his gaze away from them, 'but I noticed you before you morphed into an elf,' he reminded her as he retrieved her elbow and headed briskly for the stairs.

'It's hard to miss someone falling over their own feet right in front of you,' she said, stumbling a little in the soft boots as she struggled to keep up with him.

He slowed, a consideration that she was sure neither Rupert nor his men would show her.

'Of course I have spent the last few months being buffed and polished and waxed,' she rushed on, trying not to think about how much 'notice' he'd taken of her. How close he'd just come to 'noticing' her again—this time in an empty store with none of the constraints of shoppers pounding past them. He was the enemy, for heaven's sake, and while she wanted to throw him off the scent, she wasn't entirely sure who would be distracting who... 'My hair has been streaked, my eyelashes dyed, my eyebrows threaded and I've lost weight, too.'

'Don't tell me. You had a personal trainer.'

'Good grief, no. I've just been too busy to snack between meals.' She gave him an arch look, ran a finger over one of her well-tended brows. 'You have no idea how much time it takes to look this groomed.'

He glanced at her, taking a long look at her messy hair and clothes that not even a catwalk model could make look good.

'Forget I said that,' she said hurriedly. 'I've been deprived of chocolate for too long and it's affecting my brain.'

Suddenly desperate for the instant gratification of chocolate melting on the tongue, she stopped, forcing him to do the same, dug the chocolate finger biscuit out of her elf pouch—so much more satisfying than acorns—and unwrapped it. As she raised it to her mouth she realised that she had an audience and she snapped it in half, offering one of the fingers to Nathaniel Hart.

He shook his head, not bothering to hide a smile. And she was right. The distraction was mutual. 'Your need is greater.'

She wasn't arguing and she bit into it, struggling to contain a groan of sheer pleasure.

'Better?'

'Marginally. Don't get me wrong,' she said, licking her fingers—she'd been carrying the chocolate next to her body and it was soft. 'I enjoyed it all. The gorgeous clothes. Being made over, every single bit of me being made as perfect as humanly possible without the intervention of surgery. Who wouldn't?'

That, after all, was the dream she was selling. Buy your clothes from this store and you too can have all this.

'Surgery?'

'I drew the line at the boob job. And the spray tan. I like my orange in a glass. Or chocolate-flavoured.'

She tossed a glance in his direction, but he shook his head. 'No comment.'

'Oh, please. Everyone has an opinion.' From the editor of a magazine who was desperate to do a step-by-step photo feature of a silicone implant—and had really struggled to hide her annoyance when she'd refused to play along—to the woman who did her nails. Everyone, apparently, wanted a bigger cup size. Everyone except her. She put her hands to her waist and pushed out her chest, straining the buttons to the limit. 'Apparently my naturalness and lack of guile wasn't, when push came to shove, quite enough. But that's the Cinderella story, isn't it? She had to be transformed before she was fit for the prince. All imperfections disappearing with a wave of a magic wand. Or the modern equivalent.'

He lifted an eyebrow.

'Photoshop.'

'But he still wanted her when he saw her as she really was. In her rags and covered with ashes from the hearth.'

'Oh, please! He didn't even recognise her.' She looked at the elegant red suede shoe he was still carrying, then up at Nathaniel Hart. 'Do you want to risk it?' she asked. 'If the shoe doesn't fit, will you let me go?'

'The shoe fell out of your bag, Lucy.'

'Did you see it fall?'

'Well, no…'

'Then I believe that is what's known in legal circles as circumstantial evidence.'

'Not if I find the matching one in there.'

'The matching one is jammed in a grating two streets away.' Then, unable to bear the suspense, the teasing pretence a moment longer, 'Shall we cut the pretence? How long have I got?'

His dark brows drew together in a puzzled frown. 'I'm sorry? How long have you got for what?'

'There's no need to pretend. I know you've called him. Rupert,' she added when his frown only deepened. 'I saw you. As you left the locker room.'

'The only person I've spoken to in the last twenty minutes—apart from you—is my chief security officer. To inform him that, rather than going straight to my office, I was still in the store.'

They'd reached the Food Hall and he released her elbow, snagged a trolley and headed down the nearest aisle.

Not Rupert?

Lucy firmly smothered the little flicker of hope that he was for real, ate the second finger of biscuit for comfort and went after him.

'Nice try,' she said when she caught up, 'but you were following me. On the stairs.'

'We were going in the same direction,' he conceded, picking up a box of eggs, glancing back at her. 'What made you look back?'

'Sheer paranoia? When I ran out of that hotel I had a dozen or so people on my tail. I knew I wasn't far enough ahead to have evaded all of them. I was trying not to draw attention to myself,' she said. 'Waiting for the hand on my shoulder.'

'And you thought I was the hand?'

'Aren't you? I heard you tell Frank Alyson to keep a

look out…' She faltered as he stopped by a shelf containing breakfast cereals. She was beginning to sound paranoid. Could she have got it wrong? That he didn't have a clue what she was talking about…'You will tell me if I'm making a total idiot of myself, won't you?'

CHAPTER SIX

'YOU'RE making a total idiot of yourself,' Nathaniel said obligingly, 'but it's okay. You're scared. I don't know why and you don't have to tell me. And I had the people following you escorted from the store.'

'You did? But how did you know?'

'They weren't discreet.' The muscles in his jaw tightened momentarily. 'Of course it's likely they were replaced but you should be safe enough now that the store is closed. They'll have to accept that you aren't inside and go away.' He continued to examine the shelf. 'Be glad to in this weather, I should think.'

'I suppose.'

'As for me, I was just doing my afternoon round of the store. It was pure chance that I happened to be following you up the stairs. What's your favourite cereal?' he asked, looking back at her.

'Mr Hart…'

'Nat. This one looks interesting,' he said, taking a box from the shelf. 'It has fruit pieces and something called clusters.'

'Nathaniel…'

'What are "clusters"?'

'Not one of your five-a-day,' she snapped, beginning to lose it. No. She'd lost it the minute he'd looked at her. He was looking at her now and her mouth dried. 'I haven't the faintest idea. I've never bought fancy breakfast cereals in my life. I always have porridge.'

'Always?'

'It's cheap, filling and good for you.' And, even when you had a platinum credit card with your name on it, old habits died hard.

'It also requires a saucepan and heat,' he pointed out.

'I was quite content with the crisps and the chocolate.'

'You've eaten the chocolate,' he reminded her, replacing the fancy cereal with its fruit and clusters on the shelf. 'Porridge it is.'

'No! I don't want anything.'

But he'd tossed a smart tartan box into the trolley.

It bore about as much similarity to the jumbo pack of own-brand oats she bought from the supermarket as the Lucy B version of the cashmere dress she'd abandoned, and she was sure the packaging reflected the price.

'And, just so there's no misunderstanding,' he continued, scanning the shelves as they moved on, 'the only thing I was asking Frank to keep an eye open for was anyone else showing signs of the bug that laid Pam low.'

'But—'

'The last thing I need at this time of year is an epidemic. Staff passing it on to the children visiting the grotto.'

She looked up at him, searched his face. He submitted patiently to her scrutiny, as if he understood what she was doing. He looked genuine but so had everyone else she'd met in the last few months. All those nice people who had been lying to her.

She could no longer trust her own judgement.

'Can I believe you?'

'It doesn't really matter what I say, does it? If I've called Henshawe to tell him where you are there is no escape. If

I haven't, then you're safe. Only time can set your mind at rest.'

'So,' she asked, a wry smile pulling at her lip, 'is that a yes or a no?'

His only response was to reach for a bottle of maple syrup and add it to the trolley.

'Suppose I insisted on leaving?' she persisted. 'Right this minute.'

'I'd find you some warm clothes and then drive you wherever you wanted to go.'

'Why?'

'Because, interesting though that outfit is, I imagine you'd rather leave wearing something that doesn't look as if you've escaped from a pantomime.'

Lucy discovered that she couldn't speak.

'Because you're under my roof, Lucy. Staff, temp, customer, you're my responsibility.'

She shook her head in disbelief.

'You're afraid I'd trick you? That I'd take you to him?'

He didn't appear to take offence which, considering the way she'd been casting doubt on his character, was suspicious in itself and Lucy shook her head again. Her entire world had been turned upside down for the second time in months, but this time not for the good.

'I can't trust anyone. I thought I knew Rupert. I thought he cared for me. I don't and he doesn't. The only thing he appears to care about is his profit and loss statement.'

'Are you sure? I don't know Henshawe, other than by reputation,' he continued when she didn't say anything. 'What I've read in the financial pages. Frankly, he's not a man I'd want to do business with, but love can change a man.'

'Well, that's just rubbish and you know it,' she declared.

'The only time you can change a man is when he's in nappies.'

She saw him pull his lips back tight against his teeth, doing his best not to smile. His eyes let him down.

'It's not funny!' But she found herself struggling with a giggle. 'Rupert Henshawe is not, and never was, in love with me. What we had was not a romance, I discovered today, but a marketing campaign. That's why I gave him back his ring.'

'A masterpiece in understatement, if I might say so. You have a good throwing arm, by the way. Have you ever played cricket?'

'They showed that on the news?' She groaned, mortified at the spectacle she'd made of herself. Then she sighed. 'What does it matter? It'll be on the front page of every newspaper tomorrow morning. The only story about our relationship that wasn't carefully stage-managed by his PR team.'

'You and the PR team got lucky. Tomorrow's headlines will all be about the weather.'

'It's still snowing?'

'Deep and crisp and even,' he said. 'Traffic chaos from one end of the country to the other. It's no night for an elf to be out.' He paused. 'Especially not in something that doesn't cover her—'

'I've got the picture.' She tugged on the back of the tunic. 'Thank you.'

When she still didn't move he took her hand and pressed his phone, warm from his pocket, into it.

'If you can't trust me, take this, call Enquiries and ask for a cab firm, although I warn you you'll have a long wait in this weather.'

Calling her bluff. He knew she had nowhere to go. She

opened it, anyway. Keyed in the number for Enquiries but, before it was answered, she broke the connection.

'We both know that if I had anywhere to go, anyone to call, I wouldn't be standing here in this ridiculous outfit,' she said. 'I'd be long gone.'

Nat watched her accept the bitter truth and felt his heart breaking for her. No one should be so alone. So friendless.

'I'm sorry. It's tough when you love someone and they let you down.'

'Love is a word, not an emotion, Nathaniel. We're sold on it from the time we're old enough to listen to fairy tales. Songs, movies, books… It's a marketing man's dream. I was in love with the idea of being in love, that's all. Swept up in the Cinderella story as much as anyone buying the latest issue of *Celebrity*. It's not my heart that's in a mess. It's my life.' About to hand the phone back to him, she said, 'Actually, would you mind if I sent a message?'

'You've thought of someone?'

Why didn't that make him feel happier?

'Half a million someones,' she replied. 'My Twitter and Facebook followers. Some of them must be genuine.'

'It seems a fair bet,' he admitted. 'What will you say?'

'Don't worry, I'm not about to ask them to descend en masse on Hastings & Hart and rescue me.'

'Pity. It would make this the best Christmas H&H have ever had,' he said, then wished he hadn't.

'Sorry. While I'd like to oblige you by delivering a store full of customers at opening time, right now I'm doing my best to stay beneath the radar while I figure out what to do.'

'It's your call. What will you say?'

'*Trust no one*…springs to mind. Or does that sound a touch paranoid?'

'Just a touch.' He turned away, giving her a moment to think while he pretended to scan the shelf. 'And since Henshawe, in his statement to camera regarding your out-burst, managed to imply that you not only had an eating disorder but were mainlining tranquillisers to deal with the stress of your new lifestyle, that might not be in your best interests.'

'He did *what?*'

'He was touchingly sincere.'

Her eyes narrowed.

'I'm just saying. Having met you, I can see how unlikely that is. At least about the eating disorder,' he added, toss-ing a packet of chocolate biscuits into the trolley. The ones with really thick chocolate and orange cream in the middle. Maybe they'd tempt her to stay.

'Thanks for that!'

Lucy noted the chocolate biscuits. The man was not just eye candy. He paid attention…

'Any time. And, let's face it, you're a bit too sparky to be on tranquillisers.'

'Sparky?' She grinned. Couldn't help herself. '*Sparky?*'

'I was being polite.'

'Barely,' she suggested. 'You're right, of course. It was my mouth that got me into all this trouble in the first place. But I can see how his mind is working and that does scare me.' And, just like that, she lost all desire to smile.

'He blamed the press for causing the problems by hound-ing you out of the flat you shared with your friends.'

'If you're attempting to reassure me, I have to tell you that it's not working.'

'You didn't feel hounded?'

Nat added some crackers to the trolley, then crossed

to the cold cabinet and began to load up with milk, juice, salads, cheese.

'A bit,' she admitted, trailing after him. 'I couldn't move without a lens in my face, but since it was his PR people who were orchestrating the hysteria it seems a bit rich to blame the poor saps wielding the cameras. But I have fair warning what to expect when Rupert catches up with me.'

Nat glanced at her.

'I'll be whisked into one of his fancy clinics for my own good,' she said, responding to his unasked question.

'He has clinics?'

'He has a finger in all kinds of businesses, including a chain of clinics that provides every comfort to the distressed celebrity. A nip and tuck while you're drying out?' she said, pulling on her cheeks to stretch her mouth. 'No problem. A little Botox to smooth away the excesses of a coke habit? Step right in. Once he's got me there, he'll probably throw away the key.'

Lucy attempted a careless laugh, but he suspected that she was trying to convince herself rather more than him that she was joking.

He was more concerned why Henshawe would want her out of the way that badly—or why she'd think he would—and when he didn't join in she stopped pretending and frowned at the phone.

'How about, *I'll be back!*…?' she offered.

'Will you?' he asked. 'Go back?'

'To Rupert?' She appeared puzzled. 'Why would I do that?'

'Because that's what women do.'

'You think this is just some tiff?' she demanded when he didn't answer. 'That it'll blow over once I've straightened myself out? Got my head together?'

'It happens,' he said, pushing her, hoping that she might volunteer some answers.

'Not in this case.'

She snapped the phone shut without sending any kind of message and offered it back to him.

'Why don't you hang on to it for now?' he suggested. 'In case you change your mind.'

She looked at him, still unsure of his motives. Then she shrugged, tucked the phone into the pouch at her belt.

'Thanks.'

Her voice was muffled, thick, and he turned away, picked up a couple of apples and dropped them in the trolley. Giving her a moment. Sparky she might be, but no one could fail to be affected by a bad breakup. Especially one that had been played out in the full gaze of the media. Tears were inevitable.

After a moment she picked up a peach, weighed it in her hand, sniffed it. Replaced it.

'No good?' he asked, taking one himself to check it for ripeness.

'They are a ridiculous price.'

'I can probably manage if you really want one. I get staff discount.'

That teased a smile out of her, but she shook her head. 'Peaches are summer fruit. They need to be warm.'

And, just like that, he could see her sitting in the shade of an Italian terrace, grapes ripening overhead, her teeth sinking into the flesh of a perfectly ripe sun-warmed peach straight from the tree. Bare shoulders golden, meltingly relaxed.

Her lips glistening, sweet with the juice…

'I get why you ran out of the press conference, Lucy,' he said, crushing the image with cold December reality. 'But, having dumped the man so publicly, I don't understand why he's so desperate to find you.'

She swallowed, managed a careless shrug. 'I thought you didn't want to know.'

He didn't. If he knew, he would be part of it, part of her story. But, conversely, he did, desperately, want her to trust him and the two were intertwined.

'I have something of his. Something he wants back,' she admitted.

The file, he thought, remembering the glossy black ring binder she'd been holding up in the news clip. That she'd been carrying in her bag.

It wasn't there now, he realised.

'Maybe you should just give it back,' he suggested. 'Walk away.'

'I can't do that.'

Before he could ask her why, what she'd done with it, she was distracted by the sound of voices coming through the arch that led to the butchery.

'It's just one of the cleaning crews,' he said quickly, seizing her wrist as panic flared in her face and she turned, hunting for the nearest escape route. 'Good grief, you're shaking like a leaf. What the hell has he done to you? Do you need the police?'

'No!' Her throat moved as she swallowed.

'Are you sure? What about this?' he demanded, releasing her wrist, lifting his hand to skim his fingertips lightly over the bruise darkening at her temple.

She stared at him. 'What? No! A photographer caught me with his camera. It was an accident. Nothing to do with Rupert.' She looked anxiously towards the archway, the voices were getting nearer. 'Please…'

'Okay.' He wasn't convinced—he'd heard every variation of the bruise excuse going—but this wasn't the moment to press it. 'We're done here,' he said, heading for the nearest lift.

'You can't take the trolley out of the food hall,' she protested as the doors opened.

'You want to stay and pack the groceries into carriers?' he asked, stopping them from closing with his foot.

A burst of song propelled her into the lift. 'No, you're all right.'

'Doors closing. Going up...'

'What?' She turned on him. 'Where are you taking me?'

'Believe me, you'll be a lot safer on the top floor than the bottom one,' he said quickly. 'There'll be no security staff. No curious cleaners wondering why you look familiar. Where they've seen you before.'

She opened her mouth, closed it again, her jaw tightening as she swallowed down whatever she was going to say.

'You'd never have got away with it, Lucy.'

'You don't know that,' she declared, staring straight ahead. 'And it would test your security staff. If they found me you'd know they're as good as you think they are.'

'Believe me, they are. And you'd spend the night in a police cell.'

'Oh, but—'

'They don't call me when they find intruders, Lucy. They call the local police station and then the game would be up. If you're so sure that the cleaners would recognise you, I think it's a fair bet to assume that whoever turned up to arrest you would, too.'

She slumped back against the side of the lift. 'You're right, of course. And the elf costume would confirm everything that Rupert was saying about me. That I'm one sandwich short of a picnic.'

'It wouldn't look good,' he agreed. 'But if you really do have your heart set on spending the night in a tent, I'll go and fetch one of those pop-up ones. You can set it up on the bedroom floor.'

The lift came to a halt. *'Tenth floor... Customer services. Accounts. Doors opening...'*

'Bedroom floor?' She frowned. 'I thought the bedroom department was on the fifth...'

She stopped, blushing, remembering too late how she knew that.

'Forget the bedroom department,' he said, leading the way past the customer services department, down a corridor past empty offices. 'Have you never heard of living over the shop?'

'Over the corner shop, maybe,' she said as he used a swipe card to open a door that led to an internal lobby containing a private lift from the car park and a pair of wide double doors. 'But not...'

He keyed a number into a security pad, opened the door and, as he stood back to allow her to precede him, her protest died away.

Ahead of her was the most striking room Lucy had ever seen. Acres of limed floor. A pair of huge square black leather sofas. Starkly modern black and steel furniture. Dove-grey walls. No paintings, no colour, not a single thing to distract from the view through the soaring wall of glass in front of her. Constant movement, the ever-changing vibrant colour of the cityscape against the monochrome room.

'Wow!' she exclaimed, gazing out over a London lit up and laid out at her feet like fairyland. 'You actually live here?' she asked, moving closer.

There were lights everywhere.

Not just the Christmas lights, but every famous landmark

floodlit to show it at its best. There was traffic crossing bridges, strings of lights along the Thames. Even the aircraft coming into land, navigation lights winking, added to the drama.

And Christmas trees, everywhere there were Christmas trees.

Big ones in squares, rows of small ones atop buildings, every shape and size in gardens and shining out of windows. The colours reflected in the big soft flakes of snow falling like feathers over the city, settling on parks, covering trees, rooftops. Wiping the world clean.

He hadn't answered and she turned to him, expecting to see him smiling, amused by her totally uncool reaction.

But his face was expressionless.

'When I'm in London,' he said. 'There are stores all over the country, as well as abroad. I seem to spend a lot of time in hotels.'

'They don't all have apartments like this on the top floor?'

'No. I can say with confidence that this is unique. It was commissioned by my cousin, Christopher Hart, as part of the refurbishment of the Hastings & Hart flagship store.'

'It's amazing. I bet you can't wait to get home.'

'This isn't home…' He bit off the words as if they'd escaped before he could stop them. And when she waited for him to tell her why, 'It's a long story.'

'Is it? Well, here's the deal. You tell me yours and I'll tell you mine.'

'Long and very boring. Make yourself at…'

'Home?' she offered, filling the gap.

He managed a smile. He had an entire repertoire of them, she discovered. Sardonic. Amused. The one that lit up her insides, fizz, whoosh, bang, like a New Year firework display.

And then there was this one. The blank-eyed kind you cranked up when you didn't want anyone to know how you were really feeling. The shutters had come down so fast she almost heard them clang, excluding her. And now they were down she knew how much she wanted to go back two minutes.

'Or not,' she said when the silence had gone on for far too long.

'My problem, not yours, Lucy. Look around. Find yourself a room—there are plenty to choose from. I'll be in the kitchen.'

He didn't wait to see if she accepted his invitation, but returned to the trolley, disappeared through a door. Something had touched a raw nerve and while every instinct was urging her to go after him, put her arms around him, kiss it better, he might as well have painted a sign saying *keep out* on his back.

Instead, she took him at his word and looked around. The small flat she'd occupied at the top of Rupert's townhouse had been elegant, comfortably furnished, but this was real estate on an entirely different level.

It was the kind of apartment that she'd seen featured in the 'at home' features in *Celebrity*. So tidy that it looked as if no one lived there.

This was a somewhat extreme example, she decided. There was no Christmas tree here, no decorations. Not so much as a trace of tinsel.

Maybe, she decided, when you worked with it all day, you needed to escape. Maybe.

This might be a stunning apartment but he'd said himself that it wasn't home. So where was? She wanted to know.

Her fingers trailed over the butter-soft leather of the sofa as she turned, taking it all in and, looking up, she saw an open gallery with the same stunning view of the city. It was reached by a circular staircase and, taking Nathaniel at his word, she went up, finding herself in a space wide enough for casual seating. Armchairs in more of that soft black leather.

There was a single pair of black panelled doors. Assuming that they led to an internal lobby where she'd find the bedrooms, she opened one and stepped through.

For a moment all she could see was the blinking of the navigation lights of a plane passing overhead, then soft concealed lighting, responding to movement, gradually revealed the room she'd stumbled into.

The dark, asymmetrical pyramid of glass above her that would, by day, light the room. The tip of a landmark that rose like a spear into the sky. Silver in the rain. Bronze, gold, fiery red when struck by the sun. Never the same.

Below it was the largest bedroom she had ever seen, perfect in every striking detail. The walls were a soft dove-grey and, apart from the bed, a vast space of pure white, the only furniture was a cantilevered slab of black marble that ran the entire width of the room behind the bed.

Unable to stop herself, she opened a door that led to a pair of dressing and bath rooms. His and hers.

Nathaniel's?

No. Despite an array of the most luxurious toiletries, the designer suits, couturier dresses, in the walk-in wardrobes, it was obvious that neither of them was in use. It wasn't just the fact that all the clothes were cocooned in plastic covers.

There was no presence here. Like the rest of the apartment, it was visually stunning, austere, silent.

But here the silence was a hollow, suffocating emptiness.

Even the art was monochrome. Just one piece, a black-framed architectural impression of the Hastings & Hart building that filled the space above the bed.

The only point of colour in the room was a single crimson rose in a silver bud vase gleaming against the black marble.

She touched a velvety petal, expecting it to be silk, but it was real. The one thing in the room, in the entire apartment, as far as she could tell, that was alive and she shivered as she stared up at the drawing.

The building was a thing of light, energy, leaping from the earth. While this…

'This isn't home…'

And then her eyes focused on the signature on the drawing.

Nathaniel Hart.

Nat emptied the groceries onto the central island of the vast kitchen that he rarely used for anything other than making coffee.

He'd offered to pitch Lucy a tent but wasn't that what he was doing? Camping out. Living here but doing his best not to touch anything.

As if by not making an impression, not disturbing anything, maybe one morning he would wake up and he'd be back in his own life. The nightmare over.

Lucy closed the doors, quietly retraced her steps down to the lower floor, found the kitchen.

Nathaniel was standing with his back to the door, arms spread wide, hands gripping the counter so hard that his knuckles were white. Certain she was intruding, she took an instinctive step backwards, but he heard and half turned, his face as empty as the room upstairs.

'I'm lost,' she said quickly.

'Lost?'

'Not so much lost as confused. I went upstairs. It seemed the obvious thing to do.' She lifted a shoulder in an embarrassed little shrug.

'My fault.' He straightened, dragged both hands through his hair. 'I should have given you the guided tour instead of leaving you to find your own way around.'

'I could have found my own way. I just didn't want to blunder in anywhere else that's private.'

'It's not private. It's just…' He shook his head. 'Come on, I'll show you around.' He grasped her hand and led the way to a wide corridor with a series of doors, all on one side.

'Linen cupboard,' he said, keeping her hand tucked in his. 'Bedroom, bedroom, bedroom…' opening doors to reveal three empty bedrooms, all decorated with the same pale walls, black marble night tables, white linen as the room upstairs. 'Bedroom,' he repeated, opening the last door to reveal yet more of the same, finally releasing her hand, leaving it for her to decide whether or not to follow him inside because this was not just another bedroom.

'This is your room,' she said.

'The master suite upstairs spooked you and you don't know me.' He turned to face her. 'I wanted you to see for yourself that I have nothing to hide.'

'You don't feel like a stranger,' she said, following him, placing her hand in his. Foolish, maybe, especially considering the way her heart leapt whenever he was within ten feet of her. Yes, the room upstairs had spooked her, but it didn't seem to be doing much for him either, and his fingers closed about hers. Almost as if they were uniting against the world.

The word dropped into her chest with a thunk, but for once she kept her mouth closed, her thoughts to herself.

United…

That was what it had felt like when he'd held her on the stairs. Instinctive. Natural. There had been no barriers between them, only an instant and mutual recognition, and in another place somewhere private, they'd have been out of their clothes, not caring about anything but the need to touch, to hold and be held, feel the heat of another human body.

Not just lust at first sight. Something far deeper than that.

Slightly shocked at the direction her mind was taking, she forced herself to retrieve her hand, ignore the cold emptiness where his palm had been pressed against hers and concentrate on the room.

Square, with long, narrow floor to ceiling windows on two sides, it occupied the corner of the building.

Nathaniel had barely made an impression on it. There were a few books piled up on the marble ledge beside the bed and, taking advantage of his invitation, she ran her fingers down the spines. Art. Design. Management. Psychology. No fiction. Nothing just for fun.

The only thing that set this room apart from the others was a drawing board and stool, tucked up into the corner. As far out of the way as possible.

There was nothing else that gave any clue to the man.

A bathroom. A wardrobe-cum-dressing room, smaller than the ones upstairs. At least his clothes were lived in, used and, unable to help herself, she lifted the sleeve of one of maybe a dozen identical white shirts.

She turned, saw that he was watching her. 'Fresh air,' she said. 'It smells of fresh air. Like washing hung out on a windy day.'

'You're wasted as an elf. You should be writing copy for the manufacturers of laundry products.'

'Not me!' She shook her head. 'Sorry, I didn't mean to snap, but I'm right off the whole idea of marketing right now.'

She dropped the sleeve, stepped past him, back into the bedroom.

'Tell me, Nathaniel,' she asked as she looked around, 'did you get a discount for buying in bulk?'

'Bulk?'

'The paint. The marble. I know you designed the building. I saw your drawing. In the room upstairs.'

'I designed the building. The store,' he confirmed. 'But the apartment was private space, decorated to client specification. The idea was that nothing should distract from the windows. The colour, the movement. The concept of the city as living art.'

'Right.'

'You don't like it?'

'The initial impact is stunning. The views are incredible, but...' She hesitated as she struggled to find the words to explain how she felt.

'But?'

'But everything with colour, life, movement is happening somewhere else. To someone else. Up here, you're just...' she gave an awkward little shrug '...a spectator.'

CHAPTER SEVEN

'How long have you been here, Lucy?'

'I don't know. Twenty minutes?' She looked across at him. 'Do you want me to leave now?'

'You're not going anywhere. And I'm not offended. I was merely calculating how long it had taken you to see the fatal flaw in a design that wowed the interior design world. Was featured in a dozen magazines.'

'And was cousin Christopher pleased about that?' she asked, sensing that he wasn't entirely happy with what had been done with the amazing space he'd provided. 'He is the man whose clothes are shrouded in the dressing room upstairs, I take it?'

'He was torn, I'd say. He'd thrown open the doors to the likes of *Celebrity* magazine, wanting the world to see his eyrie. He'd forgotten that I was the one who would be credited with its creation.'

And the impression she'd gained that he didn't like the man much, even if he was kin, solidified.

'I'll bet you a cheese omelette that they all focused on the windows. That's if you'd allow anything that yellow to brighten the monochrome perfection of your kitchen.'

'I let you in,' he reminded her, 'and I promise you no one has ever looked greener, or more out of place.'

'Dressed like this,' she replied, reprising the twirl, 'I'd look out of place anywhere except your basement.'

'True.'

'Maybe you should have left me down there.'

'Maybe you should get out of it.'

Something about the way he was looking at her sent a tremor of longing through her. It was as if something had become unhinged in her brain. Shock—it had to be shock. She didn't do this. But, before she could do something really stupid, she said, 'I think we'll stick with the plan.'

Plan! What plan?

When he didn't answer she crossed to the drawing board to take a look at what he was working on. It wasn't a big project, just the front and side elevations of a single-storey house.

There was a photograph clipped to the corner of the board. Taken from a rocky ledge, the land fell away to a small sandy cove. The site for the house?

The edges of both photograph and drawing were curling slightly, as if they hadn't been touched in a long time. Yet it was here, he kept it close, and she ran a hand over the edge of the photograph in an attempt to smooth it.

'This is nice,' she said, looking back at him. 'Where is it?'

He didn't look at the picture.

'Cornwall.'

'I've never been to Cornwall.'

'You should,' he said, his face devoid of expression and for a moment she thought she'd put her foot in her mouth. Right up to her ankle. 'It's… nice.' Then she saw the tiny betraying flicker at the corner of his eye. 'And full of Cornish piskies. Dressed like that, you'd be right at home.'

He was teasing her?

'I'm not a pixie,' she said, mock indignantly, to disguise the rush of pleasure, warmth, that threatened to overwhelm her. 'I'm an elf.'

'Piskies, not pixies.' Then, abruptly, 'That's the lot. You've seen it all now. Choose a room, Lucy. Make yourself at home. I'll go and make a start on that cheese omelette I owe you.'

'You're admitting I was right?' she demanded, not wanting him to go.

'Smart as paint,' he agreed, leaving her in his room. A gesture of trust? Because she was a stranger, too. Or because he felt the same tug of desire, heat?

Except they weren't. Strangers. They might never have met before but, from the moment their eyes had met, they had known one another, deep down. Responding to something that went far beyond the surface conventions.

She looked again at the photograph.

Nice.

What a pathetic, pitiful word to describe such a landscape. To describe a house designed with such skill that it would become a part of it.

It wasn't *nice*; it was dramatic, powerful, at one with its setting.

It was extraordinary. Twenty minutes. That was all it had taken her to see through surface veneer to the darkness at the heart of the apartment.

He'd designed it as a gift for Claudia, his cousin's wife. Envisaged it filled with light, colour, life—reflecting the light, colour, life of the city. He'd been forced to watch, helpless, as Christopher had taken his vision and sucked the life right out of it. Just as he'd sucked the life right out of the woman he loved.

* * *

Lucy didn't bother to look at each room before deciding which to choose. They were all as soulless as the room upstairs.

She dumped her bag on the bed and checked out the en suite bathroom. Like those upstairs, it was supplied with all the essentials, including a new toothbrush which she fell upon with gratitude.

She'd replace it first thing…

She caught her reflection in the mirror. *First thing* suggested that she was staying. That she had taken him at his word. Trusted that bone-deep connection…

'Not bright, Lucy B,' she said. 'You are such a push-over. One smile and he's got you wrapped around his little finger.'

One look and she'd seen her engagement to Rupert for the sham it was.

But, even if he was as genuine as her instincts—and just how reliable were those dumb whoosh, flash, bang hormones anyway?—were telling her, this was, could only ever be, a very temporary stopgap.

Breathing space.

She took out her own phone and it leapt into life. Of course. Why would Rupert cut her off when it was the one way he could contact her?

There were dozens of voicemails. She ignored them. There was no one she could think of who'd have anything to say that she wanted to hear. But she opened Rupert's last message:

Henshawe 20:12. We need to talk.

Blunt and to the point, it didn't escape her that he'd waited until the store was closed, all the doors were locked and there was no chance that she was still inside before calling her.

Proof, if she needed it, that he'd had someone watching all that time, just in case.

No doubt he'd had everyone out checking anywhere else she might have taken cover, too. She guessed some of the messages were from her former flatmates, the owner of the nursery where she'd worked. Everyone who had touched her life since the day her mother had abandoned her.

No apology, but at least there was no pretence. Forced to accept that she'd somehow slipped through his fingers, he was ready to talk.

The problem there was that there was nothing he had to say that she wanted to hear.

Or maybe one thing, and that was unintentional.

Not that, in her heart of hearts, she'd needed confirmation that Nathaniel really was on the level. That he'd seen she was in trouble and hadn't hesitated to step forward.

That he was one of the good guys.

But it was good to know that her judgement wasn't terminally damaged. Not as crap as she'd thought.

She logged into Twitter. There were hundreds of messages now. And a new hashtag: *#findLucyB*

No prizes for guessing who'd come up with that one, she thought, as she logged into her diary.

Nathaniel Hart is on the side of the angels. Not only can he make the world go away with a look, but he doesn't ask unnecessary questions. Which doesn't mean I'm not going to have to tell him everything. I am. I will. But not yet.

Right now, I'm a lot more interested in his story. The man is clearly a genius architect, so what the heck is he doing running a department store—stores?

And if those clothes upstairs in the creepy

*bedroom belong to his cousin, the one who com-
missioned this apartment, where is he?*

'Can I help?'

Nat, emptying the trolley, turned at the rare sound of
another human voice in his kitchen. Lucy was standing in
the doorway, a discordant slash of garish green against the
cool grey of the slate and marble surfaces of the kitchen.

A discordant note in his life, knocking him off balance,
sending a fizz of expectancy racing through his veins.

'Shall I put these away?' She didn't wait for an answer,
but picked up a bag of salad leaves and, as she turned, he
saw that she'd taken off the felt boots and striped tights,
that the tunic barely covered her satin-skinned thighs and
that her toenails were painted a bright candy-red that would
have all the boy elves' heads in a spin. Not to mention the
CEO of this department store.

She opened one of the doors to the stainless steel fridge
and he saw her pause for a heartbeat as she realised that,
apart from bottled water, it was empty.

'You don't do a lot of entertaining, do you?'

'I usually eat in one of the store restaurants,' he said.
'It keeps the staff on their toes, knowing I might drop in
at any time.'

'Right.'

'There are eight of them to choose from,' he said, needing to prove that he wasn't totally sad. 'Everything from
Italian to Japanese.'

'Sushi for breakfast?' She didn't wait for an answer.
'The store doesn't open until ten, does it? I don't know
about you, but I'd be gnawing my fingers off by then.'

'It's just as well I ignored your demands to put the porridge back on the shelf, then.' He took one of her hands,

rubbed a thumb over the back of her slender fingers, perfect nails. 'It would be a pity to spoil these.'

'Nathaniel...' The word came out as a gasp.

'Fortunately, the staff canteen opens at seven,' he said, cutting off the little thank you speech he could see she was working up to, letting go of her hand. He didn't want her thanks. He didn't know what he wanted. Or maybe he did. He just wasn't prepared to let go of the past. Admit it. 'It takes time to get everything pitch perfect for the public.'

'Well, that makes sense, I suppose.' She sounded doubtful. 'If you don't like to cook.' She turned back to the island, continued putting away the cold food. 'What are you planning to do for Christmas? I don't imagine the store is open on Christmas Day.'

'No. Obviously, I've tried to persuade the staff that it's a good idea, purely for my own convenience, you understand, but for some reason they won't wear it.'

Bad choice of words.

She wasn't wearing nearly enough. If she was going to stay it was essential that she cover those shapely legs. Those sweet little toes with their shiny red nails. Or he wouldn't be answerable.

Nathaniel frowned and Lucy swallowed. Hard. She was totally losing it.

'I'm sorry. That was unbelievably rude of me. You've probably noticed, but I tend to say the first thing that comes into my head. Obviously, you've got family, friends.'

A cousin, at least.

'I'm never short of invitations,' he agreed, 'but, by the time the big day arrives, all I want to do is open a tin of soup.'

'You can have too much of a good thing, huh?'

'Remind me again,' he invited, 'what exactly is good about it?'

'You don't like Christmas?'

'I repeat, what's good about it?'

'Lots of things. The fun of choosing gifts for the people you love.' No response. He didn't love anyone? No... 'Planning the food?' she offered quickly, not wanting to think about the red rose in the room upstairs. 'Oh, no. You don't cook. How about a brass band playing Christmas carols in the open air? The sense of anticipation. The faces of little children.' She didn't appear to be making much impression with the things that she loved about Christmas so she tried a different tack. 'How about the profits, Nathaniel? Remind me, how much does it cost to take a sleigh ride to Santa's grotto?'

If she'd hoped to provoke him into a show of emotion, she would have been disappointed.

'Would you care to see a breakdown of the costs involved in designing and creating a visual effects spectacular that will satisfy children who've been brought up on CGI?' he enquired, clearly not in the least bit excited by the cost or the finished product. 'You're right, Lucy. Christmas is a rip-off. A tacky piece of commercialism and if I could cancel it I would.'

'I didn't say that!'

'No? Forgive me, but I thought you just did.'

'What I was doing was offering you a personal reason to enjoy it.'

'The profit motive? Sorry, you're going to have to try harder than that.'

'Okay. Come down to the grotto and listen to the little ones for whom it's all still magic, the wonder still shiny-bright.'

'At a price.'

'I know. And I wish every child had the chance to see it.' She reached up for an egg basket, hanging over the island. 'Actually, I wouldn't mind seeing it myself.' Then, because he was a cynic and she was a fool, 'Should any of them ask you, by the way, the reindeer are parked on the roof.'

'They are?'

'Well, obviously. Santa's here so where else would they be?'

'Good point.'

'And you might warn Groceries that there's likely to be a rush on chilli-flavoured cashew nuts. You wouldn't want to miss a sale.'

'That would be tragic.' Nat felt the tension ease from his jaw as his mouth hitched up in the makings of a smile. 'I know I'm going to hate myself for asking this, but why would there be a rush on chilli-flavoured cashew nuts?'

Lucy responded with a careless shrug and he found himself holding his breath, wondering what was coming next.

'I happened to let it slip that Rudolph eats them to keep his nose bright. Dido promised to keep it secret but I can't guarantee that she won't try a little one-upmanship on her sister.'

'What an interesting day you've had, Lucy Bright.'

'It's had its ups and its downs,' she admitted. 'That was definitely an up.'

'Why cashew nuts?'

'Oh, well, peanuts can be a problem. You know. Allergies…' She regarded him steadily, waiting. Then, 'Come on, Nathaniel Hart. Get with the plot.'

Realising he'd missed something, he lifted his brows, inviting her to provide the punchline.

'Elf and safety?'

It took a moment but then he shook his head. 'I do not believe you just said that, Lucy Bright.'

'Actually, neither do I,' she said solemnly. And then she snorted with laughter.

The sound rippled around the kitchen, bouncing off doors, windows, an array of steel tools hanging from the four-sided rail above the island.

Waking everything up, Nat thought, setting up a hum that seemed to vibrate through him until he was laughing, too.

'Do you have a kettle, do you know?' she asked once she'd recovered. Then, as he reached for it, 'I don't need to be waited on.'

'I do know how to boil a kettle. Tea?' he offered. 'Or would you prefer coffee?'

'Oh, tea, I think. Camomile, if you've got it. It's a bit late for coffee.'

Only if you were able to sleep.

She transferred the eggs from the carton to the basket while he filled the kettle, switched it on. Stretched up on her toes to replace it.

Her hair had dried into a froth of little tendrils that curled around her face, against her neck. All she needed were wings and a white dress and she'd look more at home on the top of a Christmas tree than dressed as an elf.

Eggs safe, she picked up a punnet of baby plum tomatoes and looked at them for a moment, then at the plain white china mugs he'd taken from the cupboard, a tiny frown buckling her forehead.

She wasn't beautiful, there was nothing classic about her features, yet there was a sparkle in her green eyes that made everything right. Made something inside him begin to bubble, catch like a motor that hadn't been used in a while, that had to be teased into life with a touch, a smile, laughing lips that begged to be kissed.

Like a limb that had gone to sleep, the return to life hurt.

He turned away, almost with relief, as the kettle boiled and reached for one of a row of polished black canisters.

'It's not camomile,' he apologised, extracting a couple of tea bags. He rarely drank tea and discovered that they were disconcertingly beige in this monochrome world. 'I'm afraid Earl Grey is the best I can do.'

'That will be lovely,' she said, joining him. A warm presence at his side.

He dropped the bags into the mugs, poured on boiling water, looked up.

'You've settled in?' he asked, trying to forget about the kiss.

She nodded.

'You've got everything you need? Toothbrush? Toiletries?'

'Yes, thanks. Everything for the guest who forgot to pack her toilet bag,' she assured him. 'Even a bathrobe. I'll replace the toothbrush.'

'No need.'

'I'd have to buy one, anyway.'

'You'll need more than a toothbrush. You'll need some clothes.' And, before she could object, 'A change of underwear, at least.'

'You have a washing machine, I imagine?'

'There was one included in the specification,' he admitted. 'Along with every other modern convenience known to man.'

'Specified by your cousin. The man with the Gothic taste.'

'Gothic?'

'How else would you describe that room upstairs? It's pure Addams family. All it needs is a belfry for the bats.'

'It would spoil the lines. And let in the rain.'

'Heaven forbid.'

He saw the question in her eyes, then the uncharacteristic hesitation as she decided against it.

'Actually, it's all black and white, glass and brushed stainless steel in the store, too, isn't it?' she said, changing tack. 'I hadn't realised before, but of course down there it's a frame for all that colour. It works.'

'Thanks for that. I think,' he said, but it gave him an opportunity to revisit the subject of clothes. 'Actually, I was wondering, in the interests of aesthetics, if I could encourage you to change into something a little less…green.'

'In the interests of aesthetics?' Her exquisitely threaded eyebrows rose in a pair of questioning little arches. 'Is that an architectural get-out-of-your-kit line, Nathaniel Hart?'

'I wasn't suggesting you stripped off here and now.' Although the idea had considerable appeal.

'Are you sure? It sounded rather like it.'

He managed a shrug. 'I was merely pointing out that they're working clothes. If you're planning to keep up the act, continue to hide out in the grotto, you're going to need them fresh and clean in the morning. House rule,' he said.

'Is that right?' For a moment he thought she was truly offended. Then she grinned. 'Well, snap, Mr Pinstriped Suit. Off with your jacket. Off with your tie and cufflinks!'

Grinning back, he said, 'I'll change if you will. Let's go shopping.'

She was still smiling, but she was shaking her head. 'Until I get a proper job, I won't have any money. And I can't take anything from you, Nathaniel.'

Why not? Presumably, she'd allowed Henshawe to dress her. Which answered that question. But didn't help with the problem.

'Be reasonable, Lucy. You can't live in that.'

'It will be a challenge,' she admitted, but there was a steely glint in those eyes now, and he battled down the frustration of having an entire store full of clothes he would happily give her, aware that this wasn't about him. This was about her. Her need to re-establish her self-esteem. Recover what had been stolen from her.

'You've got a proper job,' he reminded her, 'at least until Christmas. I'll sub you until the end of the week.'

'You're really going to let me work here?'

'Why not? You seem to have nothing better to do and an elf with a close personal relationship with Rudolph is a real find. Besides,' he pointed out, 'you owe Pam.' It wasn't playing fair, but he was prepared to use every trick in the book to keep her safe. Keep her close.

'Pam might have other ideas if she knew the truth,' she reminded him as she opened a carton of milk, poured a little into each mug. 'What is the going rate for an elf?'

He told her.

'Sorry…' she was going to turn him down? '…that's actually not bad, but even so I wouldn't be able to afford your prices.'

'There's a generous staff discount,' he said.

'For temps?'

'I'm a temp, too.' Long-term, until death us do part…

'Are you?' For a moment it was all there in her eyes. The questions that were piling up, but when he didn't answer all she said was, 'I bet you're on a better hourly rate than me.'

She handed him one of the mugs and turned to lean back against the counter to sip at her tea. He could feel the warmth of her body and he wished he'd taken her advice, taken off his jacket so that there was only his shirt sleeve between them.

'I wonder what happened to the real elf?' she said after a moment. 'The one from Garlands.'

'Maybe, given time to think about it, she didn't want to spend December in a windowless basement,' he said, sipping at his own tea and deciding there were more interesting ways of heating up his, her lips. How close had they been to a kiss on the stairs? An inch, two?

'Maybe. Or maybe, when it started to snow, she decided she'd rather go home and make a snowman.'

'Is that what you'd have done, Lucy?'

'Me? Fat chance. Every minute of every day is fully booked. Or it was. This afternoon I had a meeting with a wedding designer to explore ideas for my fantasy wedding.'

'It may still happen,' he said, glancing down at her, the words like ashes in his mouth.

'Nope. The word "fantasy" is the clue. It means illusory. A supposition resting on no solid ground.'

He wanted to tell her that he was sorry. But it would be a lie and actually she didn't look that upset. The brightness in her green eyes was not a tear but a flash of anger.

'So what should you be doing this evening? If you weren't here, tearing my life's work to shreds.'

'Now?' She pulled a face. 'I should be gussied up in full princess mode for a gala dinner at the Ritz, to celebrate the unveiling today of Lucy B.'

'With you as the star? Well, obviously, that would have been no fun,' he teased.

'Not nearly as much as you'd think. Speeches, smug PR men and endless photographs,' she said. 'Being an elf beats it into a cocked hat.'

'So you're saying that your day hasn't been a total write-off?'

'No,' she said, looking right at him. 'Hand on my heart, I'd have to say that my day hasn't been a total write-off.'

Any other woman and he'd have said she was putting a brave face on it, but something in her expression suggested that she was in earnest.

'Shame about the snowman, though,' she said, turning away as if afraid she'd revealed more of herself than she'd intended. She abandoned her mug. 'It doesn't often snow in London, not like this. I hope the missing elf did seize the day and go out to play.'

'It's not too late.'

'Too late for what?'

'To go out to play.' And where the hell had that come from? 'Build a snowman of your own.'

'Nathaniel!' she protested, but she was laughing and her eyes, which he'd seen filled with fear, mistrust, uncertainty, were now looking out at the falling snow with a childlike yearning and, crazy as it was, he knew he'd said the right thing. And, as if to prove it, she put a hand behind her head, a hand on her hip, arched a brow and, with a wiggle that did his blood pressure no good, said, 'Great idea, honey, but I haven't got a thing to wear.'

'Honey,' he replied, arching right back at her. 'You seem to be forgetting that I'm your fairy godmother.'

Before he could think about what he was going to do, he caught her hand and raced up the stairs with her.

The emptiness hit him as he opened the door, bringing him to an abrupt halt. Lucy was right. This wasn't a bedroom, it was a mausoleum. And that hideous rose...

'Nathaniel...' Her voice was soft behind him, filling the room with life, banishing the shadows. Her warm fingers tightened on his as if she understood. 'It doesn't matter. Leave it.'

'No. Seize the day,' he said, flinging open the door to

the dressing room with its huge walk-in wardrobe filled with plastic-covered ghosts. The colours muted. No scent. Nothing.

He pulled off covers, seeking out warm clothes. Trousers. He pulled half a dozen pairs from hangers. A thick padded jacket. Opened drawers, hunting out shirts, socks. Sweaters. Something thick, warm…

As his hand came down on thistledown wool, it seemed to release a scent that had once been as familiar as the air he breathed and, for a moment, he froze.

Carpe diem.

The words mocked him.

When had he ever seized the day? Just gone for it without a thought for the consequences; been irresponsible? Selfish? Maybe when he'd been eighteen and told his father that he wasn't interested in running a department store, that he was going to be an architect?

Had it taken all the courage, all the strength he possessed to defy, disappoint the man he loved, that he had never been able to summon up the courage to do it again?

'Nathaniel, this is madness,' Lucy called from the bedroom. 'I can't go outside. I don't have any shoes.'

He picked up the sweater, gathered everything else she was likely to need, including a pair of snow boots that he dropped at her feet, doing his best to ignore her wiggling toes with their candy nails.

'They'll be too big,' she protested.

'Wear a couple of pairs of socks.' Then, 'What are you waiting for? It'll all have disappeared by morning.'

'Madness,' she said, but she leapt to her feet and gave him an impulsive hug that took his breath away. She didn't notice, was already grinning as she began to tug the tunic over her head, offering him another glimpse of those full, creamy breasts, this time encased in gossamer-fine black lace.

Breathless? He'd thought he was breathless?

'Downstairs in two minutes,' he said, beating a hasty retreat.

CHAPTER EIGHT

LUCY scrambled into a shirt that didn't quite do up across the bust. Trousers that didn't quite meet around the waist, were too long in the leg. It was crazy stupid. But in a totally wonderful way.

She picked up the thistledown sweater, held it to her cheek for a moment, trying to catch a hint of the woman— thinner, taller than her—who'd owned it. What was she to Nathaniel? Where was she?

Nothing. Not even a trace of scent.

Relieved, she pulled it over her head. It was baggy and long enough to cover the gaps. She tucked the trousers into a pair of snow boots that swallowed the excess and the feather-light down-filled coat, the kind you might wear on a skiing holiday, had room enough to spare.

Hat, scarf.

She didn't bother to check her reflection in the mirror. She didn't need confirmation that she looked a mess. Some things it was better not to know. Instead, she picked up the gloves and, leaving behind her a room that no longer looked cold but resembled the aftermath of a jumble sale, she stomped down the stairs in her too-big boots.

By the time she'd re-applied lipstick to protect her lips from the cold, picked up her phone and purse, Nathaniel was impatiently pacing the living room.

'Two minutes, I said!'

About to reiterate that this was madness, the words died on her lips. He'd abandoned the pinstripes for jeans, a jacket similar to the one she was wearing. The focused, controlled businessman had been replaced by a caged tiger scenting escape.

'Yes, boss,' she said cheekily, pulling on her gloves as they used the private lift which took them straight to the underground car park.

He boosted her up into the seat of a black Range Rover, climbed up beside her.

'Better duck down,' he said as they approached the barrier.

'You don't think…?'

'Unlikely, but better safe than sorry.'

The traffic was light; no one with any sense would be out in this weather unless is was absolutely necessary.

'I think you might be optimistic about it thawing by morning,' she said.

'Want to risk leaving it for another day?'

'No way!'

'Thought not.'

Neither of them spoke again until he'd driven through Hyde Park and parked near the Serpentine Bridge.

'Oh, wow,' she said, staring across the utterly still, freezing waters of the lake. The acres of white, disappearing into the thick, whirling snow. 'Just…wow,' again as she unclipped the seat belt, opened the door, letting in a flurry of snow.

She didn't stop to think, but slid down, spun around in it, grinning as Nathaniel caught her hand and they ran across the blank canvas, leaving their footprints in the snow.

She picked up a handful and flung a snowball at him,

yelling as he retaliated, scoring a hit as snow found its way inside her jacket.

Lucy was right, Nat thought as they gathered snow, piling it up, laughing like a couple of kids. This was crazy. But in the best possible way. A little bit of magic that, like the kids visiting the grotto, was making a memory that would stay with him.

They rolled a giant snowball into a body, piling up more snow around its base before adding a head.

Drivers, making their way through the park, hooted encouragement but, as Lucy waved back, he caught her hand, afraid that someone might decide to stop and crash their snowman party.

He wasn't afraid that she'd be recognized. They were far enough from the street lights and the snow blurred everything. It was just that, selfishly, he didn't want to share it, share her, with anyone.

She looked up, eyes shining, snowflakes sticking to her lashes, the curls sticking out from beneath her hat, clinging for a moment to her lips before melting against their warmth.

'Are we done?' he said before he completely lost it and did in reality what he'd imagined in his head a dozen times: kiss her senseless. Or maybe that was him. The one without any sense. 'Is it big enough?'

'Not it. She. Lily.'

'A girl snowman?'

She added two handfuls of snow, patting it into shape, giving her curves.

'She is now.' She grinned up at him. 'Equal opportunities for all. Fairy godmothers. Santas. Snowmen. I wish we'd brought some dressing up clothes for her.'

He removed the pull-on fleece hat he was wearing and tucked it onto Lily's head.

'Oh, cute,' she said and draped the scarf she was wearing around her like a stole. Then she took her phone from her pocket and took a picture.

'Give it to me. I'll take a picture of both of you.'

She crouched down, her arm around the snow lady, and gave him a hundred watt smile. Then she said, 'No, wait, you should be in it, too. A reminder of how much trouble you can get into when you catch a stranger on the stairs.'

'You think?' he said, folding himself up beside her, holding the phone at arm's length. 'Closer,' he said, putting his arm around her, pulling her close so that her cheek was pressed against his and he could feel her giggling.

'We must look like a couple of Michelin men.'

'Speak for yourself,' he said, turning to look at her. Her eyes were shining, lit up, her mouth just inches from his own in a rerun of that moment on the stairs when the world went away.

Had it ever come back?

He fired off the flash before he forgot all his good intentions.

'How's that?' he said, showing her.

'Perfect,' she said, looking over his arm. 'Can I send them to my diary?'

'As a reminder of a crazy moment in the snow?'

'As a reminder that not all men are mendacious rats,' she said. 'That once in a while Prince Charming is the real deal.'

'No...' Not him. Wrong fairy tale. He was the Beast, woken by Beauty from a long darkness of the soul.

But she had fallen back in the snow, laughing as she swept her arms up and down to make a snow angel.

'Come on. You too,' she urged, laughing, and he joined in, sweeping his arms up and down until their gloved hands met. He looked across at her, lying in the snow, golden curls peeping out from beneath her hat, laughing as the huge flakes settled over her face, licking them from her lips.

'What do they taste of?' he asked.

She didn't hesitate. 'Happiness.' And then she looked at him. 'Want to share?'

She didn't wait for his answer, but rolled over so that her body bumped into his, her face above him.

There were moments—rare moments, perfect moments—when the world seemed to pause on its axis, giving you an extra heartbeat of time.

It had happened when he'd caught her on the stairs and, as her laughing lips touched his, a simple gift, and cold, wet, minty-sweet happiness seeped through him, warming him with her passionate grasp on life, it happened again, more, much more than any imagined kiss.

The world stood still and he seized the moment, lifting his hands to cradle her head, slanting his mouth against hers as the warmth became an inferno hot enough to touch the permafrost that had invaded his soul.

Her kitten eyes were more gold than green as she raised her lids. Then touched her lips to his cheek, tasted them with her tongue.

'One of us is crying,' she said.

He rubbed a gloved thumb over her cheek. 'Maybe we both are.'

'With happiness,' she declared.

'Or maybe it's just our eyes watering with the cold. I need to stand up before my butt freezes to the ground.' And, before he could change his mind, he lifted her aside, stood up.

'I've messed up your snow angel,' she said as he reached out a hand to help her to her feet.

'That's okay. I'm no angel,' he said.

'Who is?'

'If I had a Christmas tree, I'd put you on top of it,' he said and, beyond helping himself, he touched his knuckles to her cheek, kissed her again. Just a touch, but somehow more intense for its sweetness. A promise... 'Do you want a picture of your angel?' he asked, forcing himself to take a step back.

'Please.' Then, as if she, too, needed to distract herself from the intensity of the moment, 'I don't suppose you have such a thing as a piece of paper?'

He searched through his pockets, found an envelope. 'Will this do?'

'Perfect.' And, using a lipstick, she wrote in big block capitals: LUCYB WOZ HERE!

She propped it on the front of the snow lady, put out her hand for the phone and took a snap.

'Great. Tweet time, I think,' she said, pulling off her glove with her teeth and, struggling with cold fingers, keyed in a message.

Thanks for the good vibes, tweeps. Here's a tweetpic, just to let you know that I'm safe. #findLucyB
LucyB, Wed 1 Dec 22:43

Lucy lifted the phone, looking over her shoulder at him. 'What do you think? Will that have them all running around in the snow?'

'Is that the plan?' he asked as she pressed 'send'.

'I don't have a plan,' she said, lifting her hand to his cheek, pressing her lips against it. Then, as she looked up at him the smile died, 'Thank you, Nathaniel.'

'I should be thanking you. If it wasn't for you, I'd be inside going through the daily sales figures instead of finding my inner child.'

'Inside in the warm,' she said, turning away to give the

snow lady a hug. 'Stay cool, Lily.' Then she looked up. 'It's stopped snowing.'

'I told you. It'll all be gone by tomorrow. Everything will be back to normal.'

'Will it?'

She sounded less than happy at the prospect. Which made two of them.

'We've still got tonight. Are you hungry?'

Her eyes lit up. 'Absolutely starving.'

Diary update: *Fun and frolics in the park with Nathaniel. I didn't see that coming and neither, I suspect, did he. I have to admit that making a snowman—snow lady—in the park at ten o'clock at night in a blizzard is probably not the most sensible thing I've ever done. And it's getting hard to top the stupid ones I've done today.*

And then he kissed me. No, wait, I kissed him. We kissed each other. Lying in the snow.

'I know what this is all about, you know.' Lucy gave him a sideways grin as they stood on the Embankment overlooking the river, tucking into hot dogs. 'Why we're having hot dogs. You just don't want all that nasty bright yellow eggy, cheesy stuff in your kitchen.'

'It's not that.'

Nat took out his phone and snapped her as she sucked a piece of onion into her mouth.

'Hey, not fair!'

'One more for your fans,' he said, lifting it out of reach as she made a grab for it. 'The truth of the matter, Lucy B, is that I couldn't make an omelette to save my life.'

For some reason she seemed to think that was funny.

They'd laughed a lot.

She'd laughed at a couple of outrageous Santa incidents he'd shared from way back in the history of the store. He'd laughed at her stories about a day-care nursery where she'd worked. It was obvious how much she loved the children she'd worked with. From a momentary wistfulness in her look, how much she missed them.

As she'd talked, laughed, all the strain had seeped out of her limbs and her face and she'd told him enough about her character—far more than she realised—to reassure him that she was on the level.

'Actually, this is great. Crazy perfect.' She bumped shoulders with him. 'Thank you.'

'My pleasure,' he said, wrapping his arm around her waist, wanting to keep her close. And it was. Golden curls peeped out from beneath her hat, framing a face lit up, almost translucent in the lamplight.

And, as the strain had eased from her face, the knots deep in his own belly had begun to unravel, at least until that second kiss. At which point they had been replaced by a different kind of tension.

'I hope the missing elf had as much fun as we have,' she said. 'I owe her a lot.'

'Me too,' he said. 'I'll check with HR first thing to see if there were any messages. Deflect any problems.'

'Why?' she asked, her tongue curling out to catch an errant onion. 'Why would you do that? Any of this?'

Good question.

She looked up. 'What happened, Nathaniel? On the stairs.'

Another good question.

'I don't know,' he admitted. That something had happened—something momentous—was beyond doubt. 'I can tell you why I noticed you.'

'That's a start.'

'It was your hair... The way it seemed to float around your head like a halo. It reminded me of someone.'

Quite suddenly, Lucy lost her appetite. What had she expected him to say? That he'd been captivated at a glance. Lie to her? She'd had enough lies to last her a lifetime.

'The woman these clothes belong to?' she asked, pushing it.

'Claudia. Her name was Claudia. She was my cousin's wife.'

'You were in love with her?' Stupid question. Of course he was.

'We both were. I met her at university, dated her, but when I brought her home she met Christopher and after that it was always him. It didn't stop Chris obsessing that we were having an affair when we worked together on the store design.'

She lifted her hand to the bruise at her temple, gently rubbing her fingers over the sore spot, remembering his concern.

'He was abusive,' she said.

'I believe so. She used to brush aside any concern, say she bruised at a touch. Was always walking into things. Maybe she was. She wasn't eating properly, fighting an addiction to tranquillisers. Then one day I caught her running, terrified. I held her,' he said. 'Just held her, begged her to leave him. Not for me. For herself. And then Chris caught up with her, held out his hand to her and, without a word, she took it. Walked away with him. It was as if she had no will.' He glanced at her. 'It was just the hair, Lucy. You're not a bit like her.'

'No,' she said. 'I'm shorter, fatter...' He frowned and she rushed on, 'You're talking about her in the past tense.'

'There was an accident. Chris always drove too fast, even though he knew it terrified her. Probably *because* it terrified her. It's all about control, isn't it?' He looked away for a moment, but then looked back. 'She died instantly. He's in a wheelchair, paralysed from the neck down.'

She shivered, but not with the cold, and he turned to her, put his arms around her. Held her. Just as he'd held Claudia, she thought and, much as she wanted to stay there, in his arms, she pulled away.

'I have no reason to protect Rupert Henshawe, Nathaniel. He does not control me.'

'Doesn't he?' He shook his head, as if he knew the answer. 'Reason has nothing to do with it,' he said. Then, before she could deny it, 'It was my fault. I should never have come back. Never accepted the commission.'

'Why did you?'

'Family. Guilt. I turned my back on family tradition and it broke my father's heart. It was a way to make up for that.'

'And, after the accident, you stepped in to look after things?'

'There was no one else.'

'No one else called Hart, maybe. Is Christopher punishing you for what happened to him?' she asked. 'Or are you punishing yourself for not saving Claudia?' He didn't answer. Maybe he didn't know the answer. 'Who is it who leaves the rose, Nathaniel?'

'That's enough, Lucy,' he said sharply.

'It's him, isn't it? A daily reminder that she loved him. He can't abuse his wife any more, frighten her, hurt her, because she's beyond his reach,' she continued, recklessly ignoring the warning. 'So he's abusing you instead.'

There was a long moment of silence.

So not bright, Lucy Bright.

Blown it, Lucy Bright.

And then he touched her cheek with his cold hand. A gesture that said a hundred times more than words.

'Bright by name, bright by nature. Good guess, but you're not entirely right. I'm punishing myself for failing to protect her. But I'm punishing him, too. Even while it gives him pleasure to know that I've been jerked back into the family business, robbed of something I loved, at the same time it's eating him alive to know that I'm in control. In his place.'

'He had Claudia.'

'Yes, he had Claudia. His tragedy, and ultimately hers, is that he never believed that she could love him more than me. That he always thought of himself as second choice in all things.'

'Let it go, Nathaniel. If you don't, it will destroy you and then he'll have killed you both.'

'I know,' he said, looking at her. 'I know.' And somehow she was the one holding him. Hugging him to her, holding him safe. She could have stayed there for ever, making their own warm, safe space in an icy world. Then he dropped a kiss on the top of her head. 'Your turn, Lucy.'

'Mine?' She looked up at him.

'That was the deal. I tell you mine and you tell me yours. Tell me what happened on the stairs.'

'I...' About to deny it, she thought better of it. 'I don't know. I was in a bit of a state, confused. An emotional basket case.'

'That would explain it,' he replied dryly, 'but I have to tell you that, between your criticism of the penthouse and the basket case explanation of a stop-the-world-moment, you are not doing a lot for my ego.'

'I didn't mean...'

Lucy faltered. She didn't know what she meant. She was more confused now than she had been then. When he'd caught her, their eyes had met and the instant connection had entirely bypassed her brain.

Her response to him had been entirely physical, without thought or reason. Completely honest. Without guile. Innocent.

'I wanted you to kiss me,' she said. Then, because being honest really mattered, 'I wanted you.'

Even in the light from the street lamps, Nat could see the blush heat Lucy's cheeks. Felt an answering and equally primitive rush, a desire to recapture that atavistic moment of connection. The caveman response, with no need for words or complicated ritual.

Her honesty shamed him. He'd wanted her, too, with a raw urgency that shocked the civilised man. It was the same primal instinct that urged him to protect her. They were two sides of the same basic need for survival. Take the woman, plant your seed and then protect her against the world because she was your future. And he would. From what, he wasn't entirely certain, only that this time he wouldn't stand back. Wouldn't fail. No matter what the cost.

The 'no involvement' mantra had gone right out of the window the moment he'd suggested this mad adventure.

That first life-changing encounter had given him back something of himself. The kisses they'd shared in the snow had broken through a barrier. More would have them naked, in bed. That was why he'd stopped by the hot dog stall instead of taking her straight home.

'"I wanted you",' he repeated thoughtfully. 'Maybe it could do with a little work. I was thinking that it was one of those perfect, never to be repeated, once-in-a-lifetime moments when everything seems to drop into place.'

She pulled a wry smile. 'You'd think so, wouldn't you. But they will keep happening to me.'

'You're telling me that you keep meeting strangers you want to kiss?' he asked, his voice even, but the caveman response was, he discovered, a lot more powerful than the civilised veneer would suggest.

'Oh, not *kiss*.' Her smile deepened. 'That was a bonus feature. And of course last time it wasn't a chance encounter, but stage-managed, so actually you're right. Once-in-a-lifetime it is.'

'Stage-managed?'

'You want the story.' She nodded as if she'd been expecting that. 'I warn you that it's long. You'll probably want another hot dog. Extra onions for me.'

He returned with two fresh hot dogs, dripping with mustard and onions, and leaned back against the wall, his shoulder just touching hers. Just so that she'd know he was there.

Giving her courage to tell her story. Face the betrayal head-on.

'The Henshawe Corporation's High Street fashion chain had lost market share,' she began. 'It was no longer hot so they made the decision to give the stores a new look, a new name. Re-brand it. Take it upmarket.'

Lucy bit into the bun, chewed it for a while, watching a police launch moving slowly up the river, the lights dancing on the water, while she gathered her thoughts.

Nathaniel slipped his arm around her shoulder as if it was the most natural thing in the world.

'They went to their PR company, as you do,' she said, 'and commissioned them to come up with a strategy to launch the new brand. One that would not only garner maximum media coverage, but engage their target consumer audience of young women who read gossip magazines and aspire to be the wife, or at least the girlfriend, of a top sports star.'

'Or, failing that, one of the minor royals,' he said, raising a smile.

'You've got it.'

'So far, so standard.'

'Their first step was to set up focus groups to find out what that group were looking for. Get feedback on likely "names" to launch the new brand.'

'Classy, stylish, sexy clothes. Good value. A label with cachet. You don't need a focus group to tell you that,' he said.

'No, but they were surprised to discover that concerns were raised about sweatshop labour. And then someone said wouldn't it be great if they used an ordinary girl, someone like them, rather than a celebrity to be the face of the store.'

'What they meant was one of them.'

'Undoubtedly,' she said. 'But it gave the PR firm their hook. Their media campaign. All they needed was an ordinary girl.'

'So how did they find you, Miss Ordinary?' he asked.

'They advertised for a junior clerical assistant.'

'Interesting approach,' he said dryly. 'You ticked all the boxes?'

'Good grief, no. I wasn't thin enough, tall enough, pretty enough or even smart enough.'

It was all there in the file. Painful reading.

'I thought they wanted ordinary.'

'Ordinary in quotes,' she said, using her fingers to make little quote marks.

'You must have had something.'

'Thanks for that,' she said, waving towards the road, where the cars were moving slowly past in the slushy conditions.

'Who are you waving to?'

'My ego and yours, hand in hand, hitching a ride out of here,' she said, her breath smoking away in the cold air. Her mouth tilting up in a grin. Because, honestly, standing here with Nathaniel, it did all seem very petty. Very small stuff. Except, of course, it wasn't that simple.

'Actually, I happen to think you're pretty special,' he said, capturing her hand, wrapping it in his. 'But we both know that you're not classic model material.'

'You're right. I know it, you know it, the world knows it. But I had three things going for me.' They'd handily itemised them on a memo. 'First, I had a story. Abandoned as a baby—'

'Abandoned?'

'The classic baby in a cardboard box story, me.'

He made no comment. Well, what could anyone say?

'I had a dozen foster homes,' she continued, 'a fractured education that left me unqualified to do anything other than take care of other people's children. Not that I was qualified for that, but it was something I'd been doing since I was a kid myself.'

'You truly were Cinderella,' he said, getting it.

'I truly was,' she confirmed.

The hot dog was gone and she reached for her coffee. Took a sip. It was hot.

'Second?' he prompted.

'I had ambition. I worked in a day-care nursery from eight-thirty until six, then evenings as a waitress to put myself through night school to get a diploma in business studies.'

'Cinderella, but not one sitting around waiting for her fairy godmother to come along with her magic wand.'

He was quick.

'Cinderella doing it for herself,' she confirmed. 'Not that

it did me much good. I didn't get a single interview until I applied for the Henshawe job.'

'It's tough out there.'

'Tell me about it. I really, really needed that job and when they asked me why I wanted to work for the company I didn't hold back. I let them have it with both barrels. The whole determination to make something of my life speech. Oscar-winning stuff, Nathaniel. They actually applauded.'

'They were from the PR company, I take it?'

'How did you guess?'

'HR managers tend to be a little less impressionable. You said you had three things.'

'My third lucky break was that some woman on the team was bright enough to realise that I was exactly the kind of woman who would be walking in off the street, desperate for something to make her look fabulous. Let's face it, if the gold-standard was a size-zero, six-foot supermodel, the reflection in the dressing room mirror was always going to be a disappointment.'

'But if they compared themselves with you… Who is this PR company? I could use that kind of out of the box thinking.'

'Oh, I don't deny they're good.'

'Sorry. Your story. So, having applauded your audition, they told you what the part would be?'

'No.'

'No?'

'You're missing the point. I was going to be a genuine "ordinary" girl who had been picked from among his staff. I had to believe in the story before I could sell it.'

'Did I say they were good?'

'Oh, there's more. Someone added a note on the bottom of their report to the effect that this was going to be a real fairy tale. And then they started thinking so far out of the box they were on another planet.'

His hand tightened on hers. 'It was all a set-up? Not just the job, the discovery…'

'I had a phone call the day after my interview, offering me the job. I started the following week and I have to tell you that it was the most boring week of my life. I was climbing the walls by Friday afternoon, wondering how long I could stand it. Then I was sent up to the top floor with a pile of files, got knocked off my feet by a speeding executive and there was Rupert Henshawe, perfectly placed to pick me up, sit me in his office, give me coffee from his personal coffee-maker while his chauffeur was summoned to take me home. And, while we waited, he asked me about my job, whether I liked working for the company. I'd heard he was as hard as nails. Terrifying if you made a mistake. But he was so kind. Utterly…' she shrugged '…charming.'

'I'd heard he was a smooth operator.'

'I had flowers and a note on Saturday. Lunch in the country on Sunday. Picture in the tabloids on Monday.'

CHAPTER NINE

'ARE you telling me that you didn't have a clue?'

'Not until today,' she admitted. 'Dumb or what?'

'Don't be so hard on yourself. You saw what he wanted you to see.'

'What I wanted to believe. Until today. I was late and, since I didn't have time to go home and pick up my copy of the wedding file, I decided to borrow the one in Rupert's office. That's when I stumbled across the one labelled "The Cinderella Project".'

She still remembered the little prickle at the base of her neck when she'd seen it.

'But the romance, the engagement?'

She understood what he was asking. 'There is no sex in fairy tales, Nathaniel. My Prince Charming okayed the plan, but only with the proviso…' written in his own hand '…that he didn't have to "sleep with the girl".' More of those quote marks.

'So he's gay?'

She blinked. 'Why would you say that?'

He shook his head. 'Just thinking out loud.'

She stared at him for a moment. Was he saying what she thought he was saying? That the only reason a man wouldn't want to sleep with her was because…?

'No…'

He responded with a lift of those expressive eyebrows. 'You'd have thought someone so good at the details would have made a little more effort. That's all I'm saying.'

'Yes... No...' She blushed. 'I wasn't exactly throwing myself at him.'

'No? How come I got so lucky?' She dug him in the ribs with her elbow. In response, he put his arm around her. 'You throw, I'll catch,' he said and, without stopping to think, she stood on tiptoe and put her arms around his neck. He didn't let her down, scooping her up so that she was off the ground, grinning as he spun her around, kissing her before he set her back on her feet.

'Thanks,' she said.

'Entirely my pleasure,' he assured her, still holding her close. 'But I don't understand. If there was no great romance, no passion, why did you accept his proposal, Lucy?'

'Because I bought the fairy story.'

She was still buying it, she thought, glancing up at Nathaniel. She really needed to get a grip on reality.

'The breakup scenario is already written, by the way,' she said, before he could say anything. Pulling away. 'Apparently, I'm going to call the wedding off because Rupert is a workaholic, too absorbed in business to spend time with me. True, as it happens. Sadness, but no recriminations. Nothing sordid. Just a quiet fade out of the relationship once the stores are open and the brand established.'

'You went seriously off message this afternoon.'

'I lost the plot big time, but that's what you get for employing amateurs.'

'I can see why he's desperate to get the file back. The tabloids would have a field day with this.' And, from looking deep into her eyes, he was suddenly looking at something in the distance above her head. 'I'm not just talking about his underactive libido.' She didn't miss the edge to his voice as he added, 'You could make a fortune.'

'Yes, I could. I could have phoned one of the tabloids this afternoon. But I don't want a drama, Nathaniel. I just want to disappear. Get my life back. Be ordinary.'

'But you're Lucy B,' he pointed out.

'I know. That's why I can't let him get away with what he's doing. Why I can't just disappear. Because that's not the end of it.'

'There's more?'

'He wants his file back because all that lovely stuff about fair trade fashion is a bunch of baloney.'

'Baloney?'

'Lies, falsehoods, untruths. There is a fair trade company, but it's just a front. The actual clothes, shoes, accessories still be made by the same sweatshop workers he used for the old stuff. That's why he's desperate to retrieve the file.'

He said just one word. Then, 'I'm sorry...'

'No need to apologise. You've got it. The man has all the morals of a cowpat.' She stuffed her hands deep in her pockets. 'That's why I was so angry. Why I couldn't think straight. When the media circus took off like a rocket, bigger than anything they had imagined, and a headline writer shortened my name to Lucy B, Marketing ditched the names they'd been playing with and grabbed it. He's going to use my name—on the shop fronts, on the labels, everywhere—use me to sell his lie. That's what today's press conference was about. To unveil the look of the stores. Tell the world about the jobs he's creating, both here and in the Third World. Impress the public with his new caring image, impress the shareholders with profit forecasts.'

'That's...' For a moment he didn't seem to be able to find a word. And then he did. 'Dangerous.'

Not reassuring—she'd been a lot less bothered by the expletive—and, despite the down jacket, she shivered.

'You're cold,' he said. 'Let's go home. Get you back in the warm.'

Diary update: *I have to admit that when Nathaniel asked me if I was hungry I didn't anticipate a hot dog from a stall on the Strand, but it was junk food at its finest. And the onions were piled up high enough to bring tears of joy to the eyes of the government's diet Tsar. But then it's been that sort of day. Surprises all round. Horrible ones, delicious ones and a man a girl could love. Not fairy tale falling in love, but the genuine article.*

Will everything be back to normal tomorrow?

Can anything ever be normal again?

What is normal?

Nathaniel didn't say anything until they were near the store, then he reached out and, hand on her arm, said, 'Out of sight, I think.'

She didn't argue, but ducked down until the barrier clanged behind them and he'd pulled into a parking bay and switched off the engine. Released his seat belt.

'You saw something?' she asked as she slid down from the seat without waiting for him to help her.

Nat shook his head, put his arm around her shoulders and swept her towards the lift, wanting her inside, out of sight. Regretting the crazy impulse to go out in the snow. Anyone might have seen her.

The guy at the hot dog stall wouldn't forget two idiots who'd gone out to play in the snow, stood for ever, eating hot dogs and talking.

'What's bothering you?' she asked.

'I hadn't realised… This is a lot more serious than I thought, Lucy.'

He keyed in the code and breathed more easily when the door clicked shut behind them, shedding his coat and gloves, kicking off his boots. It was probably the first time he'd actually been glad to be home since he'd moved into the apartment. The first time it had felt like home. A sanctuary.

'You're scaring me,' Lucy said, cold hands fumbling with her zip.

He stopped her. Not cold, just shaking, he discovered and, instead of unzipping it for her, he put his arms around her, held her, because he was scared for her.

This wasn't simply some romance gone wrong. It wasn't even just an amoral PR campaign that meant heads would roll right up to boardroom level.

'Nathaniel? Now you're really worrying me!'

He let her go, unzipped her jacket, helped her out of it.

'Okay. While the fake romance would be an embarrassment to Henshawe, I've no doubt he could contain the damage, but the fair trade thing is fraud.'

'Fraud?'

'It's going to seriously damage him and the Henshawe Corporation when it gets out. The Lucy B chain will be history, his shareholders will want blood and he'll be facing a police investigation.'

'You're talking jail time?' she asked, shocked.

'He's probably shredding papers as fast as he can right now. Talking to his suppliers to cover his tracks. But, while you've got his file, written proof of what he did, he's not safe and I believe that a man who has the morals of a cowpat would go to any lengths to stop that from happening.'

'You're saying that I'm in danger?'

Before he could answer, the phone rang and he unhooked it from the wall. 'Hart.'

'Nat, it's Bryan. Sorry to disturb you, but I've just had a call from the police.'

His heart rate picked up. 'And?'

'It seems they've had a missing person report. A woman called Lucy Bright. The WAG of some billionaire. She was last seen heading this way just after four this afternoon and appears to have vanished off the face of the earth. I wouldn't have bothered you, but the timing is right and the description matches the woman you saw this afternoon.'

'Did you mention that to the police?' he asked, reaching out a hand as he saw the colour drain from Lucy's face.

'No. It might not have been her and I assumed that you wouldn't want policemen crawling all over the store talking to the staff. Or the ensuing press invasion. Not until we're sure, anyway.'

'Good call.'

'I searched the name on the internet and I'm about to send you a photograph as an email attachment. In the meantime, I've initiated a sweep of the premises, just to cover ourselves.'

'Right…' Then, 'You were in the force, Bryan. Isn't it unusual for them to get involved in something like this so quickly?'

'It depends who's missing. And why.'

Nat listened as he detailed all the likely reasons why the police had got involved so quickly. Suspected violence, theft… He never took his eyes off Lucy who, her free hand to her mouth, was watching him with growing apprehension.

'I'll get back to you. In the meantime, keep me posted.'

Lucy was numb. The minute Nathaniel had picked up the phone she'd known something was wrong. And when she'd heard him say the word police she'd known the game was up.

'The police? They've been here? Looking for me?'

'Just a phone call.'

Just!

'You've been reported missing and they're following up on a suggestion that you were last seen entering the store.'

'They're not going to give up, are they? I'm so sorry to have involved you in this, Nathaniel, but I can't believe that Rupert had the nerve to involve the police.'

'You stole a file,' he pointed out. 'One filled with sensitive commercial information.'

'I know, but…' Then, 'Are you saying that he's had the nerve to accuse me of stealing?'

'Not officially.'

'So what?'

'He could be using the fact that there has been a campaign by your fans on the social media sites to put pressure on them. Apparently, the most used hashtag in the last few hours has been #findLucyB.'

'Well, colour me surprised.'

'You're not impressed that you inspire such devotion?'

'Not desperately. I have no doubt that it was instigated by the Henshawe PR team. Why waste time looking for someone when you can persuade half a million people to do it for you? Get a little hysteria going. But I still don't understand. The police don't normally bother about missing persons unless there's blood on the carpet. Do they?' she pressed when he didn't immediately answer.

'Not normally. Not this soon. It must have been the call from your mother that did the trick.'

Lucy froze.

'My mother?'

'She gave an emotional doorstep interview, pleading with anyone who knows where you are to call her. It's probably online if you want to see it.'

'No! I don't. She's not my mother,' she said. 'I told you. I don't have a mother.'

'Lucy—'

'She's a fake,' she said quickly, all the peace, the pleasure of their evening together dissipating in that bitter reality. 'Just another lie dreamed up to keep the press engaged.' The worst one. The cruellest one. The rest she might abhor, but they, at least, had a purpose. 'What's a fairy tale without a wicked witch…?'

Except that she hadn't been wicked. She'd been fifteen. Abandoned by an abusive boyfriend. Alone and afraid.

Lies…

Before she could move, Nathaniel had his arms around her, holding her rigid body, murmuring soft calming sounds that purred through her until she finally stopped shaking. He held her while her silent, angry tears soaked his T-shirt. Held her until the tension seeped from her limbs and she melted against him.

Just held her.

It was a technique she used to calm distraught children, holding them tight so that they'd feel safe even when they fought her—her promise that, whatever they did, she would not let go. And, even as she broke down, buried her face in his shoulder and sobbed like a baby while his hands gently stroked her back, in the dark recesses of her mind, she recognized that this was something he'd done before.

That she shouldn't read more into it than a simple

gesture of comfort and gradually she began to withdraw. Ease away.

She was a survivor. She'd taken everything that life could throw at her and she'd take this, come through it. She lifted her head, straightened her shoulders, putting herself back together, piece by piece, something she'd done times without number.

But never before had the loss of contact felt so personal, the empty space between two bodies quite so cold.

Then, as she brushed her fingers, palms over her cheeks to dry them, Nathaniel took away her hands, tugged up the edge of his T-shirt and used it to very tenderly dab them dry.

'I'm sorry,' she said quickly, pulling away from him before the tears began to fall again. 'I didn't plan to weep all over you.'

His response was a crooked smile and, making a pretence of wringing out his T-shirt between his hands, making a joke of it, he said, 'Is that the worst you've got?'

She felt an answering tug at the corner of her own lips. She was still embarrassed at bawling her eyes out, but somehow it didn't seem to matter so much. Nothing seemed to matter when Nathaniel smiled at her.

And that was dangerous.

Not because he was trying to fool her, but because she was capable of fooling herself. Seeing only what she wanted to see. Hearing only what she wanted to hear.

'You have to call the police, Nathaniel. Tell them I'm here.'

'Do I?' he asked. 'I'm perfectly capable of looking a policeman in the eyes and telling him that you're not in the store.'

'No lies,' she insisted. 'Nobody lies…'

'So long as I do it before the store opens tomorrow, it will be the truth.'

'But it wouldn't be the whole truth and nothing but the truth, would it?'

'You care about that?'

'I've been living a lie for the last six months. This afternoon I lied to Pam...'

'You didn't actually lie to her.'

'I didn't tell her the truth, which is the same thing.' She'd actually congratulated herself on her cleverness, which, considering the way she'd berated Rupert for doing the same thing, was double standards any way you looked at it. 'You've been kind, Nathaniel. Not some fairy tale Prince Charming; you're the real thing. A "parfit gentil knyght". But you have the store to think about, your reputation. This is going to be messy and I don't want you involved.'

'It's odd, Lucy, but that's exactly what I told myself this afternoon when I delegated one of my staff to find you, return your shoe, offer you a pair of tights, whatever else you needed. Leave it to someone else to deal with, I thought. Don't get involved.'

'You did that?' For a moment she felt as if she was bathed in a warm blast, like opening an oven door. 'Well, I guess I will need a pair of tights—'

'I was still saying it when I had Henshawe's bullies evicted from the store,' he continued, taking her face in his hands.

'—and shoes. The boots are great, but—'

'And all the time I was driving Pam home and couldn't think of anything but the fear in your beautiful kitten eyes.' Instinctively, she closed them and felt the butterfly touch of his thumbs brush across her lids. His fingers sliding through her hair as he cradled her head. 'I was telling myself to forget it. Whatever it was. That it wasn't my problem. Don't get involved—'

'But, as to the rest,' she cut in, forcing her eyes open, refusing to succumb to his touch, his voice so soft that it seemed to be lost somewhere deep in his throat.

Forcing herself to take responsibility for what had happened. Step away.

'As to the rest,' she said as her retreat was halted by the bulk of the island unit, 'I'll swallow my pride, borrow some clothes and call that taxi. Go to the nearest police station and tell them the truth.'

It was fraud. A crime…

He'd moved with her, his hands still cradled her head, his train of thought unbroken.

'—don't get involved. Telling myself that by the time I got back you'd be long gone.'

'And in the morning,' she persisted, shutting her ears to temptation, 'you can tell the police that I'm not in the store.'

'And that's not being economical with the truth?'

'Only slightly.'

'The truth, since you're so keen on it, Lucy Bright, is that I was involved from the moment I saw you ahead of me on the stairs. Your hair floating like a halo around your head.'

'Well, that's history…'

She was trapped against the island. His hands were a gentle cradle for her face, his body was warming her from breast to knee, the silver glints in his eyes were molten.

'Now I just look like Harpo Marx…'

Not that she could have moved. Every cell in her body had given up, surrendered and, as his gaze slid down to her lips, it was only the counter at her back that was holding her up.

'Your neck...' His thumb brushed her jaw as his hand stroked her neck in a slow, lazy move that sent a wave of heat rippling down to her toes. 'Did you know that the nape of the neck is considered so erotic that geishas leave it unpainted?'

She managed a small noise, nothing that made any sense because, forget necks, napes or any other part of the anatomy, his voice, so low that only her hormones could hear, was doing it for her.

'The way your dress was slipping from your shoulder—'

'It was just a look,' she said in a last-ditch attempt to hang onto whatever sense she possessed. 'A once-in-a-lifetime, never-to-be-repeated look—'

'What are you prepared to risk on that, Lucy Bright? Truth, dare, kiss, promise...'

Her desperate protestations died as, not waiting for her answer, his eyes never leaving her lips, Nathaniel looked at her with that same intensity, the same liquid silver eyes that had turned her core molten, before slowly lowering his mouth to hers.

She watched in slow motion, knowing that it was going to happen, knowing that all she had to do to stop it was answer him.

Say just one word.

If only she could remember what it was. But her brain was lollygagging around somewhere. Out to lunch. Make that dinner...

She slammed her eyes shut a second before he made contact and her world was reduced to touch. The soft warmth of a barely-there kiss. A tingle as her lips demanded more. A breath—his, not hers. She'd sucked air in and it was stuck there as she waited for the promise.

The warmth became heat.

Her lower lip began to tremble.

Someone moaned and her tongue, too thick for her own mouth, reached for his. Touched his lip. Another moment of this torture and she was going to slither between his arms and melt into a messy puddle on the floor at his feet.

Was this the kiss? The promise? Or was it about the truth?

Right now, it didn't seem to matter much. It might be 'just a kiss' but she wanted it. Wanted it and everything that followed.

'You win,' she murmured against his mouth, her eyes still closed.

'Not entirely,' he replied, his voice more a growl than a purr as his hand abandoned her neck to capture her hip, pull her close, as the kiss became the briefest reality before he took a step back, leaving her hot and hungry for more. 'But you most certainly lost and I'm not going to be a gentleman about it. I'm claiming my forfeit.'

At which point her knees gave up the struggle and buckled beneath her.

Nat caught her as she slithered into his arms. 'Hey,' he said, 'it isn't going to be that bad.'

Her throat was thick and she had to clear it. 'It isn't?'

'What did you think? That I was going to demand your body?'

'Noooo…' Dry and thick with disappointment which if she could hear, so could he…'The police,' she muttered, grabbing for reality. 'We have to call them now.'

'You surrendered, Lucy. I won. Remember? Or shall we try that again?' He mistook her hesitation for reluctance. 'I'm going to call my lawyer,' he said, one arm propping her up, the other retrieving his phone from his jacket pocket.

'He'll call the police, reassure them that you're safe. That you'll be available for an interview, at a time convenient to you, if they want to talk to you.'

'Can you do that?'

'I can do that.'

And he did. Right after he'd caught her behind the knees and carried her through to her bedroom, set her down on the bed and pulled off the boots, taking the three pairs of socks she was wearing with them.

He'd stared at her toes for a moment, then flipped open the phone, got some lawyer out of his bed and told him exactly what he wanted. Not just straightening things out with the police—without revealing her whereabouts—but the retrieval of her belongings from the apartment in the Henshawe house.

'I'm running up a big bill, here,' she said when he'd finished.

'True. You're going to have to work right through until Christmas Eve.'

'That's not work. That's fun.'

He grinned. 'Christmas Eve two thousand and twenty.'

'That big, huh? And if I volunteer to cook Christmas lunch for you?'

'Christmas Eve two thousand and fifty.' And his smile faded. 'Here,' he said, handing her the phone. 'Keep this with you. Post the rest of your photographs. Give Henshawe a sleepless night.'

She would rather give Nathaniel one, she thought, but for once held her tongue, just watching him as he adjusted a dial on the wall and the glass darkened, blotting out the lights, the planes passing overhead.

'I'll find you something to sleep in.'

'I'll manage.'

'No doubt, but I'm not sure my blood pressure can take the strain.'

CHAPTER TEN

Diary update: *Okay, this is the last entry for today. I just peeled off the jeans, which were pretty wet around the knees. The snow had got down my neck, too. I hadn't noticed until Nathaniel left me and suddenly I felt horribly cold, so now I'm dictating this as I lie back in a gorgeously scented bubble bath...*

LUCY paused as she heard a tap on her bedroom door.

'Hello?'

'Room service.'

'I didn't—' she began, but the bathroom door opened a crack—it hadn't occurred to her to lock it—and a glossy Hastings & Hart carrier appeared, dangling from long masculine fingers.

'Pyjamas, slippers and a selection of other female necessities, madam.'

She swallowed. 'Nathaniel...'

'Two thousand and fifty-one,' he said, before any of the things bubbling up from her heart could spill over and embarrass them both.

'Two thousand and fifty-one? They had better be designer necessities,' she replied. Keeping it light, light, light...

'Down to the last button,' he assured her, slipping the handles over the door knob, where it would be safe from accidental spills—the man learned fast—and closing the door. She slid down a little lower in the bath, grinning to herself.

She waited a minute, then clicked 'record' and continued her diary update.

Right, where was I? Oh, thawing out in the bath. It's impossible to describe today, except that I'd be happy to cook Nathaniel Hart's Christmas dinner until the end of time. He is unbelievably special. And, I'm certain, deeply unhappy but tomorrow, as Scarlett O'Hara so famously said, is another day. Maybe it will bring a few answers. To my problems. And to his.

That done, she checked her tweets.

@LucyB Loved the snow lady! One of the London Parks, right? Hyde, Regency, Green? More clues! #findLucyB
jenpb, [+] Wed 1 Dec 23:16

@LucyB Hyde Park. I can just make out the Serpentine Bridge in the background. U okay, sweetie? #findLucyB
WelshWitch, [+] Wed 1 Dec 23:17

She blinked, then quickly keyed in a response, posting the pictures Nathaniel had taken.

@jenpb Hyde Park it is. Here's a pic of a snow angel I made. Tucked up safe, thanx, WW. #findLucyB
LucyB, Wed 1 Dec 23:51

* * *

*@WelshWitch Safe & well fed as u can see in this pic.
Who needs dinner at the Ritz? Night tweeps. More
in the morning. #findLucyB*
LucyB, Wed 1 Dec 23:54

Lucy climbed out of the bath, wrapped herself in the
bathrobe, brushed her teeth, did the whole cleanse, tone,
moisturise thing with the stuff provided.

Only when she was done with all that did she allow
herself the pleasure of opening the carrier.

The pyjamas were white—obviously—but they were
spattered with candy-red hearts and she couldn't wait to
scramble into them. Fasten the heart-shaped buttons.

The slippers, fuzzy soft ones that you pushed your feet
into, matched them. There was even a wrap that tied with
a big red bow.

Further down the bag she found underwear. Yummy,
silky, lacy underwear. And, right at the bottom, wrapped
in tissue, a pair of shoes. Red suede with peep toes, a saucy
bow and very high heels.

Not exactly like the ones she'd been wearing, but she
couldn't have chosen anything better for herself and she
was wearing a great big grin as, her arms full of wrap
and undies and shoes, she opened the door. And, for the
second time that day, had a heart-stop moment as she saw
Nathaniel, this time stretched out on her bed in a pair of
worn-thin joggers, a T-shirt so old that whatever had been
written on it had long since faded out, hair damp from the
shower, bare feet crossed at the ankle.

Exactly the kind of eye candy that any woman would
be delighted to find waiting for her after a delicious soak
in a scented bath.

Her pleasure was somewhat dimmed by the fact that he
was reading the file she'd carefully hidden in the locker

room, although she had to admit that the glossy black cover nicely matched the decor.

'I could have been naked,' she exclaimed. Again.

'A man doesn't get that lucky twice in one day,' he said, looking up, holding her gaze for so long that she forgot all about the file. 'But cute will do to be going on with.'

'The jammies *are* sweet,' she said when her heart had settled back into something like its normal rhythm and she could breathe again. 'I particularly love the red. It exactly matches my toenails.' She wiggled them. 'I had these done this morning. Pam made me remove the colour from my fingernails, but she missed these.'

'I can't think how,' he said, 'but I'm glad she did.' Then, 'Tell me, do you talk to yourself in the bath?'

'I was updating my diary. There was a lot to say.'

'It's been a busy day for Lucy B.'

'Buzz, buzz, buzz… Do you want to hear what I said about you?'

'Probably not.'

She told him anyway. 'I said that you were a great kisser, unbelievably special and deeply unhappy. I seem to have missed your talent with a lock pick.'

'I'm working on the happiness thing,' Nat said, grateful for the distraction of the file. 'And I didn't have to pick the lock. We keep a duplicate set of keys to the lockers. People are always losing them.'

'So? What? You wanted to check my story? See if I was telling the truth?' Her grin was long since history.

'If I'd even suspected that you were lying, Lucy, I'd have read the file in my office. I simply wanted to be sure that you had cast iron proof of Henshawe's guilt.'

'And have I?'

'Yes, fortunately. It's in the focus group section. The part where someone raised the fair trade question. There are detailed notes from the individual tasked to look into it and come up with a plan that would make them look good without compromising profits.'

'But—'

'There were a number of options. Higher prices. Lower margins. Cheaper materials. Or the handy solution that he went for. There's a handwritten note at the bottom over Henshawe's initials. "Option Four. Get on with it."'

Nat held it up for her to see and she sat down heavily on the side of the bed. 'So that's it, then. Lucy B down the pan.'

'Wishing you hadn't opened Pandora's box?' he asked.

'Good grief, no.' She looked down at him. 'You can't think that.'

'But you're not happy,' he said, leaving the question unanswered.

'How can I be? People are going to get hurt. Not Rupert. I don't care if he rots in jail,' she declared fervently and the last shreds of tension, doubt left him. She wasn't going to be seduced by the glamour, the millions. Her only thought was for the people who would be hurt when she brought the company down.

'Tell me about it,' he urged, dropping the folder and stretching out an arm, inviting her to lean back against his shoulder.

'It's always the innocents who pay,' she said, snuggling against him. 'I may have hated working there but hundreds of people—ordinary people—rely on the Henshawe Corporation to feed their families.'

'Right.'

'And it isn't just them. There are the shops. If they're not rebranded, they'll close. Hundreds of women will lose their jobs. I've met some of them and they're all so enthusiastic. So excited…'

She slipped down a little, getting more comfortable, her body heavier against him.

'Even the poor devils in the sweatshops will lose out,' he said, resting his chin on her head.

The scent of the soap she'd used was familiar, but on Lucy it was different, somehow.

'I know. But what choice do I have?' She fought a yawn. 'The man's a liar, a cheat and a crook.'

'List your options,' he suggested. 'One, you go to the police. Bring him and his company down.'

'It's too horrible to think about. Can I go to sleep now?' She closed her eyes.

'Okay. Two, you could sell him out to the tabloids, write a book, make a fortune.'

'Same result, except I get rich.'

'You could share the money amongst the people who lose their jobs.'

'Not rich enough to make a difference to them,' she said, her cheek pressed into his chest.

'No, not rich enough for that. There's option three, the one where you walk away and let him get on with it.'

'Nnngg.'

'No? How about threatening him with exposure? You could force him to clean up his act in return for playing out the role as written? Number four, sticking with the plan, but with you in the driving seat.'

'Wdntrstim,' she mumbled.

'No. Neither would I.' Then, 'What about me, Lucy? Could you trust me?'

No answer.

He didn't need one. She was curled up against him, defenceless as a baby. She'd seen through his guard, peered into his darkest places, knew him as few people did.

And he knew her, too. She lived who she was. Caring for others. even when her own world was crumbling around her.

He was, without question…involved.

And deeply happy to be so.

The engine had caught, the motor was running and the road ahead might have bumps in it but it was leading exactly where he wanted to be.

'Hey, into bed with you,' he said, tearing himself away. He didn't want to leave her, lose the soft warmth of her breast, her thighs curled against him. He wanted, for the first time in as long as he could remember, to lie beside a woman, sleep with her.

Just sleep.

Close his eyes and know she was there. Know she would be the first thing he saw when he woke. Know that he would be the first thing she saw when she opened her green-gold eyes and smile because that one thing made her happy.

But this wasn't about him. He pulled the cover from beneath her and she rolled into the warm space where he'd been lying, her face in the pillow.

'Big day tomorrow.'

'T'day…'

She was right. It was gone midnight. Or did she mean that it had been a big day today? Not just for her.

'Furs day rest life,' she mumbled.

He stood for a moment watching every scrap of tension leave her body as she melted into sleep almost before the jumble of words had left her mouth.

Today was the first day of the rest of her life. Or did she mean his?

He looked around at the room that, just hours before, had been sterile and empty. Clothes dropped where she'd left them. The bright red splash of her coat across the chair. A muddle. Untidy. Just like life.

There were no easy solutions, no perfect answers. You did what you had to do and got on with it. He'd been a successful architect, but he'd been raised to this. With no heart in it, he'd expanded the company out of all recognition. What could he do if he stopped looking back, regretting the life he'd lost and instead looked forward? Seized the day? Seized the life he'd been given?

Time to do a little homework. Arrange a meeting with the H&H trustees.

'Hey, sleepy-head.'

'Nnng…' She pushed her face deeper into the pillow. Today was not going to be fun and she was in no hurry for it to start.

There was a touch to her shoulder and, giving up, she opened her eyes, saw the tempting curl of steam rising from a bright red mug standing on the black marble, Nathaniel crouched down beside the bed.

'Nice mug,' she said.

'It matches your toenails.'

'So it does,' she said, rolling over onto her side. She was going to have to leave today and she didn't want to miss a minute of looking at Nathaniel. 'What time is it?'

'Nearly eight. I would have left you sleeping but I've got a meeting with the company trustees in a few minutes and I'm not sure how long it will take.'

'Shame,' she said. 'I was going to make you porridge for breakfast.'

'I'll cancel.' He made as if to move, but she caught his arm.

'No, you're all right. I've got until two thousand and fifty-one to convert you to oatmeal.'

'I warn you, it might take that long.'

For a moment neither of them spoke. She was thinking of forty years spent sharing breakfast with Nathaniel.

He was probably thinking *help!*

'Trustees?' she prompted.

'Hastings & Hart is controlled by a family trust. Much of the profit goes to charity.'

'That explains a lot.'

'Does it?'

It explained the sense of obligation. Why he couldn't walk away.

'I found the picture Pam took of you yesterday, by the way,' he said after a moment, 'and I've made an ID card for you, Louise Braithwaite.'

'Mmm... Yes. Sorry about that, but the name Lucy Bright was given to me by the nurses in the hospital, so that's made up, too.'

'I was going to talk to you about that. I did a little research on Henshawe last night and I saw the photographs. Are you sure that your mother is a fake?'

'It's in the file.'

'All it says is that it would make a great story if they found her.'

'And it did. Not a dry eye in the house.'

'Did you like her?' he asked. 'I mean, she did abandon you.'

'Fifteen years old with a boyfriend who'd done a runner at the word pregnancy. She could have done a lot worse, Nathaniel. I'm here. But not because of her. She's a fake. Another lie generated by Rupert's PR company.'

She threw the covers back, swung her legs out of the bed, but he didn't back off.

'Okay, I liked her. More than liked.' It wouldn't have hurt so much if she'd hated her on sight. Thought her the worst mother on earth and didn't give a damn. 'We fit.' Still he didn't move. 'I loved her, okay?'

'You look like her,' he said.

'They weren't going to pick someone who didn't, were they?'

'You've got the same hair.'

'The halo or the Harpo Marx? Hair can be fixed.'

'And eyes, Lucy. Look at her eyes. You can change their colour with contacts but not their shape. And, honestly, I know that His Frogginess is capable of it, but how could he get away with it? Truly. People know her. Her history. If she was a fake, her story was a lie, don't you think someone would have sold her out to the media?'

'Aren't you going to be late for your meeting?' she said.

'Just look, okay?' Then, letting it go, 'Your employee ID is in the kitchen with a swipe card to get you through the door between the store and the apartment. There's also a store account card in the same name so that you can get anything you need. And the keypad number for the door is two five one two.'

'Two five one two,' she repeated. 'Christmas Day? I think I can remember that.'

And she wiggled her toes at him, just to show him that she'd forgiven him for bringing up her mother.

Damn. She was doing it now.

Forgetting the quotes.

'The lawyer called first thing,' Nathaniel said. 'He's spoken to the police and also issued a short statement to the press to the effect that while you're sorting out your differences with Henshawe you're staying with a friend.'

She reached up, touched his cheek. 'A very good friend.' Then, 'Nice tie, by the way.'

He was dressed for work in a crisp white shirt and the uniform pinstripes, but the tie today was candy-red.

'I've decided that it's my favourite colour.'

'Good choice.' But, despite the tie, he looked tired and she said so. 'Did you get any sleep?'

'Not much,' he admitted. 'I had a lot of thinking to do.'

'Don't tell me—I've turned your life upside down. It's a bad habit I have.'

'No, Lucy. You've turned it the right way up. And the time wasn't wasted. I've come up with a fifth option.'

'What?' She was wide awake now.

'I'm going to be late for my meeting.' He leaned forward, kissed her cheek, headed for the door.

'Nathaniel!' She leapt out of bed and went after him. Then paused, suddenly shy. 'Your tie…' She reached up to straighten it, pat it into place, keeping her eyes on the knot, but he hooked his thumb under her chin, made her look at him.

'It'll be all right. I just need to straighten a few loose ends before I put it to you.' Then, apparently forgetting all about his meeting, he caught her close, kissed her, sweet and simple, before releasing her. 'Go back to bed, Lucy.'

'I will if you'll come too.'

'You make it hard for a man to leave.'

She grinned. 'I noticed.'

'You don't really have to be an elf, you know. You can stay here. Housekeeping will come in at about ten but, apart from that, no one will disturb you.'

Too late, she was already disturbed and the condition, she feared, was terminal.

'Frank is expecting me. I can't let him down.'

'Of course you can't. He'll feed you to a troll.' He kissed her again. 'I'll see you later.' And this time he did make it to the door, where he paused to look back at her. 'Don't do anything rash, will you?'

'The rashest thing I'm going to do this morning is put maple syrup on my porridge,' she promised.

Maybe.

Diary entry: *Woken by Nathaniel, all crisp and gorgeous and ready for a hard day making dreams come true in his palace of delights. Christmas shoppers. Children. And mine? And I'm not talking about Option Five. But I will have to decide what to do today.*

Nathaniel can't be right about my mother? Can he?

The meeting began just after eight.

Nathaniel began by offering his father, his uncles, what they wanted. A Hart fully committed to the company.

Only two men in the room did not leap to accept the gesture with gratitude, relief.

Christopher's father. And his own.

He wasn't surprised.

His uncle clung vainly to the hope that one day his own son would be able to resume his place.

His father had been hurt beyond measure that he hadn't wanted to follow in his footsteps and was sure there would be a proviso.

'What do you want in return, Nathaniel?' his father asked.

'Your agreement to a proposal.' He passed around a folder as he began to talk.

* * *

Lucy retrieved her costume from the upstairs bedroom. It seemed less daunting in the daylight, with clothes heaped untidily on the bed.

She left them where they were, but picked up the rose and took it downstairs, where she tossed it, bud vase and all, into the rubbish bin tucked beneath the sink.

Start the day with a positive action. And a proper breakfast.

She sat on a stool, spooning porridge sweetened with maple syrup into her mouth, sipping her orange juice. Flipping through her messages, reading tweets, messages on Facebook. Catching up.

There was nothing more from Rupert. Not a man to waste words on a lost cause.

There were a dozen or more from the woman who claimed to be her mother. She ignored them, instead flicking through the photographs stored on her camera. The informal snaps taken when she was off guard. Zoomed in on the eyes. Compared them.

Could Nathaniel be right?

She flicked back to her messages.

Do you want to send a message?

Did she? She thumbed in a text:

Tell me the truth. Who are you? Really?

Her thumb hovered over 'send'.

Two hours later, only Nat and his father were left in the room.

'You're in love with this girl?' His father had listened to his plan, added his opinion but, now they were alone, he'd gone right to the heart of the matter.

'I only met her yesterday.'

'You're in love with her?'

'It's a good plan.'

'Can I meet her?'

'Of course. She's down in the grotto, working as an elf.' He shrugged. 'It's a long story.'

'I've got all day.'

Lucy was sitting cross-legged on the floor, a semi-circle of children sitting around her, totally absorbed, as she sang them a song. They joined in the actions, roared with the lion, hooted with the owl, quacked with the duck.

Frank, watching with a smile stretching his face, turned as Nat joined him at the window. 'Will you just look at that?' he said.

He needed no encouragement. 'What's going on?'

'Santa's come down with the bug and I had to send him home. The replacement is suiting up, but there's a bit of a backlog. Lou sent some of the elves to organise coffee for the mothers and then rounded up the kids. I don't know where Pam found her but I'd like half a dozen more.'

'Sorry, Frank,' Nat said. 'She's a one-off and she's mine.' He turned to his father. 'And the answer to your question is yes.' Love at first sight was a concept he would have denied with his last breath. Until it happened. 'I know you'll think I'm a fool, that it's crazy, but I'm in love with her.'

'No. I don't think you're a fool. It happens like that sometimes. Magic happens. It was like that with your mother and me. Just one look was all it took.'

Just one look...

Yes.

'Any chance of you bringing her home for Christmas?'

Before Nat could answer, there was a movement from the inner sanctum and the children, almost reluctantly, began to trickle away.

'Can we borrow your office, Frank? We need to talk to her.'

'You're not going to take her away?'

'It's not up to me what she does; she's her own woman.'
A romantic maybe, but strong, too. A woman who knew
what she wanted, who never allowed anyone to control her,
use her.

'Damn women's lib,' Frank muttered, stomping off to
send her in.

'Nathaniel?' Lucy appeared in the doorway, hat slightly
askew, curls wild, tunic rucked up behind. She tugged on
it. 'Is anything wrong?'

'Nothing. My father wanted to meet you.'

'Oh.' She extended her hand. 'Hello, Mr Hart.'

'Hello, Lucy. I'm delighted to meet you. I'll leave
Nathaniel to explain the situation.' He put his hand on his
son's arm. 'Whatever you decide about the holiday. Your
decision.'

'The holiday?' she asked when the older Hart had
gone.

'We've been invited for Christmas.'

'We?'

'Us,' he said. 'It's okay. They ask me every year. They
don't expect me to go.'

'Oh.'

'You sound disappointed. Sorry, but there's no way
you're getting out of cooking Christmas dinner.'

'Shouldn't you check that I can cook before you commit
yourself?'

'I don't actually care,' he said. Then told her about
Option Five.

City Diary, London Evening Post
It was announced today that Hastings & Hart,
continuing their expansion under the steady hand
of Nathaniel Hart, have today acquired the Lucy

*B chain from the Henshawe Corporation, who are
withdrawing from the fashion business in order to
concentrate on their core business.*

*Lucy Bright, the face of Lucy B, will be taking
a more hands-on role in the business and is joining Hastings & Hart in January as a director of
the Lucy B division with responsibility for fair trade
development.*

*Rupert Henshawe is relinquishing the chair-
manship of the Henshawe Corporation with immediate effect. Shares in the company were down in
trading.*

*Slight wobble, tweeps, but the frog has been van-
quished and LucyB is back and on target. Thanks
for all the support.*
LucyB, Fri 3 Dec 10:14

Lucy flicked through her followers, picking out the ones
that were missing. Jenpb was gone. A couple of others.
But *WelshWitch* was cheering her on and, on an impulse,
she sent her a direct message. Something only she could
read.

WelshWitch Want to meet for lunch? DM me.
Fri 3 Dec 10:16

There was just one more thing to do. She scrolled
through the numbers in her phonebook and hit 'dial'.
'Lucy?'
'Mum…'
And then they were both crying.

* * *

Friday, 24th December
Appointments
09:30 Hair and stuff
11:00 Meeting with Marji from Celebrity
12:30 Lunch (with my mum!)
17:00 Reception for trustees in boardroom
20:00 Dinner in Garden Restaurant to celebrate
Hastings & Hart takeover of Lucy B launch

'Happy?' Nat said as they returned to the apartment after a Christmas Eve dinner for family and friends in the Garden Restaurant on the seventh floor—a celebration that her mother had been part of, too. Because, while Rupert Henshawe's ability to deceive had gone as far as pretending that he'd looked for her, she was the one who'd come forward when she'd read the story in the newspaper.

'Blissful,' she assured him. 'But what about you?' she asked, hooking her arm in his. 'Are you really prepared to let go of your career in architecture?'

'Says my biggest critic.'

'No. This building is amazing. The apartment is amazing. It just needs a little internal glow.'

He paused at the entrance, turned to her.

'You give it that, Lucy. It means light, doesn't it. Lucy?'

She nodded.

'Well, that's what you are. A light shining into all the dark places. You've lit up my life. Warmed my heart—'

'Nathaniel...'

'It's too soon to say this, you're going to think me a fool and, no, it's nothing to do with making you a director of Lucy B. You've earned that with your heart.'

'I'm terrified I'll get it wrong.'

'Terror is the default setting when you're at the top. But

you're not on your own.' He reached out to her hand. 'Never on your own.'

Her fingers wrapped around his and he felt the tension slide away as it always did when she was close. 'You are going to be wonderful. My father said so and he's no push-over for a pretty face.'

'I like your dad. And your mother. It was so kind of them to invite my mum for Christmas, too.'

'They knew that, wherever she was, you'd want to be, Lucy. That, wherever you were, I'd want to be, too.'

'I owe you a Christmas dinner,' she said, looking up. 'I guess that takes us to two thousand and fifty-two—'

'You think I'm letting you go that easily?' he growled. 'What I'm trying to say is that this is not a get-your-kit-off line. I love you. I loved you from the moment I first saw you.' With his other hand he reached out and touched her cheek, very gently, almost afraid that she would disappear under his touch. 'Just saying. You don't have to do a thing about it.'

'But, if I wanted to get my kit off, that would be all right?' she asked seriously. Looking up at him with those green-gold eyes, soft, filled with warmth, joy, happiness.

He swallowed. 'Your call.' Then, before she could move, 'But maybe you want to think about that. Give yourself some time.'

'And if I don't?'

'Then you can forget about flat-hunting. You won't be going anywhere.'

'If I stay here, I'll make changes,' she warned.

'You already have.' Pop music on the radio first thing in the morning. Pots of early jonquils brightening every surface. Laughter everywhere.

'Phooey. That's nothing. If I stay, I warn you, I'll want to paint the walls primrose-yellow.'

'I'll help you.'

'Hang pictures everywhere.'

'I've got a hammer.'

'Get a kitten.'

'Only one?' he asked.

'Well, they do get lonely without their brothers and sisters,' she said, a glint of mischief in her eyes. 'Two would be better.'

'Bring the whole damn litter.'

Her smile deepened momentarily and then, suddenly, she was serious. 'There's one more thing.'

'You want your mother to live with us?'

'You'd do that for me?' she asked. Then, shaking her head, she let him off the hook. 'It's not that. I want you to build the house in Cornwall.'

'For you—'

'No, Nathaniel; not for me. For you.' And, as if she knew that was the most difficult thing she'd asked, she lifted herself onto her toes and, coiling her arms around his neck, she kissed him. Giving him her courage, her strength, all her love.

There was no need. She'd been giving him that since the day she'd stumbled in front of him on the stairs. In that moment the fairy tale had changed from Cinderella to something entirely new. She'd brought the sleeping Beast back to life with a kiss, made him whole again. But he had one condition of his own.

'It's a house for a family, Lucy. I'll build it if you'll help me fill it.'

'Fill it?'

'With kittens, puppies, your mother. Our children.' There was a still moment when the world seemed to hold its breath. 'I love you, Lucy Bright. Will you marry me?'

'I...'

'It's a big decision. You'll need time to think about it.'

'Yes…' For a moment the world seemed to hang on its axis. Then she said, 'I've thought about it.' And, reaching for the single button holding together the green-gold silk Lucy B jacket that she was wearing, 'How soon can you get that door open?'

Lucy hadn't got it free when he pushed the door open, but this time he was the one who came to a shocked halt.

'A little extra glow,' she said as he took in the eight-foot Christmas tree laden with toys and candy canes and painted glass balls. A replica of the one in the grotto. Or had she just had it shifted? Frank would do anything for her.

There were swathes of greenery, a forest of plants sparkling with tiny white lights. Thick red pillar candles.

'I used my Louise Braithwaite store card,' she said. 'This is your Christmas gift from the elf.'

Then she let her jacket slip to the floor, raised her arms.

'But this one is from me. With all my heart, Nathaniel. All my love. All you have to do is unwrap it and enjoy.'

Lucy gazed at the familiar view. The rugged landscape, the deep blue of the distant sea. Familiar but different. And she smiled.

These days, when they bumped down the track in the big black Range Rover, the rocky ledge was topped by a long, low house that appeared to grow out of it. That over the years had become so much part of the landscape that it deceived the eye. The glass wall facing the sea a perfect reflection of the land. The rock and stone indivisible. One. Like the two of them.

Nathaniel turned to the rear. 'Out you get, boys. Let's get the car unloaded.' Then, as their two sturdy lads scrambled out, whooping to be free, eager to get at the sand, the sea, he reached across, laid his hand across her expanding waist, his eyes more silver than grey. 'Okay?'

'Absolutely. Our little girl and I will sit here and enjoy the view while you unload.'

'You're facing the house,' he pointed out.

'I know. It's my favourite view in all the world.' The house that he had designed for himself, built for her. More beloved than any palace. Just as he was so much more than any Prince Charming. Her rock. Her partner. Her beloved husband. The father of her children. A man at peace with life, with himself.

'Can we pitch the tent, Daddy?'

'I want to build a den.'

'What do you want, Lucy B?' Nathaniel asked, taking her hand, lifting it to his lips.

'I've got everything I ever wanted,' she said. 'How about you?'

'I have you, Lucy. Everything else follows from that,' he said, leaning across to kiss her.

HER HOLIDAY
PRINCE CHARMING

CHRISTINE FLYNN

*For the lovely ladies who have made the "Hunt"
happen, and everyone who believes in the
fairytale.*

Christine Flynn admits to being interested in
just about everything, which is why she considers
herself fortunate to have turned her interest in
writing into a career. She feels that a writer gets
to explore it all and, to her, exploring relationships –
especially the intense, bittersweet or even light-
hearted relationships between men and women –
is fascinating.

Prologue

"What's on your Christmas list this year? No matter how big or how small, you're sure to find what you're looking for at Seattle's one-stop answer to all your holiday—"

With a quick flick of the dial, Rory silenced the cheerful voice suddenly booming from her car radio. In an attempt to drown out her worries while she waited to pick up her son from kindergarten, she'd turned the music to a decibel she'd never have considered had her five-year-old been in the vehicle.

The ad had just brought to mind the one thing she'd been desperately trying *not* to think about.

She'd hoped to make the holiday special for her little boy this year. Not just special, but after last year's unquestionably awful Christmas, something wonderful. Magical.

As of three days ago, however, she was no longer sure how she would keep a roof over their heads, much less put a tree under it. Due to downsizing, her telecommuting services as a legal transcriptionist for Hayes, Bleaker & Stein were no longer required. She'd needed that job to pay for little things like food and gas and to qualify for a mortgage.

Without a job, she had no hope of buying the little Cape Cod she'd thought so perfect for her and little Tyler. She had no hope of buying or renting any house at all. Since the sale of the beautiful home she'd shared with her husband closed next week, that left her four days to find an apartment and a job that would help her pay for it.

A quick tap ticked on her driver's side window.

Through the foggy glass, a striking blonde wearing studious-looking horn-rimmed glasses and winter-white fur smiled at her. The woman didn't look at all familiar to Rory. Thinking she must be the mom of an older student, since she knew all the moms in the kindergarten class, she lowered her window and smiled back.

Chill air rushed into the car as the woman bent at the waist to make eye contact. "You're Aurora Jo Linfield?"

Rory hesitated. The only time she ever used her full name was on legal documents. And she rarely used Aurora at all. "I am."

"I'm Felicity Granger." Hiking her designer bag higher on her shoulder, she stuck her hand through the open window. The cold mist glittered around her, clung, jewel-like, to her pale, upswept hair. "But please, call me Phil. I'm an associate of Cornelia Hunt. You've heard of Cornelia, haven't you?"

Rory shook the woman's hand, watched her retract it. "I've heard of her," she admitted, wondering what this woman—or the other—could possibly want with her. Nearly everyone in Seattle had heard of Mrs. Hunt, the former Cornelia Fairchild. She'd been the childhood sweetheart of computer genius Harry Hunt, the billionaire founder of software giant HuntCom. Rory recalled hearing of their marriage last summer, even though she'd been struggling within her fractured little world at the time. Media interest in their six-decade relationship had been huge.

"May I help you with something?"

"Oh, I'm here to help you," the woman insisted. "Mr. Hunt heard of your situation—"

Harry Hunt had heard of her? "My situation?"

"About your job loss. And how that affects your ability to purchase another home."

"How does he know that?"

"Through your real estate agent. Mr. Hunt knows the owner of the agency she works for," she explained. "Harry bought a building through him last month for his wife so she'd have a headquarters for her new venture. When he learned why you couldn't move forward with the purchase of the house you'd found, he remembered Mrs. Hunt's project and thought you'd be a perfect referral. So we checked you out." Her smile brightened. "And you are.

"Anyway," she continued, anxious to get to her point. "Cornelia knows of a property for sale that you might want to purchase. She's aware of your current unemployment," she hurried to assure her, "but she said you're not to worry about that little detail right now. Just look at the place. If you're interested, suitable arrangements can be made for you and for the seller.

"It's not exactly what you told your agent you want," she cautioned, reaching into a pocket of her coat. "But it could be perfect for you and your little boy. You really do need to keep an open mind when you see it, though," she warned. "Don't judge it as is. Look for the possibilities.

"You'll be met at the address on the back." She held out a white, pearlescent business card. "The owner's representative will be there at ten tomorrow morning. A man by the name of Erik Sullivan. He's quite knowledgeable about the property, so feel free to ask him anything that will help you decide whether you want the place or not. You should keep an open mind about him, too.

"I have to run now. Double-parked," she said, explaining her rush but not the warning. "If you like what you see, I'll see you tomorrow afternoon."

Rory took the pretty little card. Neatly hand-printed on the back was an address outside Port Orchard, a short ferry ride across the sound from Seattle.

With questions piling up like leaves in the fall, she glanced back up.

The woman was gone.

Seeing no sign of her in the Pacific Northwest mist that was closer to fog than rain, she looked back to the shimmery little card.

The past fourteen months had left her without faith in much of anything anymore. The sudden, devastating loss of her husband to an uninsured drunk driver who'd run a red light. The whispered and crushing comments about their marriage that she'd overheard at his funeral. The exodus from her life of people she'd once thought of as family and friends. Each event had been shattering in its own right. Together, they'd made her afraid to trust much of anything. Or anyone.

And that had been before she'd lost the job Harvey Bleaker had said was hers for as long as she needed it.

The lovely woman with the bookish glasses had appeared out of nowhere. As if by magic, she'd disappeared into the mist the same way, like some sort of a fairy godmother dressed in faux fur and carrying Coach.

Dead certain her sleepless nights had just caught up with her, Rory dropped the card into the open compartment on the console. Whatever had just happened had to be either too good to be true or came with a spiderweb of strings attached to it.

Probably, undoubtedly, both.

Still, she, Tyler and the for-rent section of the newspaper were going apartment hunting in the morning. Having just picked up a check for the small down payment she'd put on the house she hadn't been able to buy, less fees, she had enough for three or four months' rent and expenses. In the meantime, feeling a desperate need for either magic or a miracle, she figured she had nothing to lose by checking out the address on that card.

She just hoped that this Erik Sullivan would be as accepting of her circumstances as Mrs. Cornelia Hunt seemed to be.

Chapter One

"Are we lost, Mom?"

"No, honey. We're not lost." Parked on the dirt shoulder of a narrow rural road, Rory frowned at the building a few dozen yards away. "I'm just not sure this is the right address."

"If we can't find it, can we go to the Christmas place?"

"We'll see, sweetie. We're looking for a new place to live right now."

"I don't want a new one."

"I know you don't," she murmured. Freckles dotted Tyler's nose. His sandy hair, neatly combed when they'd left the house, fell over his forehead, victim of the breeze that had blown in when she'd lowered his window to get a better look at the address on the roadside mailbox.

Nudging wisps back from his forehead, she smiled. "But we need one. And I need you to help me pick it out. It's our adventure, remember?"

"Then can we go to the Christmas place?"

They had seen a banner for a holiday festival in nearby Port Orchard when they'd driven off the ferry. Tyler had been asking about it ever since.

Everything she'd read last night on the internet made the area around the shoreline community a few miles around the bend sound nearly idyllic. The part of her that didn't want to get her hopes up knew that could simply have been good marketing by its chamber of commerce. The part that desperately needed this not to be a wild-goose chase focused on getting them moving.

"Not today, I'm afraid." She hated to say no, but housing had to be their first priority. "We don't have time."

It was nine fifty-five. They were to meet the seller's representative at ten o'clock.

Reminding Tyler of that, and agreeing that, yes, they were still "exploring," she pulled his hood over his head and glanced to the structure surrounded by a few winter-bare trees, dead grass and a wet patch of gravel that, apparently, served as a parking lot.

The address on the mailbox matched the one on the card. The structure, however, bore no resemblance at all to a residence. The two-story flat-roofed rectangle of a building faced a partial view of a little marina two city blocks away and backed up to a forest of pines.

A long, narrow sign above the porch read Harbor Market & Sporting Goods. Signs by the screened door read Fresh Espresso and Worms and Closed Until Spring.

Mailboxes farther up the road indicated homes tucked back in the trees. The only vehicle to be seen, however, was hers. With no sign of life in either direction, she was about to pull out her cell phone to check the address with Phil Granger when she remembered what the woman had said.

She'd warned her to keep an open mind when she saw the place. To look for possibilities.

The potential goose chase was also, apparently, a scavenger hunt.

A narrow driveway curved around the back of the building and disappeared down a slight hill. Thinking there might be a house or cottage beyond the gate blocking it, she grabbed the shoulder bag that held everything from animal crackers to a Zen meditation manual and gamely told her little boy they were going to look around while they waited for the person they were to meet to show up.

The damp breeze whipped around them, scattering leaves in their path as they left the car. With a glance toward the threatening sky, she was about to reconsider her plan when the relative quiet gave way to a squeak and the hard slam of a door.

Tyler froze.

Across twenty feet of gravel, she watched six feet two inches of broad-shouldered, purely rugged masculinity in a fisherman's sweater and worn jeans cross the store's porch and jog down its three steps.

"Sorry about that." His apology came quickly, his voice as deep as the undercurrents in the distant water. "I didn't mean to startle you. I keep forgetting to fix the spring."

The breeze blew a little harder, rearranging the otherwise neat cut of his slightly overlong dark hair. He didn't seem to notice the wind. Or the cold bite that came with it. All lean, athletic muscle, he strode toward them, his glance shifting between her and the child who'd smashed himself against her leg.

That glance turned questioning as he stopped six feet from where she'd rooted herself in the driveway.

"Are you Mrs. Linfield?"

Surprise colored the deep tones of his voice. Or maybe what she heard was disbelief. His pewter-gray eyes ran from the wedge of auburn hair skimming her shoulders, over the camel peacoat covering her black turtleneck and jeans and up from the toes of her low-heeled boots. His perusal was quick, little more than an impassive flick of his glance. Yet she had the unnerving feeling he'd imagined her every curve in the brief moments before she realized he was waiting for her to speak.

"I didn't think anyone was here." The admission came in a rush. "I didn't see a car, so we were just going to look around—"

"I flew over. Floatplane," he explained, hitching his head in the direction of the water. "It's down at the marina.

"I'm Erik Sullivan." Stepping closer, he extended his hand. His rugged features held strength, a hint of fearlessness. Or maybe it was boldness. Despite its lingering shadow, the square line of his jaw appeared recently shaved. He looked hard and handsome and when he smiled, faint though the expression was, he radiated a positively lethal combination of quiet command and casual ease. "I'm handling the sale of this property for my grandparents."

"You're a Realtor?"

"Actually, I build boats. I'm just taking care of this for them."

Her hand had disappeared in his.

She could feel calluses at the base of his fingers. He worked with his hands. Built boats with them, he'd said. What kind, she had no idea. The white-gold Rolex on his thick wrist seemed to indicate he was successful at it, though. The words *capable* and *accomplished* quickly flashed in her mind, only to succumb to less definable impressions as she became aware of the heat of his palm, the strength in his grip and the deliberate way he held that strength in check.

What she felt mostly, though, was a wholly unexpected sense of connection when her eyes met his.

Everything inside her seemed to go still.

She'd experienced that sensation only once before; the

first time Curt had taken her hand. It had been a fleeting thing, little more than an odd combination of awareness and ease that had come out of nowhere, but it had dictated the direction of her life from that moment on.

As if she'd just touched lightning, she jerked back, curling her fingers into her palm, and took a step away. The void left in her heart by the loss of her husband already felt huge. It seemed to widen further as she instinctively rejected the thought of any sort of connection to this man, imagined or otherwise. Because of what she'd learned since Curt's death, it was entirely possible that what she'd thought she'd had with her husband—the closeness, the love, the very rightness of the life they'd shared—hadn't existed at all.

Having struggled with that awful possibility for over a year, she wasn't about to trust what she'd felt now.

Conscious of the quick pinch of Erik's brow, totally embarrassed by her abrupt reaction, she rested her hand on her son's shoulder. Just as she would have introduced her little guy, the big man gave the child a cautious smile and motioned her toward the building.

"The main entrance to the living quarters is around back, but we can go through the market. Come on and I'll show you around."

Whatever he thought of her reaction to him, he seemed gentleman enough to ignore it.

She chose to ignore it, too.

Living quarters, he'd said?

"There isn't a separate house here?" she asked, urging Tyler forward as the sky started to leak.

"There's plenty of room to build if that's what a buyer wants to do. The parcel is a little over three acres. Living on premises has certain advantages, though." He checked the length of his strides, allowing them to keep up. "Shortens the commute."

If she smiled at that, Erik couldn't tell, not with the fall of cinnamon hair hiding her profile as she ushered the boy ahead of her.

Mrs. Rory Linfield wasn't at all what he had expected. But then, the new owner of the building next door to Merrick & Sullivan Yachting hadn't given him much to go on. He wasn't sure what the elegant and refined wife of Harry Hunt was doing with the building Harry had apparently given her as a wedding gift—other than providing Erik and his business partner an interesting diversion with her total renovation of its interior. It had been his offhand comment to Cornelia, though, about a place he'd be glad to sell if Harry was still into buying random pieces of property, that had led him to describe the property his grandparents had vacated nearly a year ago.

The conversation had prompted a call from Cornelia yesterday. That was when she'd told him she knew of a widow in immediate need of a home and a means to produce an income.

When she'd said *widow,* he'd immediately pictured someone far more mature. More his parents' age. Fifty-something. Sixty, maybe. With graying hair. Or at least a few wrinkles. The decidedly polished, manicured and attractive auburn-haired woman skeptically eyeing the sign for Fresh Espresso and Worms as she crossed the wood-planked porch didn't look at all like his idea of a widow, though. She looked more like pure temptation. Temptation with pale skin that fairly begged to be touched, a beautiful mouth glossed with something sheer pink and shiny, and who was easily a decade younger than his own thirty-nine years.

He hadn't expected the cute little kid at all.

He opened the door, held it for them to pass, caught her soft, unexpectedly provocative scent. Following them inside, he had to admit that, mostly, he hadn't anticipated the sucker punch to his gut when he'd looked from her very kissable mouth to the feminine caution in her big brown eyes. Or the quick caution he'd felt himself when she'd pulled back and her guarded smile had slipped into place.

What he'd seen in those dark and lovely depths had hinted heavily of response, confusion and denial.

A different sort of confusion clouded her expression now.

He'd turned on the store's fluorescent overheads when he'd first arrived. In those bright industrial lights, he watched her look from the rows of bare, utilitarian grocery shelving to the empty dairy case near the checkout counter and fix her focus on a kayak suspended from the ceiling above a wall of flotation devices. Sporting goods still filled the back shelves. After the original offer to buy the place fully stocked had fallen through, he'd donated the grocery items to a local food bank. That had been months ago.

The little boy tugged her hand. "Why is the boat up there, Mom?"

"For display. I think," she replied quietly, like someone talking in a museum.

"How come?"

"So people will notice it." She pointed to a horizontal rack on the back wall that held three more. Oars and water skis stood in rows on either side. "It's easier to see than those back there."

With his neck craned back, his little brow pinched.

"Are we gonna live in a store?"

"No, sweetie. We're just…" From the uncertainty in her expression, it seemed she wasn't sure what they were doing at the moment. "Looking," she concluded.

Her glance swung up. "You said this belongs to your grandparents?"

"They retired to San Diego," he told her, wondering what her little boy was doing now as the child practically bent himself in half looking under a display case. There were no small children in his family. The yachting circles he worked and played in were strictly adult. Any exposure he had to little kids came with whatever family thing his business partner could talk him into attending with him. Since he managed to limit that to once every couple of years, he rarely gave kids any thought. Not anymore.

"They'd had this business for over fifty years," he explained, his attention already back on why the property was for sale. "It was time they retired."

The delicate arches of her eyebrows disappeared beneath her shiny bangs. "Fifty years?"

"Fifty-three, actually. They'd still be running the place if Gramps hadn't hurt his back changing one of the light fixtures." Erik had told him he'd change the tube himself. Just as he'd helped with other repairs they'd needed over the years. But the Irish in John Sullivan tended to make him a tad impatient at times. "He can be a little stubborn."

"Did he fall?"

"He just twisted wrong," he told her, conscious of the quick concern in her eyes, "but it took a couple of months for him to be able to lift anything. Grandma picked up as much slack as she could, but those two months made them decide it was time to tackle the other half of their bucket list while they could both still get around."

Her uncertainty about her surroundings had yet to ease. Despite her faint smile, that hesitation marked her every step as she moved farther in, checking out the plank-board floor, the single checkout counter, the old, yellowing acoustic tiles on the ceiling. Watching her, he couldn't help but wonder how she would do on a ladder, changing four-foot-long fluorescent tubes in a fixture fourteen feet off the floor. Or how she'd wrestle the heavy wood ladder up from the basement in the first place.

Since Cornelia had specifically asked if the business was one a woman could handle on her own, he'd also thought his prospective buyer would be a little sturdier.

Rather than indulge the temptation to reassess what he could of her frame, hidden as it was by her coat, anyway, he focused on just selling the place.

"The original building was single story," he told her, since the structure itself appeared to have her attention. "When they decided to add sporting goods, they incorporated the living area into the store, built on in back and added the upstairs.

"The business is seasonal," he continued when no questions were forthcoming. "Since summer and fall recreation provided most of their profit, they always opened in April and closed the first of October. That gave them the winter for vacations and time to work on their projects."

It was a good, solid business. One that had allowed his grandparents to support their family—his dad, his aunts. He told her that, too, because he figured that would be important to a woman who apparently needed to support a child on her own. What he didn't mention was that after the first sale fell through, the only other offers made had been too ridiculously low for his grandparents to even consider.

Because there were no other reasonable offers in sight, he wasn't about to let them pass up Cornelia's offer to buy it—if this particular woman was interested in owning it. He hadn't even balked at the terms of the sale that required his agreement to help get the business back up and running.

Selling the place would rid him of the obligation to keep it up. Even more important than ending the time drain of weekly trips from Seattle to make sure nothing was leaking, broken or keeping the place from showing well was that his grandparents had been the last of his relatives in this part of the sound. Once the place was sold, he had no reason to ever come back.

Considering all the plans he'd once had for his own life there, nearly all of which had failed rather spectacularly, that suited him just fine.

His potential project had yet to ask a single question. He, however, had a few of his own.

"Have you owned a business before?"

He thought the query perfectly reasonable.

She simply seemed to find it odd.

"Never," she replied, sounding as if she'd never considered running one, either. Still holding her little boy's hand, she set her sights on the open door behind the L-shaped checkout counter. "Is that the way to the living area?"

He told her it was, that it led into a foyer.

Wanting a whole lot more information than she'd just given, he followed her with the child looking back at him over the shoulder of his puffy blue jacket.

The instant he met the child's hazel eyes, the boy ducked his head and turned away.

With a mental shrug, Erik focused on the mom. She looked very much like the spa-and-Pilates type married to some of his high-end clients. Yet the car she drove was a total contrast—economical, practical. "Are you into outdoor sports?"

"We have bicycles," came her distracted reply.

"Mountain or street?"

"Street."

"For racing or touring?"

"Just for regular riding."

"Do you know anything about mountain bikes?"

"Is there a difference?"

That she'd had to ask had him moving on. "What about hiking or camping?"

"Not so much."

"Water sports? Do you windsurf, paddleboard, water ski?"

"Not really."

He took that as a no. "Do you know anything about sporting goods?"

Clearly on a mission of her own, she answered his last query with a puzzled glance and moved past the stairs, one set leading up, the other down, and into a spacious living room.

The empty downstairs space was interrupted only by the kitchen's long island near one end and anchored by a ceiling-high stone fireplace at the other. The bare walls all bore a pristine coat of latte-colored paint.

It was toward the kitchen that she motioned. "Mind if I look back there?"

Not at all pleased with her responses, he told her he didn't and watched her head for the glass-faced cupboards.

Her sandy-haired son darted straight to one of the large picture windows lining the opposite wall.

"Have you ever worked retail?" he asked her.

"Never," she replied once more.

"Wow, Mom. Look! It has a park!"

Rory's glance cut to where her little boy pressed his nose to the wide window near the fireplace. A large meadow stretched to a forest of pines. Between the dawning potential in the place and the feel of the tall, decidedly distracting male frowning at her back, she hadn't noticed the expansive and beautiful view until just then.

What she noticed now was her son's grin.

That guileless smile added another plus to her escalating but decidedly cautious interest in what surrounded her. "It sure does, sweetie. But stay with me. Okay?"

Yanking his unzipped jacket back over the shoulder of his Spider-Man sweatshirt, he hurried to her, his little voice dropping as he glanced to the man who remained on the other side of the white oak island.

"Does he live here?" he asked, pointing behind him.

She curled her hand over his fingers. "It's not polite to point," she murmured. "And no. He lives somewhere else."

"Where?"

"I don't know, honey."

"But it's a long way, huh?"

"Why do you say that?"

"'Cause he said he came in a plane. It floated here."

From the corner of her eye, she noticed the big man's brow lower in confusion.

"He came by *floatplane*," she clarified, easing confusion for them both. "It's a plane that can land on water. It flies just like any other."

"Oh." Tyler screwed up his nose, little wheels spinning. "Why didn't he make him a boat?"

He remembered what Erik had said he did for a living.

There wasn't much Tyler heard that he ever forgot. She'd come to regard the ability, however, as a double-edged sword. While her bright little boy absorbed information like an industrial-strength sponge, there were things she knew he'd overheard that she truly hoped he'd forgotten by now. Things certain relatives had said that had confused him at the time, hurt him and made her even more fiercely protective of him than she'd been even before he'd lost his dad.

Since no response came from the other side of the island, she told Tyler it was possible that Mr. Sullivan did have a boat, but that it was really none of their business. Right now, they needed to look at the rest of the house.

There were certain advantages to a five-year-old's short attention span. Already thrilled by the "park," Tyler promptly forgot his interest in the boat their guide did or did not have and, like her, poked his head into the pantry, the mudroom and downstairs closets.

There was no denying his attraction to the cubbyhole he found in one of the upstairs bedrooms. Her own interest, however, she held in check. A person couldn't be disappointed if she didn't get her expectations up to begin with.

The property was nothing she would have considered even a week ago. It had none of the little neighborhood atmosphere she'd looked for. None of the coziness she'd craved for herself and her son. It felt too remote. Too foreign. Too...unexpected.

Her option was an unknown apartment in an as yet undetermined area near a job she still had to find.

Her hopes rose anyway, her mind racing as Erik led her back down from the three bedrooms and two baths that would be more than adequate for her and her son.

Phil had said to keep an open mind about this place.

Despite its drawbacks, it was, indeed, full of possibilities. But it wasn't just Tyler's surprisingly positive reactions or the idyllic views from some of the windows that tempered her misgivings. What Phil hadn't mentioned was that this wouldn't just be a place to live. It would be her source of income.

She could have her own business. Be her own boss. That meant the means to support her son would be dependent on her, not on someone else with obligations or agendas of their own. It would be up to her if she succeeded or failed. And while the thought brought as much anxiety as anticipation, mostly it brought a surprising hint of reprieve.

She could start over here. She could finally, truly move on.

By the time they'd worked their way back downstairs, Tyler knew which room he wanted to be his. He wasn't quite so sure what to make of their tour guide, though. Every time he'd looked over his shoulder to see if Erik was still with them, he'd moved closer to her or tightened his grip on her hand.

Considering the man's easy self-assurance, it struck her as odd that he appeared equally undecided about Tyler. Because he'd yet to say a word to her son, she wasn't sure if he simply didn't know how to relate to small children or if he was one of those people, like her father-in-law, who felt a child was to be seen and not heard and otherwise ignored until they became of an age to engage in meaningful conversation.

Maternal instincts on alert, the moment they reached the foyer, she asked Tyler to see if he could spot deer in the woods from the living room window. He was barely out of earshot when she felt Erik Sullivan's disconcerting presence beside her.

"Your son seems to like the place," he pointed out, joining her by the mahogany newel post. "What about you? You haven't said much."

Erik would admit to not being particularly adept at deciphering women, even when they did speak. *No* often meant *yes. Don't* often mean *go ahead. Nothing* always meant *something,* though finding out what that something was could be akin to pulling an anchor out of dried cement. But this woman hadn't given him so much as a hint about any conclusion she might have drawn.

"Do you have any questions?" he prompted.

"When did you say the store usually opened for business?"

"April. The first or second week."

She lifted her chin, her thoughts apparently coming in no particular order.

"Phil Granger said you know I can't qualify for a mortgage just now."

"We're aware of that," he assured her.

"Were your grandparents planning to carry the mortgage themselves?"

"A second party will carry it. So," he prodded, "you're interested, then?"

She wanted to smile. He could see the expression trying to light the flecks of bronze in her deep brown eyes. She just wouldn't let it surface.

"That depends on what they want for it. And the terms. How much are they asking?"

He should have been relieved by her interest. Would have been had she been even remotely qualified to take on the store.

"That's…negotiable."

"But they must have a price in mind."

"Do you have *any* business experience?"

It was as clear to Rory as the doubt carved in his handsome face that he had serious concerns about her ability to make a go of the store his grandparents were selling. Unflattering as his obvious skepticism was, she couldn't fault him for it. They had run the business for decades. They'd probably poured their hearts and souls into the place that had defined them for years. This man hadn't had to tell her for her to know how much the store and their home had meant to them. The shelving in the spare room upstairs—his grandma's sewing room, he'd said—had been built by his dad. The beautiful, lacquered banister beside them had been lathed by his grandfather.

He'd casually mentioned those things in passing. With his big hand splayed over the grapefruit-size mahogany ball atop the newel post, his thumb absently rubbing its shiny finish, she realized this place mattered to him, too.

Her only concern now was that he trust her with it.

She took a step closer, lowering her voice so Tyler couldn't overhear.

"It's not that I've never had a job," she informed him

quietly. "I was a file clerk while I worked on an associate's degree. After that, I spent four years as a legal secretary before Tyler came along. I went back to work transcribing documents at another law firm ten months ago. I'd still be doing that if they hadn't let me go because the firm merged and they cut my job."

Skipping over the five-year gap in her résumé, she aimed for the heart of his concern. "I've just never owned a business. Or sold anything other than whatever the PTA was selling to raise money for school projects.

"I'll admit that when I got here," she hurried on, hoping he'd overlook that last part, "the last thing I expected was a store. But you said it's a good, solid business. If your grandparents didn't usually open it until April, that would give me four months to figure out what needs to be done and how to do it." All she had to do was get past the daunting little fact that she had no idea where to start.

"Look," she murmured, too tired after too many sleepless nights to care how much of herself she exposed. "I'll admit I don't know a…a…"

"A bivy sack from a bobber?" he suggested.

"Exactly. And until now," she said, muscling on, "I'd honestly never thought about owning anything like this. The only sports I know anything about are tennis and golf." And that was only because her husband had wanted her to fit in at the club. She was so not the rugged, outdoors type. "But I'll do whatever I have to do to provide for my son.

"This could be a good place to raise him. He could help me in the store. I think he'd love that. He'd even have his own park," she pointed out, thinking of how badly she wanted them gone from the exclusive community that had come to feel like a prison. She'd hoped for a normal neighborhood, but breathing room would be a good thing, too.

"I'll never be able to replace the security he had before his dad died, but it's up to me to give him as much stability as I can." Her voice fell with her final admission. "I think I can do that here."

Her last words were as soft as the utter conviction in her eyes. Erik saw a plea there, too. Quiet. A little raw. And a lot uncomfortable for him to witness in the moments before he glanced to where her son seemed to be counting something at the window.

He'd been about that age—five or so, if he had to guess—when his grandfather had put him to work stacking canned goods on shelves. After that, he'd practically begged to come over so he could help.

He'd once thought this would be a good place to raise a child, too.

"There's one other thing," she admitted, her voice still quiet. "Tyler has never lived anywhere other than in the house we're leaving. We have to be out in three days. Until the job thing happened, I'd thought we'd be settled in our new house well before Christmas. He didn't have a very good one last year and it would be really nice to find a place that I don't have to move him from again." Practicality, or maybe it was weariness, kept her tone utterly matter-of-fact. "So how much is it?" she asked. "And how do I make this happen?"

He didn't know which struck him more just then: her absolute determination to do whatever she had to do to care for her child or the naked vulnerability lurking in the depths of her eyes.

As if she knew what he saw, her glance hit the floor.

Her determination to hide that vulnerability pulled at something unfamiliar deep in his chest, even as he steeled himself against it.

He hadn't been told how she'd been widowed. Or how long she and her child had been on their own. He had no idea if her marriage had been as good as his parents', as much a failure as his own had been or some form of tolerable in-between. He knew only from what she'd said about her child's loss that it was entirely possible she still grieved the man she'd lost, too.

He wasn't a particularly sensitive or sympathetic man. Or so he'd been informed by his ex-wife and certain of the arm candy who trolled the circles he moved in. But he wasn't at all comfortable being privy to something so personal. It disturbed him even more to find himself wondering what it would be like to mean that much to a woman.

Equally unsettling was the fact that an hour ago, she hadn't even known the store existed. "I can't give you the terms."

She hadn't a clue what she was getting into.

He knew for a fact that he was no longer comfortable with what he'd agreed to do himself.

"My agreement with Cornelia…Mrs. Hunt," he corrected, "is that she or her assistant will discuss those details with you."

Reaching into the back pocket of his jeans, he extracted one of the same pearlescent cards Phil had given her yesterday. "Did you take the ferry or do the loop through Tacoma?"

"Ferry."

"Which one?"

"Southworth. It lands at Fauntleroy."

By land or water, either way it would take her a while to get back to Seattle.

"Then I'll give you directions to their office from the dock. I have another meeting in Seattle at noon." Card in hand, he pulled his cell phone from another pocket and keyed in a number.

With the instrument to his ear, he turned away, started to pace.

Rory glanced at her watch. It was already after eleven o'clock.

She was about to mention that when she remembered his mode of transport was infinitely faster than hers. He was already into his conversation with Phil, anyway. She couldn't hear what he said, though. She knew only that he looked oddly resigned when he turned a minute later to inform her that Phil wanted to talk to her.

By the time the woman who had appeared out of nowhere yesterday told her everything was ready to proceed with the sale and confirmed their meeting that afternoon, Rory couldn't shake the feeling that nothing could possibly be as simple as Phil had made it sound—and that Erik Sullivan had more of a role in the sale than anyone was letting on.

Chapter Two

The directions Rory had been given led her to the Ballard neighborhood in northwestern Seattle and a weathered, two-story redbrick building much like the others along an old business section of the waterfront. What distinguished the structure was the trail of plaster dust and debris leading from the open front door to the Wolf Construction Dumpster at the curb.

Inside, sheets of milky construction plastic masked two stories of interior scaffolding and what appeared to be something grand under construction. The filmy barriers did little to deaden the occasional clatter and boom of interior demolition. The noise was muffled considerably, however, behind the closed door of the only completed space—an unexpectedly feminine and elegant ground floor corner conference room in shades of ivory and pale taupe with a view of a marina, Shilsole Bay and snow-capped Hurricane Ridge beyond.

The long banks of ivory-draped windows caught Tyler's

attention the moment they'd walked in. Rory had thought the boats in the inlet had drawn him. Until she noticed Erik.

A walkway ran behind the buildings. She could see him outside, pacing past the rows of windows, bare-masted sailboats bobbing in the background. Apparently oblivious to the chill, he had one hand in a front pocket of his jeans, his head down against the breeze as he talked on his cell phone.

He did not look happy.

Logic told her he could be talking about anything. But the unease joining her curiosity and uncertainty over this meeting made her fairly certain his scowl had something to do with her.

"We're so glad you liked the place," said Phil, leading her across the floor, the click of her heels on polished oak suddenly hushed by the pale blue Aubusson rug. "With everything so unsettled for you, we didn't know if you'd see the advantages of taking on a business right now. Especially one that you might not ordinarily have considered."

Wearing a cream blouse and slacks slung with a thin gold belt, the woman Rory met yesterday took her and Tyler's coats and motioned to one of the Queen Anne chairs at the circular conference table. The light from the ornate crystal chandelier above it made the mahogany surface gleam like glass. "Cornelia did feel you'd consider it, though," she added, "given your circumstances."

"Which are very close to what mine were at one time," came a voice from a small alcove.

A statuesque, elegantly mature lady in pale lavender cashmere emerged from the washroom, carrying roses she'd just freshened. Her silver-blond hair was coiled in a chic chignon at her nape. Diamonds glinted from her ears. The rock on her left hand, a huge pink diamond surrounded by a dozen of brilliant white, flashed in its platinum setting as she set the vase on a marble credenza with a quiet clink.

"Please pardon the mess out there, Rory. We're a work in progress at the moment. I'm Cornelia Hunt," she said, intent on putting her guest at ease as she held out her hand. "It's a pleasure to finally meet you."

Feeling a distinct connection to Alice after she'd slipped down the rabbit hole, Rory clasped the woman's hand. She had dressed that morning in a casual black turtleneck and skinny denims to look at properties and apartments, not to meet well-dressed ladies in what could have passed for a drawing room in a palace.

"The pleasure's mine," she returned, fighting the urge to curtsy.

"You only met briefly, so I'll officially introduce you to Felicity Granger. Phil is my assistant. She's also an academic counselor at the university. She's really rather brilliant at helping others with their life decisions, so I brought her in to help me with my work." Her green eyes seemed to twinkle as she smiled. "What have you been told about the arrangements so far?"

"Hardly anything. The man who showed us around... Erik," she identified, still aware of him pacing, "wouldn't even give me the price."

"I don't doubt that you have questions," Cornelia conceded. "I'll have Phil start answering yours and explain the details while I get us some coffee. Or would you prefer tea?"

Rory told her coffee was fine, thank you. And that yes, cocoa for Tyler would be nice. Even as she spoke, she wasn't at all sure what struck her as more incongruous just then: that Cornelia Fairchild Hunt, the very pleasant wife of a reportedly eccentric computer-genius billionaire, was getting her coffee. Or the mound of dingy canvas mail sacks piled beside a delicate French provincial writing desk.

On the desk's surface, dozens of what appeared to be opened letters teetered in stacks.

Phil took the chair next to Rory. Seeing what had her attention, she adjusted her overlarge glasses and leaned toward her.

"There was an article in the Seattle *Washtub* recently about how Cornelia helped a young entrepreneur get the break she needed with her business. Ever since then, requests have poured in by email and snail mail for her in care of the newspaper and the offices of HuntCom asking for her help from other young women. And for them. Like you," she explained. "The reporter who wrote the article said she's bringing another sackful over this afternoon."

"A reporter is part of this?"

"Don't worry," Phil hastily assured. "Cornelia wants to stay under the radar with her project and she trusts Shea Weatherby to help her with that. As for anyone else we might need to talk with, we only identify our clients to those directly involved in her situation."

The assertion was hugely reassuring to Rory. She'd already supplied enough fodder for gossip in certain social circles to last a lifetime. Nearly every member of those circles would have sold their summer homes to mingle with a Hunt, too. But all that mattered to her just then was that this meeting was confidential. Her relationship with her in-laws was strained enough without word getting out and embarrassing them because their son's widow apparently needed to be bailed out by strangers. For Tyler's sake, she needed to make as few waves with them as possible.

Thinking about her in-laws reminded her that she needed to call them about Christmas.

"The volume of requests Cornelia is receiving," Phil continued, mercifully sidetracking her from the stomach-knotting thought, "is why she needed to hire help. I just love what she's doing."

"I really am at a loss here," Rory admitted. "What *is* she doing?"

"She's being what the first woman she helped called her," her assistant replied. "A fairy godmother."

She had a fairy godmother?

"On to the details." Phil pushed a pale blue folder toward her, the snowflake polish on her nails glittering. "If these terms are agreeable to you, Cornelia will purchase the property you saw from the owners and you will purchase it from her for the amount stated on line one. To keep everything legal and as simple as possible, your down payment will be one dollar. Your balance will be interest-free with the first payment due September first. You'll have had five months of cash flow by then."

Disbelief held Rory's tone to nearly a whisper. The number couldn't possibly be right. "The property has to be worth three times this."

"Oh, it is. And that's what Cornelia will pay the owners for it. But that's your price. Of course, there is more to the sale."

Ah, yes, Rory thought, unable to understand why Cornelia would take such a loss for her. The strings.

"Cornelia has added a few perks," Phil chose to call them. "She believes the best route to success is to have a good adviser. Since it's understandable that you'd know little about this particular business and since the Sullivan's grandson is reasonably acquainted with it, she arranged for Erik to be your mentor for the next six months. He'll help you with your inventory, suppliers, getting part-time help and whatever else it will take to get your new venture up and running.

"The two of you can determine how often you need to meet, but there will be a status meeting here once a month.

Of course, I'm available to both of you together or individually at any time. At the end of the six months, if you're on track with your business plan, Erik will have fulfilled his mentor agreement, and you'll be on your own. All we ask," she concluded, as if she'd rather expected the stunned silence coming from beside her, "is for your discretion in discussing the work we do here."

Phil sat back, smiling.

Rory couldn't seem to move.

Poof. Just like that. The property her little boy had fallen in love with that morning—and the business that came with it—could be hers.

The reality of it didn't want to sink in. Yet even in her disbelief what registered most was that her new life included a man who she strongly suspected didn't want to work with her at all.

"This Erik," she said, caution competing with amazement as Cornelia joined them with a tray of tall porcelain mugs. "May I ask the terms of his agreement with you?"

Taking the chair on the opposite side of her, Cornelia passed mugs to her and Phil. "It's nothing complicated. I just requested that he help you with the business if I buy the property for the Sullivans' asking price."

"But why did he agree to that?"

"Because he wants a decent price for his grandparents and I offered him one. He's been taking care of the property for them, so I also imagine he'd like to be free of that responsibility. I don't think he begrudges his grandparents his time. He sounds quite fond of them," she offered, approval in the soft lines of her face. "But he's a busy man."

Rory remembered his strong, workingman's hands, the calluses she'd felt brush her palm. Right behind the thought came the disquieting memory of what his touch had elicited. "He said he builds boats."

"Oh, they're more than boats. He and his business partner build world-class sailing sloops. Their boatworks is down past the marina, but their sales and rental office is next door. J.T., one of my stepsons," she said, identifying Harry's second oldest, "commissioned one from him years back. He said Erik is the only man he'd ever do business with on a handshake. If you knew my stepson, you'd know that respect for someone's character doesn't get any greater than that."

Her carefully penciled eyebrows arched as she offered cream and sugar. "Did you find him disagreeable?"

Disturbing, yes. Disagreeable? She couldn't honestly say they'd disagreed about anything. "No."

"Are you not wanting help?"

Rory shook her head. She'd be a fool to turn it down. "I'm sure he has far more information about how the market is run than anything I can even begin to find on my own."

The unguarded admission brought Cornelia's smile back. "Then it's a win-win for everyone."

Baffled by the woman, more uncertain than she wanted to admit about her mentor, Rory touched the handle of her mug. "Please don't think I'm not beyond grateful, Mrs. Hunt—"

"It's Cornelia," the woman said graciously.

"Cornelia," Rory corrected. "But I'm having a hard time making sense of all this. I understand from Phil that you helped someone else when she needed it. But why do you want to help *me* like this?"

"Because I can," she said simply. "My Harry gave me a ridiculously large amount of money for a wedding gift. Since I have the means, I decided to make it my mission to offer deserving young women a hand up when the going gets rough for them, or when they just need the right break.

"In your case," she admitted, "I know all too well what it's like to be financially strapped and the only parent. My first husband was a dear, but he left me in a real financial bind when he died. I had to sell my home, just as you've had to do. And I had to work hard to raise my girls."

She gave Rory's hand a pat, drew back her own. "From what we learned about you from your real estate agent—and other resources," she admitted, making it clear she thoroughly vetted the recipients of her largesse, "I don't doubt that you'll do what you must to make it work. Erik has proven himself to be an excellent businessman," she assured, as the opening door let in the back-up beep of a truck. "I'm sure you can trust him to help you succeed.

"Can't she, Erik?" she asked the man himself as he walked in.

Seeming oblivious to the way his presence suddenly filled the space, much less to the faint tension leaking from him in waves, Cornelia raised an eyebrow in his direction.

"Can't she what?" he replied.

"Trust your business judgment."

"It hasn't let me down so far."

The disarming smile he gave Cornelia and Phil seemed to come easily. The wattage, however, lowered considerably when it settled on her. Having met her eyes long enough to make her heart jerk, Rory watched him lower his glance to the older woman's coffee.

"Mind if I get some of that?"

"Not at all. The pot is fresh."

His heavy footsteps muffled by the carpet, Erik headed for the coffeemaker in the alcove. Behind him he could hear the elegant matron and the bookish blonde he'd met last week explaining that the paperwork for Rory's mortgage would be handled at a title company Monday afternoon. Since he had power of attorney for the sale for his grandparents, he and Cornelia had already agreed to take care of their business there that morning.

The Hunt name tended to eliminate delays.

He could hear the low, soft tones of Rory's responses, but he had no idea what she said. He was too busy telling himself that the next six months wouldn't be as bad as he'd feared.

They'd probably be worse.

He didn't question the sincerity of the rather shell-shocked-looking young woman reading the papers in front of her. Her determination to do what she had to do for her child had been nearly tangible to him. But her impulsiveness had raised about a dozen red flags.

Women spent more time making up their mind about buying a pair of shoes than she had about taking on something that would require a nearly 24/7 commitment. Especially at first. He knew. He ate, slept and breathed his own business. And that business was something he'd wanted since he was a kid. She'd only wanted the store since she'd learned about it that morning. She'd even admitted to knowing nothing about what she'd agreed to get herself into—which meant she'd take far more time than he'd planned on devoting to the care and feeding of her education.

It was that last part that he'd explained to his business partner when he'd called a while ago to tell him he'd still be tied up for a while. Pax had said not to worry about what he'd committed himself to. He'd cover for him if he needed time during the day to work with the store's new owner.

Though they'd never talked about the reasons for it, Pax knew how badly Erik wanted to be out from under that property. And why. They'd grown up together. Pax had been his best man. He'd also gone through the ugliness of his divorce with him by letting him take on however many projects it took to keep him too exhausted to think about anything else.

It had been seven years since the demise of his eight-year marriage, and Erik had long since recovered from what he had no intention of ever repeating again, but he already felt guilt about the time he'd be taking away from work. Especially with an April delivery date on their present work under construction, another client waiting for his final blueprints and two others hovering in the wings to get on their list.

Then there were their evening commitments with past and future clients. The holiday party season had just started—and Merrick & Sullivan Yachting never missed a business or philanthropic commitment.

With the women still talking, and feeling the tension creep up his back, he took his filled mug to the nearest window and rubbed at his neck. He'd do what he had to do where the woman behind him was concerned, and hope she wasn't the sort who required a lot of hand-holding to come up to speed. Heaven knew he wasn't a coddling sort of guy.

Erik took a sip of the coffee that was infinitely better than the sludge he and his partner had been brewing since their secretary had gone on maternity leave. It didn't help the situation that Mrs. Rory Linfield had a son. He'd made it a point over the past several years to avoid women with children. They tended to want more of a commitment than he was interested in. But that deliberate lack of exposure left him feeling less than capable when it came to anyone under four feet tall.

With his pretty little project deep in conversation, he looked out over the blue-tarped sailboats yawing in their slips. He and Pax had pulled their rental fleet out of the water last month, but farther up the shoreline, he could see the point that anchored the rest of their operation: the boatyard where they stored their boats over winter and the boatworks where they built their custom sailing yachts, one sloop at a time.

"How come that boat has a Santa on it?"

The little boy had walked over from two windows

down. Now, with his chin barely clearing the window-sill, the sandy-haired child pointed to a row of decorated sloops in the marina. Several had colored lights anchored fore and aft from the mainsail mast. One had a blow-up Santa at the helm.

Erik gave a shrug. "Some people just like to decorate their boats this time of year."

"How come?"

"Because they entertain on them," he said, thinking of the cocktail parties he and his partner had hosted on their respective sloops for their clients over the years. They had one scheduled next week. "Or maybe they're going to be in one of the boat parades." The floating parades were legend around the sound during the holidays.

The little boy's brow furrowed. Digesting what he'd been told, he said nothing else. For about five seconds, anyway.

"Do you have a boat?"

"I do."

"Do you decorate it?"

"I have."

"Do you put a Santa on it?"

"No."

"Oh," the child said.

He took another sip of coffee, waited for another question. When none was forthcoming, Erik tried to focus on the conversation behind him.

The small voice immediately cut in.

"I'm glad your house has a fireplace. So Santa can come down," Tyler explained, still looking out the window. "Mom said he can visit without one, but it's easier when he has a chimney."

It took a moment for the boy's conversational leap to make sense. Apparently since Santa was on his mind, any context was fair game.

"I've heard that about chimneys, too," he assured him. "And the house you saw isn't mine. It's my grandparents'."

The distinction apparently didn't matter.

"We have a fireplace in our house. But we didn't have a tree last time for him to put presents under." The small voice sounded utterly matter-of-fact. "Mom said this year won't be sad. We get a tree no matter what."

His mom had mentioned that he hadn't had a very good Christmas last year. Sad, the child had just called it. Yet Erik didn't let himself consider why that had been. Telling himself that her personal business was none of his, he murmured a distracted, "That's good," to her son and focused on the only business of hers he needed to be interested in. The store.

Cornelia had asked for his presence in case Rory had questions for him. He figured now was as good a time as any to see what those concerns might be.

The three females at the table glanced up as he approached.

It was Rory's dark eyes that he met.

"Is there anything you want to ask me about the property?"

Her shell-shocked look had yet to fade. With her ringless hand at the base of her throat, she slowly shook her head. "I don't even know where to start right now."

"Make a list as things occur to you," he told her. "I'll come by the market next week and we can go over it.

"The sale is being expedited," he told her, knowing now that part of the appeal of his grandparents' home, for her son, anyway, had been the fireplace his own family had gathered around at Christmas. "You can move in whenever you're ready. I'll check my schedule and Phil can set us up with a day and time next week to go over inventory."

He set his coffee on the table with a decisive clink and pulled his business card from his pocket. Walking around the table to give it to her, he watched her rise. As she did, his glance slid over what her coat had hidden earlier. The long black turtleneck she wore skimmed her feminine curves, molded the sweet shape of her hips.

She had the body of a dancer. Long, lithe and sexy as hell.

Masking his misgivings about having to deal with her, feeling them mount by the minute, he ignored the vague tightening in his gut. "Do you need help moving in?"

"No. I'm… No," Rory repeated, hating how flustered she felt. "But thank you." The last thing she wanted was to impose on this man. Considering what he'd been asked to do for her, she'd be obligated enough to him as it was. "I'd planned to be out Monday, so I've already arranged for movers."

She pushed back her bangs, revealing the pinch of her brow. "You really don't mind if I take things over before the sale closes?"

"You said you want to be settled before Christmas." He assumed now that that desire had something to do with putting up a tree. "The earlier you start, the sooner you can be."

Rory swallowed. Hard.

"Thank you."

He held out his card. "My office and cell numbers are on here. Call me if something comes up. I'll leave a key under the rock by the back porch. You'll get a full set at closing." His fingers brushed hers. Her skin felt cool to him, soft, and though he was trying not to notice anything in particular about her, he could have sworn he felt her trembling.

Without looking up, she palmed his card and clasped both hands in front of her.

"You're sure you're covered on the move?" he asked

"I'm positive. I arranged everything a couple of weeks ago."

Standing as close as he was, he caught the tremor in her

breath as she eased it out. He didn't doubt she felt overwhelmed with all that was happening for her. Yet she managed to maintain the composure that had her graciously assuring Cornelia that she truly needed nothing else as far as help was concerned. Something about that composure seemed practiced to him, though. It was as if she'd found herself in overwhelming or uncertain situations before and wasn't about to let anyone see how unsettled she really was.

She wouldn't look at him again. She seemed to know what he'd seen, and felt totally embarrassed being so exposed. A huge burden was being lifted from her slender shoulders, but she wasn't letting herself feel the relief of that weight. It appeared that admitting the scope of that relief would be admitting how truly desperate she'd begun to feel. So she just kept it all in, as if that was what she'd become accustomed to doing anyway, and turned to the women.

With a choked little laugh, she said she had no idea how to thank them.

Leaving her to figure it out, he looked to the matriarch running the show, thanked her for the coffee and headed for more familiar territory.

He'd given his word that he'd help. And he would. He never promised anything he didn't intend to deliver. But when he showed up for the meeting Phil arranged for him with Rory the following Wednesday, he discovered something about his charge that he hadn't anticipated.

The young widow with the sweet, sharp little boy might have looked as fragile as sea foam, but she had a stubborn streak as wide as Puget Sound.

Chapter Three

Erik hesitated at the store's front door. For years he'd simply walked in when the business had been open. After his grandparents had moved, he'd let himself in with his key. Since the sale had closed two days ago, he no longer had the right to come and go as he pleased from a place that had been part of his life for as long as he could remember.

The odd sense of having been displaced lingered as he rapped his knuckles on the frame of the screen door, and promptly disappeared the instant the inside door swung open. Even with her pretty features schooled into a smile of greeting, the unease in Rory's guarded expression made him suspect she was already having second thoughts about what she'd taken on.

Or so he was thinking when she let him in and his glance cut from the black hoodie and yoga pants molding her curves to the furniture behind her.

It looked as if every possession she owned sat piled in the interior of the market. Bedroom sets, tables, chairs, boxes.

"You said you didn't need any help moving in."

Good morning to you, too, Rory thought. "I didn't think I did," she said, stepping back for him to pass.

Deliberately overlooking the accusation shadowing his rugged features, she crossed her arms over her hoodie and the teal turtleneck and thermal undershirt layered beneath it. She wanted to believe her shiver had more to do with the chill in the large space than with the big man in the waffle-weave pullover and charcoal cargo pants. After all, the thermometer by the dairy case did read forty-nine degrees.

The man should wear a coat, she insisted to herself. It was easily ten degrees colder outside.

She turned on her heel to lead him inside where it was warmer. "The college kids I hired were only available long enough to drive the U-Haul over and unload it into the market," she explained, heading between the packing boxes that formed an aisle to the interior door. "It wasn't until we got here that they told me they wouldn't have time to carry everything to the rooms. They did take one of the beds upstairs, though." The thud of heavy hiking boots echoed behind her. In running shoes, her footsteps barely made a squeak. "A mattress, anyway," she qualified. "And a box of bedding." That had been huge.

Spending the past couple of nights on a hard floor would have guaranteed even less sleep than she usually managed. Even with a reasonably comfortable place to rest, she'd spent most of both nights trying not to disturb Tyler and listening to the building's unfamiliar creaks and groans while hoping to heaven she could make this store work.

"They'll come back to finish sometime next week," she continued, "so I've been taking in what I can by myself. Tyler's helping." Boxes too heavy to carry she'd emptied one armload at a time. The method wasn't the most efficient, but she now had one bathroom in order and the kitchen organized, except for the table and chairs. The old refectory table weighed a ton. She knew—she'd tried to move it last night.

She chafed her arms along her sleeves, winced a little when she rubbed a spot above the elbow that now sported the bruise she'd earned in the attempt. She had a matching one on the back of her shoulder. No longer hearing Erik's footfalls, she glanced around to see that he had stopped.

Across ten feet of worn plank flooring, she saw his dark eyebrows merge. "Isn't the furnace working?"

"It's working just fine."

"Then why is it so cold in here?"

"Because I'm not heating this big space until I have to. Fuel's expensive. By the way," she added, gratitude slipping into her voice, "thank you for having the tank filled. You saved me from running out of oil." She'd always had electric heat before. Not accustomed to an oil furnace, she hadn't realized the need for fuel until the man who'd performed the building inspection Sunday had showed her the tank and pointed out the gauge.

"The driver of the truck wouldn't leave an invoice," she told him. "So if you'll tell me what I owe you, I'll give you a check."

"You don't owe me anything."

"Yes, I do."

"No," he insisted, "you don't. Just think of it as a move-in present."

He obviously considered the matter settled. There seemed no doubt of that as he turned away to ponder the height and breadth of the obstacles blocking his view of the back of the store.

As appreciative as she was for his thoughtfulness, she couldn't accept his gift.

"Look." Hugging her arms a little tighter, she stepped in front of him. "I'm already not sure how I'll repay you for helping me get to know the store. I know you agreed to do it to help your grandparents sell this place," she conceded, which meant his benevolence definitely wasn't personal, "but I'd rather not be any more obligated to you than I already am. Or will be," she qualified, because other than make her acutely aware of his reluctant and very male presence, he hadn't done anything yet. "Okay?"

For a moment, he said nothing. He just let his deceptively easy glance slip over the quiet determination in her eyes before he headed to the checkout counter.

"Then don't accept it as a gift. Accept it because I'd rather work out here with heat."

Confusion preempted further defense. "I thought we were going to go over the inventory."

"That's the plan."

He carried a briefcase. A rather hefty one of scarred butterscotch leather and straps with buckles that had far more character than the sleek, unscuffed ones carried by other men she knew. As he set it on the scratched counter, she could see his burnished initials, worn shiny in places, above the equally worn lock. A section of stitching on the side looked new, as if it had recently been repaired. The case was old, she thought. It had history. And part of that history seemed to say that he'd rather keep and care for what he had than replace it.

Not appreciating how he'd dismissed her attempt to establish an understanding, she didn't bother to wonder why she found that so appealing.

"I thought we'd work where it's already warm. Inside," she pointed out, ever so reasonably. "We can sit at the island and go over the books in there."

"I meant the physical inventory. The stuff that's on the shelves and in the bins back there." He hitched his thumb over his shoulder. "I have a printout of what came with the sale, but those items have been sitting around for a year. You'll want to discount some of what you have and replace it with new merchandise. Things like sinkers, bobbers and leaders are fine, but creels and some of the stock that isn't packaged looks shopworn."

Rory hadn't a clue what he was talking about.

"Fishing gear," he explained, apparently sensing that.

Undaunted, she picked up a couple of the boxes from the cracked surface. She'd already decided the old laminate needed to go. "Then we'll work here at the counter."

The boxes had been emptied, Erik realized when she easily lifted two marked *Dishes* from where his grandfather had once kept displays of bug repellent and sunglasses. She removed two more, adding them to the only space available without blocking either doorway: the tops of three tall stacks of red-and-green bins marked *Christmas*.

She had to stretch to get them there. Jerking his glance from the enticing curve of her backside, he reached past her.

"Let me get that."

"Already have it," she insisted, and having placed the boxes, turned right into him.

Rock had more give to it.

The thought occurred vaguely as she bumped into his chest. Promptly bouncing back, she gasped a breath when his quick grip tightened on her upper arms. Her heart had barely slammed against her ribs when he pulled her forward to keep her from hitting the bins behind her and bringing the empty boxes down on their heads.

The freshness of soap and sea air clung to him. With her pulse scrambling, his grip tight on her bruise, she had no idea why the scents even registered. Her hand shot up, covering the back of his where it curved over the tender spot on her arm.

The pressure of his fingers eased.

With their bodies inches apart, she went as still as stone. Or maybe he froze first. She just knew that one moment she'd been intent on doing whatever she needed to do to make it clear that she wouldn't waste his time, and the next, the tension in his body and the warmth of his hands had seeped through to her skin, making her conscious of little more than…him.

Erik's eyes narrowed on hers an instant before she ducked her head. Slacking his grip, he dropped his hands. There'd been no mistaking the way she'd winced when he'd grabbed her.

Without thinking, he reached toward her again, touched the back of her hand where it now covered where his had been.

He hadn't thought he'd grabbed her that hard.

"Are you okay?"

At the concern in his voice, the caution in his touch, her head came back up. "I'm fine." Wanting to convince them both, she smiled. "Really."

His brow pinched as he drew his hand away once more.

Rory's breath slithered out. That small contact had been far too brief to elicit the loss she felt when he stepped back. Yet that sense of loss existed, sinking deeper into her chest with every heartbeat—unexpected, unwanted and feeling far too threatening under his quiet scrutiny.

A certain numbness had protected her since she'd lost what had felt like the other half of herself. Yet, as with the first time this man had touched her, something about him scraped at the edges of that barrier, made her conscious of things she truly didn't want to consider.

Out of nowhere, the need to be held sprang to mind. It was such a simple thing, so basic that she'd never truly considered it until it had been found and suddenly lost— that need for security, comfort, a sense of oneness. But she knew how rare it was to find that sense of belonging, and the need didn't feel simple at all. Not when she realized she was actually wondering what it would feel like to be folded against Erik's broad, undeniably solid chest. A woman would feel sheltered there. Safe from what troubled her. And for a few moments, anyway, free of the need to stand alone.

Shaken by her thoughts, by him, she started to move back, as much from the need behind the unexpected admissions as from the man who'd prompted them. The stacks behind her allowed her no escape at all.

His scrutiny narrowed. "If you're okay, why are you still holding your arm?"

She was holding in his touch. Realizing that, hoping he didn't, she promptly dropped her hand.

"It's nothing." Rattled, trying not to be, she shrugged. "It's just a little sore."

"Why?"

"Because I landed against the corner of a dresser." She was just tired. Tired and apparently in need of some downtime with her yoga mat. If she could find it. Or, even better, some fudge. The one thing she did not need was to think about this man's chest, his arms or the way he was scowling at her. "I was trying to move a table and lost my grip.

"So," she said, fully prepared to move on so he'd move himself.

He didn't budge. "Which table?"

Trapped between the counter, bins and boxes, she leaned sideways and pointed toward the eight-foot-long, solid oak-and-iron refectory table jammed between a bedroom set and the dairy case. "That one."

His scowl deepened as it swung back to her. "You tried to move that yourself?"

"It wasn't going to go inside on its own."

Forbearance entered his tone. "You said you were going to wait for the kids who moved you here to help with the heavy stuff."

"What I said," she reminded him, just as patiently, "is that they'd be back next week."

"When next week?"

"When they can fit it in."

"Meaning this could all be here a week from now," he said flatly. "Or the week after that."

She didn't particularly appreciate the cynical certainty in his tone. Especially since she was trying not to dwell on that discouraging suspicion herself.

"What about your friends?" he asked, clearly prepared to pursue other possibilities. "Have you asked any of them to help you?"

"I'm sure everyone's busy."

"Do you know that for certain?"

She could omit and evade. No way could she lie. Thinking of the few people she still thought of as friends, she muttered, "Not exactly."

"Then ask."

She started to say that she didn't want to. Fearing she'd sound like a five-year-old, not liking how he prodded at her defenses, she ignored the command entirely.

Since he had yet to move, she ducked around him. "I'll go turn on the heat."

She would do her best to cooperate with him for his help with the store. She could cut corners somewhere else to keep expenses down.

"I only took two bar stools inside, so there are a couple more back there we can bring up to sit on. I'm going to tell Tyler I'll be out here. He's watching a DVD on my laptop."

Erik watched her slip behind the counter, his focus on the resolute set of her shoulders as she disappeared inside. Her son was undoubtedly watching her laptop because her television was buried somewhere in the stacks beyond him. He also gave the guys she'd hired about a fifty-fifty chance of returning to finish their job.

He didn't care what she said. She did need help here. She just didn't want to ask for it.

Considering that she hadn't wanted to accept his little housewarming present, either, he couldn't help but wonder if the woman was always unreasonable, impractical and stubborn, or if some less obvious trait compelled her to refuse assistance when she clearly needed it.

What she needed now was some serious muscle.

Judging from the size of the decidedly upscale sofa and armchairs, sections of wall units, tables and a huge mirror sitting between the rows of shelving, there had been significant space in the house she'd left behind. The larger of two armoires was the size of a king-size mattress. He had no idea where she was going to put that. It might have fit in the largest of the bedrooms upstairs, but it would never make the bend at the top of the staircase.

He pulled his cell phone from his pocket, checked the time before scrolling through his contact list.

He'd just ended his call when she hurried back through the door.

"I have a friend on the way to help with the heavy stuff," he announced. "You and I can take care of the rest of it." Pushing up his sleeves, he motioned to an overstuffed, roll-armed, oatmeal-colored chair blocking a bedroom set. "Where does that go?"

Beneath a dusting of dark hair, his forearms were roped with sinew and muscle. They looked every bit as strong as she imagined them to be, but it was his left arm that had her staring. A silvery scar, hook shaped and wide, slashed from wrist to elbow.

"Just part of a collection. Caught a jib line when it snapped," he said, seeing what had her attention. "It couldn't be helped." His glance slid pointedly to the sore spot on her arm. "Unlike banging yourself up trying to move something you had to know was too heavy for you.

"So where do you want it?" he asked. "The living room?"

His presumption made her let the table reference go.

"You don't need to do this." *Part of a collection,* he'd said. He had more injuries like that? "And you definitely didn't need to call your friend."

Unease over what he'd done had collided with a hint of concern for the scar. Or maybe what he saw was embarrassment warring with interest. Whichever it was, he could practically see her struggling to decide which should take precedence as she moved with him toward the chair. The process, he thought, was rather fascinating.

"Yeah," he muttered, undeterred. At least she now had some color in her cheeks. "I did. I can't get those dressers up the stairs by myself."

"I meant, you didn't need to impose on him at all. I can't ask you to do this," she stressed, only to have him hand her the chair's seat cushion.

"You didn't ask," he pointed out.

"You know what I mean," she muttered back, arms wrapped around the awkward bulk.

"What I know is that there's no way to go over the inventory when we can't even get to it. So, yeah. I do need to do this." Challenge lit the chips of silver in his steel-gray eyes as he pulled one of her arms free and handed her the wide back cushion, as well. His glance slid to her biceps. "You're skinny, but you have more muscle than I'd thought. This'll go faster if you help."

Over the tops of the pillows, Rory could have sworn she saw challenge shift to a smile. Too disconcerted by him and what he'd done to stand there and make certain of it, she turned with the cushions and headed for the door.

She'd admit to having lost a couple of pounds in the past year or so, but no one had called her skinny since sixth grade.

"Which room do you want the twin bed in?" she heard him call.

"The one next to the master," she called back.

She had no intention of arguing with him. Not just because she didn't want to appear difficult. Or because he had a valid point about not being able to get to the inventory. As unsettled as her life felt—would always feel, she feared—getting the visible chaos under control would be huge. Tyler having his own bed that night would be nice, too.

Focusing on her son distracted her from the man carrying up her little boy's bed. For all of five minutes. The moment Tyler saw his bookshelf going up the stairs, he wanted to help. Wanting to keep him out of Erik's way, since she was trying to stay out of it herself, she waited until the piece was in place, then put him to work filling the shelves with his toys. While Erik moved on to tackle the living room furniture, she carried in lamps, pictures and, now that she could get to it, her box of potted herbs for the kitchen windowsill.

They didn't work together so much as they worked around each other. Erik clearly just wanted to get the job done so he could get on with the job he was there to do. Hating how she'd inconvenienced him, she just wanted to get it done, too.

An hour later, she'd returned to the base of the stairs for the rolled-up dinosaur posters she'd left there when muffled male voices drifted from inside the store.

"No way is this thing going up the stairs," she heard Erik insist. "Not without a saw."

"She might take exception to that," came the sensible reply. "How about through the bedroom window? Aren't there picture windows on that side of the house?"

"We'd have to take the window out and bring over a

crane, but it might be doable. The boys could load the EZ-Rig on a trailer and one of them can drive it over."

"That would do it." The unfamiliar voice paused. "There just isn't enough time to do it today. Not if you want the rest of this cleared out. That party starts at six."

Not totally sure what had the men talking about bringing in heavy equipment, equally concerned by mention of a prior obligation, Rory left the posters and poked her head inside the store. In the bright overhead lights, she saw Erik facing the large cherry armoire that blocked one of the grocery aisles. He stood in profile to her, his arms crossed over his broad chest, his wide brow furrowed.

He seemed totally occupied with logistics. She just couldn't see whom he was talking with. Whoever it was remained hidden by the sizable piece of furniture.

Needing to remove the apparent complication, she scooted past the checkout counter. "If it can't be carried up, just leave it. Or move it out of the way if you need to. I'll figure out what to do with it later."

Erik's glance caught hers as an athletic-looking male in worn denims and a plaid flannel shirt stepped from behind the armoire. The man had a scant inch on her mentor in height, which put him in the range of six-three or so, and the same imposing, broad-shouldered, leanly muscular build that spoke of intimate familiarity with hard physical work. Or a gym.

Beneath his wavy, wood-brown hair, his eyes narrowed an instant before he smiled. That smile seemed as easygoing as the man himself when Erik introduced him to her as Pax Merrick.

"My business partner," Erik added.

Pax reached out. "And partner in crime."

Shaking her hand, he gave her a quick once-over, the kind men who enjoy women often do, along with a rakish wink. "We go back a long way. You're Rory," he said, sparing his partner the introduction, along with whatever he could have added about their apparently extensive history.

Her glance bounced between the two unquestionably attractive, undoubtedly successful, probably rather fearless males. With the sense that their history might be rather intriguing, she offered Pax an apologetic smile of her own. "I'm really sorry to cut into your day like this."

"Not a problem. He'd do the same for me," he admitted, eyeing her with no small amount of curiosity. "You're really taking over this place?"

Something in the man's tone gave her pause.

"I am," she replied. "Why?"

"It'll seem really different, is all. I used to hang out here with Erik when we were kids. We built our first boat in Gramps's garage down there. And this store... It was just the Sullivans here all those years. They had sort of a mom-and-pop thing going," he explained, looking her over as if to verify some preconceived impression. "Down-to-earth. Comfortable, you know? I never thought about it being run by someone..."

Like you, she was sure he'd been about to say, only to be cut off by the quick-but-subtle slicing motion Erik made across his own throat.

"...else," he hastily concluded. "But if Erik's going to teach you the ropes," he hurried to add, "I'm sure you don't have a thing to worry about. The guy's got the patience of Job."

Meaning he thought she was going to require...what? she wondered, swinging her glance to Erik. Patience of biblical proportions?

Erik pointedly ignored her. "Are you going to help me move this, Merrick?"

"Absolutely. I'm on it."

As if wanting to muffle his partner, Erik motioned to the furniture the large piece blocked. "As soon as we get this out of the way, we'll take up your son's dresser," he told her. "Where do you want those bookcases?"

"In the spare room across from Tyler's." *Please,* she might have added, but his friend's insinuation still stung.

"Is there a bed that goes in there?"

"I don't have a spare bed anymore." She nodded toward the headboard and nightstands an aisle over with the same carving as the armoire. "That's a set we had in a guest room. I'll use it for my room now."

She'd sold the bed she'd slept in with Curt for so many years. Its new owner had picked up all the master bedroom furnishings the morning her movers had come. She'd sold the bulk of her other possessions to an estate broker she'd met at the country club to which she no longer belonged. Had it not been for Tyler, she'd have sold everything and bought only what she'd need to start over. But too much had changed for him already for her to indulge the need she felt to shed all the reminders of a life that no longer was.

Taking a deep breath, she pushed her hand through her hair and looked over to see Erik still watching her.

"I take it you've downsized."

"You have no idea," she murmured back.

She couldn't imagine what he saw in her expression, but she saw something in his that looked remarkably like understanding. It was as if he knew what it was like to walk away from the trappings and reminders of a former life. Whether he'd had no choice or the choice had been solely his, she had no idea. All she felt with any certainty as he shoved up his shirtsleeves to get back to work was that he wanted no part of those reminders now.

The realizations gave her pause. As she turned away herself and headed inside to pick up the posters, so did her disquiet over his partner's unwitting revelations. The fact that Erik had obviously implied to his friend that she would require considerable patience was merely annoying. She also questioned just how patient he actually was, given his steamroller approach to getting her things moved out of his way. But what truly troubled her was what his friend had said about her mentor's grandparents having been there for so long.

She hadn't even considered what her neighbors and customers would think of someone new running a business that might well be some sort of institution in the area. She'd already been wondering if she could keep it open year-round, and added that to her list of questions for Erik. Her newly heightened concerns about fitting in she'd have to add later, though, when she wasn't busy keeping Tyler out of the way of all the testosterone hauling bedroom furniture up the stairs.

Every time they clamored up the stairs and down the hall with another piece of something large, he'd dart to the door of his new bedroom to watch them go by.

Pax joked with him, noticeably at ease with small children. Erik, preoccupied, said even less to him than when he'd been around him before. He'd given him a half smile on their first pass, which had put a shy grin on Tyler's face, then barely glanced at him at all.

Because her little boy continued to wait in his doorway for "the man with the boat," it soon became painfully apparent that Tyler was hoping Erik would acknowledge him again—which had her feeling even more protective than usual when he asked if he could help him.

"I don't think so, sweetie. They're in a hurry," she explained, brushing his sandy hair back from his forehead. "When people get in a hurry, accidents can happen."

"If I be careful can I help?"

Erik heard the tiny plea drift down the hallway. Focused on getting Rory's possessions out of the way of the inventory, he'd paid scant attention to the child other than to make sure he wasn't where he could get something dropped on him.

But now they needed tools. Deciding to save himself a trip and do something about the dejection he'd heard in that small voice, he called, "Hey, Tyler. Can you do something for me?"

A nanosecond later, little footsteps, muffled by carpeting, pounded down the hall.

Tyler appeared in the doorway of the master bedroom, shoving his hair back from the expectation dancing in his eyes. Rory was right behind him, unmasked concern in hers.

Erik crouched in his cargos, his forearms on his thighs, hands dangling between his knees. Behind him, Pax continued squaring the bed frame to the headboard.

Rory's glance fixed on his as she caught her son by his shoulders. "What do you need?"

Whatever it was, she seemed prepared to do it herself. She had mother hen written all over her pretty face.

"Let him do it. Okay?"

The little boy tipped his head backward to look up at his mom. "Okay?" he echoed. "Please?"

For a moment, she said nothing. She simply looked as if she wasn't at all sure she trusted him with whatever it was he had in mind, before caving in with a cautious okay of her own.

It didn't surprise him at all that, physically, she hadn't budged an inch.

"There's a red metal box at the bottom of the stairs," he said to the boy. "It has socket wrenches in it. It's kind of heavy," he warned. "Do you think you can bring it up?"

With a quick nod, Tyler turned with a grin.

"No running with tools!" Rory called as he disappeared out the door.

"'Kay!" the boy called back, and dutifully slowed his steps.

Caught totally off guard by what Erik had done, Rory looked back to the big man crouched by her bed frame. He was already back to work, he and his partner slipping the frame parts into place and talking about how much longer it would take them to finish.

Not wanting to be in their way herself, she backed into the hall, waiting there while Tyler, lugging the case with both hands, grinning the whole while, made his delivery.

When he walked back out of the room moments later, his expression hadn't changed. She couldn't remember the last time her little boy had looked so pleased. Or so proud.

"Erik said I did good."

She knew. She'd heard him.

"Can I show him my boat?"

"Maybe some other time. He's really busy right now," she explained, then added that *she* really needed his help finishing his room.

Helping his mom wasn't nearly the thrill of helping the guys. Especially when Erik called for him again ten minutes later, this time to carry down the tools he'd had him bring up.

From where she stood on a chair adjusting the ties on a primordial-forest curtain valance, she watched Tyler walk by his bedroom door with both hands again gripping the handle of the red metal box. Right behind him came Erik, telling him he'd take the box when they got to the stairs so he wouldn't lose his balance with it.

Right behind Erik, Pax paused and poked his head into the room.

"I've got to run, Rory. No need to stop what you're doing," he called, because she'd done just that. "We have a client's Christmas party tonight or I'd stick around and help. Erik's going to finish up."

She'd forgotten they had plans. Groaning at the lapse, she left the last tie undone and headed for the door.

Erik had disappeared into the store. Tyler, now empty-handed, stood in the entryway as Pax passed him, ruffling his hair on the way.

"What can I do to repay you?" she called.

"Do you bake?"

"What's your favorite cookie?"

"Any kind that goes with coffee." Grinning, he disappeared, too.

Erik eyed his buddy as Pax walked into the store. "If she has any spare time," he insisted, setting the toolbox on the counter, "she'll need to spend it out here."

"Hey," his shameless partner said with a shrug, "if she wants to bake me something, it'd be rude to refuse. So how much longer will you be?"

Erik flatly rejected the odd sensation that hit out of nowhere. It almost felt like protectiveness. But just whom he felt protective of, he had no idea. The woman wasn't Pax's type at all. "Half an hour at the most."

"You taking a date tonight?"

"Yeah," he muttered, the word oddly tight. "What about you?"

"I'm leaving my options open. I'll cover for you if you need more time," he added, his smile good-natured as he headed out the store's front door.

Erik wished he'd left his options open, too. Though all he said to his partner was that he'd catch up with him at the party and turned back to what was left of his task.

The aisles were finally clear. The inventory visible. Except for the large armoire they'd moved to the empty space near the front door and the boxes and bins Rory had said she didn't need just yet, mostly those marked *Christmas*, nothing else needed to be carried in. Except for her monster of a dining table, which they'd put in place, he and

Pax had carried the rest of the furniture in and left it all wherever it had landed in the living room.

His briefcase still lay on the checkout counter's marred surface, its contents untouched.

Burying his frustration with that, he glanced up to see her watching him uneasily from the inner doorway. More comfortable dealing with logistics than whatever had her looking so cautious, he figured the furniture in the living room could be pushed or shoved into place. It didn't feel right leaving her to do it alone. It wasn't as if she'd call a neighbor for help with the heavier pieces. She didn't even know them. And she'd seemed inexplicably reluctant to call in a friend.

"Where do you want the sofa? Facing the window?" That was where his grandparents had always had theirs.

Rory wanted it to face the fireplace. She just wasn't about to impose on him any more than she already had.

"I'll take care of it," she insisted, because he had that purposeful set to his jaw that said he was about to get his own way. Again.

"What about the big cabinet?"

"It's fine where it is. For now," she conceded, not about to tell him she wanted it moved across the room to the stair wall. "I'm hugely grateful for your help with all this, Erik. And for your friend's. But I'd just as soon not feel guiltier than I already do for having used your time like this. You came to work on the business. Not to help me move in. You need to go now."

One dark eyebrow arched. "I need to go because you feel guilty?"

"You need to go because you have a date."

She'd obviously overheard his conversation with his partner. Not that it mattered. Like Pax's unveiled allusion to the care and feeding Erik had told him he was sure she'd require, nothing had been said that he'd rather she hadn't heard. He'd bet his boat she already suspected he wasn't crazy about being there, anyway.

"Right." He wasn't in the habit of leaving a woman waiting. "We'll get to the inventory later this week. I won't have time until Friday."

"Friday will be fine. I'll be here. And thank you," she added again, touching his arm when he started to turn away. The moment he turned back, she dropped her hand. "For letting Tyler help," she explained. "I haven't seen him smile like that in a really long time."

Thinking the cute little kid had just wanted to be one of the guys, he murmured, "No problem," and picked up the toolbox and his briefcase. There was no reason for her to be looking all that grateful. Or all that concerned.

Still, as he told her he'd call her later and turned for the door, adding, "Bye, sport," for the little boy who'd just appeared behind his mom, cradling a toy boat, he really wished he didn't have the date with the bubbly event planner he'd taken out a couple of weeks ago. He didn't know the striking blonde all that well, but she'd been easy on the eyes, into sailing and, had he been interested in pursuing her hints, not at all opposed to a little casual sex.

He just hoped she'd need to make it an early evening so there'd be no awkwardness at her door. His head wasn't into games tonight. He wasn't much up for a party, either, though he wasn't about to stand up a client.

For reasons he didn't bother to consider, what he wanted to do was stay right where he was.

Chapter Four

The last thing Rory wanted Friday morning was to be late for her meeting with Erik. Or for him to be on time.

As she turned her car into her gravel parking lot, she realized she wasn't getting her wish on either count.

She'd also just confirmed her suspicions about the gleaming white seaplane she'd seen tied to the dock at the bottom of the rise. It was Erik's. He was on her porch, leaning against a post.

The fact that her mentor flew his own plane meant that he hadn't had to queue up for the ferry or get caught in traffic the way she and the rest of the mortals had crossing the sound and navigating surface streets that morning. It also meant that it had only taken him minutes to make the flight that was now a ninety-minute-each-way expedition for her to Tyler's school.

Hating that she'd caused him to wait, she left her little car in the otherwise empty lot in front of the store rather than park it in her garage and hurried toward where he'd straightened from the post. "I'm sorry I'm late. I was the last car off the ferry," she called, praying he hadn't been there long. They'd agreed on eleven o'clock. It was only a few minutes after. Still… "How long have you been here?"

The ever-present breeze ruffled his dark hair as he pushed his cell phone into a front pocket of his jeans and picked up his worn briefcase.

"Long enough to figure out you weren't going to answer the back door or the one to the mudroom. I didn't realize you'd be gone. I was just going to call you."

His cloud-gray eyes slid from hers as a muscle jerked in his jaw. His skin looked ruddy from the chill. In deference to the cold, he wore a leather flight jacket—open, though, as if in defiance of the need for it.

She hadn't thought of him as defiant before. Or rebellious, or rash, or anything that might even hint at irresponsibility. He seemed too much in control of himself for that. Yet the finely honed tension surrounding him alluded to a sort of restiveness that implied far more than his impatience with her, and made her acutely aware of how restless a man with flying and sailing in his blood might be. Restless. Daring. Bold.

She couldn't remember the last time she'd felt anything that wasn't tempered by the numbness that lingered deep inside her. And she'd never felt bold in her life.

What she felt most was simply the need to keep pushing forward. Especially now. Forward was good. Looking back made it too easy to fall apart.

He didn't need to know that, though. As she crossed the porch planks, searching her crowded key ring for the unfamiliar key, she figured all he needed to know was that she would make this venture work. Exactly how she would do that was as much a mystery to her as the dawn of creation, but she figured the basics would be a good place to start. And basically, she knew she needed this man to help make it happen.

His footsteps echoed heavily as he came up beside her, his big body blocking the wind whipping at her hair. "Where's your son?"

"At school. He only has tomorrow and next week before winter break, so we're commuting."

"To Seattle?"

Conscious of him frowning at the top of her head, she tried to remember if the key she'd just selected was for the store's front door, its emergency exit, the door to the house or the side door to the garage.

"I don't want him to miss working on the holiday projects with the other kids. He already missed the first of the week because of the move and he really wants to help decorate the school's big tree." He wanted a big tree, too, he'd told her. A *huge* one. How she'd make *huge* happen currently fell in the mystery category, too. "Since he won't be going back there after Christmas, it's about the only thing keeping his mind off the need to change schools right now."

"How long does that take you?"

"An hour and a half, if you include queuing up for the ferry."

"You're spending three hours over and back in the morning, and another three hours every—"

"That's just today," she hurried to assure him. "I'll usually only make the round-trip once. Kindergarten is only four hours, so I'll run errands while he's there." And maybe see if she could slip into her friend Emmy's yoga class, since seeking calm seemed more imperative by the moment. "A friend is picking him up with her son this afternoon. He'll play at their house until I get there."

His tone went flat. "So you came all the way back just to keep this appointment."

"You said it was the only time you had this week."

"You could have told me you'd be in Seattle," he insisted. "I never would have expected you to come back here for this."

"You said we had to go over the inventory. We have to do that here, so there was no point in mentioning it."

The key didn't work. Her head still down, his disapproval doing nothing for her agitation, she picked out another.

Before she could try that one in the lock, Erik reached over and snagged the wad of keys by the purple rhinestone-encrusted miniflashlight dangling below them.

"That's to the garage." He paused at the practical bit of bling, chose one beside it. "You want this one."

He held a duller brass key by its blade.

"Next time something like this comes up," he continued, biting back what sounded a lot like frustration, "mention it."

All her rushing had left her jumpier than she'd realized. Or maybe it was the edginess in him that fed the tension she did not want to feel with this man. Taking the key, conscious of how careful he'd been not to touch her, she forced the hurry from her tone.

"My schedule is my problem, not yours. I'll make sure it doesn't interfere with what you need to show me here. Not any more than it has already," she concluded, since last time he'd wound up hauling in her furniture.

Trying not to give him time to dwell on that little failure, she slid the key into the lock.

As the lock clicked, he moved behind her. Reaching past her head, he flattened his broad hand on the heavy wood door.

His heat inches from her back, the nerves in her stomach had just formed a neat little knot when he muttered, "Then let's get to it," and pushed the door open.

Intent on ignoring the knot, disconcerted by their less-than-auspicious start, she hurried into the store to the warning beeps of the alarm system.

With the front display windows shuttered for the winter, the only light came from what spilled in behind them. Relying on that pale shaft of daylight, she headed straight for the checkout counter and the inner door behind it, mental gears shifting on the way.

Feeling his scowl following her, she deliberately sought to shift his focus, too.

"I'm going to start the coffee. While I do that, would you look over the floor plan I came up with? It's right here on the counter." Fluorescent lights buzzed and flickered as she snapped switches on. Punching the security code into the pad by the inner door, the beeping stopped. "I'll be right back."

In less than a minute, she piled her purse, coat and scarf onto the dining table, flipped on the coffeemaker she'd already filled and grabbed the tape measure she'd left on the island.

She'd barely turned back into the store when the hard line of Erik's profile had her freezing in the doorway.

He'd tossed his jacket over the far end of the U-shaped counter's now-bare surface. Without it, she could see *Merrick & Sullivan Yachting* discreetly embroidered in sky-blue on the navy Henley hugging his broad shoulders. Ownership, she thought. He had a definite sense of it. He had it stitched on his shirt. His initials, she'd noticed before, were on the latch of his briefcase.

On the scarred beige countertop lay the file she'd left open. His frown was directed to the new floor plan she'd come up with.

"You did this?" he asked.

With a vague sinking feeling she walked around to him. She might not know anything about the little doodads in the bins and on the Peg-Boards hanging in her new store, but she was a consumer with her fair share of shopping hours under her belt. If the interior didn't have some appeal, people might run in to buy what they needed, but they wouldn't stick around to browse and buy more.

"The store needs updating," she said simply, certain he could see that himself. "I thought it might make the space more interesting to have three shorter horizontal shelving units in back than that one long one down the middle. The floor space along here," she said, pointing to the front and back walls on the drawing, "would be a little narrower, but the endcaps would allow for ninety-six more inches of display space. I could use part of the longer piece—"

"I'm not asking you to defend this," he interrupted mildly. "I'm just asking if you drew it."

Erik's only interest when he'd first arrived had been in tackling the task they hadn't even started the other day. As far as he was concerned, they were already behind schedule if she was to open in April. Not wanting to fall further behind and risk her not making a success of the business, he'd just wanted to get in, get out and get back to work until the next time he had to meet with her. It had been that ambivalent sort of annoyance eating at him when he'd realized what she'd done to accommodate him.

The trip by air between the store and Seattle was nothing for him. Minutes from takeoff to touchdown, depending on head- or tailwinds and whether he left from his houseboat on Lake Union or the boatworks in Ballard. The drive and a ferry ride for her was infinitely less convenient. People commuted from the inner islands every day. But she had actually come back from Seattle just to meet with him, and would have to return later that day to pick up her son.

Even the time it would normally take her on other days seemed an enormous waste of time to him. She was right, though. How she did what she needed to do was her problem. Just as it was his problem, not hers, that he didn't want to consider changing the store from exactly as it had been for decades.

The need to play nice so they could reach their respective goals wasn't what had his attention at the moment, however. It was the detail in the drawing. It hadn't been generated using a computer program. The floor plan had been drawn with pencil on graph paper. While the layout was admittedly simple, the measurements and identity of the elements were all perfectly drawn and precisely printed. It had the touch of a professional.

"Oh," she murmured, apparently understanding. "I took a drafting class a few years ago. We'd thought about building our own home and I wanted to understand what the architect was talking about." She gave a shrug, the motion nowhere near as casual as he suspected she intended it to be. "We never got to the blueprint stage, though. We bought instead."

We.

The freshness of her soap or shampoo or whatever it was clinging to her skin already had him conscious of her in ways he was doing his best to ignore. He'd caught the light herbal scent of her windblown hair when she'd pointed out the walls on the drawing. He caught it again now. Whatever it was she wore seemed too subtle to define. But the elements managed to hit his gut with the impact of a charging bull.

Telling himself he didn't need to know anything about her that didn't apply directly to his reason for being there, he deliberately overlooked her reference to the man she'd married—along with the subtle havoc she wreaked on certain nerves—and indicated a rectangle she'd drawn by the front door.

"So what's this?"

"That's the armoire over there. It just needs to be moved

back against that wall and down a few feet and it'll be perfect. A couple of neighbors stopped by to welcome me yesterday. Actually, I think they came to check me out," she admitted, because their curiosity about the "single woman who'd bought the store" had been so obvious. "But one of them mentioned that she makes organic soaps and creams. She has a friend up the road who makes candles for craft shows. I thought I'd see what else is made locally and put a gift display in it."

He eyed her evenly. "This isn't a boutique."

"Are you saying it's a bad idea?"

He wasn't going to commit to anything yet. He was still back on her having taken a drafting class just because she'd wanted to understand her architect.

"When did you do this?"

Realizing he hadn't shot her down, a hint of relief entered her eyes. "After Tyler went to sleep in the evening. And between 1:00 and 3:00 a.m."

Sleepless nights, he thought. He'd once been there himself. Having one's world turned upside down did tend to promote a certain degree of restlessness. He figured it didn't help matters she was trying to sleep in an unfamiliar house, in a bed she apparently wasn't accustomed to, either. She'd said the one she was now using had been in a guest room.

The thought of her in bed, tossing, turning or otherwise, had him reaching for his old briefcase.

"Let's get to the inventory. Once you know what you have to work with here, you'll know what you need to order and how much shelving space you can actually use."

"So you think this floor plan might work?"

The layout of the shelves his grandfather had built had served its purpose effectively for years. Changing anything about it hadn't even occurred to Erik. The old-fashioned footprint of the place was simply part of the store's personality. It always had been.

He'd thought it always would be.

He gave a mental snort, blocking his reaction to the change as irrelevant. No one knew better than he did how transient "always" could be. The store was hers now, he reminded himself yet again. She was free to do anything she wanted as long as she could turn a profit.

"It might. Probably," he conceded, because her plan would certainly better define the grocery section from the sporting goods. Using the big armoire to promote local artisans wasn't a bad idea, either.

Still, there was no denying the reluctance in his agreement. He could practically hear it himself. He also couldn't help but notice the small smile Rory immediately stifled.

It pleased her to know that her first instincts and efforts toward her new business were good ones. It didn't feel good to him, though, to know he'd deprived her of sharing that pleasure with the only person available. He was her mentor. He was supposed to be encouraging her. Showing a little enthusiasm.

Before he could tell her just how good her instincts probably were, she'd crossed her arms over the glittery designer logo on her hoodie and moved on.

"Before we start the inventory," she prefaced, "would you tell me about the customs your grandparents had here? One of the ladies I met said she hoped I'd have a farmers' market on the porch like the Sullivans did every summer. The other one said that the Harbor Market lighted walking kayak was missed in the Chimes and Lights parade last week."

She hadn't realized such an object even existed until Edie Shumway, the fortysomething community volunteer and, Rory suspected, neighborhood busybody, had explained what it was. Apparently Erik's grandfather and one of his cronies from the local lodge provided propulsion for the Christmas-light-covered kayak—which explained the two holes she'd finally noticed in the bottom of the one hanging from the ceiling in the back of the store.

"I'm going to call the lodge and see if I can get a couple of volunteers to walk it in the parade next year. I'll provide candy for them to throw to the kids, and get elf hats like Edie said they wore. But I need to know what else your grandparents did that I should do, too."

Erik hesitated.

"I'm not totally sure what you're after."

"Anything they did for holidays, or for community events. Or things they did every year that people looked forward to."

"Like the kayak and the elf hats," he concluded.

"Exactly. I want to belong here," she explained, as if that need meant as much to her as financial success. "I want us to fit in. The other day, your friend implied that this place was sort of an institution around here. If there are customs your grandparents had that their neighbors and customers looked forward to, then I'll keep them up the best I can."

"You want to maintain my grandparents' traditions?"

"If you'll tell me what they were."

Erik was not a man who impressed easily. Nor was it often that a woman caught him so off guard. Even as the businessman in him commended her approach to public relations, a certain self-protectiveness slipped into place.

Resting one hip on the counter, he crossed his arms over his chest, conscious of her honest interest as she waited for whatever he might be willing to share.

"They always gave suckers to the little kids." A few innocent memories would cost him nothing. And possibly help her bottom line. "And ice cream bars. Locals always got a free one on their birthday." His grandma had kept a calendar under the cash register with the regular custom-ers' birthdays written on it. Anniversaries were there, too.

He told her all that, ignoring an unwanted tug of nos-talgia as he began to remember traditions he'd taken for granted, then forgotten. Or noticed but overlooked.

"They always opened the week of the spring sailing re-gatta in April, so they hung nautical flags along the porch and a life preserver by the door. For the Fourth of July they hung bunting and handed out flag stickers," he said, mem-ories rushing back. He'd loved the Fourth as a kid. Lying on his back in the grass to watch the fireworks over the sound. Or better, being out on the water in a boat, watch-ing them explode overhead.

"And every fall," he continued, thinking her little boy would probably like it, too, "the porch would be full of pumpkins and hay bales and they'd serve cups of cider."

With her dark eyes intent on his, she seemed completely captivated by the small-town customs he hadn't considered in years. She also appeared totally unaware of how close she'd drawn to him as he spoke. As near as she'd come, all he'd have to do was reach out and he would know for certain if her skin felt as soft as it looked.

As his glance slid to the inviting fullness of her bottom lip, he wondered at the softness he would find there, too.

Her lips parted with a quietly drawn breath.

When he looked back up, it was to see her glance skim his mouth before her focus fell to his chest and she took a step away.

"What about Thanksgiving and Christmas?" she asked, deliberately turning to the file on the counter. "Aside from the kayak."

Forcing his attention back to her question, he stayed right where he was.

"Thanksgiving was just the fall stuff. But the day after, Gramps would string lights along all the eaves and porch posts and set up a Christmas village with a giant lighted snowman." There had been a time when he and his dad had usually helped. That was back when Thanksgiving dinner had always been here. Christmas had been at his parents' house, around the bend and in town a couple of miles. After the aircraft company his dad worked for had transferred him to San Diego a few years ago, he'd headed south for that particular holiday.

"The store was closed for the season by then, so I don't think they gave anything out. At least, not the past several years." He hadn't been around to know for sure. Seattle was only twelve miles as the crow flew, but he lived his life what felt like a world away. Unless his grandparents had needed something before they'd moved south, too, he'd given this place and the areas around it as little thought as possible. And he'd never given it as much thought as he had just now. "But a lot of people drove by to see the light display."

Whatever self-consciousness she'd felt vanished as she glanced back to him. "Where are the lights now?"

"They were sold."

"The snowman, too?"

"Everything. They had a garage sale before they moved."

For reasons he couldn't begin to explain, he wasn't at all surprised by her disappointment. What did surprise him was that he actually felt a twinge of it himself.

"Tyler would have loved to have a big snowman out there," she said. "And the village. He gets so excited when he sees Christmas decorations."

Threading her fingers through her hair, she gave him a rueful smile. "Unfortunately, I'd thought I was moving somewhere a lot smaller, so I sold everything for outside except a few strings of lights."

With the lift of her shoulder, she attempted to shrug off

what she could do nothing about now, anyway. "What else is there I should know?"

From the pensiveness in her voice, there wasn't a doubt in his mind that she was still thinking about how her little boy would have loved what his grandparents had done.

"I can't think of anything right now." Wanting to get her mind off what she couldn't do for her son, and his thoughts off her mouth, he rose from his perch. "But if I do, I'll let you know."

"One more thing," she said as he turned to his briefcase. "Everything I've heard so far tells me this will be a good place to live. But what do you think about it? The community, I mean."

Just wanting to get to work, he opened the case with the snap of its lock. "It is a good place. I grew up in town, but I was around here a lot, too. I even came back after college." Paper rustled as he pulled out a sheaf heavy enough for a doorstop. "Pax and I first went into business about a mile down the road." The stack landed on the counter. "You and your son should be fine here."

Considering that Erik had apparently lived much of his life there, it seemed to Rory that the entire area had to mean a lot to him. "Why did you leave?"

He pulled another stack of paper from his scarred briefcase. For a dozen seconds, his only response was dead silence.

"Didn't your business do well?" she prompted.

"The business did fine."

"Then if this is a good place to live and your business was doing well, why did you go?"

The defenses Erik had attempted to ignore finally slammed into place. He knew her question was entirely reasonable. It was one he'd want answered himself were he on the other end of their agreement. Yet as valid as her query was, it bumped straight into the part of his life that had led to an entirely different existence than he'd once thought he'd be living by now.

His plans had been unremarkable, really. No different from half the guys he knew: a good marriage, build boats, a couple of kids, maybe a dog. The one out of four he did have was 90 percent of his life. It was a good life, too. The rest he'd written off completely years ago.

"It has nothing to do with here."

"What did it have to do with, then?"

"Nothing you'd need to be concerned about."

"How can I be sure of that if I don't know what it is you're not telling me? If you were getting your life established here," she pointed out, "it's hard for me to imagine why you'd leave. You seem too much in command of yourself and everything around you to do that if you'd really wanted to stay. That's why your reason for leaving is important to me." She tipped her head, tried to catch his glance. "Was this place lacking something?"

She'd stated her conclusions about him more as fact than compliment. As if she saw his influence over his surroundings as basic to him as his DNA. He'd have been flattered by her impression of him, too, had it not been for how much control he'd actually given up to save the marriage that had ultimately ended anyway. He could see where she deserved something more than he'd given her, though. After insisting his business had been fine there and that she would be, too, he did feel somewhat obligated to explain why he hadn't stuck around himself.

"It didn't lack for anything," he admitted. At least, it hadn't as far as he'd been concerned. "I left because my ex-wife wanted to teach in the city for a few years before coming back to raise a family. Those few years led to a few more and she changed her mind. About coming back and about the family," he admitted, making a long story as short as possible. "When we left here, the business had barely gotten off the ground. But by the time I realized we weren't coming back, Pax and I were established in Ballard. We had a good location. We had good people working for us. So it made sense to stay there. Like I said, my leaving had nothing to do with anything around here."

Thinking he'd covered all the bases, he added two more stacks of papers to the first.

"She was a teacher?"

"Kindergarten," he said without looking up. "She was great with kids."

Her voice went soft. "You wanted children?"

A folder landed on the pile. "Let's get to this, shall we?"

He'd said as much as he was going to. He'd closed the door on all the excuses Shauna had come up with to delay having a baby, and on how he'd hung in there because he'd promised to be there for better or worse. She'd kept asking him to bear with her on the baby thing. Especially after his business took off. She'd eventually changed her mind about a baby, but only after they'd divorced and she'd remarried. He'd realized then that it wasn't that she hadn't wanted children. She just hadn't wanted his. She'd had no problem, however, keeping the house and a hefty chunk of their assets.

Frowning at his thoughts, he turned the whole stack of what he'd unloaded toward Rory. The past was just that. Past. Over. Done.

Rory saw a muscle in his jaw jerk.

The demise of his marriage evidently hadn't been his choice.

She thought that an incredibly sad thing to have in common. She'd had no choice in hers ending, either.

"I'm sorry about your wife."

"Ex."

"Ex-wife," she corrected. She spoke quietly, feeling bad for having pushed, worse for what she'd discovered. He'd once had plans to build his life in the fiercely beautiful surroundings where he'd grown up, but circumstances had forced him to move away, and move on. Just as circumstances had forced her in an entirely different direction than she would have chosen, and led her to the very place she strongly suspected he truly no longer wanted to be.

"Marriage can be complicated," she said, beginning to appreciate the roots of his restiveness. "That must be why it's never easy no matter how it ends."

The furnace kicked on with the rattle of the floor vent behind the counter. His head down, his hand on the printout, Erik slowly ruffled a corner of the pages with his thumb.

He'd heard understanding in her voice, suspected he'd see it in her fragile features were he to look up. She seemed to think they shared the same kind of pain.

He didn't want that kind of sympathy. He didn't want to poke around at what he'd finally grown so far beyond, or into what was undoubtedly fresher and more painful territory for her. And he definitely didn't want to be as curious as he couldn't seem to help being about her, or the man she'd married. She'd once spoken of her child's loss. There'd been no doubt in his mind at the time that she hurt for her son. He just hadn't considered how the boy's pain could easily compound the depth of the loss she felt herself.

Mostly, though, he didn't want her getting so close, or to get close to her. Emotionally, anyway. Physically would be just fine. Heaven knew he was aware of her in ways he had no business considering. But she didn't seem anything like many of the women he knew, those looking for a good time, no commitments involved. Not that he'd been intimate with anyone in longer than he cared to remember. He didn't want any commitments, either. Still, he'd grown tired of the games, the shallow conversations and walking away feeling little more than…empty.

He gave the top folder a nudge. "I'm sorry about yours, too," he admitted, because he didn't need to know the details to feel bad for her. "And you can have a good business here," he assured, because it was his job to help her make that happen. "We just need to get to work so we can make sure of it.

"This is my grandfather's business plan," he said, opening the folder. "Since you're new to all this, it'll be your bible. We can tweak it as we go, but to get you up and running, it'll be simpler not to deviate from it too much at first. This—" he pulled the top printout forward "—is a stock list of the groceries they kept on hand, divided by type and vendor. Dairy, produce, snacks, staples, that sort of thing.

"This printout," he said, indicating the tallest stack of paper, "is your sporting goods department. There are certain vendors you'll need to order from weeks or months in advance. Others can ship in twenty-four hours. You'll want to get their new catalogs. Gramps said they're all online, but some will mail hard copies. You'll need to establish accounts in your name with all of them."

He handed her a CD. "It's all on here for ordering and bookkeeping purposes. Look through it, list your questions and we'll go over them later. I want to get you started on the physical inventory. You need to know what you have on hand, so it's as good a way as any to get your feet wet."

The change of subject was as subtle to Rory as the slam of a door. He would share anything that would help her make a success of the business. But his personal life was now off-limits. Despite how deftly he'd closed off his past, however, he'd revealed wounds that might well have taken years to heal. Family mattered to him. His dreams had mattered. Once.

She'd give anything to know how he'd survived knowing that the woman he'd married had no longer loved him.

For her, even harder than Curt's death was the knowledge that he might not have ever loved her at all.

The deep tones of Erik's voice somehow overrode the sick sensation that inevitably came with the thought. Or maybe it was simply his no-nonsense presence that managed to keep that awful feeling at bay.

"We can start with things you can probably identify even if you've never used them. Camp stoves, lanterns, backpacking gear," he said. "Or go with something that might be more of a challenge. Your choice."

He was there to teach her what she needed to know to reopen the store, not about how to live with questions that could now never be answered. From his deliberate allusion to her lack of knowledge about certain outdoor activities, she had the feeling, too, that he intended his baiting to pull her out of her thoughts. If not for her sake, definitely for his own.

Since he had far more experience with both the store and self-survival, the least she could do was follow his lead.

"More of a challenge."

He said he wasn't surprised.

First, though, she brought them each a cup of coffee, his black, hers with milk, which they took with a section of the printouts and a notepad to the back of the store. It was there that he told her he needed to leave by two o'clock, which, thankfully, was a few minutes before she needed to leave to catch the ferry to pick up Tyler. So for the next hour, she learned to identify lures, hooks, rods, reels, creels, the difference between a bobber and a sinker and the different weights of leader—which would be important to know, he told her, if a customer came in asking for twenty-pound test. At least now she'd know they were asking for fishing line.

"If someone wants fish, wouldn't it be a whole lot more convenient to buy it from a grocery store?"

Towering beside her, he remained focused on a column of item numbers. "Might be convenient, but it wouldn't be nearly as much fun."

"I take it you've never been to Pike Place Fish Market." She focused on a page of her own. "You pick out the fish you want and the guys behind the cases toss it down the line to the scale. You get it wrapped, packed, you don't have to gut it and the show is free. That's fun enough for me."

With that even-eyed way he had of looking at her, he slanted her a tolerant glance. "You're missing the point."

"The point being?"

"Being in the great outdoors. The thrill of landing a thirty-pound salmon, or pulling an eight-pound rainbow trout from a freshwater stream."

"The guilt of taking Nemo from his mother," she muttered.

"What?"

"Never mind. I doubt that you know him."

"Please tell me that's not the approach you're going to take with your customers," he muttered back, just before his glance dropped to her mouth—which had the odd effect of shutting her up and getting her back to verifying counts.

They didn't have time to move on to the modest sections of hiking, camping or boating equipment before she noticed the time. Since she had to drive right past the marina at the end of the street, and he'd tied his floatplane there, she asked if she could give him a ride and save him the two-block walk in the misty rain.

Conscious of the time himself, he told her that would be great. She could go over the rest of the inventory on her own and call him with any questions. They'd meet again next week after she'd gone over the business plan. He also asked if he could take the drawing of her new floor plan with him.

Thinking he intended to give the layout she wanted some thought, she handed it over, along with a travel mug of coffee since he seemed to like hers. Minutes later, he'd just tossed his briefcase into the back of her fuel-efficient little car and folded his big frame into the passenger seat when her cell phone chimed.

One glance at the caller ID had her bracing herself an instant before she dropped the phone back into her bag, started the engine and backed up. The phone continued to chime as she pulled onto the wet two-lane road and headed down the rise.

Erik's glance cut from her purse to her profile.

"I'll call her back," she said. "It's Audrey. My mother-in-law. She's calling about plans for Christmas." The woman was actually returning Rory's call, something it had taken her three days to do. The conversation would be short, but it wasn't one she wanted to have with Erik in the car.

"She *was* my mother-in-law," she corrected. Technically, Rory was no longer related to the Linfields. Audrey had apparently pointed that out to Lillian Brinkley, the wife of the country club president, who had ever so thoughtfully shared it in the ladies' room with two other members of the socially connected among the mourners at Curt's funeral. Rory had been seeking a few minutes of quiet while closed in a stall at the time.

According to Audrey, via Lillian, Rory's vows with her son had been "until death do them part." They'd parted, however sadly. End of legal relationship.

As strained as her relationship with Curt's parents had always been beneath the polite manners and civility, Rory hadn't doubted the remarks at all.

"She's really only Tyler's grandmother now." That was the only part that mattered, anyway.

The wipers swiped at the heavy mist on the windshield. Through the veil of gray, the little marina came into clearer view. Erik barely noticed. For a couple of hours he'd caught glimpses of a woman whose guard with him had begun to ease, a smart, savvy woman who possessed no small amount of determination, ingenuity and a remarkable willingness to step beyond her comfort zone.

What he saw now was a woman doing her level best to mask disquiet. He'd seen her do it before, for her son's sake. Her attempts seemed to work fine on her five-year-old, but Erik recognized strain when he saw it. With her eyes on the road, he watched her take a deep breath, slowly ease it out.

Whatever was going on with Tyler's grandmother had her hands going tight on the wheel.

The heater whirred in its struggle to produce warmth, gravel crunching beneath the tires as she pulled to a stop by the wooden stairs that led to the long floating dock. In the choppy, chill water of the sound, his white Cessna Amphibian floated and yawed where he'd secured it at the end of the pier, well away from the few sport boats moored there this time of year.

He almost always felt better flying from this place than toward it.

"Thank you for your help today," she murmured, her hands now tucked at her waist, her shoulders hunched against the still-cold air. "I'll come up to speed on everything as fast as I can. I promise."

The bravado behind her smile pulled at protective instincts he'd rather ignore. He knew she wanted to belong there, in a place she'd known absolutely nothing about until last week. He knew she wanted to make a good home for her son. He suspected, too, that she could use a little reassurance on both counts.

After all, she was pretty much on her own here.

"I'll pass that on to our benefactor," he promised back, wanting to keep his purpose there in perspective. "And for what it's worth, Rory, you and your son really should do well here." He hesitated, perspective faltering. "I'd always thought it was a good place to raise a child."

He reached for the door, cold salt air blasting in as he opened it. "I'll call you next week. In the meantime, call me if you have questions." He climbed out, then ducked his head back in to retrieve his case from the backseat. "Thanks for the ride."

Rory had barely opened her mouth to tell him he was welcome before the door closed. In the space of a heartbeat she'd swallowed the words and was staring at his broad, leather-covered shoulders as he headed for the weathered stairs.

He'd made it halfway down the dock, his long stride sure and certain despite the drift and roll beneath his feet, when she finally put the car into gear. Even with the surface beneath him shifting with the unpredictable current, the man seemed as steady as a rock.

I'd always thought it was a good place to raise a child.

The admission had cost him. She felt as certain of that as she did of her gratitude for his having shared it. He knew his opinion mattered to her. She'd told him so herself. But sharing that particular thought had also demanded a hasty retreat back to the world he now lived in, back to a world so different from what he'd once wanted.

What stung, though, wasn't how anxious he'd been to retreat to the life he'd created for himself. It was the sharp, undeniable feeling that he had quite deliberately retreated from her.

Chapter Five

Rory returned the call to Curt's mother within a minute of dropping off Erik at the dock. When Audrey didn't answer, she left a message saying she was sorry she'd missed her and asking her to please call back as soon as it was convenient.

Despite two other attempts to reach her, it apparently hadn't been "convenient" for four days.

The conversation they'd had still had Rory reeling three hours later. Thanks to the distraction a text from Erik provided, however, at that particular moment she didn't have to struggle to mask the resentment, offense and indignation she wasn't about to impose on her little boy, anyway.

"Is Erik at our new house now, Mom?"

Following the beam of her headlights through the steady rain, she murmured, "Probably, honey."

"Can I help him again?"

"We'll have to see. I'm not sure why he's coming."

The text she'd received from Erik that morning hadn't given her a clue.

Am in mtgs. Need to know if you will be home around 6.

She'd texted back that she'd be there by 6:15 p.m.

His reply had been a wholly unenlightening See you then.

Since he'd indicated he'd be in meetings, she hadn't called to see what he wanted. She hadn't talked to him at all since he'd closed her out at the dock last week, even though he'd told her to call if she had any questions.

She had dozens. Between online catalogs and searches, she'd figured out the answers to most of them, though, and talked herself out of contacting him about the rest. Those she simply added to her list to ask at their next meeting. Partly because they weren't urgent. Mostly because she suspected that what she really wanted was more of the relief she'd so briefly experienced when he'd assured her that she and Tyler would be all right. The sensation hadn't lasted long enough to do much more than tease her with the hope of finding the security she hadn't truly felt in forever, but she desperately needed to feel something positive about the more personal aspects of her life—and that wasn't something she should be seeking from him at all.

There also existed the unnerving little fact that she'd just wanted to hear his voice—something she insisted she shouldn't even be thinking about, considering that she was nothing more than an obligation to him.

That glaring bit of reality mingled with her turmoil over her in-laws as she turned onto the gravel drive just past the store. Through the silvery drizzle, her headlights illuminated a black, bull-nosed pickup truck loaded with something large covered in plastic.

She'd barely pulled into the garage and gathered her

groceries from the backseat when Erik strode up and plucked the heavy sack from her arms.

"Anything else back there?" he asked.

Raindrops glistened in his dark hair, beaded on his leather jacket. His impersonal glance swept her face, his brow pinching at whatever it was he saw in her expression.

Not about to stand there trying to figure out what that something might be, she turned away. "Just one bag. I can get it."

Ignoring her, he reached into the car as Tyler raced around the back bumper and came to a screeching stop.

One strap of his green dinosaur backpack hung over his shoulder. The other dangled behind him as he looked up with a shy "Hi."

Erik straightened, looking down at the child looking up at him. "Hi yourself, sport."

Anticipation fairly danced in her little boy's hazel eyes.

As if unable to help himself, Erik smiled back and held out the bag of apples he'd snagged off the seat. "Do you want to take this?"

At Tyler's vigorous nod, he waited for the child to wrap his arms around the bag, then nudged him toward the warmth of the house. With Tyler doing double time to match Erik's long strides, Rory punched the remote to close the garage door and hurried to catch up, clutching her shoulder bag and keys.

She couldn't believe how pleased Tyler looked to see him.

"Were you on the ferry?" she asked, torn between her son's growing fascination with the man and trying to imagine why he was there.

"I took the long way around. I had a meeting in Tacoma," he told her, speaking of a town at the south end of the sound, "so I drove. Jake was on it, though. He should be right behind you."

"Jake?"

"One of our craftsmen." Rain glittered through the pool of pale yellow light that arced from the neat back porch. Even in that spare illumination, Erik could see strain in the delicate lines of her face, could hear it in her voice. "I'll explain when we get inside."

He watched her hurry ahead of him. Her head down, she unlocked the door and ushered Tyler inside, reminding him to wipe his feet on the way.

The mudroom, with its pegs for coats, cabinets for storage and the double sink his grandmother had used for repotting plants, opened into the kitchen. The warmer air held the same welcome it always had, but no longer did it smell of the pine disinfectant his grandmother had used with abandon when mopping the floors. Now lingering hints of lemon soap gave way to scents of cinnamon and orange as Rory distractedly flipped on lights and told him to set the bags anywhere.

The island of the neatly organized kitchen seemed as good a place as any. As he set the bags on the laminate surface, his glance cut to where she'd left on a lamp at the far end of the long, open space.

She'd just moved in last week, yet everything appeared to be in order. Furniture had been pushed, pulled or shoved into place. Drapes and pictures were hung. Not a box remained in sight.

Not a hint of what had once been familiar remained, either.

The walls had been bare for over a year. Having walked through that empty space a dozen times, it no longer felt strange without the chaos of floral patterns and knick-knacks his grandparents had acquired living there. But with that blank canvas redecorated, the sense he'd had the other day of no longer belonging there, of having lost a piece of himself, threatened to surface once more. He didn't doubt that it would have, too, had the unexpected ease of what she'd created not distracted him from it.

The well-defined spaces now bore his student's decidedly understated stamp. The heavy wood pieces he'd carried in were dark and substantial enough to make a man feel comfortable, but balanced by shades of ivory and taupe that felt amazingly…restful.

The rustic refectory table with its high-backed chairs held a large pewter bowl filled with glittered pinecones and cinnamon potpourri. Beyond it, the deeply cushioned sofa faced the stone fireplace at the end of the room. A long, narrow sofa table behind it held a trio of thick cream-colored candles. The two armchairs he'd brought in had been positioned to one side, a heavy end table stacked with books and a chrome lamp between them.

He turned to see that she'd left her raincoat in the mudroom. The apples and her shoulder bag had landed on the desk by the now child's-art-covered refrigerator—mostly red-and-green construction paper bells. Sinking to her heels in front of her little boy, she worked his jacket's zipper.

"You've been busy."

Oblivious to what had his attention, conscious only of his presence, Rory understated considerably.

"A little," she replied, thinking of the day she'd had and how desperately glad she was for it to be nearing its end. "I had a meeting with the probate attorney." Now that the house had sold, she'd had more paperwork to sign. "And I had to go to the bank to close the safe-deposit box, then go straighten out my medical insurance."

The good news was that she could pay the attorney's fees and increased insurance costs from the proceeds of the sale of the house. The not so good part was that both cost more than she'd expected—which meant she'd have to forgo the new sign and new shelving she'd hoped to have for her store's grand opening. And buy a considerably smaller Christmas tree than a version of the megadollar, floor-to-ceiling noble fir that had so mesmerized Tyler at his school. She'd already ruled out buying more outdoor lights to pay for the ferry rides.

Budget concerns, however, had taken a backseat to the varying degrees of anger and hurt she'd been busy stifling all afternoon. Thanks to Curt's mother.

"After I picked Tyler up from school," she continued, "we dropped off library books and went grocery shopping before we caught the ferry."

"And saw Santa ringing a bell at the store," supplied Tyler, still in Christmas mode. "Not the real Santa," he explained. "Mommy said he was a helper." He gave a sage little nod. "The real Santa has lots of helpers."

"Be tough to do all he does alone," she explained. Her little boy's zipper now freed, she rose and headed for the bags. "I hope the milk stayed cold."

Erik had never seen her in a suit and heels before. A crisp white blouse peeked from beneath the black jacket that curved at her waist and hugged the hips of her slim pencil skirt. Black tights covered the long, shapely line of her legs. As he glanced up from her spike-thin heels, he had to admit he hadn't seen her truly upset before, either. Though she definitely was, and trying hard to hide it.

"I meant you've been busy around here."

Apparently realizing the extent of her preoccupation, she met his eyes and promptly closed hers with a sigh.

"Can I have an apple?" Tyler asked.

She forced herself to brighten. "You'll ruin your appetite, sweetie." Taking his head between her hands, she kissed the top of it, hard, and tipped his face to hers. "Hang up your jacket and empty your backpack. Dinner will be ready in a few minutes."

With Tyler dragging his jacket into the mudroom, she reached into the nearest bag to unload groceries. She'd just put the milk in the fridge and grabbed two boxes of cereal when she turned on her stylish heel.

The boxes landed on the counter three feet from where Erik watched her with his hands in the pockets of his cargos. The stance pulled the sides of his jacket back from the navy pullover covering his chest and made his shoulders look broad enough to bear the weight of the world.

It seemed terribly unfair just then to be taunted by the memory of how very solid his chest had felt. Especially when she so badly wanted to be held against it. But fair hadn't been a big part of her day.

"I'm sorry." She shook her head, the neat wedge of her hair swinging. "You didn't drive all the way here to watch me put away groceries." She tried for a smile. "May I get you something? Juice? Milk?" Neither sounded very adult. "Coffee?"

He took a step toward her. "I didn't come to interrupt. I just want to drop off your shelving."

"My shelving?"

"The three units for the back of the store. I had a couple of the guys work on them with me over the weekend. With Christmas coming, they were up for the overtime. One of the units is in the back of my truck. Jake is bringing the rest."

Disbelief cut through the anxiety that sat like a knot beneath her breastbone. They'd barely discussed her layout to update the market. Though he'd said it would probably work, he hadn't even bothered to tell her whether or not he liked the idea. All she'd done was show him her sketch, explain why she wanted it and all of a sudden the shelving she'd felt certain would now have to wait had materialized. He made it happen just like that, as if he was some sort of…fairy godfather.

The man fairly leaked masculinity. As utterly male as he was and so *not* fatherly in the way he'd checked out her legs, the thought would have made her laugh had she not felt like crying.

"You made my shelves?"

"You wanted them, didn't you?"

She wanted world peace, too, but that didn't mean she expected it to happen.

She raked her fingers through her hair, wondering if they were a gift, which she couldn't accept without reimbursing him. Wondering, too, how much he'd paid his men, since it was undoubtedly more than she could afford.

"Yes. Absolutely. I'm just…" *Speechless,* she thought. "Thank you," she concluded, because she had no idea what else to say before the ring of his cell phone had him pulling the instrument from his pocket.

After two short beeps and a glance at the text, he muttered, "Jake's out front," and dropped the phone back into his pocket. "I'll be back in a few minutes. Then you can tell me what's wrong."

Certain he was referring to her less than gracious reaction, she said, "Nothing is wrong. You just caught me off guard. I never expected you to make the shelves—"

"I meant what was wrong with you when I got here."

Oh. That.

Thinking him far too astute, uncomfortable with that, too, she turned for the cereal. "It's nothing."

Moving with her, Erik stopped scant inches from her back. With Tyler just around the corner, he lowered his voice to nearly a whisper. "Lying is a bad example to set for a child."

Conscious of his warm breath moving her hair, her head still down, she lowered her voice, too. "Then how about it's nothing I can talk about in front of him?"

"That's better." Taking a step back, he indicated the door near the stairway. "I need to get into the store. Mind if I go in through the living room?"

Since he tended to do what he wanted to do anyway, she was a little surprised that he'd asked. Mostly, she was just conscious of how close his muscular body still was to hers. All she'd have to do was turn around…

She shook her head, swallowed hard. "Not at all."

"Give me half an hour. I'll be back."

Twenty minutes was actually all the time it took him and his employee to unload the sections of the three shelving units from a company vehicle and the back of Erik's truck. It wasn't long enough, however, for Erik to question why he couldn't leave well enough alone with the woman he'd spent the past few days trying not to think about at all. Not beyond her needs for the store, anyway. He'd told her to call him if she needed anything. Since she hadn't, he'd assumed she was doing fine.

Except she clearly was not. Even when he let himself back inside, greeted by the scent of something delicious, there was no mistaking the disquiet she was still trying to hide.

Tyler smiled from where he sat on the dining room side of the island. Beyond him, light glowed through the glass-paned white cabinets, revealing neat stacks and rows of plates and glasses.

"Mom's making mac and cheese. It's my favorite. You want some?"

"Mom" had shed her jacket and heels. She stood across from them in her stocking feet, stirring a pot on the stove. The cuffs of her white blouse had been folded back. A green dish towel had been tied into an apron at the waist of her skirt. Erik knew she'd heard him come in, but it was her son's innocent invitation that had her looking over her shoulder with apology in her expression.

"I told him you probably already had plans," she said,

sounding as if she fully expected his refusal and had already prepared her son for it. "But he wanted to ask anyway."

Had this been any other woman, any other child, Erik knew without a doubt that he'd have done what she obviously expected and come up with some excuse for not being able to stick around for dinner. With just the three of them, the beat of the rain against the windows and the cozy warmth of the kitchen countering the cold outside, the scenario felt entirely too domestic for him.

He wanted to know what had upset her, though. If for no reason other than to be sure it wouldn't impede her progress with the store. Or so he told himself. He also knew she wasn't going to say a word about whatever it was as long as her son was present.

Then there was the little boy himself. With Tyler looking all hopeful, he simply didn't have the heart to say no.

"Mac and cheese, huh?"

Again, the quick nod. "It's really good."

"Then I guess I'd better stay." He looked to the woman at the stove, caught the strain countering the softness of her smile. "That okay, 'Mom'?"

Her hesitation held uncertainty, and collided with something that looked suspiciously like gratitude for indulging her child. "Of course it is. Tyler?" she asked. "Let's move your place mat to the table and get another one from the sideboard for Erik."

Erik tossed his jacket across the stool next to where Tyler sat. As he did, the boy scrambled down and grabbed his pine-green place mat from the island. Intent on his mission, he laid it on the heavy oak table, then pulled a matching one from a long drawer in the printer's cabinet his mom had pushed to the wall by the stairs.

He'd just set the mat across from the other when he looked back to the man tracking his progress. "Do you want to see my boat?"

Erik hadn't a clue what had prompted the question. Seconds ago they'd been talking about food. With a shrug, he said, "Sure," and the little boy was off.

Wondering if the kid's energy ever ran low, he walked over to where Rory spooned dinner into two shallow pasta bowls.

"What can I do?" he asked.

"You've already done it," she said quietly. "He's wanted to show you that boat ever since you said you build them. After you told him about the boats outside Cornelia's office, it was nearly all he talked about." She turned, a bowl in each hand. "But if you want, set these on the table for the two of you while I slice another tomato. That would be great."

Handing them over, she slipped past him to take two salad plates from the cupboard.

"Where's yours?"

"I'm not hungry. What do you want to drink?" she asked, pointedly avoiding his scrutiny as he set the bowls on the table.

Walking toward them with his toy, Tyler announced that he wanted milk.

Rory told him she knew he did. As she set salads of tomatoes, herbs and olive oil above their place mats, she also said she knew he really wanted to show Erik his boat, but right now he needed to sit down and eat his dinner before it got cold.

She appeared as calm and unruffled to Erik as he'd always seen her with her son. Still, he recognized restlessness when faced with it. There was no mistaking the nerves that had her too keyed up to sit down herself. She seemed to be using motion as a means to keep that tension under control as she started pulling measuring cups, flour and a big wooden spoon from cabinets, cupboards and drawers.

Intimately familiar himself with the cathartic effects of

movement, specifically his usual morning run or sanding teak until his arms ached, he said nothing about her joining them. While she moved about the kitchen side of the island, he turned his attention to the boy who'd docked his little blue plastic boat on the table between them.

His fork in his fist, Tyler stabbed a noodle. "It's my Christmas boat."

It certainly was.

The miniature ski boat held a hunk of clay middeck. A peppermint-striped straw stuck up from the little blob like a mast. More clay anchored a bit of pencil-thin neon-green tinsel from bow to mast and mast to stern.

He'd rigged the tinsel on it just like the lighted boats they'd talked about in Cornelia's office.

Erik couldn't believe how deeply touched he was by the boy's innocent desire to share something of his with him. Or how humbled he felt by the innocent expectation in the child's eyes.

The silence coming from the table had Rory nearly holding her breath as she waited for Erik to acknowledge what her son had shared.

He finally picked up the toy, turned it in his big hands.

She could have hugged him when he said, "Now that is one awesome sailboat."

Tyler beamed.

Rory felt her heart squeeze.

Setting the child's handiwork back on the table, Erik pointed his fork at the bow. "Do you know what that's called?" he asked.

"The front?"

"That, too," came his easy reply. "But in nautical terms, the front of a boat is called its bow."

"What's 'not-cul'?"

"Nautical," Erik emphasized with a smile. "It means things relating to boats and sailors," he added, which led

Tyler to ask what the back was called. That led to a discussion of stern, port, starboard and keel, the latter of which his ski boat didn't have, but which Erik fashioned out of a paper napkin just so Tyler would get the idea of what one looked like.

When Rory casually mentioned that she was going to have to reheat their dinner if they didn't start eating, conversation turned to the merits of shell-shaped pasta over elbow while they cleaned their bowls. Over pudding for dessert, talk then turned back to the boat—specifically the differences between sail and motor.

Her child ate up the attention her mentor so generously bestowed while she put cranberry muffins into the oven to have with breakfast and cleared their dishes. By the time she'd finished cleaning up the kitchen and removed the muffins from the oven twenty minutes later, it was nearing Tyler's bedtime, and she didn't want to impose on Erik any further.

"It's time to put the boat away," she finally told him. "Say good-night to Erik now, okay? And go brush your teeth. I'll be up in a few minutes to tuck you in."

She'd thought he would do as she'd asked and simply say good-night. Instead, with his toy under one arm, he walked to where Erik stood by the island and wrapped his free arm around the man's thigh. "'Night, Erik," he said.

She wasn't sure who was caught more off guard by the unexpected hug—her or the man who went completely still a moment before his big hand settled on Tyler's head.

"'Night, sport," he murmured back. "Thanks for showing me your boat."

Tyler tipped back his head, gave him a smile. "You're welcome."

Her conversation with her former mother-in-law already had Rory's maternal instincts on high alert. Torn between allowing the draw her child obviously felt toward someone who would be out of their lives in a matter of months and the need to protect him from it, she took him by his little shoulders and eased him back.

"Teeth," she reminded him, and turned him around to get him headed in the right direction.

"Can I read?" he asked on his way.

"Until I get there," she called after him.

"'Kay," he called back and disappeared up the stairs.

"He's a neat kid." The admission came almost reluctantly, as if he hadn't wanted to be as impressed—or touched—as he was by a five-year-old. "I don't know how long it's been since he lost his dad, but you seem to be doing a great job with him."

It had been fourteen months that sometimes felt like mere weeks. Sometimes, strangely, as if it had been years.

"It was a year ago in October. And thank you," she offered at the compliment. "Thank you for being so nice to him, too. I'm sure you had other things to do tonight, but you just made his week. He's not around men very often," she said, compelled to explain why her son had monopolized his evening. "And he really misses his dad."

"I imagine he does." The agreement brought a frown. "What about relatives? Grandfathers? Uncles?"

She shrugged. "My parents are in Colorado." This month, anyway. Heaven only knew where they'd be this time next year. "I'm an only child. So were my parents. So that's it for my side. Curt's family is in Seattle, but his parents aren't…available." Pushing her fingers through her hair, she could practically feel the hurt building in her chest. Even with Tyler out of earshot, her voice sank at the heartlessness of what had been said. "Actually," she conceded, "they don't want anything to do with him."

He took a step closer, his brow dropping right along with his voice. "Why wouldn't they want to see their grandson?"

The need to restrain her resentment pushed hard. The

hurt pushed back. It was Erik's expression, though, the un-questioning disapproval in it, that urged her on.

"Until a few hours ago, I'd thought it was just because of me," she admitted, pride biting the dust. "I don't care about having a relationship with Curt's parents for myself. I gave up wanting their acceptance a long time ago. But they're family. Tyler's, anyway," she clarified, reminded again of how succinctly her change in status had been pointed out to Audrey's friends. "For his sake, I did want him to have a relationship with them. I wanted him to have traditions.

"Especially this time of year," she hurried on. "Curt and I barely had time to start our own and my parents never had any." None that counted, anyway. None she wanted to pass on. "But as much as anything, I'd hoped he'd have a sense of being part of more than just him and me."

This wasn't the first time she'd mentioned traditions to him. The last time he'd been there, she'd made learning those his grandparents had maintained over the years a huge priority. But discovering why she apparently lacked those bits of history herself—and, if he had to guess, the sense of belonging that came with sharing them—would have to wait. He was far more interested in what had her looking agitated enough to pace the walls.

Until a few hours ago, she'd said.

"Does this have something to do with that call from his grandmother when you dropped me off last week?"

It had everything to do with it. It also surprised her that he remembered it.

"I finally talked to her this afternoon. I already knew she didn't want me to be part of their Christmas Day," she told him, hating how she'd even let that matter to her. "But I'd hoped I could stop by for an hour or so with Tyler on Christmas Eve so he could spend some time with them. Audrey hadn't sounded thrilled with the idea when I first asked," she admitted, understating considerably, "but she'd said she'd get back to me. She called while I was on my way from the lawyer's to pick up Tyler at school."

Rory would be forever grateful that Tyler hadn't been in the car at the time. She had known for years that the senior Linfields hadn't approved of her. She'd just had no idea until that call how little they'd cared about the child their son had so dearly loved. "She and Curt's father decided it best that there be no further contact between us. She said it was just too painful for them to see me or 'the boy.'"

The hurt she felt for her son shadowed her eyes, filled her hushed voice as slights of past years could no longer be ignored.

"I should have seen this coming." She turned toward the rack of muffins cooling on the counter. Turned right back. "Nothing about this ever came up while Curt was alive, but since his death they haven't wanted to spend any time with Tyler at all." Twice she had arranged to meet them. Once for Curt's father's birthday so Tyler could give him the present he'd made for him, a collage of photos of Tyler and his dad. Once for a trip to the zoo. Both had been canceled by last-minute calls from Audrey. "I'm just glad I hadn't told him we'd be seeing them at Christmas. It's so much easier on him to not get his hopes up at all than to have him be disappointed all over again."

She turned back to the muffins, brushed a couple of crumbs from the counter into her palm, took two steps to the sink.

"What are you going to tell him if he asks about seeing them?"

"I don't know. I haven't had time to figure that out."

"Maybe they'll change their minds."

With a glance toward him, the crumbs landed on white porcelain.

"Only if you believe in hell freezing over."

The rush of water in pipes told her the child under discussion remained occupied in the upstairs bathroom. Still, her voice grew quieter as agitation had her turning away, turning back once more.

"Audrey said that they feel no bond with him." She spoke bluntly, as Audrey had. "That they never have. She said they tried while Curt was alive, for Curt's sake, but with him gone, there was no need to keep up the pretense. He's not their son's blood, so they want nothing to do with him. Apparently, they already amended their will to delete Curt's 'legal offspring.' Heaven forbid 'the boy' should get a penny of their precious money."

Caution crossed the hard angles of Erik's face.

"Not their son's blood." He repeated her words slowly, as if to make sure he hadn't misunderstood. "He's not Curt's child?"

As upset as she was, as insulted and offended as she was for her son, that caution barely registered. "Not biologically. We adopted him. We've had him since he was two days old," she explained, going with the bonds that really mattered. To her, anyway. "We didn't know until after a year of trying that Curt couldn't have children. It wasn't anything we ever discussed with anyone," she added in a rush. "We just said that the opportunity to adopt came up and we couldn't say no. After nearly four years and no other children, I'm sure his parents figured the problem was with me.

"Not that it matters," she muttered, hugging her arms around her waist. "And not that I'll ever tell them otherwise. They hadn't liked me the minute they found out I was Curt's secretary and not a lawyer myself. You could actually *see* them withdraw when they found that out. It got even worse when they found out my 'people' weren't the right pedigree. But Tyler's a *child*," she insisted, only to forget whatever else she'd been about to say when she realized all that she'd said already.

Erik looked as if he wasn't about to interrupt her. Though one dark eyebrow had arched significantly, at which detail she couldn't be sure, he was clearly waiting for her to continue.

Appalled by the scope of personal detail she'd just dumped at his feet, she closed her eyes and turned away. Rubbing her forehead, she muttered, "I cannot believe I just told you that."

His hand curved over her shoulder. The comforting weight of it barely registered before he turned her back around.

"Which part?"

"About Curt's…"

"Inability to father a child?" he asked when her voice drifted off.

She gave a nod, not at all sure how she felt having divulged something that, until moments ago, had been only between her, her husband and their fertility doctor. She felt just as uncertain about the odd sense of loss that came as Erik's hand slid away. "And about how his parents felt about me."

He didn't seem terribly interested in that. "Curt was a lawyer?"

Of all the questions he could have asked, he'd gone straight for what had been so hugely important to the Linfield family status. "Corporate. His father's a litigator."

"His mother?"

"She's into charities."

"What about brothers, sisters?"

"A brother. He took after their dad. His life is the firm and his wife is from money. She and Audrey adore each other."

"So they had a problem with you not being equal, or whatever the hell it was?"

Among other things, she thought, though she wasn't

about to get into everything she'd overheard in that bathroom stall before she'd opened the door and watched Audrey's friends go pale.

She'd said more than enough already.

"Seems so," came her embarrassed agreement.

Quick, assessing, his glance swept her face. As if looking for where the problem might lie, apparently finding
nothing in what he knew of her, utter certainty entered the
low tones of his voice.

"Then this is their loss. Not yours." Lifting his hand as
she lowered her head, he caught her chin with one finger,
tipped her head back up. "And for what it's worth, everything you've said stays right here." He brushed the back
of his finger along the curve of her cheek, only to catch
himself and still the motion scant seconds later. Drawing
back, he settled both hands on his hips. "All of it."

At the gentleness in his touch, her shoulders had risen
with her indrawn breath. They now fell with a soft "Thank
you" that had as much to do with his unexpected defense
of her as his assurance that her secrets were safe with him.

She couldn't deny how good his support felt. She was
also rather horrified by how badly she wished he would
stop looking at her as if he wanted to touch her again, and
just do it. She felt terrible for her child. Totally powerless
to give him the family he'd once had, imperfect as parts of
it had been. Knowing what she knew now, she didn't want
him around the Linfields anyway. Yet what made her ache
the most just then was what Erik had so inadvertently done.

Simply by touching her, he'd reminded her again of how
long it had been since she'd been held. There had been
brief hugs at Curt's funeral, many of them awkward, most
of them part of the blur that awful time had become. She
couldn't remember the last time she'd felt any measure of
comfort from a man's touch. She couldn't even remember
the last time she'd been in Curt's arms. Or the last time

they'd made love. She could easily recall the last kiss Curt had given her, though. She'd played it over a thousand times in her head. As rushed and preoccupied with work as he'd been in the mornings, it had been little more than his customary peck on her cheek on his way out the door.

After what she'd overheard, she couldn't think of that kiss without wondering if it hadn't been tolerance more than preoccupation underlying those absentminded good-byes. But the awful possibility that the man she'd adored had merely endured living with her had existed since the day she'd buried him.

She shoved back the memories, fought the threatening ache.

"This is so not what you signed on for, Erik." She shook her head again, tried to smile. "Thank you for listening. And for your help. And for the shelves. I still can't believe you did that. Just tell me what I owe you." She'd add it to what she owed him for the oil. "And thank you for having dinner with my son," she hurried on, because that had been huge. "I'm sure you'll think twice about sticking around for a meal in the future, but if you do happen to stay, I'll make a point of not burdening you with my baggage."

Despite her attempt to brush off the pain of what she'd shared, she looked as fragile to Erik as the thin silver chain resting below the hollow of her throat. He didn't want her thanks or her money. What he wanted was more detail, not less. He especially wanted to know what she felt about the man whose privacy she still protected. He didn't question why that mattered to him, or ask anything about Curt now. He was too busy hating how the man's family had rejected her and the child she clearly cherished.

He'd never have guessed Tyler was not biologically her own. He'd just figured the boy had come by his fairer coloring from his father.

"What I signed on for was to make sure you can make

a success of the business. I'll do what I have to do to make that happen. I'm not taking your money, Rory. The shelves are just part of the service."

He could see her protest forming even as he lifted his hand to her cheek once more. It was as apparent as her disquiet that she didn't want to feel more obligated to him than she already did. Yet that protest died as he curved his fingers beneath her jaw and touched his thumb to the corner of her mouth.

"As for your son, he doesn't need people in his life who don't appreciate him." Having made her go still, he drew his fingers toward her chin. "And you have too much else to do to waste any more energy on people who don't appreciate you, either. Got that?"

She swallowed, gave him a small nod. Other than that questionable agreement she simply stood there, looking very much as if she was afraid to move for fear that he would.

He'd been physically aware of her since the moment they'd met. Knowing she wanted his touch made that awareness tug hard. She looked very much as if she needed to be held. Needed to be kissed. It was that stark vulnerability that drew him as his hand cupped the side of her face.

Lowering his head, he brushed his lips over the soft part of her mouth.

He heard her breath catch, felt it ease out, the warmth of it trembling against his cheek.

Rory wanted to believe it was just anxiety catching up with her as she slowly leaned toward him. Longing curled through her, a subtle yearning to simply sink into the incredible gentleness in his touch and let it take away the ache in her chest.

But that ache only grew.

So did the need for him to make it go away.

She leaned closer, drawn by that need, by him. As she

did, his fingers eased through her hair, tipping her head and causing her to cling a little more tightly, to kiss him back a little more deeply.

It was kissing him back that turned the ache to something less definable. Shattering sweetness gave way to confusion. She craved the feel of this man's arms, his strength, his self-possession. She just hated how needy she felt, and how badly she wanted him to make all the hurts and the doubts go away.

The pressure of her nails pressing into her palm suddenly registered. So did the realization that all that kept them from cutting into her flesh was the fabric wadded in her fists.

Beneath his own hands, Erik felt tension tightening the slender muscles of her entire enticing body. Before he could ease back himself, she'd released her death grip on his sweater and ducked her head.

Her quiet "I'm sorry" sounded like an apology for everything from the desperation he'd felt building in her to the way she'd bunched the front of his pullover. To remove any possible wrinkle she might have left, she hurriedly smoothed the fabric with the palm of her hand.

As if suddenly conscious of her palm on his chest, or possibly the heavy beat of his heart, she jerked back her hand and stepped away.

Erik moved with her, canceling that negligible distance. There wasn't a doubt in his mind that he'd just added to the chaos of all she was struggling with. That hadn't been his intent at all. Not totally sure what his intention had been, feeling a little conflicted himself, he lifted her face to his.

"Hey. It was just a kiss," he murmured, attempting to absolve them both. Just a kiss that had done a number on his nervous system, he qualified, but her decidedly physical effect on him was beside the point. "No apology necessary. Okay?"

Unlike her unease, her nod was barely perceptible.

"I'll call you in a couple of days." Aware of how she barely met his eyes, he consciously lowered his hand. He shouldn't be touching her at all. "Can you finish the inventory by Friday afternoon?"

As segues went, he knew his was positively graceless. All he wanted at the moment, though, was to get past the awkwardness that had her protectively crossing her arms as she pulled composure into place.

"I'll have it finished."

A wisp of her shiny bangs had fallen near the corner of one eye. Instincts that still wanted physical contact with her had him starting to nudge it aside. More prudent senses had him dropping his hand an instant before the small voice coming from the top of the stairs would have had him dropping it anyway.

"I'm ready to tuck in, Mom."

She took another step away. "I'll be there in a minute," she called toward the stairs. Brushing at the taunting wisp, she looked back with an uncomfortable smile. "He has to be up early in the morning."

"Then I'll get out of your way so you can take care of him. I'll let myself out," he said, stopping her as she started for the door. "Just say good-night to him for me."

His jacket lay on the stool behind her. Reaching around her, careful not to touch, he snagged it and backed up. "Thanks for dinner," he added, and walked out the mudroom door, wondering what in the hell he thought he'd been doing when he'd reached for her in the first place.

He had no one but himself to blame for the tension that had his entire body feeling as tight as a trip wire. He was messing where he had no business going. Even if she wasn't so obviously not the sort of woman a man could have a brief, casual affair with, she was just now moving on from a loss that had affected her in ways that went far beyond anything she'd shared with him.

He couldn't even pretend to understand how she felt, or to know what she needed. Whatever it was, he couldn't give it to her anyway. He didn't know how. Even if he did, he suspected she wouldn't let him close enough to try. She didn't want to rely on anyone she didn't absolutely have to. He could appreciate that. He'd been there himself. As it was there were only a handful of people he truly trusted—and not one of them was a female he wasn't related to or who wasn't in his employ. He suspected, though, that her walls weren't nearly as thick as those he'd erected around his heart. There was no denying how vulnerable she was right now.

He wasn't about to take advantage of that, either. He also wasn't going to do anything else to potentially screw up his relationship with her as her mentor and jeopardize his agreement with Cornelia.

That was why he'd told his lovely protégée that he'd call in a couple of days instead of meeting with her. If he wasn't near her, he wouldn't be tempted to touch.

That didn't stop him from being touched by her, though. Or by the little boy who'd strung Christmas tinsel on his toy boat.

He knew Rory wanted her son to have traditions. Knowing how tight her money was, and how badly she wanted this season to be special for the child, he decided there was no reason he couldn't give them one of the traditions that had long belonged there anyway.

Chapter Six

She never should have said she'd have the inventory finished by Friday. She should have asked for another day at least. As much as she required his expertise, she'd just made it a point to accommodate Erik's schedule any way she could.

Had she been thinking, she would have realized how impossible that deadline was. But she'd been too rattled by the needs she'd felt in his arms and the kiss he'd dismissed as inconsequential to consider everything else she'd committed to do before Friday—which happened to be Tyler's last day at his current school.

Given the occasion, guilt over not having kept her word to Erik would have to wait. Her little boy was not taking this latest transition well at all.

The familiar faces and routines at Pine Ridge Day School were the last constants in the life they were leaving behind. As a child, she'd had considerable practice dealing with such separations. Her parents' nomadic lifestyle had made a new school or two every year her norm, and they'd tried to ease those transitions. But her little boy had never known that sort of instability. Even after his father had died, she'd managed to protect him from the biggest upheavals and keep his routine as consistent as possible. Until they'd had to move, anyway.

As she'd feared he would, he started missing his playmates the minute he'd fastened himself into his car seat in the back of their car and they'd pulled out from the portico.

A quick glance in her rearview mirror caught his pensive expression. He looked the way he had driving away from their old house a couple of weeks ago. Solemn and a little uncertain.

"We can always come back for a visit, Ty," she assured him, heading for the freeway and the ferry. "Just because you'll be going to a new school doesn't mean you won't ever see your old teachers or classmates again."

"They'll still be there?"

"They'll still be there," she promised. It wouldn't be like when he'd lost his dad. There wasn't that sort of finality to this parting. She needed him to understand that. "We can come back after the holiday to say hi, if you want."

"Will the tree be there, too?"

The tree. Ten feet of pine studded with a thousand white lights and draped with paper chains and cutouts of students' handprints. It graced the main building's foyer.

"The tree won't be there, honey. Everyone takes Christmas trees down after the holiday. But everything else will be the same."

"Nuh-uh," he replied, picking at the knee of his khaki uniform pants. "I won't be there anymore."

No, she thought with a sigh. He wouldn't be, and the silence that followed hinted at how very much that new change disturbed him.

Thinking the Christmas carols playing on the radio

might distract him, she turned the volume up over the hum of the heater and encouraged him to sing along.

That didn't work. Neither did any of her other attempts to console, cajole or otherwise ease away his dispirited expression.

Fighting discouragement herself, she finally conceded that she had no idea just then how to make everything better for her little boy.

That disheartening fact had just registered when her eyes widened on what should have been nothing more than the dusk-gray shapes of the road, the woods and the distant rectangle of Harbor Market & Sporting Goods.

Peering past the headlights, she heard Tyler's sudden "Oh. Wow!"

Wow, indeed.

The market stood glittery bright in the encroaching dark. Every pillar, post and eave, its roofline, even the chimney had been outlined with twinkling white lights. The bare branches of the apple tree at the near end had been wrapped in peppermint stripes of white lights and red. It was the snowman beyond it, though, that had her attention. Glowing blue-white, his top hat cocked at an angle, the tall, grinning Frosty stood as bold and impressive as the only person she knew who would have put it there.

The light on her answering machine was blinking when she finally coaxed Tyler out of the cold and into the kitchen. Hitting Play, she heard Erik's recorded voice say he was checking to see if she'd finished the inventory and ask when she'd be available to discuss the business plan. He mentioned nothing about the dazzling Christmas lights that hadn't been there when she'd left that morning.

She hit Redial. Apparently taking his cue from the number on his caller ID, he answered with an easy, "You're home."

"We just got here. Erik," she said, her tone half laugh, half hesitation, "I can't believe what you've done."

"Is that good or bad?"

"I don't know." She honestly had no idea how to weigh her son's reaction against her next electric bill.

"Does Tyler like it?" he asked while she figured it out.

"Like it?" *This is* ours, *Mom?* he'd asked, his eyes huge. "He hasn't stopped grinning since we got here. He's practically stuck to the window right now watching the icicle lights."

The sequential lights strung along the overhangs looked like dripping ice. Even the back of the house had been decorated. They'd noticed the lights wrapped around the side of the building the moment they'd driven up the rise. "He loves the snowman."

"You said he would have liked the one my grandparents had," he reminded her over the drone of what sounded like an electric saw. "My grandfather always put theirs facing the sound, but I had it put farther back on the lot, thinking Tyler could see it from the window."

Truly torn by what he'd done, she dropped her scarf on the phone desk and unbuttoned her coat. When they'd talked about his grandparents' traditions with the store, he'd seemed to see maintaining them mostly as a good approach to business. Yet her mentor's gift clearly had less to do with marketing than with the little boy pressing his nose to the glass.

She didn't want his thoughtfulness to mean so much. She just wasn't able to help it. Not with her little boy so totally captivated.

"How did you get it done so fast?"

The drone beyond him grew quieter. Nearer, voices rose, then faded.

"This close to Christmas, lighting companies are usu-

ally finished putting up decorations and are just waiting
to take them down. I called a company a client uses, told
them what I wanted, gave them the building measurements
and they did their thing."

Just like that. With one phone call, he'd managed to do
what she hadn't been able to do no matter how hard she'd
tried and totally distracted her son from his dejection.

"It's just lights, Rory."

The man had a serious gift for understatement. He'd
used the same think-no-more-of-it tone right after he'd
proved that the shell of control she fought to maintain
around her life was about as thin as paper.

It was just a kiss, he'd said.

He was only being kind when he'd reached for her. Just
as he was only being kind when he'd overlooked how she'd
practically crawled inside his shirt when she'd kissed him
back—shortly before he'd pointedly minimized the moment of comfort, security and whatever else she'd felt in
his arms.

He, on the other hand, apparently hadn't felt much of
anything at all, other than anxious to get out of there.

But this wasn't about them. Not that there *was* a them,
she insisted to herself. This was about what he'd done for
her child.

"It's more than lights, Erik. To us, anyway." He had to
know that. "And Tyler loves them." That was all that she
would let matter at the moment. For her son's sake, she
wasn't even going to panic over the electric bill. Yet. "So
thank you. From both of us."

"You're welcome. Listen," he continued over the thud
of heavy boots on metal stairs, "I have to get back to the
payroll right now, but we need to discuss your business
plan and address inventory. I have to be in Tacoma before

noon tomorrow, so let's do it over the phone. Are you okay for an eight-thirty call? That'll give us a couple of hours.

"You there?" he asked when she hesitated.

"Can we make it Sunday?"

"Sunday's not good for me."

"Actually," she began, wondering if Sunday involved the woman he'd taken out last week, "I'm not quite finished with the inventory." She hated telling him that. "I'd have finished last night, but we had to bake cookies."

With the bang of a door, the noise and conversations beyond him died.

"*Had* to?"

"I told Tyler's teacher I'd bring treats for his class today. And I'd promised him he could help. So, yes," she insisted. "I had to."

She'd also brought cookies for the staff—which meant she'd spent the past two afternoons and evenings baking and filling tins and decorating twenty-two gingerbread girls and boys. With Tyler's help, the project had taken twice as long as it might have, but she'd wanted something for him that she'd never had as a child, holiday memories of flour on noses, sugar sprinkles, the air scented with vanilla and spice. Her mom's idea of baking had been heating a muffin in the microwave.

"What about tomorrow? Will you have it finished by then?"

Juggling guilt and priorities, she rubbed the ache brewing beneath her forehead. "I told Tyler we'd get our tree tomorrow. I'm going to work in the store tonight after he goes to bed," she explained, hoping to minimize the delay to Erik's schedule. "After we get the tree decorated, I'll finish whatever I haven't done in the store. I've been working out there after he goes to sleep, but I ran out of hours in the past couple of days.

"Since Sunday isn't good for you," she hurried on, easily

able to imagine a scowl etched in his too-handsome face, "I'll be ready Monday for sure." That would also give her time to read the business plan she'd tried without much luck to study on the ferry and after Tyler had gone to bed. Having to look up terms like *gross margin, inventory turns* and *marketing mix* had also slowed her down considerably. So did being so tired her eyes blurred.

She hated the plea that entered her quiet "Okay?"

Leaning against the edge of his desk, Erik stared past the schematics on his drafting table to the black-framed photos of Merrick & Sullivan racing sloops lining the pearl-gray wall. To his left, the windows of his office, like those of the other offices lining the catwalk, overlooked the production floor a story below. Those on his right exposed the lights of other industrial buildings lining the night-darkened waterway.

The pleasure he'd felt knowing the snowman had been a hit with Tyler had rapidly faded to something far less definable.

When he'd left her place the other night, his only thoughts had been about doing what he could to make the kid's Christmas a little better, and his need for physical distance from the boy's mom. He'd wanted to focus on his work and his world and to get her out of his head for a while. He was good at that. Focusing his thoughts, his energies.

He usually was, anyway. His days were crowded enough to prevent more than a fleeting thought of her undeniably feminine shape, or the way her bottom lip curved when she smiled. But she was messing with his nights, too, driving him from his bed to pace the floor or exhaust himself with his weights before sleep would finally drive her from his mind.

He never should have kissed her. If he hadn't, he

wouldn't know the sweetness of her mouth, the feel of her satin-soft skin, how perfectly her body fit against his.

Now, frustrated on a number of levels, he pushed from his desk, jammed his fingers through his hair.

"Forget Monday," he muttered. Just because he would have preferred she keep her focus on his schedule didn't mean she could make it her priority.

In roughly two weeks she'd lost her job, sold her home and was settling into a place that hadn't even been on her radar until his amazingly generous neighbor had decided to help them both out. In between, she seemed to be doing everything she could to ease the transition for her son while dealing with the former in-laws from hell and getting a business she knew nothing about back up and running.

No way could he justify pushing her just because he wanted his obligations there over and done with.

"The store can wait for now. We'll pick up after Christmas."

Pure skepticism shaded her quiet "Seriously?"

"Seriously," he echoed. "You and Tyler have a good time picking out your tree. There's a great tree lot on Sydney Road. It's only a few miles from you. Old family operation. Tell them you bought John and Dotty Sullivan's store. I imagine they'll give you a good price on a little one."

"I'll do that. And thank you. Thank you," she repeated, sounding relieved beyond belief by the reprieve he'd offered. "But the tree can't be little. Tyler has his heart set on the tallest one we can fit into the room."

Erik's voice went flat. "The ceilings in there are nine feet high."

"Then I guess we're getting an eight-foot tree. That'll leave room for the angel."

"And you're hauling it how?"

"The only way I can," she replied, ever so reasonably. "On my car."

The thought of eight feet of freshly cut conifer atop twelve feet of rounded, lime-green Bug drew his quick frown.

"Have you ever driven with a tree strapped to your roof?"

"Not exactly. No," she finally admitted, leaving him to assume that her husband had been behind the wheel. He also figured that the guy had transported prior trees on something considerably larger than what she drove now. Or they'd had it delivered, given what she'd said about the sort of family she'd just shed.

"Then you need to know that the weight affects the way a car handles. Especially if it's windy, and we have a wind advisory for the weekend. Make sure they net it for you. It'll be easier to manage that way. And take a blanket to protect your roof. Have someone help you secure it, too. You want it tied tight so it doesn't slip."

She hadn't thought about the weather. Rain at least part of the day was a given. It was the Northwest. She didn't like wind, though. It made inclement weather that much more miserable.

"Did you *promise* Tyler you'd have it up tomorrow?"

"It was the only thing I could think of to take his mind off having to change schools."

"Did it work?"

Her little boy hadn't budged from the window. He hadn't even taken off his jacket.

"Not as well as your lights did."

The admission would have made him smile, had he not just caught the hint of defeat in her voice. Or maybe what he heard was simply fatigue.

"Tell you what." Totally sabotaging his plan to stay away, he did a quick reschedule. "I'll only be a half an hour away from you tomorrow. What time will you be at the lot?"

"About the same time you said you have to be in Tacoma."

"I'm just picking up parts from a machinist. I'll leave earlier and be at the lot about twelve-thirty." It would take an hour to pick up the tree, an hour plus to get back. That left him plenty of time to drop off the parts at the boatworks, get home, shower, change and get to yet another client's holiday party. At least this time he didn't have to pick up a date. He didn't have one.

"You don't have to do that, Erik. You've done enough," she insisted, obviously referring to the lights. "We'll manage."

"We? You mean you and Tyler?"

"We're the only we here."

"Look." He was really getting tired of the I-don't-want-to-be-obligated-to-you tone that had slipped into her voice, but he had neither the time nor the inclination to argue with her. "You've said you want this Christmas to be good for your son. I assume that means you don't want him to have memories of his mom having a meltdown because his tree fell off the car and the car behind her hit it and turned it into kindling. Or because the thing weighs a ton and she can't get it into the house. Or into the tree stand, for that matter. You have a tree stand, don't you?"

"Of course I do. And I don't have meltdowns," she replied. "Especially in front of my son."

"No. You probably don't," he conceded, not at all sure whom he was annoyed with. Her. Or himself. "You just suck it up and try to deal with everything on your own. It's fine if you want to be independent, Rory. I'm sure you have your reasons for being that way. But this isn't about creating an obligation, or you owing me if I help you. It's about Tyler. All I want to do is help with the tree. For him. Okay?"

Silence.

About the time he thought she might simply hang up, she said, "Okay. For Tyler."

"Good. I'll be at the lot tomorrow with my truck." With a glance at his watch, he winced. "Right now I've got to get to this payroll. I'll call you when I'm on my way."

He should probably apologize.

The thought crossed Erik's mind every time he noticed the wary way Rory watched him the next afternoon. He just wasn't sure exactly what he should apologize for. He hadn't said a word to her that wasn't absolutely true. And she'd definitely needed the help.

The rain came in fits and starts. The weather was cold, the temperature dropping, the wind blowing, and the tree Tyler had selected after carefully checking out the small forest under the huge canvas tent was not only the eight-foot maximum she'd given him, but rather wide. Even tied up to make it more manageable and tarped to keep it dry, with the heavy wind gusts, getting it to her place on the rounded roof of her car would have presented a definite challenge. So would the task of her and Tyler unloading the thing and carrying it into the store to get it into its heavy iron stand, a task that involved sawing off a couple of lower limbs and trimming the thick trunk to make it fit before tightening the screws into place.

Mother and son wrestling it into the house on their own would have presented its own set of frustrations. Especially since carrying it into the house through the store— which had been easier than putting it in the stand in the garage and carrying it through the mudroom—involved hoisting the stand end of the eighty-plus pounds of bushy branches, trunk and iron to his shoulder while she brought up the rear with the top end and Tyler ran ahead of them to open the door.

He said nothing about any of that, though. It wasn't necessary. The process proceeded far easier with his truck and his help, and that was all he'd wanted: to make something a little easier for her and her son—and to offset his guilt over having pushed her about the store to the point where she'd given up sleep.

"Where do you want it?" he asked.

"In the corner by the fireplace. On the towel so the stand doesn't stain the carpet."

"Can I help?" called Tyler.

"Just stay back for a minute, sport. I've got it." He told Rory, "You can let go."

Behind him, Rory stepped back as the weight lifted from her shoulder. With a quiet whoosh of branches and the thud of heavy metal on towel-covered broadloom, the stand hit the floor and the tree popped upright.

The whole room suddenly smelled like a pine forest.

Beside her, her little boy grinned. "It's really big, huh?"

Not just big. For the space, it was huge, definitely larger than what they would have wound up with had Erik not been with them. Fuller, anyway.

She'd realized within minutes of arriving at the tree lot that what she'd promised her son would have been a nightmare to manage on her own. On their own, they also would have wound up with something more in the five-foot range.

"Thank you," she said to Erik's back.

He turned, pushing his windblown hair back from his forehead.

"No problem. This is the fourth tree I've hauled this month." He wanted her to know that what he'd done wasn't a big deal. Not to him, anyway. Certainly nothing she needed to feel obligated to him for. "The one at work, a neighbor's and one of Pax's cousins'."

"Do you have a tree?" Tyler wanted to know.

"I don't usually put one up."

"How come?"

"Because I'm not home in the evenings much this time of year and I go to my folks' for Christmas."

Her little boy's brow pinched. Before he could voice whatever had him looking so concerned, Erik motioned to the single green bin sitting near the fireplace.

"You want the rest of those?" he asked her, referring to the others still stacked in the store.

She started to tell him she could bring them in herself. Thinking it wiser to accept his help than risk resurrecting the tension that had ended their phone call last night, she said, "Please," and hurried after him to help.

Tyler wanted to help, too, so she had him carry in their new two-foot-high, red-velvet-clad Santa with its price tag still attached while they brought in the bins filled with the lights and ornaments she'd need for the tree.

The only other thing she needed, other than for the heavy caution between them to ease, was to start a fire in the fireplace to take the deepening chill off the room. While Erik went back for the last bin, she crumpled newspaper under some of the kindling she and Tyler had found by a cord of split logs in the lean-to behind the garage.

Erik had barely walked back in when he shot a narrowed glance at the parka she still wore. Tyler hadn't taken his off yet, either.

"Did you turn off the heat?" he asked, hoping she hadn't gone that far in her efforts to conserve.

"I turn it down when we leave, but it's always colder when the wind blows. It just hasn't been this windy. Or this cold. It's freezing out there."

The house had always been drafty. As his grandmother had done on especially cold days, Rory had closed her heavy drapes over the big expanses of glass to insulate from the chill. With the wind that blew the rain against the windows stirring the fabric, he figured he should probably check the weather stripping.

Just not now. For now, all he'd do was make sure she had enough firewood and get out of there.

"There's plenty," she assured him when he said he'd bring some in. "Tyler and I carried a load into the mudroom this morning."

"Can we decorate now?" Tyler asked. "If you don't have a tree," he said to the man checking his watch, "you can help decorate ours. Mom said she'd show me her magic ornaments. You want to see 'em?"

"Magic ornaments?"

"Uh-huh. They're in here." With his arms still wrapped around the Santa, he bumped his little boot against a bin she'd brought in that morning. "She showed me a heart and a bell. I get to see the rest when we put them on the tree."

He looked eager and hopeful and was still running on a sugar high from the hot cider and big candy cane he'd been given at the tree lot.

"We've kept Erik long enough, honey." She hated to burst his little bubble, but with Erik frowning at the time, it seemed apparent he was anxious to go. She felt anxious for him to go now, too. Every time she met his glance she had the uncomfortable feeling he was wondering how she would ever manage there on her own. Or thinking about how much longer the project had taken than he'd probably planned. "He said he had to leave by four," she reminded him. "Remember?"

"But he doesn't have his own tree, Mom. We're s'posed to share."

They were indeed, which left Rory at a loss for a reasonable rebuttal. She didn't doubt her child's disappointment. Yet that disappointment didn't seem to be only for himself. It was as much for the man she sincerely doubted needed anything from them at all.

"I suppose I could stay a little longer," he said to Tyler,

touched by the child's concern, ignoring her. "How much do you think we can do in thirty minutes?"

"We have to put the lights on before we can do anything," she pointed out to them both. Thirty minutes would barely get them going.

"Then I guess that's where we start." He looked to where she suddenly stared back at him. "Unless you hadn't planned on doing this right now."

He had accomplished his mission: delivering the tree. It hadn't occurred to him that he'd even want to stick around and decorate the thing. Especially with Rory stuck somewhere between grateful for his help, not wanting to have needed it and uncomfortable with his presence. Her little boy's excitement with the process, though, and his innocent desire to share that experience with him held far more appeal just then than heading home to get ready for yet another evening of schmoozing and champagne. Even if he didn't leave for another half hour, he'd barely be late. He just wouldn't stop by the boatworks.

Both males expectantly waited for her reply. That Erik seemed to want to stay caught her totally off guard. Considering how he'd practically bolted out the back door the last time he'd been there and how annoyed he'd sounded with her on the phone yesterday, she'd thought for sure that he'd be on his way as soon as he'd delivered Tyler's tree.

Not about to deliberately disappoint her son, and determined to not upset the precarious equilibrium between her and her mentor, she lifted both hands in surrender. "If we're doing lights, we need a chair," was all she had to say before Tyler started pulling off his coat and Erik started heading toward the dining room table.

On his way, he pulled his cell phone from the front pocket of his jeans.

"I need to tell Pax I won't be in today," he told her, punching numbers. They didn't need the parts until Monday, but his partner would be expecting him. "Just give me a minute."

Taking her animated little boy's jacket, she slipped off her own and headed into the mudroom to hang them up. As she passed Erik, she heard his easy "Hey, buddy" before he relayed his message, told him where he was and added that he'd see him "later at the party."

Marveling at the man's social life, and unsettled to find herself wondering yet again about the woman he'd taken out last week, she walked back into the kitchen moments later to see him still on the phone.

"No, I'm not 'seriously preoccupied,'" he good-naturedly defended. "I've just been getting a tree into a stand. What are you talking about?

"You're kidding," he muttered, and headed for the dining room window.

The moment he pulled back the closed drape, she heard a soft ticking against the glass. Little was visible in the gray light beyond. Blowing rain obscured the view.

His brow furrowed. "Turn on the TV, will you?" he asked her.

"What's going on?"

"Everything's closing down," was all he said before she grabbed the TV's remote.

With Erik joining her on her left, still listening to Pax, and Tyler smashed against her right leg, hugging Santa, the three of them watched the churning weather map on the screen while the authoritative voice of the weatherman warned everyone to stay off the roads. The ticker on the bottom of the screen listed temperatures in various degrees of freezing in Seattle and surrounding areas as the voice went on about predicted accumulations of freezing rain or sleet. Another voice took over as the picture switched to a weather cam with a blurry image of a multicar pileup on I-5.

A viewer video showed the sleet-shrouded image of a ferry rocking at its landing.

"What about the Narrows Bridge?" she heard Erik ask Pax.

The furrows went deeper. "Got it. Sure. You, too, man," he concluded, and ended his call.

Sensing the adults' concern, Tyler pressed closer as he looked up. "Is this a bad thing, Mommy?"

It wasn't good. "It's okay, honey. The weather is just causing a few problems," she explained even as more personal complications dawned.

"Nothing you need to worry about, sport."

Peering around his mom, Tyler looked to the man smiling over at him.

"All you need to worry about is finding a place to put that big guy." Erik nodded to the Santa that was nearly half Tyler's size. "Then we can start on the lights."

His concerns appeased, Tyler plopped his Santa on the floor beside him. Suggesting he put the decoration somewhere a little more out of the way, Erik turned to Rory.

"Pax said they're closing the airport, bridges, ferries and freeways. The roads are all iced." His partner had gone over to their client office. The one by Cornelia's. Now he was stuck there.

Given that the bridge he himself needed to take to get back was closed and that the ferry would be down, he seemed to be stuck where he was, too.

He could usually roll with anything. He just wasn't quite sure how the woman who'd just drawn a deep breath and turned away felt about having him there for a little longer then she'd expected. She didn't say a word as she knelt beside one of the bins and popped off the lid to reveal dozens of neatly wrapped strings of lights.

"We're having soup and sandwiches for dinner," she finally said.

Lifting out two strings, she stood up, turned to face him. "Since it seems you're here for the night, you can stay in my room."

His left eyebrow arched.

Mirroring his expression, determined to prove she could hold her ground with him, Rory added, "I'll sleep with Tyler."

Chapter Seven

Rory left the door to Tyler's room halfway open and paused at the top of the stairs. Her little boy had fallen asleep within seconds of his head hitting the pillow. No surprise considering how exciting the day had been for him and how hard he'd fought to stay awake after supper to finish the tree.

From downstairs, the television's barely audible volume told her Erik had switched from *How the Grinch Stole Christmas* to the news.

She hated the ambivalence creeping back as the low tones mingled with the beat of the sleet on the roof, the muffled sound of it pinging against the upstairs windows. The thought of riding out the ice storm in a still unfamiliar house would have had her anxious on a number of levels, had it not been for Erik.

She felt safe with him there. Physically, anyway. And there wasn't a single part of her being that didn't want exactly what he had just helped her provide for Tyler: an afternoon and evening of moments he might always remember as special.

That, in a nutshell, was her problem. His presence provided as much comfort as it did disquiet. Tyler had turned to her every time he'd had a question about where an ornament should go, but it had been Erik's assistance or advice he'd sought if he couldn't get it on a branch, and his approval he'd wanted with nearly every accomplishment.

She didn't want him being so drawn to the man.

She didn't want to be so drawn to him herself.

Wishing she still had her chatty little boy as a buffer, she headed down the steps, stopping when she reached the foyer.

Erik stood with his back to her, his heavy charcoal pullover stretched across his broad shoulders, his hands casually tucked into the front pockets of his jeans as he faced the talking head on the television. The size of the blaze in the fireplace indicated that he'd added another log. Strewn around him were empty bins and ornament boxes. In front of the sofa, the large, square coffee table held a red candle in a beribboned glass hurricane and the last of the crystal icicles waiting to be hung on the brightly lit tree.

As if sensing her presence, Erik turned toward her. She immediately turned her attention to cleaning up the mess.

"Is he asleep?" he asked.

"We barely got through brushing his teeth."

"I'm surprised he made it that far." Seeing what she was doing, and how deliberately she avoided his eyes, he picked up a bin that had held the faux evergreen boughs now draped over the stone fireplace mantel, set it in the entry and put another on the coffee table for her to fill with what she collected.

"Thanks," she said quietly.

"Sure," he replied, and finally found himself faced with what he'd managed to avoid the past few hours.

It had felt strange decorating her tree. Partly because he'd never helped decorate one with a small child buzzing around his knees, partly because the feel of the room with her understated touches in it was completely different from what it had been years ago. What he'd felt most, though, was the need to get past her guardedness with him. That caution still tempered her smiles, and made him more conscious of little things like how her animation had died when she'd opened a bin to see a Christmas stocking embroidered with *Dad.* Her wariness with him wasn't anything overt. It wasn't even anything someone else might notice. Probably something even he wouldn't notice, if he hadn't known he was responsible for it.

He never should have kissed her. The thought had crossed his mind a thousand times in the past few days, usually right behind the memory of how she'd practically melted in his arms. He'd yet to forget the sweet taste of her, the perfect way she'd fit his body. It was as if the feel of her had burned itself into his brain, leaving nerves taut, distracting him even now.

He shouldn't have gotten so annoyed with her on the phone last night, either, though he was pretty sure that same sort of frustration had been at least partially to blame. But the storm wasn't letting up anytime soon, the thickening ice made escape next to impossible and he didn't want this evening to be any more difficult than it needed to be. Short of apologizing to her, which he had the feeling would only make matters worse, especially for the kiss part, he'd do his best to put her at ease with him some other way.

She'd just reached up to hang a fallen ornament high on the tree. As it had every other time she'd reached that high, the motion exposed a thin strip of pale skin between the hem of her short white turtleneck, shorter green vest and the dark denims hugging her sweetly rounded backside.

"So," he said, forcing his focus to something he wanted

to know, anyway. "What's with the 'magic' ornaments?" He nodded toward the empty shoe box on the end table. "You told Tyler all those you took out of that box appeared out of nowhere."

The tiny crystal ice skates, the little Eiffel Tower stamped *Paris, Texas,* the miniature pink-and-white cupcake—all the ornaments in her "magic" collection looked much like the other decorations sparkling on the tree. Yet she'd even handled them differently, more carefully, he supposed.

"That's because they did," she replied, lowering her arms to pack up more empty boxes. "It didn't matter where my parents and I were, every Christmas morning I'd open the door and there would be a package with a gold box tied with a red bow. Inside would be an ornament that had something to do with where we were staying. Or something I was into at the time."

"Did your parents leave them there?"

"They had no idea who sent them. There was never a return address."

"So that's why you call them magic," he concluded.

"It was more than that." Conscious of him watching her, she packed the boxes into the bin he'd set on the coffee table. "It was what I felt when one of those little packages appeared. That's what made them magic. At that moment, no matter what town we were in, with Mom and Dad mine for the day and that gift in my hands, I had the feeling that everything was right in my little world." That was the feeling she wanted Tyler to know. He deserved that. Every child did. "I wound up with fourteen of them."

"It sounds like you moved around a lot."

"We did. Mom and Dad still do." Their mailing address was their agent's. "They're musicians."

His brow furrowed. "So what's wrong with that?"

The question brought a quick frown of her own. "I didn't say anything was wrong with it."

"I didn't mean you. You said the other day that Curt's parents had a problem with you being his secretary instead of a lawyer. That things got worse when they found out your 'people,'" he repeated, making air quotes, "weren't the right pedigree. What's wrong with being a musician?"

Her instinctive defense eased with his mystified tone. Marginally.

Apparently he had her a little edgier than she'd realized.

"There wouldn't have been anything wrong with it if they'd played the violin or French horn in a symphony, but Dad plays bass guitar and Mom is a singer in a rock band. That was not the image Audrey wanted their friends to have of their son's wife." She closed the lid on the now full bin and moved to fill another. "On the rare occasion mention of my family came up, she said they were in the music industry and changed the subject."

Unlike nearly everything else she'd exposed about herself the last time Erik had been there, she'd forgotten she'd even alluded to her parents. She'd be the first to admit that their decidedly bohemian lifestyle hadn't provided the most stable environment, but it wasn't as if they'd tattooed her forehead and named her Moonbeam or Thistleweed. They were good people who just happened to be creative, extroverted free spirits who'd never figured out which of them possessed the recessive "conventional" gene each accused the other of passing on to her. They were her mom and dad. She loved them. She didn't understand them, but she loved them.

"Are they any good?"

"They're very good."

"Where do they play?"

"Sometimes they get a gig doing backup for tours," she told him, grateful for the ease of his questions as they worked. Relieved, too, that he wasn't letting her dwell on her former in-laws' biases.

Trying to appear as comfortable with their present situation as he did, she looked around for anything she'd missed. "Mostly they're on a circuit where they play small venues for a few weeks at a time."

"That had to make for an interesting childhood," he muttered, and handed her the stack of boxes from the sofa.

"I suppose it was." After adding what he'd given her to the last bin, she snapped on its lid. "I just never knew where we'd be next, or how long we would be there." *Fluid,* her mom liked to call their lives.

"But a little gold box showed up everywhere you went." The container now filled, Erik picked it up to stack with the others. "Just trying to get the rest of the story," he explained, and waited for her to move so he could carry it to the door.

She stepped aside, pretty sure he would have moved her himself if she hadn't.

With him carrying away the last bin, she scooped up a few of the crystal icicles and snowflakes still on the coffee table, started hanging them on the tree. "They showed up every year until I stopped traveling with my parents," she told him. "Mom and Dad had been playing in Seattle and I didn't want to move around anymore. I'd just turned eighteen, so I stayed here when they left for their next engagement. That was the first Christmas a package didn't show up. We finally figured out it was their booking agent's wife who'd been sending them. Apparently, he represented a few other artists who traveled with their kids and she did it for all of them."

"Nice lady." Erik came up beside her, pulled one of the icicles from her hand. "So where will your parents be this Christmas?"

"Colorado. They're booked through New Year's."

He glanced at her profile as she lifted another bit of crystal above her head to hang on a high branch. She wouldn't have family around, he realized. Not liking that thought, not questioning why, he took the icicle from her and hung it below the white angel on top. As he did, he caught the clean scent of something herbal mingling with pine. Her shampoo.

The fragrance was subtle. Its effect on him was not.

Intent on ignoring both, he took one of the snowflakes. "So what will you and Tyler do? Go to a friend's house? Have friends over?"

He was just making conversation. Rory felt certain of that. And the question seemed casual enough. It was his nearness, and the answer, that gave her pause.

"We'll just stay here. My girlfriends from Tyler's school will both be out of town."

"What about other friends?"

"Except for work and Tyler's school, I wasn't involved in much the past year. Most of the other people I socialized with were in Curt's circle. Members of the firm and their spouses," she explained. "I don't belong in that group anymore."

For a moment Erik said nothing. Beyond them, the low voice of the weatherman droned on, the fire snapped and crackled. He could let it go, move on to something less personal. His mention before of the man she'd married— his relatives, anyway—had dented the calm facade she'd worn for her son the past few hours. But her guard with him had finally slipped, and his curiosity tugged hard.

"You said Curt had a different area of practice," he reminded her, "but was he in the same firm as his father and brother?"

With a faint frown, she handed him the last two ornaments she held and turned to pick up more for herself.

"Different firms. Both firms belong to the same country club, though. It's where the guys play racquetball and squash and wine and dine their clients. For the most part," she qualified, moving back to the tree. "Curt liked us to entertain at home." He'd seemed proud of her skills as a hostess, too, she thought, only to banish the memory before others could take hold. The moment she'd seen his stocking a while ago, the old doubts had rushed back, adding a different sort of disquiet to an already challenging day.

"You lived in the same circles as his parents?"

"It's not like we saw them all the time," she replied, hearing the frown in his voice. "But the wives of some of the partners in Curt's firm were on the same committees as Audrey and her friends. The ones who don't work outside their homes, anyway. Symphony. Heart Ball. That sort of thing."

"And you?"

"I was on them, too. For a while." She'd done her best to help Curt's career any way she could. They'd been a team that way, a more intimate extension of the partnership they'd developed when he'd been her boss and she his secretary. Or so she'd thought. "Our personal friends were more into getting together for dinners, or taking the kids out for lunch after T-ball."

"What about them?"

"What do you mean?"

"Why don't you ask them over? I bet Tyler'd be up for it."

She was sure he would. It just wasn't that simple. And what Erik was asking was really quite sweet. Surprising. Unexpected. But sweet—if such a word could be applied to the six feet plus of disturbing male quietly messing with her peace of mind.

It seemed he didn't want her and her son spending Christmas Day alone.

"That's the group I don't belong to anymore." The other one, the country club set, she'd never really had. "I was part of a couple with Curt," she explained, wondering how long it had taken the man beside her to think of himself as an *I* rather than a *we* after his wife had gone. "After he died, the guys didn't have their colleague and I was a reminder to the wives of how their lives would change without their husbands. Or how their lives might not even be what they'd thought they were," she concluded, only to find herself in the one place she hadn't wanted to go.

The place where so many questions begged for answers that would never come because the only person who could provide them was no longer there.

She wasn't at all sure how their conversation had taken such a swerve.

"What part wasn't what you thought it was?"

Her eyes met his, old pain quickly masked as she glanced away.

"All of it." She gave a brave little laugh, tried to smile. "So any advice you have about how to move beyond something I can't do a thing about would be greatly appreciated. Something more immediate than a five-year plan would be nice."

Perspective. That was what she needed. Since she couldn't imagine how she'd ever have it where her marriage had been concerned, the least she could do was maintain some about the too-attractive man who'd kissed her senseless four days ago and now acted as if nothing had happened at all—which she would be eternally grateful for, if she could somehow forget it herself. He was her mentor. Granted, he was her business mentor, but maybe the more she reminded herself of his place in her life, the less she'd be affected by things like the swift concern lowering his brow. Since his place in her life was to provide advice, she might as well take advantage of his counsel.

"Do you want to be a little more specific?" he asked.

Pretty certain the tensions of the day had just caught up with her, she dropped her glance to the slender ornament between her fingers. What she wanted had nothing to do with the store. But Erik did have a certain amount of experience in this particular area. He'd lost someone who'd once been important to him, too.

"I overheard some things at Curt's funeral that I can't seem to forget. About our marriage," she explained, her voice quietly matter-of-fact. "Since he's not here for me to ask about them, I think what I really want is to know how long it will take before the answers don't matter so much."

Erik watched her blink at the ornament, her eyebrows knitted as she stared down at what she held.

She'd never told him what had happened to her husband. Neither Phil nor Cornelia had mentioned it, either. And he hadn't wanted to ask. It had seemed to him that the less he knew about her, the easier it would be to keep her pigeonholed as a project, a duty. Something with a start and end date that required nothing of him in between but a little business advice and elbow grease.

It would have helped enormously if her little boy had been a brat.

It would have helped even more had she not been trying so hard to move on.

"What happened to your husband, Rory?"

Her focus remained on the light reflecting off the crystal. "He was on his way home from work. It was late and a drunk ran a red light." The twin slashes between her eyebrows deepened. "He was dead at the scene."

The unnatural calm in her voice belied how totally her world had shattered at that moment. That same stillness held her there, motionless except for the movement of her finger along the spiral facets.

"And what had you heard that you couldn't ask him about?"

She barely blinked. "That he'd married me to spite his parents.

"It was after Curt's funeral," she added quietly. "At the reception." His parents had wanted the reception after the service at the club. She hadn't cared where it had been held, had been fine with going in whichever direction she'd been pointed. Other than Tyler, she hadn't cared about anything at all.

"I was in the restroom when some other women came in. They didn't know I was there because I overheard one of them ask how long Curt and I had been married. One of Audrey's friends told her, then said I was nothing like the women he'd usually gone out with. Refined women, she'd called them. I heard someone else say that everyone knew he'd married me just to spite his parents. Apparently, not long after Audrey heard we were dating, she started setting him up with women she thought more appropriate. The more polite consensus was that he'd married me to get her off his back."

That was the only clear memory she had of that entire day. So much of it had been a fog of hugs, sympathetic murmurings and just wanting to find the friends watching Tyler and get her son out of there.

She absently hooked the icicle she held onto the nearest branch. "He'd never told me his mother was doing that. But it could certainly explain why he'd wanted to elope." She'd thought at the time that his idea to run off to Lake Tahoe had sounded wonderfully romantic. But at barely twenty-one, what had she known?

"I'd been happy. I'd thought he was, too." Her hand fell, her voice along with it. "He'd always put in long hours. But that last year he'd put in even more. He'd been trying to make partner," she said, though she had no idea why the detail even mattered now. "After hearing those women, I couldn't help wondering if he was really away so much because of work. Or because he just didn't want to be there with me and I'd been too naive to realize it."

Her throat felt oddly tight. It had been well over a year since she'd verbalized that fear. She'd found out later that some of their friends had heard the rumors that day, too. Audrey, grieving herself, and in an apparent effort to save face for both of them, had even called her the next day to apologize for her friends' "lack of sensitivity at such a time." She had not, however, denied their conclusions.

Rory swallowed. Hard.

Feeling nearly as bewildered and betrayed as she had that awful afternoon, she pushed her fingers through her hair, trying desperately to force a smile. "I think now would be a really good time for you to give me the estimate I'm looking for. Six more months? A year? Please just don't say 'never.'"

For long seconds, Erik said nothing. He remained an arm's length away, his thoughts about the women's thoughtlessness anything but charitable, and fought the instinct to pull her into his arms.

He'd had closure when his marriage had fallen apart. He'd had answers to his questions. After he'd divorced, there had been no doubt in his mind that his marriage had been irreparably broken. The way this woman's had ended, she was left with questions that could never be answered.

Not by the man she'd married.

He seriously questioned Curt having had any ulterior motive when he'd married her. There was far too much about her to be attracted to, too much to truly care about.

Since the guy wasn't around to tell her what all those things were, he'd just have to enlighten her himself.

"Come here."

Taking her by the hand, he led her toward the wing chair by the sofa, muting the television on the way, and nudged her to the cushion. With his side to the fire, he hitched at the knees of his jeans and sat down on the heavy hassock in front of her.

Resting his forearms on his thighs, he clasped his hands loosely between them. "You want my take on this?"

Her arms crossed protectively at her waist, she murmured a soft, "Please."

"For starters," he began, being as objective as possible, "it's far more logical to conclude that he married you not to spite his parents, but *in* spite of them. You're beautiful, smart and easy to be with. For the most part," he qualified when she blinked at him in disbelief. "You can be pretty unreasonable at times," he pointed out, mostly so he wouldn't have to consider how unwillingly drawn he was to her himself. "But, trust me, he was attracted to you. He had to be." Especially if she'd showed up at the office looking the way she had the other night in that suit and heels.

"As for what those big mouths in the bathroom said about you being different," he continued, "you probably were. If he'd been going out with society types or old money or whatever his mother considered 'refined,' you'd have been a breath of fresh air."

A few years out from leaving the mobile nest of her fairly unconventional parents, there probably hadn't been an ounce of pretension about her. Even now, the polish he suspected she'd acquired in her husband's circles seemed as understated as her quiet sensuality. There was something about her that defied definition. It was almost as if her desire for permanence had forced her from her parents' artistic, nomadic lifestyle to seek stability in the urbane and conservative and she'd yet to find where she was comfortable in between. What truly impressed him, though, was the strength that pushed her past what many would see as totally daunting obstacles, along with a seemingly innate ability to nurture, to ease and to make a man feel as if every word he uttered mattered.

The way she made him feel just then.

"He might not have even realized how constrained he

felt until you came along." Thinking of the emotionally vacant relationships he personally limited himself to, he cleared his throat, glanced from the quiet way she watched him. "You went to work as his secretary. Right?"

Looking a little doubtful about his assessment, she gave a small nod. "He'd been there four years."

"So even before you came along, his career choices made it pretty clear he had a mind of his own. It sounds like he was willing to follow the family profession, but on his own terms. When he did meet you, I doubt he gave a second's thought to what his mom and dad would think. By the time he realized he wanted you in his life, their opinion might have mattered to him, but not as much as you did."

He knew for a fact that the physical pull between a man and a woman tended to lead the way where the sexes were concerned. If Curt had been half the man Erik suspected he was, he'd have had as hard a time as he was at that moment keeping his hands to himself. On the parental objection front, he couldn't imagine his own folks finding any fault with her at all.

"As for eloping," he continued, not at all sure where that last thought had come from, "he probably knew his parents wouldn't be willing participants, so it just made sense to avoid the problem. Most guys I know prefer to duck all the big wedding plans, anyway. Unless that's what his fiancée really wants," he qualified, because he'd given in on that one himself.

A bit of red glitter clung to one knee of her jeans. With the tip of her index finger, she gave it a nudge. "I didn't care about anything big, Erik. I just wanted to marry him."

He had no idea why that didn't surprise him. What did was how a while ago, he'd wanted details. Now, he did not.

"A little more insider info here," he offered, despite a stab of what felt suspiciously like envy. "Men aren't that complicated. If Curt was like most of us, if he was work-ing longer hours, he was just doing what he needed to do to get ahead in his field and provide the kind of life he wanted for his family. It's what a guy does," he said sim-ply. "Our egos tend to be tied to what we do for a living. But our work is also how we take care of the people we care about."

As if he'd just touched on something familiar, her glance lifted, then promptly fell.

She'd forgotten how often Curt had told her that he wouldn't be putting in those hours forever. That soon he'd be a partner and they could afford a bigger house, better cars, the kinds of vacations he wanted them to take. So many times he'd told her he was doing what he was doing for them.

She'd loved him for that. But she also remembered tell-ing him she couldn't imagine living in a house larger than the one they had. She'd been fine—more than fine—with everything they'd already possessed.

"I think he needed bigger and better more than I did."

"That's entirely possible." Erik watched her nudge again at the bit of sparkle, the rest of her fingers curled into her palm. "A lot of people measure their success by their acqui-sitions. Especially if the people around them do the same thing." He wouldn't be in business himself if there weren't people who wanted to own the exclusive sailing sloops he loved to build. "That doesn't mean he wasn't thinking of you. And Tyler. And don't forget, he also cared enough about what you had together to work through the…ah… baby problem you two had," he decided to call it, "and adopt that great little guy upstairs."

What she had recalled moments ago had put a micro-scopic tear in the doubts that had caused her to question nearly every memory. Erik's conclusions had just ripped that hole wide.

She had no secrets from this man, she realized. There was nothing of any import about her he didn't know and, in some inexplicable way, seem to understand. Because of that he had just reminded her of a time when she had known without a doubt that her husband loved her. Curt had been so worried about losing her, of her thinking less of him because he couldn't give her the child they'd both wanted so much. Yet the struggles, disappointments and finally the joy of Tyler had only brought them closer.

So many details of her married life had faded in the past months. So much had been lost or skewed by second-guessing and uncertainties. But that much she remembered with crystal clarity, and while the memory was a bittersweet reminder of what she had lost, it also felt mercifully…healing.

"As for the rest of it," he said quietly, "if you were happy and if he seemed happy with you and Tyler, that's all that matters." Without thinking, he reached over, traced his finger over hers. "If you'd stop looking for ways to explain what you heard, I think you'd probably know that."

The tip of his finger moved over her knuckles, his touch gentle, reassuring. His strong hand looked huge next to hers, and she wanted badly to absorb his certainty as he uncurled her fingers and rested his palm on the back of her hand.

"Do you think you can do that?" he asked.

Watching his fingers curve around hers, she gave another little nod.

"That's a start, then," he murmured.

He had no idea how far beyond a start he'd led her.

At that moment, with Erik doing nothing but holding her hand, she couldn't help but think of how Curt would have really liked this man. She could have hugged him herself for defending Curt the way he had—had she not already been wishing he would hold her.

He tipped up her chin, curved his hand to the side of her face. "Are you okay?" he asked.

Her heart gave an odd little bump. "Sure."

"You're a really lousy liar."

She had no idea what he saw in her expression. She just knew her throat felt suspiciously tight as his dark eyes narrowed on hers.

"You'll be all right, Rory. I don't know how long it will take for you," he admitted, surprising empathy in the deep tones of his voice. "It was a couple of years before I realized I was having a good time again. But you'll get better before you even realize it's happening."

Her head unconsciously moved toward his palm. The heat of his hand felt good against her cheek, warm, comforting. Grounding. At that moment, she just didn't know if it was that anchoring touch or his confident assurance that she needed most. She felt relieved by that contact. It was as if he was letting her know she wasn't as alone as she so often felt. She craved that security as much as she did his disarming gentleness when his thumb brushed the curve of her jaw and edged to the corner of her mouth.

His eyes followed the slow movement, his carved features going taut as he carried that mesmerizing motion to her bottom lip.

Her breath caught. When she felt his thumb give a little tug, her heart bumped hard against her ribs.

An instant later, his jaw tightened and his hand fell.

At his abrupt withdrawal, disappointment shot through her. Swift and unsettling. She wouldn't have pulled away, wouldn't have done a thing to stop him had he moved closer. Knowing that, embarrassingly certain he did, too, Rory rose before he could and reached for an empty mug on the end table.

"Sorry," she murmured. "I said I wouldn't do that again. Dump on you like that, I mean."

When she turned back, Erik had pushed himself to his feet.

Beyond his broad shoulders, a log broke in the fireplace, embers spraying upward. The tick of ice blowing hard against the window grew more audible with another gust of wind.

The storm added yet another layer of unease.

"I asked," he reminded her.

"That's true." Hoping to shake how he unsettled her, she tried for a smile. "So it's your fault."

She was talking about his uncanny ability to uncork her most private concerns. From the way his glance dropped to her mouth, he seemed to be thinking more of the seductive pull snaking across the six feet of tension separating them.

Or maybe it was just her own tension she felt.

"Just part of the service."

He'd only been doing his job.

The reminder had her ducking her head as she turned away. It didn't matter that she'd wanted his kiss, or how badly she'd wanted him to hold her. It didn't even matter that she didn't trust what she'd felt when she'd been in his arms before, that almost desperate need to hide in his strength.

He'd offered her his help, a little comfort and his experience. What he wasn't offering was a refuge, and she had no business thinking of him as one.

"If you don't mind, I think I'll just say good-night now," she murmured. "You're welcome to stay down here and watch TV if you want. My bedroom is the one—"

"I know where your bedroom is, Rory."

Of course he did.

"The sheets are clean and I put clean towels in the master bathroom." Her bathroom wasn't very big, but he already knew that, too. "I set out a new toothbrush for you."

"I'll figure it out," he assured her. "Is there anything you want me to do down here?"

"Just bank the fire."

The rest could wait until morning.

The telltale muscle in his jaw jerked. "Consider it banked. I'll take care of that," he said, taking the mug from her. "You go on up. I'll catch the news for a while and turn off the lights."

He obviously felt the need for a little space, too.

More than willing to give it to him, she started for the stairs.

The silence behind her and the faint ticking of ice against glass had her turning right back.

"Is the roof up there okay? It can handle the weight of the ice, can't it?"

"The roof should be fine."

She lifted her chin, turned back again.

Another step and she turned right back. "Is there anything I can get you before I go up?"

He'd barely met her eyes again before he shook his head and turned away himself. "I don't need a thing," he assured her. "Just go to bed. I'll see you in the morning."

Chapter Eight

For Rory, sleep rarely came easily. When it did, it was usually fitful, an often futile exercise where the loneliness she could sometimes mask with activity during the day reared its ugly head at night to haunt her. But she must have been asleep. Something had just wakened her, a distant, cracking sound followed by an odd, heavy silence.

With Tyler's back tucked against her, she blinked into the dark. Realizing that it shouldn't be that dark since his night-light should have been on, she reached for her robe at the foot of the twin bed.

She had no idea what time it had been when she'd heard Erik come up the stairs and close the door at the end of the hall. She'd lain there listening to the sound of water in the bathroom pipes and the heavy creak of floorboards as he'd moved around her room. When silence seemed to indicate that he'd gone to bed, she'd attempted to block further thought in that direction by listening to her son's deep, even breathing and the wind gusting like muffled cannon blasts against his bedroom wall beside her.

The ice pelting the window had no longer sounded as sharp, as if the buildup had muffled it. The only thing that had allowed her to not feel as anxious as she might have about the fury outside had been thinking about the man down the hall being so near.

Now she heard nothing at all.

There was no clock in Tyler's room. Quietly, so as not to wake her sleeping child, she pulled on her robe and found her way to the door.

The moment she opened it, she realized the electricity had gone out. The night-light in Tyler's bathroom across the hall wasn't on. Neither was the one in the outlet down by her room. The hall was as black as pitch.

She kept a flashlight in her nightstand, another in a drawer in the kitchen. Without questioning why she didn't head for her room, she edged toward the stairs, her hand sliding along the wall to guide her to the handrail.

"Rory?"

Her hand flattened over the jolt behind her breastbone. "Erik," she whispered, turning toward his hushed voice. "Where are you?"

"By your bedroom door. Where are you?"

"By the stairs," she whispered. "What was that noise?"

"It sounded like a tree went down. My guess is that it took out a power line." Across twenty feet of dark came the soft, metallic rasp of a zipper. "Do you have a flashlight up here?"

It seemed he'd just zipped up his jeans. Thinking he could well be standing there shirtless, she murmured, "The nightstand on the left. In the drawer."

She heard him move inside, and his mild oath when he bumped into something, the end of the bed, probably. Moments later, shadows bounced around the room and a flash of bright light arched low into the hall. Following that blue-white beam, he walked up to her, his undershirt and sweater in his free hand, and handed her the light.

She kept the beam angled down, the pool of it at his feet. Still, there was more than enough illumination to define every superbly sculpted muscle of his chest.

Deliberately, she moved her glance to the heavy sports watch on his wrist. "Do you know what time it is?" she asked.

"Almost seven."

It would be getting light in less than an hour.

He dropped the sweater. In two quick motions he shoved his beautifully muscled arms into his long-sleeved undershirt.

"When you did the walk-through with the building inspector, did he say anything about the generator? It should only have taken seconds for it to take over."

The generator? "He said it was set to come on for a few minutes once a week," she told him, scrambling to remember as she watched him pull his shirt over his head. "To make sure it'll be available when I really need it," she added.

Erik's dark head popped out, rearranging his already sleep-mussed hair. His jaw was shadowed, hard and angular in the dim light. "Has it been working?"

"I don't know." The gray metal generator on the slab at the back of the building hadn't been on her priority list. It hadn't been on her list at all. Until now. "I think he said it's set for either Tuesday or Wednesday mornings. We haven't been here then."

He swiped the sweater from where it had landed near her beam-lit, glittery-red toenails. Rising, his glance skimmed the length of her pale robe, only to jerk away before he met her eyes.

She'd barely realized he looked nearly as tense as he

had when she'd left him last night before he dragged the sweater over his head and tugged it down. "I'll check the transfer switch. Then I'll get a fire going.

"I just need this." He took the flashlight from her. "Give me a minute and you'll have enough light to do whatever you need to do up here. The hall light won't work, but the bathroom lights will. Did he explain how the standby works?"

A transfer switch sounded familiar. The guy who'd inspected the building a couple of weeks ago had pointed it out. It was in one of the electrical panel boxes in the basement.

"I think so. I don't remember everything he told me," she admitted. "We looked at a lot around here that day." There'd also been Tyler to calm. He hadn't liked the huge, shadowy space. "There was a lot to take in."

Something shifted in Erik's expression. She knew he'd been aware of how overwhelmed she'd been by Cornelia's intervention, and by how suddenly she'd found herself in a place she'd known nothing about at all. It stood to reason there were a few things she might have missed, or had forgotten. As it was, she could have managed on her own to start a fire to keep Tyler warm. She just had no idea what to do about the generator—which meant, right now, she couldn't fix this particular problem without him.

She didn't doubt that he knew that, too, as he followed the beam of light down the stairs, pulled on the heavy boots he'd left at the bottom and disappeared into the dark.

Feeling at a distinct disadvantage where he was concerned, and hating it, she turned in the dark herself, working her way first to Tyler's bathroom, then back to his room. She'd just started to put on the clothes she'd left on his play table last night when she heard his bedclothes rustle.

"Mom? I'm a-scared."

"It's okay, honey. I'm right here. The power went out," she explained, her voice soft, "but it'll be back on in a minute." Leaving her robe on, she found her way to him, hugged his warm little body to hers. "You don't need to be afraid." Forcing a smile into her voice, she murmured, "You know what?"

His response was the negative shake of his head against her neck.

"I have a big surprise for you."

"Is the tree all done?"

"It is. But that's not the surprise."

She felt him pull back. "Is he here?"

He. Erik.

The man's presence was not at all the news she'd hoped would get his morning off to a better start.

"He's downstairs," she told him, and felt certain he'd have scooted off the bed that very moment had he been able to see where he was going.

She'd thought to tell him her surprise was the big adventure the day might be, since making an adventure of uncertainties, for the most part, had taken his mind off his fears and insecurities before. Since Erik had unknowingly just accomplished that for her, she told him they'd just wait right where they were while his idol turned the lights back on.

Instead of electric lights, however, it was the beam of the flashlight that illuminated the hall outside the open door.

The beam swung inward, causing Tyler to bury his head in her chest at the momentary brightness and her to block the sudden flash with her hand.

"Sorry," Erik muttered. He aimed the beam at the rumpled bedding on the trundle. "It's not the switch. I'll have to wait until it's light out to see what the problem is."

The circle of light bouncing off the cerulean sheets

filled the room with shades of pale blue. Along the far wall, he watched Rory cuddling her son on the higher bed, her hair tousled, her hand slowly soothing the child's flannel-covered back as Tyler turned to smile at him.

It hit him then, as they sat huddled in the semi-dark, that all they really had was each other. He'd realized that on some level last night when he'd prodded her about where they'd spend Christmas. But seeing them now, realizing how much she'd lost and how vulnerable she could easily feel being that alone here, drove that reality home.

The troubling protectiveness he felt for her slid back into place. That same protectiveness had been there last night, protecting her from him.

He'd had no business touching her last night. All he'd wanted when he'd met them at the tree lot yesterday was to make sure she could give her little boy the Christmas she wanted for him.

All he'd wanted last night was her.

There hadn't been a trace of defense in her pretty face when he'd touched her. Nothing that even remotely suggested she would have stopped him if he'd pulled her to him. He'd known when he'd left there a few days ago that distance was his best defense against complications with her. Especially since the not-so-subtle needs she aroused in him simply by her presence had a definite tendency to sabotage objectivity where she was concerned.

Having sabotaged the distance angle himself simply by showing up, it seemed like some perverted form of justice that distance was going to be deprived him for a while.

"Do you have another flashlight up here?" Objectivity now appeared to be his only defense. And objectively, she truly needed far more help from him than a little tutoring with the store. "Something stronger than this?"

"The only other I have is just like that one. It's in the kitchen in the phone desk drawer."

"You need something brighter. I'll get one of the camp lamps from the store and bring it back for you to use up here."

She didn't know she had camp lamps. But then, she hadn't finished her inventory, either.

"We'll wait," she told him, then watched him leave them, literally, in the dark.

There was something he wasn't telling her. She would have bet her silk long underwear on that, had she not needed to wear it under her favorite gray fleece sweats to keep warm.

She couldn't believe how quickly the house had cooled. She turned the thermostat down every night, but without the furnace running at all, the temperature inside had dropped ten degrees within the hour.

She'd compensated by bundling Tyler in long johns, fleece pants, heavy socks, slippers, an undershirt, thermal shirt and sweatshirt and parking him under a blanket in front of the blaze Erik had built in the fireplace.

The only layer Erik had added was his jacket when he'd gone out a few minutes ago. He'd already left it in the mudroom when the thud of his heavy-treaded work boots announced his return.

"This is the last of the wood you brought in yesterday. I'll get more from the shed in a while."

The drapes were still closed, but the edges of the room were no longer dark. The fire had grown to throw flickering light into the room. The camp light that now occupied the dining table illuminated from that direction much like a table lamp.

Tyler smiled up at him.

"Can we turn on the tree?" he wanted to know.

He hadn't been talking to her. "We don't have electricity yet," she reminded him anyway. "Why don't you read

Frosty?" With the suggestion, she handed him his new favorite picture book. "And I'll get you something to eat."

Concern suddenly swept his little face. Dropping the book, he shoved off the blanket and headed for the wall of drape-covered windows.

"Is there a problem with the furnace, too?" she asked Erik, wondering what her little boy was up to. Wondering, too, if a problem with the furnace was what the larger male wasn't sharing. "It's oil. Not electric. Shouldn't it be working?"

Tyler pulled back the living room drapes. Dawn lightened the window, but the coating of frost and ice on the glass made it impossible to make out anything beyond it.

The logs landed with quiet thuds at the far end of the hearth. "The furnace is oil, but the fan and pump are electric. You need power to pump the oil and push out the hot air."

Great, she thought. "Oh," she said.

Tyler let go of the drape. The heavy fabric still swung slightly as he ran to the dining room window next to it and pulled back the drape there.

"How come I can't see it?" he asked.

"See what, honey?"

"The snowman. He has lights."

"Hey, Tyler. I heard your mom say she'd get your breakfast. How about we get that out of the way before we tackle anything else?"

At the obvious change of subject, Rory's glance darted to Erik. It was met with the quick shake of his head and the pinch of his brow.

He moved to her side, his voice low. "I don't think you'll want him to see it yet. Give me time to fix it first. I haven't been all the way around the building, but some of those gusts last night were pretty strong. You might want to take a look from the store porch.

"So," he continued, brushing off his hands as he walked over to the child smiling up at him. "Why don't you show me what kind of cereal we're having?"

Totally distracted by his friend's attention, Tyler dutifully led the way to the pantry while Rory grabbed a flashlight and headed for the door into the store. On the way, she could hear Erik asking questions about flakes versus puffs and Tyler answering like an expert before she closed the inner door and hurried by flashlight beam to the outer one.

She'd barely opened the store's front door and screen and crossed her arms against the freezing air when she froze herself.

The world outside had been transformed into a wonderland as disheartening as it was beautiful. In the pale twilight, the stubbles of her lawn appeared to be a blanket of clear marbles. Across the ice-glazed street, every bough on every tall pine, every branch of every winter-bare tree, every leaf on every bush had been encased in a robe of ice.

In between, the ice-coated electric line sagged heavily from pole to pole—except for where it dangled loose a few feet from the tangle of branches of an oak tree now uprooted from her yard and lying across the road, blocking it completely.

Near the entrance to her driveway, half of the maple tree that would shade it in summer lay squarely in it.

Clouds filtered the cold sunrise, but the sky to the east was lightening enough to add hints of color to the gray when she carefully edged her way over the icy boards to the end of the porch and looked toward the meadow. It was there that she saw the snowman that now rested in parts not far from the still upright and remarkably unbroken apple tree. The white chicken-wire, light-encrusted balls had separated when they'd blown over and were now frozen in place with boughs that had flown in from the grove of pines beyond.

Erik had suspected that seeing the dismembered decoration would have upset her little boy. He was right. And though what she saw distressed her, too—especially when she thought of what had to be an identical mess of toppled debris on the other side of the building—she wouldn't let herself think about how she was going to clean it all up right now. Mother Nature froze it, and she'd thaw it, too. She'd worry then about taking care of the scattered and broken boughs, branches and trees. Right now she couldn't let herself think about anything beyond going back inside, making sure the guys were fed and figuring out how to make coffee without any power.

The rest of it was just too daunting.

"Thank you," she said softly on her way past Erik the moment she walked back in.

He stood at the island, Tyler a few feet away at the silverware drawer. "No problem." He searched her face quickly, looking to see how she was taking what she had seen.

Not sure what to make of the deceptive calm she diligently maintained around her child, he turned with two boxes in his hands. "Cereal?"

"Sure." Doing her best to ignore the knot of anxiety in her stomach, she reached for bowls and bananas. "What kind are you having, Ty?"

"Both," her son announced.

"We're mixing 'em," Erik explained.

The camp light now stood on the kitchen counter. In that relative brightness, Tyler's eyes fairly danced.

The dark slash of Erik's eyebrow arched. "Is that a problem?"

For a moment she thought the suggestion must have been Erik's, until she considered that Tyler could have come up with the idea and Erik had decided to let him think the notion a good one. Looking between the two of them, she decided it could go either way. And either way, as protective as Erik had been of her son's feelings moments ago, and sensing that what that mountain of muscle really needed was to be outside and moving, she couldn't think of a thing to say but, "Of course not."

Being deprived of his usual five-mile morning run did nothing to help Erik escape the restiveness nagging like a toothache as he headed into the early morning light. The bracing air felt good, though. He didn't even mind that the ground felt like a skating rink beneath his boots. His balance on it was as sure as on a yawing sailboat—managing that shift and roll was second nature to him.

Where he was out of his element was figuring out how to stay objective about the woman inside when he'd been kept awake half the night by her scent on her sheets and thoughts of her tantalizing little body playing havoc with his own.

When he had first agreed to help her, he hadn't considered how much her education would require beyond a business plan and inventory. But the scope of his responsibility had finally hit him. It had taken both of his grandparents to maintain their store and their home. For her to make it here, she'd need to be as self-reliant as they had been.

What he also hadn't considered until a while ago was how much more difficult her tasks might be because part of her focus would almost always be on her child.

Ten minutes and another trip to the basement later, she had power—which was one less thing he needed to be concerned about before he headed back upstairs to see her by the light switch in the dining room.

"You fixed it." Relief lit her guarded smile as she pushed the toggle. "I heard the refrigerator come on. And the furnace."

From where he'd stopped in the entryway, he watched her glance up at the still dark fixture above the long table.

"That light is off circuit right now," he told her. "The only overhead light you have up here is in the kitchen. Besides the bathroom lights upstairs, you have one live outlet in each bedroom. All the appliances up here have power. So does the water heater in the basement, but the washer and dryer don't."

The minor inconveniences barely fazed her. "What was wrong with the generator?"

"The fuel line valve from the propane tank had been left in the off position. It could have been turned when the servicing company filled it, or by the inspector when he checked it out. Either way," he said, conscious of her concentration, "it would be a good idea for you to check it the next time it's filled. I'll show you later how to thaw the valve in case it ever freezes in place again. Right now there are a few things I want to show you in the basement."

"I wanna go to the basement," Tyler announced.

Rory looked to where he had just jumped to his feet. "I thought you didn't like the basement."

With a small shrug, he walked up to Erik.

"It's okay," was all Tyler said, but it was infinitely more obvious than Erik's faint smile that it was only okay because of the big guy.

With more immediate concerns to deal with, she knew she couldn't afford to worry about that growing attachment now. His new hero had the vaguely impatient look of a man on a mission as he led them down the steep stairs and across the concrete floor.

Because Tyler wanted to see what he was talking about, he scooped him up, catching his small hand to keep him from touching anything, and proceeded to describe how the transfer of the power between the generator and the grid took place and how this system had a double-pole, double-throw transfer switch gear as a safety feature because it was the best way to prevent shock or electrocution.

Her son looked fascinated by what the big man holding him so easily was saying about currents, shutoffs and sensors. And while she grasped the basics of what she needed to know, much of the detail escaped her just then. She had no problem, however, recognizing when something could be dangerous. As the day wore on, she even found herself wondering if there was any double sort of safety feature a woman could use to protect herself from the effects of a man who had the disturbing ability to draw her to him even as he pushed her away.

"I just want to know how to use a regular saw. Okay? The one you used to trim the trunk on the Christmas tree would work fine."

"It would work on the smaller branches," Erik agreed, the icy breeze carrying away the fog of his breath, "but not for those you need to cut to get something this size moved. If you're serious about this, a chain saw is faster and a lot less work."

Concern clearly battled her determination.

"If I'm using that, I won't be able to hear Tyler if he needs me. And I can't have him right with me, because I don't want him anywhere near that thing."

"I'll show you how to use the handsaw." He didn't hesitate to offer the assurance, aware himself of the child on the porch, breaking ice off the fir boughs she'd collected for a wreath. "But you should know how to use this, too. We'll be where you can keep an eye on him."

He watched Rory look from the wicked-looking chain saw blade to the long tangle of ice-coated limbs that had split away from the maple on the far side of the drive. A slash of exposed, raw wood on the heavy trunk mirrored the ragged tear on the thick branch where it had fallen from the tree's side.

He'd already cut up the branch that had fallen atop it with the now-silent saw he'd borrowed from her neighbor. He'd heard the saw's droning buzz when he'd come outside a couple of hours ago to fix Frosty and put a little physical distance between himself and his charge. Being near her in the confines of the house had left him too edgy, too restless. Outdoors, he at least had the buffer of space.

His glance slid from her burgundy fleece headband and jacket to the hem of her jeans. Since she'd kept herself occupied away from him for the better part of the morning, he suspected she'd been after a little distance, too.

Apparently having reassessed her options, and with her immediate concern addressed, she anchored the toe of her black boot in the loop of the saw's handle. "So," she gamely began, "I start it by putting my foot here?" she asked. "And pulling on this?"

Catching her arm as she reached for the starter pull, he turned her in the churned-up gravel to face him. "You start by putting on these."

He tugged off his heavy leather gloves, then slipped the clear safety goggles Ed Shumway also loaned him from around his neck.

Teaching her how to use a saw hadn't been on the agenda he'd outlined for himself that morning, but she'd wanted to know how to use one to clear the property after it thawed. Since he didn't much care for the thought of her outside sawing and hauling limbs by herself, he'd already planned to have the mess cleared for her. This wasn't the only storm she'd likely ever encounter, though. And he wouldn't be around once she was on her financial feet. If she was going to be self-sufficient, it was his job to give her the tools she'd need to make that happen.

Reaching toward her, he looped the goggles' wide elastic strap around the back of her head. Not giving her time to take off her gloves to adjust the bright orange band, he did it himself and settled the clear skilike goggles in place.

"Keep in mind that the barter system still works for a few things around here, too," he informed her, tucking back a strand of the dark hair he'd dislodged from the fleece covering her ears. "Someone should be willing to take care of all these trees for you in exchange for a load or two they can sell or use for firewood."

Far too conscious of the softness of her skin, the silk of her hair, he deliberately dropped his hand.

Pulling his gloves from where he'd tucked them under his arm, he jerked them back on and nodded to the saw. "Now you can start it."

Rory braced herself. Not so much for what she was about to do, but because everything about this man had her feeling so off balance.

He'd given her his jacket a while ago. He stood there now in his heavy charcoal pullover and jeans, seeming totally unfazed by the cold and the almost familiar ease with which he'd touched her.

"Hold the blade straighter," he called over the din of the idling motor. With his broad chest pressed to her back, he reached his arms around her, placed his gloved hands over hers and adjusted her angle.

"Ready?" he asked, his breath warm through the soft knit covering her ear.

Conscious of his body enclosing hers, she gave a tense little nod.

She wasn't sure which disconcerted her more, the thirteen pounds of suddenly screaming machine, or the man surrounding her, making sure she didn't hurt herself with it. With the blade engaged, metal teeth spinning, the chain bit ice. A quick spray of what looked like snow and wood chips flew.

"Keep your grip steady." He spoke near her cheek now, his body still at her back as he eased his hands to her shoulders. "You need to keep it from bucking back if you hit a knot. Keep it under control."

Control, she thought. She hadn't felt "in control" in ages.

"Like this?" she called, handles in a death grip, her eyes glued to the blade sinking into the wood.

"Just like that," he called back and, just like that, the weight of the free end of the limb cracked it downward and the blade went through.

A second of disbelief was replaced with a grin as she swung toward him.

"Don't!" His hand shot forward, the side of his face bumping the corner of her goggles an instant before his hand caught hers to hold the saw in place. Bent against her, he'd turned his head to hers, his lips inches from the startled part of her own.

"The brake," he said. With a small movement of his hand, the throttle dropped back to idle. "You need to set it as soon as you finish your cut. It's safer that way."

She realized now why he'd stayed behind her. Had she swung around, she could have caught him with the blade in his thigh.

Taking the idling machine from her, he shut off the motor, set the saw on the ground.

In the sudden silence, she could hear her heart hammering in her ears. Shaken from the start he'd given her, horrified by what she could have done to him, she dropped her glance to the short placket on his pullover as he rose and turned to her.

"Erik, I'm so sorry."

His forehead furrowed as he pulled her hand from her mouth and lifted the orange band at her temples. Removing the goggles, he looped them over the fabric covering his forearm.

"Hey. It's okay." Hating how he'd killed her quick smile, he touched his gloved finger to her high cheekbone. It was there that the goggles would have bumped. "We hadn't gotten to that part." Another second and they would have, he thought, searching her pale features. He just hadn't expected her to get excited about felling a limb. "Next time you'll remember."

He couldn't feel the smoothness of her skin through the thick suede. He could imagine it, though. Just as he could too easily imagine so many other things he knew he shouldn't be thinking about her.

Detachment wasn't an option at the moment. Not with her looking so frightened by what she could have done. "Right?"

Beneath his hand, he felt her faint nod. What he noticed most, though, was how her head turned toward his hand, as if somewhere in her subconscious she craved that unfettered contact, too.

She'd done the same thing last night, right about the time he'd been thinking about reacquainting himself with the feel of her mouth. Heaven knew how tempted he'd been to do just that. But he acknowledged now what he hadn't then. It hadn't just been complications with her he wanted to avoid. He hadn't wanted her thinking of anyone but him when he kissed her. And last night had been far more about easing the doubts that had haunted her for so long than whatever it was that kept him from caring about how easy she was to touch.

Rory watched his glance shift over her face. She had no idea what he was thinking, what it was vying with the concern so evident there, but from the way his eyes narrowed on her cheek, he seemed to be looking for a bruise.

"It didn't hurt," she told him, praying she hadn't caused him one as she unconsciously lifted her hand to his temple.

"I don't see a mark," he murmured. "But that doesn't mean you won't have a bruise later. You should get some ice on it." He gave her an encouraging smile. "There's plenty of it."

She felt far too concerned to smile back. "I don't see one on you, either," she told him, tipping her head to get a better look. "Not yet, anyway."

Erik's smile faded. He couldn't remember the last time a woman had touched him simply to make sure he was okay. There was caring in that touch, a hint of worry, a little gentleness. As complex as it seemed, it was really such a simple thing. Something basic. Yet her unveiled concern pulled hard at something deep inside him. Something he hadn't been sure still existed, and which would have felt decidedly threatening had he had time to consider what it was.

"Mom? Come help me?"

At her son's request, Rory's hand fell. Only now aware of how she'd reached to be sure Erik was all right, and of how they must look standing there checking each other out, her glance darted to where Tyler stood by a stack of pine on the porch.

He wanted help with the wreath.

Taking a step back, she called that she'd be right there.

Erik met her lingering disquiet.

"Stop worrying. You're quick. You'll get the hang of this," he insisted. "We'll give it another try later. In the meantime, you did fine. Really."

"Except for the part where I nearly disabled you," she muttered, half under her breath.

"I had you covered, Rory. You were a long way from anything like that."

A split second was hardly a long way. She'd have

pointed that out had his assessment of her capabilities not just registered. It was like last night, she thought, when he'd talked her through the doubts and turmoil of the past year. It seemed he didn't want her doubting her abilities, or herself, about anything.

He clearly expected her to challenge his last claim. The quick part, probably. She couldn't. Last night he had called her beautiful, smart and stubborn. The stubbornness she would concede. That he thought her beautiful and smart still left her a little stunned. But what mattered to her most was that for him to feel so certain about her meant he might actually believe in her himself.

Until that moment, she hadn't realized how badly she wanted that sort of faith—that trust—from him.

"I'm going to go help Tyler now."

His eyes narrowed on hers. "You're good, then?"

He wanted to know if she believed what he'd said.

I had you covered, Rory.

"I'm good," she said, and with him already turning to his task, she headed for the porch to rescue the boughs and her rosy-cheeked child.

He had her back. He wasn't going to let anything bad happen as long as he was there.

He couldn't begin to know how much that assurance mattered to her.

Chapter Nine

Erik had told her not to worry.

Rory wasn't sure she knew how to do that. The unwelcomed trait had become second nature. Yet what concerned her far more than her lack of skill with gas-fueled equipment was how she found herself wishing Erik's solid presence could be part of the community that encouraged her with its potential.

Ed Shumway, the neighbor who'd loaned Erik the saw, was married to Edie, the loquacious neighbor who'd first welcomed her to the neighborhood. He had come to repay Erik for his assist moving a limb from his garage that morning. Having heard on the news that it would be at least two days before crews could get in to restore power, he'd brought his bigger saw to help him clear the uprooted oak from the road that was their main access to town.

Even for her neighbors who didn't have access to TV news, word traveled fast by cell phone. Crystal Murphy, her laugh infectious and her carrot-red hair clashing wildly with her purple earmuffs, brought her four-year-old son to play with Tyler while her husband, Tony the roofer, joined the men. Her mom was at their house a quarter of a mile away with their two-year-old. They didn't have power but that seemed just fine with them. They had a woodstove and kerosene lamps and Crystal confessed to liking the throwback lifestyle. She turned out to be the candle maker Edie had told Rory about.

Jeremy Ott came for the same reason as Tony and Ed. Talia, his wife, who taught riding lessons at the stables a mile farther up, had braved the cold with her five-year-old twins because Edie had mentioned that Rory had a son their age.

Edie herself showed up with her two children, twelve and six, and a half gallon of milk. With all the children, hot cocoa went fast.

Even with all the activity, Rory found her attention straying to the man who stood just a little taller than the rest.

It was nearing four o'clock when the women stepped out onto the porch to see how much longer the men would be. The kids were warming up in front of the TV, under Edie's preteen's supervision, and it would be dark soon. There were suppers to prepare.

Rory doubted that Erik had taken a real break since lunch. All she'd noticed him stop for was to stretch his back or absently rub his neck before tossing aside another log or attacking another limb on the downed oak.

She was standing by the railing between Crystal and Edie when he made a V of his arm and hitched his shoulder before putting his back into hefting another chunk of tree. He and Tony were hauling cut sections of limbs to the side of the road while the other two men continued decreasing the size of what had blocked it.

Seeing who had Rory's attention, Edie flipped her braid

over her shoulder and tipped her dark blond head toward her. A navy Seattle Seahawks headband warmed her ears.

"He's an attractive man, isn't he?"

"Who?" asked Talia, leaning past Crystal.

"Erik," the older woman replied.

Rory gave a noncommittal shrug. "I suppose." *If you like the tall, dark, unattainable type,* she thought. Suspecting her neighbor was fishing, she glanced to Edie's nearly empty mug. "More coffee?"

"I'm good. Thanks." The loquacious woman with the too-keen radar kept her focus on the men methodically dismantling the tree.

"He and his business partner have done quite well for themselves, you know."

"I'd say they've done extremely well," Crystal emphasized. "Pax—his business partner," she explained helpfully to Rory, "is from here, too. I've heard they're both millionaires."

"I've met Pax. Nice guy," Rory admitted. What she didn't mention was that she already knew that Erik had means—that he even had friends among the very rich and famous.

She had been surrounded by the well-to-do, and those intent on joining their ranks, from the moment she'd married until she'd moved mere weeks ago. The understated way Erik used his wealth and the way he didn't balk at getting his own hands dirty just made her forget that at times.

Edie gave her a curious glance. "Would you mind a personal question? I didn't want to ask when I first met you," she explained. "I mean, I did, but it didn't seem appropriate at the time."

Rory smiled, a little surprised by the request for permission. "Ask what?"

"How long you've been widowed."

"A year and two months."

"That's too bad."

"It really is," Crystal agreed. "I'm sorry, Rory."

"That has to be so hard." Talia placed her gloved hand over her heart. "I don't know what I'd do without Jeremy."

Edie shook her head. "I meant it's too bad it hasn't been longer. I was just thinking how nice it would be if you two hit it off. I'm sorry for your loss, too," she sincerely assured Rory. "But I imagine you need a little more time before you start thinking in that direction."

"I don't know about that," Talia piped in. "My uncle remarried six months after my aunt passed."

"I think men do that because they don't know how to take care of themselves," claimed Edie.

Crystal frowned. "I thought that the men who married fast like that were the ones who'd had good marriages, so they weren't afraid to jump back in."

"If that's true," Talia said, leaping ahead, "then the opposite could explain why Erik hasn't remarried. I've never heard what happened with him and…what was her name?"

"Shauna," the other two women simultaneously supplied.

"Right. She wasn't from here," she explained to Rory. "They met one summer and she moved here after they married, but they left for Seattle after a year or so. My point, though," she claimed, getting to it, "is that maybe his experience has put him off women."

"Oh, I wouldn't say he's off women," Rory admitted. "We've had a couple of meetings where he had to leave because he had a date."

Talia shrugged. "Well, there goes that theory."

"That doesn't mean he's not gun-shy," Crystal supplied supportively.

"True. But Rory's not looking right now," Edie reminded them. "Anyway, I was just thinking it would be nice if Erik would come back. I can't imagine that he ever would," she insisted, certainty in her conclusion. "Not with his business so well established over in Seattle. But he still seems to fit in so perfectly here."

The woman who'd brought up the subject of her potential availability had just as abruptly concluded it. Relieved to have escaped matchmaking efforts, for a while at least, and not sure how she felt having reminded herself of her mentor's social life, Rory found herself silently agreeing with her well-intentioned neighbor.

Erik did seem to fit in. But then, he'd been raised there. Without letting herself wonder why, she'd also wondered if there was ever anything about this place that he missed. Or if his emotional barriers kept him from even noticing.

It hadn't sounded to Rory as if the women knew the other, more personal reasons why he wouldn't be coming back. The dreams he'd buried there. Still, Edie was right. Everything Erik cared about was in Seattle.

And everything she now cared about was here, she thought, and went back to looking a little concerned about him again.

"Why didn't you stop?"

"Because we were almost finished."

"You were out there another two hours, Erik."

"That's close enough to almost. I'll be fine after a hot shower. How did it go with the neighbors?"

The man was hopeless.

"It was nice." You escaped the part where Edie wanted to make us a couple, she thought, but other than that... "Crystal is going to bring me samples of her candles to see if I'd be interested in selling them. And Talia's twins go to the school I enrolled Tyler in. We're going to carpool."

She frowned at the way he cupped his neck as he sat down at the island. He'd said he'd be fine, though. The man had a scar as wide as Tyler's tired smile on the inside of his forearm. It was visible now where he'd pushed up his sleeves. He knew how much discomfort he could handle.

"What are you grinning about, bud?" he asked, tired but smiling himself.

Tyler took a deep breath, gave a decisive nod. "This was the best day ever."

"Wow. That's pretty cool." Forearms resting on either side of his heaped and steaming bowl of stew, he looked over at the little guy who'd mimicked his position. "What made it so good?"

Tyler looked over his shoulder at the white lights softly illuminating the room behind them. The fire in the stone fireplace crackled and glowed.

"My tree. And the ice on everything. And my new friends." He wrinkled his little brow, thinking. "And Mom, 'cause I got cocoa two times. And you."

"Me?" Erik exhaled a little laugh. "What did I do?"

"Well," he began, pondering. "You fixed things. And you made Mom laugh."

Erik's glance cut to where she sat at the end of the island, back to the child between them. "I did?"

"Uh-huh," Tyler insisted, his nod vigorous. "When you dropped your coat on her."

Though Erik looked a little puzzled, Rory knew exactly what Tyler was talking about. The two of them had just gathered boughs for the wreath. She'd been sorting them on the porch, her head bent over their project, when Erik had walked up behind her and asked if she'd take his jacket. With her back to him and him in work mode, she'd no sooner said she'd be glad to when he'd unceremoniously dropped it over her head.

He'd meant it to land on her shoulders. But she'd looked up just then. Heavy and huge on her, she'd practically disappeared under the soft black leather.

She'd already been smiling at what he'd done and gone

still at the unexpectedness of it when he'd lifted the back of the collar and peeked around at her.

"You okay in there?" he'd asked, and the smile in his eyes had turned her smile into something that had sounded very much like a giggle.

She hadn't giggled since she was sixteen.

Erik apparently remembered now, too.

Looking over at Tyler, he gave his little buddy a knowing nod. He remembered the bright sound of that laugh, of hearing a hint of lightness in it he suspected she hadn't felt in a very long time.

"She needs to do that more often," he decided, and after arching his eyebrow at her, suggested Tyler finish his stew before he went after it himself.

Rory glanced away, stabbed a piece of carrot. She wished he wouldn't do that—arch his eyebrow at her that way. Something about the expression seemed teasing, playful and challenging all at once. Except for the challenging part, it also tended to disarm her and she'd been having a hard enough time remembering why she needed to keep her emotional guard in place with him pretty much since he'd strong-armed her into trying Ed's saw. Or maybe the problem had started last night, when she'd unloaded on him. Again. Or yesterday, when he'd sided with Tyler about the size of the tree.

There were reasons. Compelling ones, she was sure. She just couldn't remember them as she gave him her most charming smile and told him there was more stew if he wanted it.

He had seconds, told her it was great, then finished the bit in the pot before she carried his and Tyler's bowls to the sink.

"What Tyler said about it being a good day," he murmured, handing her his milk glass when she came back for it. "It was." He kept his focus on the glass and her hand, his tone thoughtful, as if he was a little surprised by that perception. Or perhaps by the admission.

"Now," he continued, moving past whatever had prompted it, "if you don't mind, I'm going to get that shower. You wouldn't have a spare razor, would you?"

She told him she did. A small package of them was in the drawer below where she'd left the toothbrush on the counter for him last night. She didn't bother telling him they were hot pink.

It did Rory's heart good to know her little boy had had such a good time that day. It did something less definable to it to know Erik had somehow appreciated it, too. Something that fed an unfamiliar bubble of hope that common sense told her was best to ignore. But with Tyler pretty much worn out and in need of a bath, she gave it no further thought. By the time she'd helped him with his bath and his prayers, it was all he could do to keep his eyes open.

Erik seemed to have had the same problem. When she finally came back down the dimly lit stairs, the fire was nearly out and Erik had fallen asleep in front of the television.

He lay stretched out on the sofa in his jeans and pullover, one leg angled with his bare foot on the cushion, the other foot on the floor. With his dark head propped on the curved arm of the sofa, one arm thrown over his eyes, his other hand splayed on his stomach, it looked as if he'd intended to catch something more entertaining than the weather report before turning in for the night.

The volume on the detective series had been muted, though.

They hadn't talked about it, but there had been no question that he would stay again that night. The negligible melt that afternoon had started refreezing the lower the sun had sunk and, last they'd heard, it was taking forever to get anywhere on the roads. Those that were open, anyway.

That was why he'd followed the Otts home in his monster of a truck, because they'd made the drive on balding tires, and dropped off the Shumways since it was dark by then and they'd all walked earlier.

His breathing was deep and even as she picked up the television's remote and turned off the set.

As exhausted as she suspected he was, she didn't want to wake him. She shouldn't stand there thinking about what a beautiful man he was, either. Or how kind and generous he truly seemed to be even when he didn't want her getting too close. There was something terribly intimate about watching him sleep. Something that might almost have felt intrusive had she allowed herself to remain there any longer.

She lifted the soft throw blanket from the arm of the chair, moved back to lift it over him. Smiling a little at his freshly shaved face, she eased the covering over him. When he didn't move, she let out the breath she hadn't even realized she'd been holding and carefully lifted her hand to his head.

Her fingers had just skimmed the barely damp hair he'd combed back from his forehead when she went still. She hadn't been thinking. She'd simply started to do what she always did with Tyler when she tucked him in and brushed back his hair. The gesture was one of simple affection, of taking care.

As oblivious as he remained to her presence, she let her fingers slip over the soft strands, then curled her fingers into her palm as she stepped away and quietly headed for Tyler's room. Since she felt pretty certain Erik would wake up at some point and head for bed himself, she left the tree lights on so he'd be able to see.

It was to that soft light that he awoke a little after midnight, along with a cramp in his neck and an ache in his back that, he realized an hour later, made sleep impossible.

* * *

Rory heard the faint tap on the door, blinked into the shadows. It had been raining for a while now. She'd lain there, listening to the steady sound of it, imagining the drops taking all the ice away, before the new additions to her usual anxieties about what she'd taken on ruined the little exercise. Everything always felt so much more overwhelming alone at night. With Erik there, she'd at least been able to manage the more restful thoughts for a while.

Hearing the tap again, she slipped from the trundle by the night-light she'd moved to the only working outlet in the room and opened the door.

Her glance collided with Erik's solid, shadowed and bare chest. Down the hall, light from her bathroom filtered through her bedroom door, too dim to reveal more than curves and angles and the shadow of his forearm as he gripped his neck.

He stepped back as she stepped out and pulled the door closed behind her.

She hadn't grabbed her robe. Shivering a little, she crossed her arms over the sleep shirt that barely hit her knees. "Are you just now coming up to bed?"

"I came up a while ago. Do you have anything I can rub on my shoulder?"

He still hurt. Pretty badly, she assumed, to have come seeking help. Feeling guilty that he'd hurt himself helping her, feeling worse because his discomfort was bad enough to keep him from sleep when she knew how tired he must be, she headed for her bedroom door and the bathroom right inside.

The light above the vanity cut a swath across the near edge of the queen-size bed that had once occupied her guest room. If the rumpled purple comforter and sheets were any indication, whatever sleep he had managed had been as fitful as hers tended to be. As she turned into the bathroom, she noticed his nearly dry socks, his long-sleeved undershirt and a pair of gray jersey briefs on the towel rack above the heater vent. With the washer and dryer off circuit, he'd had to improvise.

Realizing what he wasn't wearing under his jeans, she quickly opened the medicine cabinet, pulled out a tube and turned to hand it to him.

He'd stopped in the doorway beside her.

The light was infinitely better here. There were no shadows to hide the broad expanse of his beautifully formed chest, the flare of dark hair, the impressive six-pack of his abdomen or the fact that while he'd zipped his pants, he hadn't bothered with the button.

Her glance jerked up. His hand still clasped his shoulder, his fingers kneading the tight muscles there. But it was his cleanly shaven jaw that held her attention. The hard line of it looked tight enough to shatter teeth. The way he arched his back and promptly winced made it evident his shoulder wasn't the only problem.

His frown of discomfort shifted to the pastel tube he took from her.

"What is this?"

"Herbal cream. I bought it when I pulled a hamstring."

"When?"

"It wasn't anything I did here," she assured him, since she had been known to acquire a bump, bruise or strain herself during her move. "It was in a yoga class. It'll help," she insisted, pretty sure he'd had something more industrial strength in mind.

The skepticism carving deep lines in his face remained as he held up the tube and backed into the bedroom to let her pass. A gravelly edge of fatigue roughened his voice. "I appreciate this. Sorry to wake you."

She didn't bother telling him that he hadn't. Or that she

was actually grateful for the reprieve from her sleepless-
ness. All that concerned her now was that he was in pain.

"Where do you need that?"

He'd moved to the foot of her bed, away from the narrow shaft of light spilling across the bedding at the corner. Her bare feet soundless on the carpet, she stopped
three feet away.

"By my right shoulder blade."

He wouldn't be able to reach there. Not very well, anyway, as stiff as he appeared to be.

"Do you want me to do it?"

He didn't look as if he thought that a very good idea.
"I'll manage."

"You're sure?"

"Yeah. I've got it," he insisted, only to wince again the
instant he moved his hand in that direction.

Not allowing herself to overthink the situation, she took
back the tube. Twisting off the cap, she squeezed a hefty
dab of the white cream onto her fingertips and handed the
tube back to him.

"You have no business calling me stubborn, you know
that?" With him filling the space in front of her, she added,
"Turn around," and after a second's hesitation on his part
found herself faced with his broad and sculpted back.

In the filtered light, the view of him half naked was no
less unnerving, but at least he couldn't see how hard she
swallowed before she reached up and spread the cream between his shoulder blade and the long indentation of his
spine. His skin felt as smooth and hard as granite when
her fingers slipped upward.

Traces of rosemary and mint mingled with the scents
of soap, shampoo and warm, disturbing male.

Silence didn't seem like a good idea.

"Why is it that when I came literally a split second from
wounding you, you said I wasn't even close? You actually

did hurt yourself," she pointed out, rubbing the cream over a knot the size of an egg, "and your 'almost' is two hours."

He lowered his head, gave a small groan with the movement.

"It had to do with circumstances."

She was about to tell him he'd have to do better than that when he sucked in a breath.

She went still. "Did I push too hard?" she asked instead.

His breath leaked out, the tightness in his back audible in his voice. "In a good way."

She'd smoothed her fingers alongside the wide curve of his shoulder blade, the long muscle there as unyielding as the bone beside it. Repeating the motion, keeping the same pressure, she felt his broad back rise as he drew another deep breath, then slowly released it.

What she was doing felt good to him. So she did it again, slower this time. It felt good to her, too, she realized, easing her motions even more. Though she'd tended to fight his efforts, he had been taking care of her in one form or another since the day they'd met. As little as there seemed to be for her to do for him in return, as little as he seemed to want from her beyond what centered on their professional relationship, the least she could do was take care of him now.

"What about the other side? Is it sore?"

"Not as bad."

Meaning it hurt there, too.

Reaching around him, she held out her hand. "I need more cream."

"You don't have to do this," he told her, but even as he spoke, he uncapped the tube and squeezed the analgesic onto her fingers.

"You hurt yourself helping me," she pointed out. "So, yeah, I do." As tall as he was, her elbows were even with her eyes as she raised her arms to work on the other side.

He seemed to realize how far she had to reach.

The bed was right there. "So it's guilt motivating you," he concluded, and sank to the nearest corner. He straddled it, his legs planted wide.

She sat down a little behind him. With one leg tucked under her, the other dangling over the foot of the mattress, she rested her hands on his shoulders to knead the knots with her thumbs.

"Must be," she conceded as he lowered his head again. "Especially since I know this isn't how you'd planned to spend your weekend."

She'd thought before that there were reasons she needed to keep her guard in place with this man. She just hadn't bothered recalling them at the time. With the feel of his big body relaxing beneath her hands, her palms tingling as much from the feel of him as from friction and herbs, it seemed wise to recall those points now.

Reminding herself of the subtle but definite distance he'd put between them last night helped her remember why that need was there. Recalling her comment to the girls about his dates helped, too. There were other reasons, she knew. Even more compelling ones. But for the moment, the last one served her purpose perfectly.

"I'm sorry you missed your party."

"Everybody missed it."

That would be true, she thought, now working her fingers up the cords at the back of his neck. "I'm sure your date was disappointed."

For a moment Erik said nothing. Her fingers were making slow little circles at the base of his skull, reversing their motion to follow the rigid cords to where they met the equally taut muscles in his shoulders.

"I didn't have a date," he finally muttered.

She kept moving down, past the sore spot on the right,

but before he could wish she'd stayed there, she'd continued lower, working her magic along the sides of his spine.

What she was doing felt like pure paradise. She had wonderful hands. Soft. Surprisingly strong. Yet incredibly gentle as she lightened her touch to soothe away the worst of the soreness, then gradually increased the pressure again.

He'd felt a different sort of gentleness in her touch before. He'd thought he'd been dreaming, that he'd only imagined her touching him with even more tenderness—until he'd opened his eyes to see her turning away. The brush of her fingers over his forehead had brought something he couldn't remember ever experiencing from a woman's touch. A feeling of ease, of comfort.

There had been a disturbing contentment to the feeling that didn't coincide at all with the direction his thoughts headed now, but something in him craved that kind of caring. Something undeniable and essential and that should have felt far more threatening than it did with the feel of her small hands unhurriedly working over his back.

The ache running from his neck to the bottom of his ribs had started to ease, the tightness there no longer threatening another spasm. An entirely different sort of tension replaced it as her fingers methodically moved over his skin, massaging toward the base of his spine.

His breath slithered out when she stopped well above the waistband of his jeans. Still, the thought of her dipping her hand lower had every other muscle in his body going taut.

"I thought you might be taking the woman you'd gone out with before," she said into the quiet. "Is she someone you've been with a long time?"

There was nothing deliberately sensual about her touch as she worked her way back up. Nothing provocative in the quiet tones of her voice. Yet the question added a certain strain to his own.

"I haven't been with anyone in a long time, Rory."

Her hands had reached his shoulders. Feeling her go still at the status of his sex life, or maybe the fact that he'd so frankly admitted it, he turned as he spoke, catching her wrist as her hand fell.

"Why the questions?"

Beneath his grip, her pulse jumped.

Rory wasn't sure how to answer. She hadn't expected him to tell her how long it had been since he'd slept with a woman. That hadn't been what she was asking. Or maybe it had been and she just hadn't let herself acknowledge her need to know. The queries had started out simply as a defense against the undeniable emotional pull she felt toward him. She hadn't allowed herself to consider why his being in a relationship with someone should even matter to her. But it had. And he wasn't. And all she could do now was scramble for an explanation that wouldn't betray how very much he already mattered to her. And he did, in ways she was only beginning to comprehend.

"I guess I wanted to know if you were involved with anyone." She lifted her shoulder in a shrug. "Just curious, you know?"

In the pale light, she looked impossibly young to him. Incredibly tempting. Mostly, she looked much as she had last night. Far more vulnerable than she wanted to be, and trying hard for a little bravado.

He saw weariness in her guileless features. He'd heard that same drained quality in her admission. It was almost as if as late as it was, as long as the day had been, she was simply too tired to keep the bravado in place.

"I'm not," he assured her. "I haven't been involved with anyone in years." Involvement implied an attachment he'd avoided for the better part of a decade. A need to be there for someone. A need to let that someone count on him to be there for her. A need to know she'd be there for him.

He'd had absolutely no interest in that sort of commitment. Until now.

"Just curious, huh?"

"A little."

If she'd been trying for nonchalance, she failed miserably.

"You know, Rory," he murmured, self-preservation fighting the need to tug her toward him. "Now would probably be a good time for me to let you get back to bed."

"Probably," she agreed softly. "But I think I'll just go downstairs and read for a while. Seems like a good night to tackle the business plan." She lifted her chin, gave him a tiny smile. "I tried, but I can't sleep."

The simple admission pulled at him, the helplessness in it, the weary frustration of trying to escape what kept a person from rest. What got him, though, was the loneliness she tried to hide with the quick duck of her head.

She'd made no attempt to reclaim her hand, and he couldn't quite make himself let go. Unable to shake the thought of how alone she'd seemed cuddling her son on the boy's bed that morning, realizing how she undoubtedly spent many of her nights, he put self-preservation on hold.

"So what kept you awake? Old worries?" he asked, because he knew how long she'd struggled with them. "Or new ones?"

"Both."

"Today probably didn't help."

He probably hadn't helped. He just wasn't sure how else he could have accomplished what they'd both needed for her to know. Yet while he'd been busy making sure she was aware of everything that needed to be done around the place to keep it up and how to take care of the problems she could expect, the weight of even more responsibility had piled on her shoulders.

"Today was actually a good day." He and Tyler weren't

the only ones who'd thought so. "The worry part is just always there. It's okay during the day when I'm busy, but at night…"

"You can't shut it off," he concluded for her.

"I managed for a few minutes tonight. But then it all came right back."

"What was it about tonight that helped?"

She lifted her glance.

"You," Rory said quietly. Of everything he had done for her in the past two days, everything he'd done in the weeks before, what he had done since yesterday had mattered to her the most. "You being here."

Especially tonight, she thought. Tonight, for a while, anyway, because of him she'd been able to shut everything out and concentrate on nothing but the soothing sounds of the rain still pattering on the roof. Because he was there, because he had her back, because he had everything under control, for the first time in well over a year she'd had a day when she hadn't had to make every decision on her own. She hadn't had to worry about how she would get a tree home for her son, or get one out of her driveway. Or remove the one that had blocked the street. Because of him, they had heat and lights. And for that day, anyway, she hadn't had to handle everything thrown at her alone.

Erik brushed the back of her hand with his thumb, conscious of the small weight of it where he held it on his thigh. The thought that he had somehow given her some measure of relief had just made it that much harder to let her go. Not until she was ready, anyway.

"Do you want to go downstairs?" he asked.

She met his eyes, looked away with a small shake of her head. "Not really."

"Do you want to go back to Tyler's room?"

Another small shake. "Not yet."

"Are you cold?"

"A little."

He knew what she needed even before he asked. He asked anyway. "Could you use a pair of arms?"

That was all he was offering. Just to hold her. This wasn't about wanting her between her sheets. Heaven knew it wasn't about self-protection. It was about giving her a break.

She didn't have to say a word for him to know that his arms were exactly what she needed. But her quiet "Please" was all it took for him to rise and turn out the bathroom light. The night-light now filtering through the doorway cast the room in shadows.

"Come here," he said, and tugged her to her feet.

Leading her to the side of the bed, he pulled the comforter over the sheets and propped both pillows against the headboard. He didn't want her in the bed, just on it.

The distinction seemed just as clear to her as she snagged the wadded throw blanket from the foot of the bed and sat against the far pillow, hugging her arms around her knees when the mattress sank beneath his weight. With his back against his pillow he drew the throw over them both and pulled her knees toward him, his arm low around her back, his hand at the curve of her waist.

"How's this?" he asked, coaxing her head to his shoulder.

He felt her sigh, the long, quiet leak of air leaving her nearly limp against the side of his body.

For a moment, Rory couldn't say a word. She could barely believe she was actually where she had so badly wanted to be. It didn't matter that his jeans felt rough against her bare calf, or that the contrast of his heat and the cool air against the back of her neck made her shiver. She could hear the heavy beat of his heart beneath her ear, could feel it where her hand rested on his hard, bare chest. It didn't even matter that for some strange reason her throat had suddenly gone raw, making her quiet "Good" sound a little tight.

His chin brushed the top of her head as he settled himself more comfortably.

"Good," he echoed, slowly skimming his hand over her upper arm.

She swallowed, then made herself take a deep, even breath. "Erik?" she finally said.

"Yeah?"

"Thank you."

A tired smile entered his voice. "For holding you?" It was hardly a hardship, he thought. She felt wonderful curled up against him. Small, feminine, trusting. The only difficult part was trying not to think of how curvy she truly was with his hand at the dip of her waist, inches from the curve of her hip.

Wanting distraction, he smoothed his hand back up her arm. The herbal scent of her hair teased him, filling his lungs every time he breathed.

"For all of it. But yes." Her tone grew muffled. "For this, too."

He wasn't sure what all she meant. It could have been anything. He just forgot to wonder what might have meant so much to her when he caught the hitch in her voice.

He started to tip up her chin.

She wouldn't let him. Instead, he cupped his hand to the side of her face, brushed it with his thumb and caught the moisture gathered at the corner of her eye.

His heart gave a strange little squeeze. "Hey." *Don't do that,* he thought. He could handle anything but tears. "What's wrong?"

"Nothing. Honest," she insisted, keeping her head right where it was. "Absolutely nothing is wrong." She tried to draw a deep breath, made it halfway before it caught. Swallowing, she tried again. "For the first time in…forever," she said, because that was how it felt, "right now there really isn't a thing wrong."

Which was what had brought the sting behind her eyelids, she realized. Not because of sadness, fear or grief. But because of an amazing, unfamiliar and totally unexpected sense of relief. She knew it wouldn't last long. That it couldn't. It was just for now. While he held her. So just for now, relief was what she felt.

"Then why tears?"

Because of what you let me feel, she thought. "Because I'm tired," was easier to admit to him.

She felt his lips against the top of her head. "Then go to sleep."

"I don't want to."

The slow shake of her head brushed her hair against his chest. Letting his fingers sift through that dark silk, he gave a small chuckle. "Why not?"

"Because I don't want to miss you holding me."

It had to be the hour, the lateness of it, the need for sleep himself. Or maybe it was his need to let her know he'd be there for her in the morning if she'd just let herself rest, but he didn't question what he did as he slipped down, bringing her with him.

His lips grazed the spot on her cheek where they'd literally bumped heads that morning. "You shouldn't say things like that."

Turning her face to him, she whispered, "Why not?"

He'd been about to tell her to go to sleep, that he wasn't going anywhere. But with her sweet breath filling his lungs, the feel of her supple little body playing pure havoc with his intention, he leaned closer.

"Because you'll make me forget why I shouldn't do this," he murmured, and brushed his mouth over hers.

Once.

Again.

"Or this." He carried that gentle caress between her eyebrows, to the space where the twin lines formed when she was worried.

He cupped his hand at the side of her face.

"Or this."

The admission vibrated against her mouth a faint second before he increased the pressure ever so slightly. His lips were firm, cool and far softer than anything that looked so hard had a right to be, but it was the feel of him tipping her head to gain the access he wanted that had her reaching for him herself.

Relief gave way to something infinitely less soothing. It barely occurred to her that this was exactly what she *hadn't* wanted when she found herself opening to him, flowing toward him, kissing him back. She'd known what she would feel if she ever got this close to him again. And she'd been right. She felt everything she had when he'd kissed her before: that deep, awful longing, the yearning to simply sink into his compelling strength, his incredible gentleness, and have him take away the ache in her chest. To relieve the void, the emptiness. Only now with her fingers curling around his biceps and his hand slipping to the small of her back, pulling her closer, the hollowness inside her seemed to be receding, and the emptiness felt more like…need.

When he lifted his head long moments later, his features had gone as dark as his voice. "I think you'd better remind me."

Her own voice came as a thready whisper. "About what?"

He touched the first of the short line of buttons on her nightshirt. His fingers trailed down, found her soft breasts unrestrained beneath thermal cotton.

His lips hovered over hers. "Why we should stop."

Surrounded by his heat, that warmth gathering low in her belly, her voice went thin. "I don't remember."

She didn't know what he saw in her shadowed face when he lifted his head. Whatever it was caused his body to go beautifully taut before his hand slipped over her hip.

"Me, either. But if you do," he warned, the low tones of his voice sounding half serious, half teasing, "stop me."

She was about to tell him that wasn't going to happen, but he lowered his mouth to hers just then and she almost forgot to breathe.

There was no demand in his kiss. Just an invitation to a heady exploration that was deep, deliberate and debilitatingly thorough.

Winding her arms around his neck, she kissed him back just a little more urgently. With him, because of him, she finally felt something other than alone and uncertain, or the need to be strong.

She'd been so frightened by her doubts, so afraid that what she'd thought had been real in her marriage hadn't been at all. If she'd been so wrong about all of it, that meant she couldn't trust her judgment about anything, or anyone, else. But he'd helped her see that she hadn't been wrong about what had mattered most. And more important than anything else he'd taught her, he was teaching her to trust in herself.

She could love him for that alone.

The thought had her clinging a little more tightly, kissing him a little more fiercely. It hurt to know how much of herself she'd let others take away from her. But he was taking that pain away, too, allowing parts of her to come back, allowing feelings she hadn't realized she still possessed to finally surface. For the life of her she had no idea why those thoughts made the back of her eyelids start to burn again. She just knew that at that moment, nothing mattered to her so much as the sense of reprieve she was only now beginning to feel. And the fact that it was he who had finally allowed it.

Erik caught her small moan as she pressed closer. Or maybe the needy little sound had been his own. There wasn't a cell in his body that wasn't aware of how beautifully female she was, and of how badly he wanted her beneath him. To him, she was perfect. Small, supple and infinitely softer than his harder, rougher angles and planes.

He would have just held her if that had been what she'd wanted. It would have about killed him, but he'd have done it. Yet, incredibly, she seemed to hunger for the feel of him as much as he ached for her.

Stretched out beside her, he drew his hand over the nightshirt covering her belly, letting it drift upward, pulling soft cotton away with it. He kissed her slowly, tracing her soft curves, allowing himself the sweet torture of finally knowing the silken feel of her body, the honeyed taste of her skin. He didn't know what to make of the tears he tasted again at the corners of her eyes when he kissed her there, or the almost desperate way she whispered, "No," when he started to pull back to make sure she was all right. Slipping her fingers through his hair, she drew him back to her, meeting him in a kiss that nearly rocked him to his core.

Gritting his teeth against the need she created, he skimmed the bit of silk she wore down her long legs. It landed somewhere beside the bed, along with his jeans.

He'd left his billfold on her nightstand. Some miracle of common sense made him drag himself from her long enough to fumble for the small packet inside. He'd barely rolled their protection over himself when she curled into him, seeking him as he sought her.

The intimacy of gentle exploration had created its own tormenting heat. What they created as they moved together now, his name a whisper on her lips, had him thinking he'd never be able to get enough of her before that heat turned white-hot and he was barely thinking at all.

Chapter Ten

Rory burrowed deeper under her comforter. A delicious lethargy pulled at her, coaxing her back toward sleep. But she heard voices. Male ones. One sweet, the other deep.

Sleep was suddenly the last thing on her mind.

Tyler was awake. Erik was with him. Through the two-inch-wide gap he'd left between the door and the jamb, she could see the light from Tyler's bathroom faintly illuminating the hall. The gap in the curtains next to the bed revealed a thin sliver of gray.

It was daylight. That meant it was somewhere after seven-thirty. She couldn't remember the last time she'd slept that late.

She threw off the covers. Nearly tripping over her nightshirt, she snatched it up and moved to the door. They were just disappearing down the stairs, Tyler in his pj's, Erik in his undershirt and jeans. From the conversation, it sounded as though they were discussing breakfast. Specifically, which one of them got to slice the bananas.

Minutes later, thoughts of how she'd practically fallen apart in Erik's arms adding to the anxiety of wanting to hurry, she'd pulled herself together enough—in the physical sense, anyway—to head into the hall herself.

Slipping a blue corduroy shirt over a cotton turtleneck and yoga pants, she could hear her little guy as she reached the first step.

"Can I help you work today?" he asked. "An' can you help put my train around the tree?"

The low tones of Erik's voice drifted up the stairway. "I think all I'm going to do out there this morning is check the gutters. It's too dangerous for you to help."

"Why?"

"Because it's a long way up there."

"How come you need to check 'em?"

"Because I need to see if the weight of the ice pulled them from their brackets."

"Why?"

She heard a deep, indulgent chuckle. "Because if they're not lined up right, the rain will pour straight off the roof instead of draining to the downspouts and get you and your mom all wet."

Her foot hit the bottom step just as she heard a pondered little "Oh."

Tyler hesitated. "Can we do the train after, then?"

Across the entry, she could see Tyler sitting in front of the lit tree, the blanket she'd covered Erik with last night wrapped around his shoulders. Expectation beamed from his little profile.

Erik sat on the edge of the hearth, his gray undershirt stretched across his broad shoulders as he closed the glass doors on the growing fire.

"I'll have to see how it goes, but I don't know that I'll have time for that, Ty." He picked a stray bit of bark from the stone beside him, tossed it onto the logs in the curved wood basket. "Now that the rain's melted the ice, I need to finish here, then get to my own place."

"You're going home?"

There was no mistaking her son's disappointment at that bit of news. She heard it in his small voice, could practically feel it in him as she watched Erik look up at her an instant before Tyler turned and looked up himself.

Shoving her fingers through her hair, partially undoing what she'd managed to arrange with a few random strokes of a brush, she found it infinitely easier to meet Tyler's sad little face.

"Good morning, sweetie," she murmured, bending to give him a hug. "How did you sleep?"

"Good," came his usual, though decidedly disheartened, reply.

She nudged back his hair, wanting to ease away his sudden seriousness. What Erik had done hadn't been deliberate. There had been nothing but kindness in his voice as he'd explained why he wouldn't be staying. But the painful proof of how her little boy could come to rely on him, could even come to love him, only added to the confusion of wants and uncertainties tearing at her as she kissed the soft, tousled hair at the crown of his head.

"I'll help you with your train later, okay?"

"'Kay," he reluctantly replied.

"So, what's up down here?" she asked him and, as casually as she could, straightened to meet the caution in Erik's smile.

He rose himself, all six feet plus of him, and came to a stop in front of her.

His gray gaze skimmed her face. Slowly assessing. Unapologetically intimate. "The plan so far was to turn on the tree, then build a fire." His eyes held hers. "Then what, Ty?" he asked, since the child hadn't answered his mom.

"Breakfast," came the slightly more enthused reply. "And cartoons?" he added hopefully from below them.

"And coffee?" Erik asked with that disarming arch of his eyebrow.

"Definitely coffee," she agreed.

Grabbing the remote, she punched in the channel she usually only let Tyler watch as a treat. With him on his way to the sofa with his blanket, she headed for the kitchen, Erik's footfalls behind her matching every heavy thud of her heart.

She pulled the carafe from the coffeemaker, turned to see him watching her from beside the sink.

Holding the carafe under the faucet, she turned the water on.

"Why didn't you wake me?" she asked, her hushed voice muffled further by the sound of running water.

"Because I was already awake. When I heard him in the bathroom, I figured he'd come looking for you, so I intercepted him before he could. I thought you might not want him to find us in bed together.

"Besides," he added quietly, "you were out. You barely moved when I pulled my arm from under you."

The reminder of how she'd fallen asleep tucked against his side, their bare limbs tangled, had heat rising in her cheeks.

"I can't believe I didn't hear him." It was so unlike her not to hear her son. "I never sleep that hard." Except with this man beside her, she obviously had.

"Thank you for the rescue," she all but whispered.

He turned off the water for her. With Tyler hidden by the sofa, he lifted his hand, curved his fingers at the side of her neck.

"I'm going to leave in a while," he told her, brushing his thumb over the lobe of her ear. "Pax said everything was okay at the boatworks yesterday, but I have some things I need to do. There's something here I want to check first, though. Is there anything you can think of that you need me to do before I go?"

In the past eight hours, his touch had become as exciting to her as it was calming, as disturbing as it was comforting. He had reawakened her heart and her senses and she'd never felt as confused as she did now, standing there desperately wanting him to pull her to him and hoping he wouldn't.

He'd said he needed to leave, that he had things he needed to do. He'd already talked with Pax, asked about the condition of their properties, their business. She'd heard him tell Tyler that he needed to check on his own place. She knew his entire life was on the other side of the sound. In her need for the temporary escape he'd offered, she'd forgotten that for a few critical hours last night.

"You don't need to check my gutters, Erik."

"Yeah, I do," he said, thinking of her lovely, long limbs and how perfect they'd felt wrapped around him. He'd really prefer that none of them got broken. "It'll save you having to do it yourself."

"I'd have to do it if you weren't here."

The hint of defensiveness in her tone sounded all too familiar.

"But I'm here now," he pointed out, looking a little more closely to see the unease he'd missed in her moments ago.

"You can just tell me what I'm supposed to look for. I'll need to know, anyway."

Caution curled through him. "It's raining out there."

"So I'll wait until it stops."

"That could be June."

He had a point. She just wasn't prepared to concede it. "Is there a particular bracket you noticed?"

There was. The one at the front of the garage that would keep water from pouring over her and Tyler when they came and went from the car. He'd noticed it yesterday and had meant to walk around the garage and the main building to see if any other gaps were visible. But this wasn't about a bracket. It wasn't about a gutter. From the uncertainty underlying her quiet defensiveness, he'd bet his business this wasn't about anything but what had happened between them last night.

Not totally sure what he felt about it himself, not sure what to do about any of it with Tyler wandering over in search of cereal, Erik decided it best to just go do what he'd planned to do anyway.

"I'm going to get the ladder from the basement. I'll be back when the coffee's ready."

It took eight minutes to brew a full pot of coffee. It was another ten before she heard the rattle of the ladder being propped against the wall in the mudroom and the faint squeak of the door to the kitchen when it opened.

Tyler had just handed her his empty bowl and was on his way past the island to go get dressed when she heard him tell Erik he'd be right back.

"Take your time, sport." Ruffling the boy's hair as he passed, Erik looked to where she again stood at the sink.

Still holding the bowl, she watched his easy smile fade to something less definable as he pushed back the navy Merrick & Sullivan ball cap he'd taken from his truck. It looked as if he'd shaken the rain from his cap and swiped what he could from his leather jacket. Beneath it, the charcoal pullover he'd pulled on before he'd gone out was dry, but the darker spots on the thighs of his jeans and the hems looked damp.

"You have two broken brackets," he told her, conscious of Tyler still moving up the stairs. "I'll pick up new ones and be back with them in the morning. I leave for my folks' house in San Diego tomorrow afternoon, so that's the only chance I'll have."

She set the bowl in the sink, picked up the mug she'd taken out for him and poured him his coffee.

Tomorrow was Christmas Eve.

She held the heavy mug out to him.

"You know, Erik," she said as he took it, "you really don't need to come all the way over here to fix those brackets."

The mug settled on the counter beside her.

"I know I don't. And I don't need you telling me that," he insisted, and skimmed her cheek with his knuckles.

The small contact compounded the anxiety knotting behind her breastbone.

Taking a small step back, needing to break his touch as much as the hold he'd gained on her heart, her voice dropped to an agonized whisper. "I can't do this."

Even as his hand fell, his shoulders rose with a slow, deep breath. His hard, handsome features were suddenly impossible to read.

"By 'this' you mean the sex."

"No. Yes." Shaking her head, she shoved her fingers through her hair. "I mean, it's not just that. Making love with you was amazing," she admitted, because it had been. "It's that I can't let myself feel what I'm starting to feel for you." What she already did feel, she thought, and which totally terrified her. "I can't let myself count on you to do things for me. Or for you to be around to talk to. Or for you to be here. If I do, it would be too easy to rely on you even more."

Apparently nothing she'd said explained why she was withdrawing from him. If anything, Erik just looked a little mystified. She figured that was because of what she'd admitted about the sex part. But then, she always had had a problem filtering what she said to him.

His eyes narrowed on hers. "Why not?"

Crossing her arms over the knot in her stomach, her voice dropped another notch. "Because I'm not going to set myself up to lose something I don't even have. It doesn't make sense to do that," she admitted, not sure she was making sense to him. "I can't do that to myself. And I definitely can't do it to my son. It will only hurt Tyler if I let him grow any more attached to you than he already is, Erik. I know people will come and go from his life. People already have, but I've never seen him take to anyone the way he has to you." She'd done a lousy job of protecting herself. That failing would not keep her from protecting her son. "Since the arrangement between us is temporary anyway, it just seems best to back away and keep business…business."

Her heart hurt. Rubbing the awful ache with her fingertips, she watched his jaw tighten as he stepped back.

Erik wasn't at all sure what he felt at that moment. He wasn't even sure what he felt for this woman, beyond an undeniable physical need and a sense of protectiveness he wasn't familiar with at all. All he knew for certain was that they had stepped over a line she clearly had not been prepared to cross.

Recriminations piled up like cars in a train wreck. He'd known all along that it would be a mistake to get involved with her. He'd known from the moment he'd met her that she was dealing with far more than he'd gone through when his marriage had ended. What he didn't understand was how he could have forgotten that his sole goal in agreeing to help her was to have no reason to return to this place once his obligation to Cornelia had been satisfied.

The fact that he hadn't considered any of that last night had his own defenses slamming into place. Having done enough damage already, he wasn't about to complicate their relationship any further. Or let her push him any farther away.

"Just answer one question for me."

"If I can."

"Last night. The tears. Were they because you were thinking of Curt?"

He figured he had to be some sort of masochist for wanting to know if that was what really had been going on with her while they'd been making love. No man wanted to think a woman had another man on her mind while he had her in his arms. Still, for some reason he couldn't begin to explain, he needed to know.

For a moment, Rory said nothing. Partly because the question caught her so off guard. Partly because it was only now that she realized her only thought last night about the man she'd married was how Erik had lessened the void he'd left.

She couldn't begin to explain everything she'd felt last night. Or what she felt now because of his question.

It seemed easiest to just go to the heart of what he really wanted to know.

"The only person in that bed with me was you, Erik."

He heard something a little raw in her quiet reply, something that made her look as if he'd just totally exposed how absorbed she'd been in only him—which was no doubt why she stood there with her arms crossed so protectively and her eyes begging him to go.

He could hear Tyler racing down the stairs.

"We're supposed to meet with Phil after the first of the year." He spoke the reminder quietly, as conscious of the child coming toward them as he was of the definite need for distance. "I don't remember the date, but I'll get it from her. We can figure out our work schedule from there."

"Can we do the train now?"

Tyler had stopped at the end of the island, his expectant glance darting from one adult to the other. He'd pulled on pants and a green thermal shirt and held a red flannel shirt in his fist.

"I have to go now," Erik told the grinning little boy. "But I heard your mom say she'd help you."

His smile fell. "You have to go?"

"Yeah, bud. I do." Unprepared for how the child's disappointment affected him, not sure what to make of the strange hollow in his chest, he tousled his sandy hair one last time, gave him a smile and let himself out through the store.

"Erik! I was just going to call you!"

Erik turned from where he was locking the front door of Merrick & Sullivan's client office. Phil had just emerged from the silver Mercedes parked behind the construction Dumpster in front of the building next door. The tails of her white scarf flew in the breeze as she hurried around to the sidewalk. "Do you have a minute?"

He didn't feel particularly sociable. What he did feel was defensive, edgy and impatient to be on his way. Still, he made himself smile. "Sure," he called back, pocketing his keys. Hunching his shoulders against the chill, he headed to where she'd stopped by Cornelia's building's front door. "What's up?"

"Let's get out of the cold. I'll make us some coffee."

"A minute is really all I have, Phil. I'm leaving to see my folks in a couple of hours."

"Oh. Well, then." Hitching her bag higher on her shoulder, she crossed her arms over her furry white coat. Beneath her matching hat, her eyes smiled through the lenses of her bookish, horn-rimmed glasses. "Rory said you were there when I called the other day. The power being out everywhere had us concerned about her and her son," she explained, "but some neighbors were visiting so I knew we didn't have to worry. We didn't have a chance to really talk, though. Is everything all right with the property?"

Realizing she was checking up on Cornelia's investment

threatened to turn his mood even more restive. "There are a few downed trees and a loose gutter, but no structural damage," he told her, thinking that was about all she'd be interested in. "I heard the power was restored a while ago."

He'd learned that from Ed, who'd done as Erik had asked him to do and called when the area had gone back on the grid. Since he'd told his old friend about Rory's unfamiliarity with the generator when he'd borrowed his saw, Ed hadn't questioned his concern about wanting to make sure there were no other glitches.

Erik hadn't let himself question his concern, either. He'd tried hard to keep thoughts of her and Tyler to a minimum.

"That's good to know. Just one other thing, then, and I'll let you go." She flashed him a smile as she crossed her arms tighter, anxious to get out of the wind. "I take it the two of you were working when the storm hit," she said quickly, making it apparent that Rory hadn't mentioned his insistence about helping with their Christmas tree. "So, how do you think she'll do? Or is it too soon to tell?"

He wanted to say she'd do just fine. She certainly didn't lack for aptitude or the determination to succeed. She even had the incentive of keeping a roof over her son's head pushing her. It would be a challenge doing it on her own, but she'd make a living there. With the connections she was establishing, she'd probably even make a life.

He brushed past the thought that she'd be making that life without him. He had a life of his own right where he was. He had work he loved, a great business, good friends. He had money and the freedom to come and go pretty much as he pleased. His obligation to the woman messing with his carefully constructed status quo ended once they had the business established. Once it was, he could walk away and never go back there again.

"Is there a problem, Erik?"

"No. No," he repeated, waiting for the quick shutdown

of feeling that normally reinforced his last thought. "I'll make it work."

I will. Not *we*.

Phil apparently heard the distinction.

"Isn't she cooperating?"

Not when she was giving him grief about helping her, he thought.

"She just needs a break right now," he decided to say. "With her little boy and the holidays, it just seemed like a good thing to do."

"Was that your idea?"

Initially, it had been. For the business part, anyway.

"The decision was mutual."

"So when do you meet again?"

"Whenever we're scheduled to be here."

"That will be the fifth."

"That soon?"

"At two," she added, and cocked her head. "Do we need to meet before then? We certainly can, if there's ever a problem," she hurried on, having caught his lack of enthusiasm for the meeting. "Part of what we do for our ladies and their mentors is help them work through challenges. Differences of opinion can arise over anything from creative priorities to scheduling—"

"It's nothing like that."

"May I ask what it is?"

It was clearly too late to deny a problem even existed. But all he would admit was, "It's complicated."

"I see." Adjusting the frame of her glasses, she peered at him with interest. "Do you have a solution to the problem?"

He wasn't sure there was one. Not for the two of them. "Not yet."

"Can you work together?"

"Yeah. Sure. There's always email and the telephone." He'd given his word. He'd hold up his end of the deal. For his grandparents. For her. "She wants the business to work. That's what I want, too."

She considered him for a moment, her head tipped thoughtfully, the fine fibers of her white hat fluttering. "You know, Erik, when I gave Rory the address of your grandparents' property, I suggested she look for the possibilities. We knew what she would see when she got there, and that it would be nothing she could have imagined she would want.

"What she'd been looking for was a small home for herself and her son," she confided, "but her needs changed when she lost her job. To see the potential in that property, she had to let go of a mind-set that focused on what she had been looking for and what she now needed. To find the solution to your problem, maybe you should look at the possibilities, too."

She smiled then, gave a little wave of her white-gloved hand. Crystals shimmered on its cuff. "I've kept you long enough," she said. "You have a plane to catch. And I need to get inside before I freeze. Have a safe trip. And merry Christmas."

He thanked her. Added a quick "You, too" and started to turn away.

As he did, his glance caught on the gold plaque engraved with three letters above their doorbell. He'd been curious about it ever since it had gone up last week.

"Hey, Phil," he called, catching her unlocking the door. "What does FGI stand for?"

"It's who we are," she called back. "Fairy Godmothers, Incorporated."

His forehead furrowed. As near as he'd been able to figure out, he'd thought they were in some sort of mortgage business. "Fairy Godmothers? Don't they have something to do with pumpkins?"

"And helping dreams come true." With a charming smile, she disappeared inside.

Mentally shaking his head, he strode toward his truck at the curb in front of his office. He had no idea how anyone over the age of ten could possibly believe in fairy tales, happily ever afters or that other impossibility that Rory had once imagined, Christmas magic. As for dreams, they died by the thousands every day. Reality simply wore them down, if it didn't kill them outright. He knew. He'd spent years in the emotional limbo that remained after his vision of his future had turned to ash. But he'd glimpsed those dreams again, and what Phil had said about possibilities now gave him pause.

She'd said Rory had to let go of a mind-set that focused on what she had been looking for and what she needed now. She'd had to be open-minded enough to see what would be possible living in a place she'd have never considered, rather than writing it off as not what she'd had in mind.

He certainly hadn't considered any sort of personal relationship with her when they'd first met. But one had evolved in spite of him. To see the possibilities in it, he'd need to get past the defenses he'd spent years honing before he could be open to what those possibilities were.

Part of the problem there was that he had no desire to give her a chance to push him any farther away.

The other part would be getting Rory to see past whatever it was holding her back from him to see their potential, too.

Rory had hoped for snow. For Tyler's sake, because that was what he'd said he wanted for Christmas. But Christmas morning had dawned with a gray sky that promised little beyond more rain.

Until a week ago, every other time she'd asked him what he wanted Santa to bring, all he'd wanted was a big tree.

The day after Erik had left, he'd told her he'd changed his mind. Since he already had the tree, what he wanted Santa to bring was Erik.

She'd explained that Erik would be with his parents for Christmas, so Santa wouldn't be able to bring him. Though decidedly let down by that bit of news, he'd decided later that he wanted snow.

All he seemed to want as far as a gift was concerned were things beyond her power to give him.

Without any sort of hint for something that Santa could bring down the chimney, she, being Santa's helper, had left him a mini kick scooter that he could ride between the counters in the store while she worked to get it ready. He'd been excited when he'd come downstairs a couple of hours ago to see it by the tree. He'd been tickled to see that Santa had eaten all but a few crumbs of the cookies they'd left out for him, and awed and delighted by the small tuft of faux-fur trim that appeared to have snagged on one of the fireplace stones when the jolly old guy had departed.

What had truly thrilled him, though, had been discovering the present from Erik among the others from her and her parents beneath the lit and glittering branches. It had been delivered yesterday with a note asking her to please put it under the tree for him to find Christmas morning. Except for the "Thanks" he'd scrawled at the bottom, that was all the note had said.

Tyler had declared the huge pop-up book about sailboats his "very favorite" and gone through every page with her while they sat on the sofa.

It had been only two days since Erik had left her standing in the kitchen feeling as if the world was falling out from under her all over again. Two long nights of missing him more than she'd thought humanly possible. The man was a rock. A truly decent guy. And while she suspected he was fiercely loyal to those he cared about, he held back from needing anyone himself—from needing her, any-way—in the way she now knew she needed him. It wasn't about survival. She could survive on her own. It was about the need to share, and he had worked his way into her life and into her heart as if he was simply meant to be there.

That had only happened with one other man.

Too unsettled to stay still any longer, she left Tyler with his book and cleaned up the bright paper wrappings and ribbons from the carpet.

She had no idea how to repair the damage done to their relationship. He was her mentor. He'd become her confidant. His voice had been one of experience and his advice had been invaluable where other situations were concerned. She just didn't know how to ask what she could possibly do to make things right between them when he was part of the problem, even though she'd picked up the phone a dozen times to try. He had no responsibility to her beyond the agreement he'd made with her benefac-tor, and now even that part of their relationship had been jeopardized.

The two-tone chime of a bell startled her from her pain-ful thoughts. She'd only heard the chime ring twice be-fore: the first morning she'd met Edie, when the woman had stopped by to welcome her to the neighborhood, and two days ago when Talia had brought the twins over to play. Erik had explained that the service bell was used for after-hours deliveries. A few of the locals obviously used it as a doorbell to save themselves from having to walk around back.

Thinking it might be one of the neighbors she and Tyler had delivered Christmas cookies to yesterday, she headed through the store and opened its front door.

No one was there.

Stepping out, the cold breeze tugging at her hair, her

glance caught on a small package on the weathered plank boards.

The little gold box was tied with a red bow.

Now conscious of the dark truck in the parking lot, her heart beating a little too fast, she picked it up.

The neat print on the back of the gold tag read "I want you to find it again."

She knew exactly what *it* was. It meant the inexplicable feeling of magic she'd told Erik she'd once known every Christmas. The feeling of everything being right in her world. He knew it was the feeling she'd wanted her son to know and something she'd given up hope of ever experiencing again herself.

Yet that sense was what she felt now as she lifted the lid on the box to find a glittery little life preserver on a thin gold cord.

She had the feeling he was only letting her know he'd help her stay afloat with the business. And that was huge. But the way he'd done it had her closing the box and holding it with both hands to her heart.

It was only then that she looked to where Erik unfolded his arms and stepped away from his driver's side door.

Gravel crunched beneath his hiking boots as he moved past the bits of storm debris still strewn over the wet grass. Dark plaid flannel hung open over a navy Henley shirt, his broad shoulders looking impossibly wide as he climbed the steps and stopped in front of her.

He hadn't been at all sure what to expect when he'd left the box for her. He'd just wanted her to discover it the way she had the others she'd told him about. They seemed to have appeared out of nowhere, she'd said, so that sense was part of what he'd wanted to give her, even if only for a moment.

He knew he could have just left it for her. But that would have defeated another part of his purpose. He'd needed to see her reaction to his gift so he'd have some idea of what to do next. It was so unlike him not to have a clear plan, but he felt much as he suspected he would setting sail without a compass or preparation. He wasn't totally sure how to get where he wanted to go, or if the waters he'd face would be calm, rough or totally unpredictable.

Encouraged by the way she held his gift, he quietly said, "Merry Christmas."

"Merry Christmas," she echoed, still clutching the little ornament. Caution merged with disbelief. "What are you doing here? I thought you were in San Diego."

"I was. I spent Christmas Eve with my family and caught the first flight out this morning. I don't want to keep you from Tyler. I just wanted you to have that."

Rory watched him nod toward her clutched hands. She could have hugged him for his gift. The reserve carved in his expression held her right where she stood.

Considering the bated relief she felt at his presence, her "Thank you" seemed terribly inadequate. "Do you want to come in? Tyler loves his—"

Erik was already shaking his head. "There's one other thing." More than one, actually, but he wanted them alone right now. "The other day, you said you didn't want to set yourself up to lose something you don't even have. You said it would be a mistake for you to count on me. I understand the need to protect yourself," he insisted. He'd mastered that one in spades himself. "And I get the reasons you don't want Tyler to start believing I'll be around for him. But I'm not all those other people who've let you down, Rory.

"You seem so certain the only way you can create stability for yourself is to keep anyone who could rock your boat at arm's length. But you've rocked mine, too. You already have me," he admitted. "I figure the least we owe each other is a little time to reconsider our positions before we totally blow something that could have a lot of potential."

She looked at him warily, a betraying glint of a smile in her eyes. "You think we have potential?"

"Yeah," he said. "I do."

She'd rocked his boat. The thought made relief harder to suppress. His admission that she already had him made it nearly impossible.

She took a step closer. "If I let myself count on you," she began, already wanting that more than he could possibly know, "what are you offering to reconsider?"

"Are we negotiating?"

"Apparently," she replied, holding his gift even tighter.

She couldn't begin to identify what she felt as the tension left his handsome features. Reprieve, for certain. But something that felt suspiciously like hope had risen right behind it. He didn't want them to close any doors.

Lifting his hand toward her, he curved it to the side of her face.

"In that case," he said, more relieved than he could have imagined when she tipped her cheek toward his palm, "you should know I've already considered how much my hang-ups were getting in the way of possibilities where we were concerned. I've spent years thinking I just wanted to be away from here. But once I moved past thinking about what I'd wanted and considered what I might need, I realized that what I needed was another chance with you.

"You made me realize how much I still want a family. And a home here. It's not just the place," he assured her. It was how she made it feel. Comfortable. Familiar. As if he belonged there. "It's you. And Tyler."

He knew he already had a good life. Until he'd met her, he'd just refused to let it matter that he didn't have anyone to share it with. He'd work or play late so that he was too tired to care that he had no one to come home to who actually cared that he'd had a great day or a bad one, or whom he could care about in return.

"We're good together. If we want to make this work between us, we can. I'm in love with you," he confessed, finally acknowledging what he'd denied to his partner well over a week ago. Pax had somehow known that she was the woman he'd been waiting for, though he hadn't realized he'd been waiting for her at all. "All I'm asking is if you're willing to try."

Rory knew his walls had existed far longer than hers. Yet he'd just put his heart on the line for her. Her own heart feeling full enough to burst, she went up on tiptoe, curved her arms around his neck and hugged him hard.

Folding her to his chest, his hold just as tight, he chuckled against the top of her head. "That's a yes, then?"

"Absolutely."

"Are you okay?"

She nodded against his shoulder. "I'm falling in love with you, too, Erik. I think that's what scared me. I knew the day we met that it could happen, but I wasn't ready for it. It happened so fast."

Drawing a deep breath, she lowered herself to her heels and let her hands slide to his chest. Still holding the little box, she met his eyes. "I think I panicked," she explained.

He brushed back the hair the breeze fluttered across her cheek.

"I know you did." She'd been no more prepared than he'd been to put a name or label on what had seemed to be growing more complicated by the moment. A little apprehension on her part hadn't been surprising at all. He hadn't dealt with it all that fearlessly himself. "We'll take it slow now. Okay? No pressure. No rush. We'll just take our time and stay open to possibilities."

"Possibilities," Rory repeated. "That's what Phil told me I should look for here." She'd only been thinking about the property, though. As Erik smiled into her eyes and drew his hand to the back of her neck, Rory remembered that the woman had also warned her to keep an open mind about him.

"She told me that, too," he told her, and lowered his mouth to hers before she could say another word.

There was relief in his kiss as he pulled her closer, and promise, hunger, possessiveness and need. It was the need she felt most. His, definitely, but her own, too, in the long moments before he lifted his head and eased back far enough to release her hands from where they'd been trapped against his chest.

"What?" he asked, seeing the question in her flushed features.

She looked at the little gold box, lifted off its lid. Suddenly she felt certain the little life preserver didn't represent what she'd thought.

Erik's voice was quiet. "You said there was a time when you could always count on something like that being there for you Christmas morning."

Her smile came easily at the reminder. "I thought this had something to do with the store. Something about keeping it afloat. But it's a lifeline, isn't it?"

"It is," he murmured, touching his lips to her forehead. "I'm just not sure which one of us I thought needed rescuing."

"Erik!"

In a flash of maroon fleece and gray denim, Tyler bolted through the door onto the porch.

"Hey, buddy!"

"You're here!"

"I'm here," Erik agreed, and pulled him between them for a hug.

It was then that Rory felt what Erik had wanted her to glimpse again.

At that moment, all felt truly, completely and utterly right in their little world. That was the magic, and it was the most wonderful gift of all.

As they headed in from the cold, it started to snow.

Epilogue

"Why are we waiting in here, Erik?" Confusion shadowed Rory's smile. "We've said hi to Phil and Cornelia," she pointed out, their purpose at the FGI office accomplished. Or so she'd assumed.

"We'll go in a couple of minutes. This is just some of that year-end stuff I need to take care of."

He'd been busy with work off and on for the past week. That afternoon, though, he was going to show her and Tyler where he built boats.

As if anxious to get business behind him, he tugged her closer to where he stood by a gold filigree chair. "Do you want to spend tomorrow night on my houseboat? Tyler might get a kick out of the fireworks."

Tomorrow was New Year's Eve. "He'd love that. I'd love it," she stressed.

She hadn't seen his place yet, though he had warned her it was small. By land-standards, anyway.

"Then that's what we'll do."

Looking more preoccupied than impatient, he glanced to the open door of the room the elegant older woman presently used as her private office. The space off the lovely conference room wasn't much bigger than a closet, but it apparently served her purpose until the major construction behind the sheets of heavy plastic in the entryway would be completed.

Beyond them, Phil and a petite, honey-gold blonde sat beneath the crystal chandelier at the mahogany table. On its surface, hundreds of letters from the mailbags mounded by the delicate French writing desk teetered in stacks. Others had been sorted into piles as the women carefully read each one.

Cornelia had introduced the pretty woman with Phil as Shea Weatherby. She was the reporter who'd written the article that had resulted in the continuing deluge of mail from prospective Cinderellas, or "Cindies," as Rory had just learned her fairy godmothers called the ladies they sponsored. She'd also just learned she'd been their second success.

As focused as Shea appeared to be on her reading, she seemed even more intent on ignoring Pax. Erik's business partner had come over with them after Erik had showed her and Tyler around their client office next door. Pax had used the excuse of needing a decent cup of coffee, something he apparently mooched off the women with some regularity. Yet it was as obvious as the charmingly devilish smile that clearly wasn't working on Shea that she was the reason he was hanging around with Tyler by the pretty little Christmas tree, checking out the boats beyond the window.

"Do you mind if I ask what we're waiting for?" Rory ventured.

"Not at all," came Erik's easy reply. "I just need to give Cornelia a check and pick up a deed from her. I'm paying off the mortgage on your property so you can stop worrying about it."

He was paying off her mortgage? "I never said I was worried."

The look he gave her said she couldn't possibly be serious. "Honey." Brushing back her bangs, he planted a kiss on the furrows between her eyes. "You've never had to tell me when you were concerned about something. I can see it. This way, the pressure's off."

"You're giving me the place?"

"Consider it a pre-engagement present."

She opened her mouth, closed it again.

"Pre-engagement?" she finally asked.

"Yeah. You know. It comes before an official engagement. If you want, I can hold off titling it to you until then. Either way, the property is yours to do with as you please."

He'd figured they could eventually live together there or he could have a bigger house built back by the woods. Whichever she wanted. With the boatworks here, he'd commute by plane most of the time. If she decided to sell or lease the place, that was her call, too. He just wanted them together. But he'd already gotten way ahead of where he figured she mentally was with their relationship.

Seeing that he'd left her a little speechless, he figured it best to change the subject. He'd told her they wouldn't rush. That they could take their time.

"Hey. Ignore me. I was just in business mode," he explained. "I hadn't intended to bring that part up until you got used to me being around." He hitched his head toward the open door. "I'm going to see what's holding up Cornelia."

He gave her a kiss, quick and hard, and turned away.

Catching his arm, she turned him right back. "I'm getting used to you," she assured him. "How long an engagement are you talking about?"

"However long you need."

Christmas morning, he'd given back to her a feeling she'd thought she'd never know again. Now he was ready to offer himself, along with the gift of time, to accept what, in her heart, she already knew.

"Then, I have no problem discussing it now." Some things, simply felt, simply were…right. "All you have to do is ask."

His eyebrow arched. "Seriously?"

"Seriously," she echoed.

With now familiar ease, he slipped his arms around her, drew her close. "In that case, I'm ready if you are."

The teasing in her expression met the smile in his. Narrowing her eyes, she tipped her head as her hands flattened on his chest. "That's a proposal?"

"It's due diligence. I don't want you to shoot me down."

"Never," she murmured. "I love you too much."

"I love you back, Rory." There'd been a time when he couldn't imagine ever saying anything like that again. Or, ever feeling what he felt with her. "And just for the record," he said, glancing toward Tyler before lowering his head to hers, "you made me believe in the magic, too."

* * * * *

A PRINCESS BY CHRISTMAS

JENNIFER FAYE

In another life **Jennifer Faye** was a statistician. She still has a love for numbers, formulas and spreadsheets, but when she was presented with the opportunity to follow her lifelong passion and spend her days writing and pursuing her dream of becoming a Mills & Boon author, she couldn't pass it up. These days, when she's not writing, Jennifer enjoys reading, fine needlework, quilting, Tweeting and cheering on the Pittsburgh Penguins. She lives in Pennsylvania with her amazingly patient husband, two remarkably talented daughters and their two very spoiled fur babies, otherwise known as cats – but, shh…don't tell them they're not human!

Jennifer loves to hear from readers – you can contact her via her website: www.JenniferFaye. com

CHAPTER ONE

AT LAST HE'D lost them.

Prince Alexandro Castanavo of the Mirraccino Islands stared out the back window of the cab as it snaked in and out of traffic. He'd never driven in New York City but his concern deepened when they swerved to the berm of the road. While all of the other traffic was at a standstill, they kept rolling along.

When the cab suddenly jerked to the left, Alex's shoulder thumped into the door. He reached for the armrest and his fingertips dug into the hard plastic. What had he done to deserve the cabbie who thought he was a grand prix driver?

Alex jerked forward as the car screeched to a halt in front of a traffic light. At least the guy obeyed some traffic rules. Another glance out the rear window revealed a bread delivery truck behind them. He breathed a sigh of relief. No one was following them. But then again, how could they? He doubted many people drove as erratically as this cabbie.

"You can let me out here?"

"No. I get you there quick."

Alex reached for his wallet, but before he could grab it, the car lurched forward. He fell back against the seat. What was up with this guy? Didn't he know that he'd make more money by taking his time?

"You don't have to hurry."

The man grinned at him in the rearview mirror. "Hurry? Sure. I hurry."

Alex inwardly groaned. He was about to correct the man when he realized that every time the man spoke, he took his eyes off the roadway. It was best not to distract him if Alex wanted to reach his destination in one piece.

He silently sat in the backseat while the cabbie jockeyed through the streets of Manhattan. Alex stared out the side window as a fine snow began to fall. Cars and people abounded in every direction, seemingly undisturbed by the deteriorating weather. Garlands and festive wreaths adorned the fronts of buildings while pine trees and shiny ornaments decorated the shop windows. Christmas was definitely in the air, even though it was still a few weeks away.

City life would definitely take a bit to get used to. Not that he planned to live it up while in town. Unlike his usual need for high visibility on behalf of the kingdom, this trip required stealth maneuvers, especially since he'd gone against protocol and stolen away without his security detail. Although in his defense, it was a necessity. Trying to elude the paparazzi was tricky enough, but doing it with an entourage would be impossible.

Soon the stores faded away, traffic thinned out and rows of houses dotted each side of the street. One last glance out the rear window assured him they hadn't been followed. At last, the tension in his neck eased.

When a loud clicking sound filled the car, he noticed they'd turned onto a cobblestone roadway. It was a narrow residential road with no parking on either side.

Alex sat up a little straighter, taking in the sweeping willow trees on either side of the street. This must be the exclusive neighborhood of Willow Heights, aptly named.

The homes in this area sat back off the road. They were older mansions that were well kept and still stunningly beautiful. Being here was like stepping back in time. A wrought-iron signpost came into view. It stood in front of a stone wall and read: The Willows.

Alex glanced up at the stately home with its old-world charm. He wasn't sure what he was expecting. When the problem at the palace had come to light, there had been no time for detailed planning. He'd moved directly into action. His mission was to draw out this game of cat and mouse with the press—not knowing how much time would be needed to resolve his brother's latest fiasco.

The driver turned in to the gated driveway. "That is some swanky place. You some rich muckety-muck?"

He wasn't sure what a muckety-muck was, but it didn't sound good. "No."

"You stay long?"

He wished he knew. "I'm not sure."

"When you need a ride. You call. Freddy take you."

English might be Alex's second language, but this man made him feel as if it was his first—the broken English combined with a very heavy accent left Alex struggling to understand what the cabbie was trying to say. But one thing he knew was that he wouldn't be summoning Freddy for another ride—anywhere.

The paved driveway led them to a spacious three-story flagstone mansion. By the looks of it, this place dated back a century or two. The owner certainly had done a fine job keeping up the outside. Ivy grew up one wall and its vines were dusted with snow. It didn't even come close to the enormity of his family's palace, but the large, sweeping porch draped with garlands gave the place a warm, homey feel.

The car pulled to a stop and the driver cast him a big, toothy grin. Alex reached for his credit card to pay the fare but paused. On second thought, he grabbed some cash from his wallet. It was best to keep his true identity under wraps for now.

Once he and his luggage were settled on the sidewalk, the cab raced off down the driveway. Alex's shoulders slumped as the adrenaline wore off and fatigue weighed him down. He stifled the urge to yawn. He'd never been so happy to have his feet on solid, unmoving ground; now he just had to find his room and get some shut-eye before he dropped from exhaustion.

"Welcome," chimed a sweet voice.

He turned, finding a young woman coming up along the side of the house, lugging a big cardboard box. Her reddish-brown ponytail swayed as she made her way toward him. Her beauty captivated him, from her pink-stained cheeks to her full rosy lips.

Her breath came out in small white puffs in the frigid air. Her forehead creased with lines of exertion from carrying a box that was far too big for her.

Alex sprang into action. "Let me take that for you."

She looked hesitant but then relented. "It goes on the front porch."

"Your wish is my command."

They strolled side-by-side along the walkway. She cast a curious glance his way. "Are you all right? You looked a little shook up when you got out of the cab."

"You wouldn't believe the cab ride I had here." He stopped at the bottom of the steps. "I think the cabbie drove off the road more than he drove on it."

"I take it you didn't enjoy your adventure?"

"Not at all. I am very grateful to be here in one piece. Remind me to think twice before I call that cab company again."

The young lady smiled and he found himself smiling

back. This was not good. He knew better than to encourage the attention of women. It only complicated things when they wanted more than he could offer.

He forced his lips into a flat line as he moved onto the porch. The box landed with a thunk. He turned around to find the young woman standing just behind him.

As he dusted off his hands, he took in her white winter jacket with the logo for The Willows stitched in blue thread on the chest. His gaze skimmed downward, catching her snug jeans and the wheat-colored work boots that completed her ensemble. He drew his gaze up from her peekaboo curves. At last his gaze made it to her eyes—her big brown eyes. He wondered if she knew how beautiful she was. The guys must go crazy over her.

"Thank you for the help." Her gaze strayed to his luggage and back to him. "Can I help you? Are you part of the wedding party?"

"No, I'm not." His voice came out deeper than normal. "I want to check in."

"Rooms are by reservation only."

This young woman must be mistaken. "I have a reservation. Now, if you could point me in the direction of the person in charge."

The young lady pulled off a glove and held out her hand. "You're speaking to her. I'm Reese Harding. And you would be?"

He stepped closer and wrapped his cold fingers around her warm ones. Her skin was smooth and supple. He resisted the urge to stroke the back of her hand with his thumb. When his gaze caught hers, he noticed the gold flakes in her eyes.

"Allow me to introduce myself. I am P—" He caught himself just in time before blurting out his formal title. It took him a moment to recall the alias he'd used on the registration. He'd borrowed his mother's family name. "Alex DeLuca."

Then, realizing he'd held on to her hand longer than necessary, he released his hold on her. He never let a woman affect him to this extent. Being awake more than twenty-four hours was definitely impacting him. If only he could sleep on planes, it'd help.

"You own this place?" he asked, just to make sure he understood her correctly.

"Yes, I do."

His brows gathered as he studied her. She certainly seemed awfully young to be running her own business. "If you don't mind me asking, how old are you?"

"I can assure you I'm older than I look."

Well, now she had him curious. "And that would be—"

"Twenty-five." Her dimpled chin lifted. "Don't tell me you're going to card me too?"

"Um…no." He glanced away. He was letting himself get off track. It must be jet lag, because he wasn't here to pick up women—even one as captivating as the woman standing before him. "About the room—"

"The place is full up until Monday."

"Monday?" That was impossible. The muscles in his neck and shoulders tightened. "I made the reservation for today."

"If you'd like to make another reservation, I can check our calendar." She turned and stepped inside.

He strode after her, closing the door behind him. "I assure you I have a reservation, if you'd just check."

With an audible huff, she stopped in the foyer and turned. "Listen. I don't have your reservation. In fact, I've never spoken to you in my life. I would have remembered the accent."

He would have remembered her honeyed voice, too.

She was as attractive as she was frustrating. "Someone else must have taken my reservation. Surely you're not the only person who works here." Then again, this place was smaller than he'd been expecting. "Are you?"

Her forehead crinkled. "No, I'm not. But anyone you'd have spoken to would have checked the online system and known we were booked."

Not about to give up, he thought back to the phone call when he'd made the reservation. "It was a woman I spoke to about getting a room. She sounded a bit older than you. She took my information."

She frowned. "Maybe you do have a reservation. It's possible it didn't get entered in our system." She lowered her head and shook it. "But it doesn't change the fact that I don't have anywhere for you to stay. We are hosting a wedding this weekend."

He'd boarded three different flights today just to be sure he'd lost the paparazzi. And he'd suffered through a long layover in the Atlanta airport, cramped in a chair. All he wanted to do now was enjoy a warm meal and a soft bed. He held back a yawn. Rather make that a soft bed and then the warm meal. Anything else was unacceptable.

He straightened to his full six-foot-three-inch height and pressed his hands to his waist. He swallowed his frustration and strove for a professional tone. "What about my deposit?"

Her lush lips gaped and her face paled. "You made a deposit?"

"Yes. Check your computer."

Her eyes widened. "Mr. DeLuca, I'll definitely check into getting you a full refund. I'm truly sorry for the inconvenience."

He glanced around at the historic mansion. His gaze scaled up the rounded staircase, taking in the stained-

glass window on the landing. There had to be room somewhere—even if it took a bit of juggling.

"Since you've already accepted my money and this
place looks spacious enough, I am sure you can set up
accommodations for me until this wedding is over." He
flashed her one of his camera-ready smiles. "After all, I
traveled a long way to get here. Now I expect you to hold
up your end of the arrangement."

Her lush lips pressed into a firm line as though she
were considering her options before speaking. "Why
don't you follow me into the lobby while I clear up this
snafu?"

Without another word the spitfire strode away. Her well-
rounded hips sashayed from side to side like the metro-
nome from the days when he'd been forced to take piano
lessons. Only the swing of her backside mesmerized him
in a way the silly rhythm keeper from his childhood never
did. He stared at her until she disappeared back down the
hallway.

Alex gave himself a mental jerk. He couldn't let himself
get distracted—no matter how beautiful the distraction.
He had a job to do. A mission to complete. His sole duty
was to protect the crown of the Mirraccino Islands from
a messy scandal—one that would most certainly rock not
only the palace walls but also the entire nation.

CHAPTER TWO

REESE HARDING STRODE to the back of the mansion, trying
not to let the tall, dark stranger get under her skin. All the
while, she ignored the prickling sensation at the back of
her neck. Let him stare. She wasn't going to go all soft
because he was drop-dead gorgeous and his mere touch
made her fingers tingle.

Her gut told her that he was used to getting what he
wanted—when he wanted—but it wasn't going to happen today. There honestly was no room. And by the way
he could make her heart race with just a look, it was for
the best.

Reese marched into the office just off the kitchen. She
suspected that her mother had accepted his reservation.
If that were the case, Reese might very well have a legitimate problem. And she'd have no one to blame but herself.
When her mother had finally come out of the dark place
she had disappeared to after Reese's father unexpectedly
died, she had been so excited to see her mother's desire to
help with the inn that perhaps she'd let her mother have
too much freedom.

"Hey, honey." Her mother peered in from the kitchen.
"What are you doing? You just tracked a trail of snow over
my clean floors."

"Sorry." Reese continued rummaging through the

stacks of bills and correspondence on top of the big oak desk. "I need to find something."

"Can I help?" Her mother's face lit up. "I'm feeling like my old self now and would really like to be more helpful around here. I could organize the office for you."

"Mom, we talked about this. I like it the way it is. I can usually find what I'm looking for." And she would this time, too, if Mr. DeLuca didn't have her all flustered. "Besides, we don't want to rush things. You're doing so well and all, I just don't want—"

"I know, honey." Her mother patted her back. "It's just nice to be needed. So what are you looking for?"

"There's some guy waiting in the foyer claiming to have a reservation for tonight. Do you recall taking a phone call from an Alex something or other?"

Her mother's graying head tilted to the side. "I'm not sure. A lot has been happening around here lately."

Reese stopped shuffling through the papers in the organizer and looked directly at her mother. "This is important. Think real hard. Did you take a reservation from a man with a foreign accent?"

Her mother's forehead crinkled. "When would he have called?"

"Last week." Reese grabbed another stack of papers, looking for anything that would confirm that man's words.

"Seems to me I might recall speaking to someone with a foreign accent. I remember because the connection wasn't very good."

"Really? You remember him?"

"If I took his reservation, the money will be in the computer."

Her mother was right. She was wasting her time searching through all of those papers. She could pop on the computer and confirm Alex's deposit had been made. She pushed a button to start the computer.

"I'll leave you alone to figure things out." Her mother made a beeline for the door.

Reese logged into the resort's financial account. There was indeed a deposit—a huge deposit. Surely she'd misread the amount. Even after she blinked and refocused, the same enormous dollar figure remained. Her heart picked up its pace as excitement coursed through her veins. There was more than enough cash here to rent out the entire mansion for a month.

She then checked the inn's online reservation system. There was no mention of Mr. DeLuca. How was that possible?

After some quick sleuthing, she determined that her mother had bypassed the online reservation system and taken his information over the phone manually. Oh, what a mess! She'd have to sit her mother down and have a firm talk about procedures so they could avoid these issues in the future.

Still, this influx of cash was just what they needed to pay the upcoming tax bill, not to mention the bank loan. *Calm down. You're getting ahead of yourself.*

It wasn't like she could accept his money. She didn't have one single room to offer him. All she could do was offer Mr. Sexy Accent a full refund and hope he'd go away quietly.

But nothing about the man said he'd easily back off from what he wanted. Everything from the man's every-strand-in-its-place dark hair to his tailored white shirt that covered an obviously buff chest and down to his polished dress shoes said he was used to getting what he wanted when he wanted and the way he wanted it.

Nonetheless, she didn't have the ability to accommodate

him, much less the obviously large party that he planned to host. With a weary sigh, she grabbed the checkbook to write out the refund. The pen hovered over the check and her grip tightened as she thought of turning away all of that money.

She wrote out his name and the amount. Life wasn't fair. In the past year or so, with the economic downturn, she'd had a hard time attracting people to The Willows and now she was having to turn away this obviously affluent guest because of a clerical error.

She really did feel bad for him. Then a thought occurred to her. The least she should do was help this man locate some other reasonable accommodations.

Armed with the check and her address book, she returned to the foyer. Upon finding her mother and Mr. DeLuca conversing in lowered voices, she paused by the staircase. Neither of them seemed to notice her presence. What in the world was her mother saying that was so engrossing? The man rocked back on his heels and laughed. The sound was deep and rich.

When she stepped off the carpeted runner and onto the dark, polished wood floor, her boots made a sound. Both her mother and Mr. DeLuca turned her way. Reese's hold on the sizable check tightened. It was best to get this over with quickly.

The man caught her gaze with his deep blue eyes. She was struck by their vibrant color, but beyond that they told her nothing of the man's thoughts. Talk about a poker face. What sort of things did this international hunk keep hidden from the rest of the world? And what twist of fate had brought him to her doorstep?

The rise of his brows had her averting her gaze, but not before her pulse spiked, causing her heart to flutter. Why was she so intrigued by this stranger? So what if he came from another land and had the sexiest way of rolling his *R*s? He was still just a guy and she wouldn't let herself want something that she knew could never be. Her attention needed to remain on the mansion and keeping it afloat.

"Ah, there's my daughter." Her mother leaned toward Mr. DeLuca as though they were old friends. "I'm sure she'll have cleared everything up for you. It was nice to meet you. I hope we can talk again." Her mother's eyes twinkled as a mischievous grin played across her lips.

Once they were alone, Reese pulled her shoulders back. "Mr. DeLuca, I've verified your reservation and I must apologize for the inconvenience this has caused you. My mother made a mistake when she gave you the reservation. She didn't realize that we already had a prior commitment."

The man remained silent, not appearing the least bit interested in helping her out of this awkward situation. She held out the hefty check, but he didn't make any attempt to accept it.

"This is the full amount you paid. I double-checked." When he still didn't move, she added, "The check will cover your full deposit."

"I don't want it."

"What? Of course you do. That's a lot of money."

Tired of playing word games, she stepped up to him and stuffed the check in his hand. For the second time in less than an hour, his touch caused a jolt of awareness to shock her nerve endings.

Her gaze lifted and she noticed his eyes were bloodshot, as though he'd been up all night. Then she noticed the lines bracketing his eyes and the dark shadow of beard trailing down his squared jaw. She was tempted to reach up and run her fingertips over the stubble.

She clamped her hands together. "If you'd like, I have

the phone numbers of other facilities around the city that might be able to accommodate your party—"

"That won't be necessary," he said firmly. "I am staying here as arranged."

"But—"

"There are no more buts. I am staying." He pressed the check back into her hand. "And don't tell me again that there is no room. Your mother informed me otherwise."

"She did what?"

He sent her a knowing smile. "She told me there's a bedroom available. It's in some private apartment until one of the guest rooms opens up."

What in the world had gotten into her mother? Sure, she used to be impulsive back before the disaster with Reese's father, but since then she'd been so reserved, so quiet. Now she was getting active in the inn, which was great, but why in the world was she handing out her daughter's bedroom to this total stranger?

Reese shook her head, trying to dispel the image of this tall, dark, smooth-talking stranger in her bed. "She shouldn't have done that, not without talking to me."

His voice softened. "She seemed certain you wouldn't mind. After all, it's only until the other guests check out."

"But that's days away. They aren't leaving until Monday." And the apartment was so small that they'd be bumping into each other, day and…night. She swallowed hard.

At that moment, approaching footsteps sounded on the stairs. Relieved at the interruption, Reese turned away. Sandy, in her blue-and-white maid's uniform, descended the steps with her dark brown ponytail swinging back and forth. The young woman's eyes lit up when they landed on their latest guest. It would appear that being left in the lurch by the father of her child wasn't enough to make Sandy immune to Mr. DeLuca's charming smile.

"Do you need something, Sandy?" Reese asked, hoping the girl would quit openly ogling the man.

Sandy came to a stop next to them. "I…uh…finished cleaning all of the rooms." She tore her gaze from Mr. DeLuca and turned to Reese. "Do you need anything else today? I don't mind staying longer."

"Thanks. But we're good. Enjoy your evening off."

"Um…sure. Thank you." Sandy almost tripped over her own feet as she kept glancing over her shoulder at Mr. DeLuca.

Reese turned back to him, refusing to let his tanned features, mesmerizing blue gaze and engaging smile turn her into a starstruck teenager. "Where were we?"

"We had just resolved my accommodations until the wedding party checks out. Now, if you'll show me to my room."

She pressed her lips firmly together, holding back her response until she gave it some thought. The truth was most women would probably stumble over themselves to have this hunk of a man sleep in their bed. But she wasn't most women. Men couldn't be trusted—no matter how well you thought you knew them.

But this arrangement was all about business—nothing more. What was a few nights on their old, lumpy couch? As it was, she didn't sleep all that much anymore. The concerns about meeting this month's payroll on top of the loan payment kept her tossing and turning most nights.

"I must warn you that the room is nothing special. In fact, it's rather plain."

"Is it clean?"

She nodded. The linens had just been changed that morning. "But I'm certain it won't be up to the standards you're used to or even the normal standards of The Willows. And…and—"

"And what?"

She shook her head. "Nothing important."

She couldn't bring herself to let on that it bothered her to share her tiny apartment with him. And no matter how much she reminded herself that it was business, it still felt personal having him slide between her sheets and lay his head on her pillow. Her pulse picked up its pace. Her gaze strayed to his bare ring finger before she realized her actions and refocused on a nondescript spot just over his left shoulder.

Maybe if he wasn't drop-dead gorgeous she wouldn't be overreacting. But for the first time since she'd started the inn, her hormones were standing up and taking a definite interest in a man. Not that he'd be interested in a college dropout like herself—even if quitting school hadn't been a choice but rather a necessity.

He looked pointedly at her. "If you have something else on your mind, you might as well get it out in the open now."

Heat crept up her neck as her fingers tightened around the check. No way was she confessing to her nonprofessional thoughts. "I was just concerned about where the rest of your party would be staying."

"There's no one else coming. I am the only guest."

"Just you?" Her gaze moved to the check that was now a bit wrinkled. "But this deposit covers all six rooms."

"I am a man who values his privacy."

That or he was so filthy rich that he didn't have the common sense God gave a flea. But hey, who was she to argue with some sheikh or eccentric recluse?

But the money in her hand came with some sticky strings. She'd have to open her home up to him for five days and four nights. She suddenly regretted not doing more with the upkeep of the apartment. But her limited funds had to go toward the debts her father had left as her inheritance. Soon the creditors would be calling and she wasn't sure what she would tell them.

She glanced up at the staircase and balcony with the large stained-glass window. Her mother's family had owned the mansion for generations. She didn't want to think about the tailspin her mother would go into if they had to turn this place over to the bank—not now that her mother had almost recovered from her father's deception. So if it took bunking with this man to secure the necessary funds, she didn't see where she had much choice in the matter.

"Well, Mr. DeLuca, it looks like you've rented yourself a mansion."

What would it be like having a sexy roommate? Did he sleep in boxers? Or perhaps in the buff? And more importantly, did he walk in his sleep? Heat swirled in her chest and rushed up her neck. After all, a glimpse wouldn't hurt anyone.

The lines on the man's tanned face eased and a hint of a smile played at the corners of his full lips. "Now that we're housemates, you may call me Alex."

She wasn't so sure getting personal with him would help her roving thoughts, but she wasn't about to turn away his kindness. "And you can call me Reese."

CHAPTER THREE

THIS WAS WHERE he was to stay?

Alex followed Reese into the tiny apartment. He wondered who lived here or if it was just kept as a spare unit. Although seeing the older furniture and the coziness of the place, it didn't resemble any of the inn's photos he'd observed online. This place definitely wasn't meant for guests.

Reese swung open the door to a small bedroom. "This is where you can sleep."

He stepped up behind her in the doorway and peered over her shoulder. The decorations consisted of miniature teddy bears of all colors and designs. He'd never seen so many stuffed animals in one room. It was definitely interesting decor.

The most important feature was that it had a place for him to sleep. In the middle of the room stood a double bed sporting a royal-blue duvet with white throw pillows. Definitely nothing fancy, but at this point it didn't matter. He didn't think he could take one more step.

And to be honest, staying in these private quarters, as primitive as they were, would only make him that much harder to find. It'd been way too easy to tease the press with a juicy morsel of information about how he'd lost his heart to an American. But what no one knew was that he wanted no part of the *L* word. He'd witnessed firsthand how devastating it could be when you've lost the one person you loved with all of your heart. He refused to let himself become that vulnerable.

"Dinner is at six." Reese backed out of the doorway. "Do you need anything else?"

He stepped past her and hefted his suitcase onto the bed. "Your mother mentioned the room has a private bath."

Reese's brows rose sharply. "She was mistaken."

"I don't think so. She sounded quite certain."

Reese crossed her arms and tilted her head until their gazes met. "Well, she was mistaken, because she was talking about her room and she's not about to give it up to you or anyone."

"You seem very protective of your mother."

"She's all I've got in this world." And without another word, Reese turned and left.

Alex stood there staring at the now empty doorway, mentally comparing the image of the smiling older woman with the very serious young woman who seemed less than happy to have him here. There was a definite resemblance between the two as far as looks went, but the similarities stopped there. He rubbed the back of his neck before stretching. He was probably making too much of the first meeting. He'd see things clearer in the morning.

At last, he gave in to the urge for a great big yawn. The unpacking could wait. After being in transit for much longer than he cared to remember, it'd feel so good to lie down and rest. Just for a moment. After all, it was almost dinnertime.

He leaned his head back against the pillow. Maybe this trip wasn't going to be as bad as he'd imagined. For the time being, he could be a normal person without people looking at him with preconceived notions of what a royal should say or do. For just a bit, he'd be plain old Alex. A regular citizen. A mere tourist. Something he'd never been in his whole life.

The next morning, Alex awoke with his street clothes still on. He'd only meant to lie down for a moment. His stomach rumbled. He hadn't even made it to dinner. Then the events of the prior evening started to play in his mind.

He groaned as he recalled how in his exhausted state he'd been less than gentlemanly, demanding to have his way. He scratched at his two—or was it now a three?—day-old beard. He definitely owed Reese an apology.

After a hot shower and a much-needed shave, he started to unpack. He moved to the dresser and pulled out a drawer. He froze when he spotted a light pink lacy bra. What in the world?

His gaze moved to the right, finding a matching pair of undies. They weren't much more than a scrap of lace with a couple of pink strings. Immediately the image of Reese came to mind. This must be her bedroom. And these were her things. He slammed the drawer shut, but it was too late. His imagination had kicked into overdrive.

Not only had he been unfriendly last evening, but he'd even stolen her bed right out from under her. He groaned. He wasn't so sure an apology was going to be enough to earn his way into her good graces.

He removed a pair of jeans and a sweater from his suitcase—the clothes he'd borrowed from his brother. They were more casual than his normal wardrobe, but this trip called for a very casual appearance. He and his fraternal twin, the Crown Prince Demetrius Castanavo, still wore the same size. Not that his brother would even notice the missing clothes, much less care about them. He had more important things on his mind at the moment.

Alex's next task was styling his temporarily darkened hair. He didn't want anyone to recognize him too soon. Let the paparazzi continue with their hunt. After all, the fun was in the chase. And it'd take them awhile to find him in this out-of-the-way inn.

As he worked the styling gel into his hair, he mulled over his brother's situation. He sympathized with Demetrius. The thought of being responsible not only for the royal family but also for an entire nation was, to say the least, a bit overwhelming. He just hoped Demetrius would come to terms with his inherited position as crown prince and not cause any further incidents—such as the potential scandal everyone was working so hard to cover up.

Next Alex added some saline drops to his eyes to refresh the colored contacts similar to the ones he'd used while he'd been on vacation a few months back. He blinked a couple of times, then inspected his image in the mirror. A smile pulled at his lips. For today, he was no longer Prince Alexandro. He was just plain, ordinary Alex. But first he had some royal business to attend to.

He stepped into the living room and heard a knock at the door. A man handed him a tray of food and Alex's mouth watered. It'd been a long time since he'd been this hungry. He thanked the man and barely got seated on the couch before he took his first big bite.

After finishing every last drop of the herb soup and devouring the turkey sandwich, he logged on to his computer. He scanned one news site and then another and another. His plan wasn't working. The paparazzi weren't following his jaunt to the U.S. the way he'd hoped they would. In fact, he'd fallen out of the headlines. This was not good. Not good at all.

He'd definitely have to up the stakes if he wanted to gain the press's fleeting attention. Uncomfortable with the idea of throwing out a juicy bit of information, he nonetheless started typing a note from a fictitious palace employee to a popular internet gossip site about his recent "activities." This was the only way to keep them from sniffing out the truth—the scandal that was his brother's life. He just wondered what lengths he'd have to go to in order to keep up this charade.

He was able to keep working into the afternoon and catch up on some important emails related to Mirraccino's shipping commerce. Once he'd pressed the send button on the last email, he made his way downstairs. He'd just found his way to the kitchen when Reese came rushing out of it carrying a stepstool. All bundled up in her coat and fuzzy pink earmuffs, she came to a halt when she noticed him blocking the hallway.

"Good afternoon." Her voice was cool and there was no hint of a smile on her face.

This would be so much easier if he hadn't stumbled upon her skimpy undies. Even now he wondered if she had on a matching blue set. Or perhaps she preferred deep purple. Or maybe they were polka-dotted.

"Could you move aside? I was on my way out the door."

He gave himself a mental jerk. He wasn't ready for her to go—not yet. "I smell something delicious. The aroma wafted the whole way upstairs. What is it?"

She lowered the collapsible stool to the floor and leaned it against her leg. "It's homemade marinara sauce. But it's not ready yet. If you want to make yourself comfortable in the living room just off the foyer, I'll make sure someone lets you know when dinner is served."

"Do you want to join me?"

"I can't. I'm headed outside to do some work." She hefted the silver stool.

"But I wanted to speak with you."

"Can it wait? I have a couple of things I need to do before dinner."

"Of course." He kept what he hoped was an impartial expression on his face. "It's not urgent. May I help you?"

She shook her head. "I've got it."

As she headed for the front door, an uneasy feeling came over him. The ladder looked as though it'd seen far better days. Combine that with the ice and snow and it'd undoubtedly add up to trouble. Perhaps this was a way he could earn himself some points with her. But more than that, something told him Reese could use a helping hand— even if she was too stubborn to admit it.

As it was, he'd never been any good at just sitting around doing nothing. If he'd been at the palace, he'd be busy dealing with one situation or another. His country was quite involved with the exportation of its fine wines and fruit as well as being a shipping mecca. But he had to keep in mind that while he was in New York, he was plain Alex on holiday. Still, that didn't mean he had to sit around doing nothing.

He rushed off to grab his coat from the apartment. On the way back down the stairs, he happened upon a young man rushing up the steps, taking them two at a time. The guy had stress marring his face as a distinct frown pulled at his mouth. The guy grunted a hello as he rushed past. Alex couldn't help but wonder if that was the groom.

Why in the world did people put themselves through such stressful situations? He had no intention of saying *I do* any time soon—if ever. He'd seen firsthand how powerful love could be. And when it was over, it left people utterly devastated.

If he took the plunge it would be for something other than love—something worthwhile. After all, a meaningful union was what was expected of a prince. It was his duty.

Lost in his thoughts, Alex yanked open the front door. His hand grasped the brass handle on the glass storm door and pushed. At that moment, he saw Reese off to the side. The door bumped into the stool with her on it. The contraption teetered to the side. Reese jumped off just in time.

"Are you okay?" Alex rushed to her side.

"I'm fine." But she didn't look happy to see him—not that he could blame her.

"I didn't expect to find someone standing in front of the door."

"It's my fault, I should have moved over to the side a little more, but I was having problems stringing the lights right above the door."

He glanced at them. "They look all right to me."

"Look at them from down here." She led the way into the yard, oblivious of the deepening layer of snow.

Alex followed her. When he turned back, he found she'd transformed the porch into a beautiful winter scene. There was garland lining the front of the porch. Small artificial pine trees strung with white lights stood guard on either side of the front door. And then there were strands of white twinkle lights the whole way around the porch, giving it a soft glow.

As Reese stood there puzzling over how to finish stringing the lights, her full lips pursed together. If he were impulsive—like his twin—he might consider stealing a kiss just to see if her lips were as sweet as they looked.

Alex turned to look out over the quiet street. The thought of kissing her still pulled at his thoughts. Besides probably earning him a slap for his effort, he knew kissing her was the sort of spontaneity that had gotten his brother in a world of trouble. Alex still didn't understand how the crown prince could elope with a woman he had only known for a handful of weeks. Frustration churned in Alex's gut. No one would want an impulsive ruler, including Alex himself. That's why the elopement had to be dealt with immediately and quietly without the encroachment of the press.

Alex glanced in Reese's direction to find her big brown eyes studying him. Her gaze was intense and put him off center because it was as if she could see through him—see that he was a fake. Or maybe it was his guilt from not introducing himself properly as the prince of the Mirraccino Islands that had him uneasy.

But it had to be this way. Keeping his identity hush-hush was of the utmost importance. He didn't know this woman any better than a person on the street. There was no reason to take her into his confidence and expect her to keep it. To her he was nothing more than a paying customer—end of story.

Her brow crinkled. "Is something wrong?"

"Not that I can think of."

"Okay. I just thought with you standing out here in the cold instead of inside in the warmth that you must need something important."

This was his opening. He didn't have a lot of practice at apologies and for some reason he really wanted to get this right.

"There's something I have to say." When he had her full attention, he continued. "I am sorry about our first meeting. I was way out of line."

There was a flicker of something in her eyes, but in a blink, it was gone. "Apology accepted. But it wasn't all your fault. You were expecting a room to be waiting for you. No one could blame you for being upset."

"But then to kick you out of your own bed—"

"Don't worry. I don't sleep much anyway."

Before he could inquire about her last statement, she

headed back to the porch to adjust the strand of lights on the banister.

"What do you think?" Reese returned to his side.

He didn't really notice a difference. "Looks much better."

"I don't know." She crossed her arms and studied the lights strung from one end of the porch to the other. "It's not perfect, but I guess it'll have to do."

"Do you always decorate so elaborately?"

She shrugged. "I wouldn't bother, but each home along Cobblestone Way is expected to light up their homes for the holidays."

Reese climbed on the unstable stepstool. When she swayed slightly, Alex rushed to her side.

"Let me do that for you." He held out his hands for the string of lights.

"Thanks, but I've got it. I know exactly how they go."

Instinctively he placed a hand on her hip to steady her while with his other hand he gripped the stool. The heat of her body seeped through her jeans and into his hand, sending a strange sensation pulsating up his arm.

She glanced down at him and their gazes caught for a second more than was necessary. Then she turned away and attempted to string the lights on three little hooks above the door.

"There. That should do." With his hand aiding her, she climbed down the few steps. "Would you mind plugging them in?" She pointed to the outlet on the other side of the porch.

He was glad to help, even if it was just something small. And the fact that this independent woman let him do anything at all must mean that he was making a little bit of progress with her. He liked that thought—not that he was going to let this budding friendship go too far. But it would be nice to have someone around with whom he could strike up a friendly conversation. He quickly found the end of the extension cord and plugged in the additional string of lights.

He turned around to find that she'd returned to the front lawn to inspect her own handiwork. Deciding that she had the right idea, he did the same. He glanced up at the house, finding it looked just as good as before. "You did a great job."

"It's no big deal. But it's nice to know that someone enjoys my efforts."

"Do you need help with anything else?"

"Actually, I do."

Her answer surprised him. "Tell me what you need."

"After dinner, I need to go get a Christmas tree."

She was going to chop down a tree? She might have the determination, but he wasn't so sure that she had the physical strength. He wondered whom she would turn to if he wasn't here. The thought of her leaning on another man didn't sit well with him.

Ignoring the bothersome thought, he followed her back to the porch and helped collect her supplies. "I must admit this will be a first for me."

"Where exactly are you from?"

He didn't want to lie to her, but he knew that he couldn't be totally honest. With his accent there was no way he could pass for an American. There had to be a way around this tricky topic.

He decided to turn things around. "Where do you think I'm from?"

"I don't know." She tilted her head to the side and eyed him. "Let me think about it."

Spending time with Reese could be trickier than he'd imagined. He didn't want to lie to her, but telling her about his homeland was not an option. Maybe he should have stayed in the apartment and avoided her altogether. He inwardly groaned. As if that would be possible with them being roommates.

Besides, he already had a date with her. Correction. He had plans with her.

Oh, boy, was he in deep trouble, and it was only his second day in New York.

CHAPTER FOUR

THIS WASN'T A good idea after all.

Reese closed the side door to the garage and inhaled a steadying breath. She'd been far too aware of Alex at dinner. The deep rumble of his contagious laughter. The way his eyes crinkled at the corners when he smiled, making him even more handsome—if that was possible. And the way he listened to her as though each word she uttered truly mattered.

This was not good.

What had she been thinking inviting this man to go pick out a Christmas-tree with her? It wasn't as if she needed any help. Since her father's death, she'd been managing everything on her own. Why should that change now?

But she reasoned that Alex was an important guest. His enormous fee would help her meet this month's bills… she hoped. It was definitely a good incentive to make his stay here as pleasant as possible. And perhaps he'd recommend his friends stay at The Willows the next time they visited the city.

And if they were all as easy on the eyes, she wouldn't complain. After all, looking didn't hurt anything. It was getting involved with men that set you up for a world of pain. Just ask her mother. And even Reese had been involved with someone after her father died who'd promptly dumped her when he found out she wasn't a rich debutante. The memory still stung. How could she have been so foolish as to fall for her ex's promises?

In the end, she'd learned an important life lesson—don't trust men with your heart. Eventually they'll hurt you when you least expect it.

As for Alex DeLuca, she was so far out of that man's league that it was laughable. So what was she worrying about? She could relax and enjoy having some company for once.

She pressed the automatic garage door opener and started the truck. It coughed and sputtered and the breath caught in her throat. *Please don't let this be another thing I need money to fix.* As though in response to her silent prayer, when she turned the key again the engine caught. She exhaled a pent-up breath and put the vehicle in drive.

In no time at all, Alex was seated next to her. "Reese, thank you for allowing me to ride along."

The *R*s rolled off his tongue in such a divine way. She stopped herself just short of swooning. He could definitely say her name as often as he wanted. Realizing that she was letting her thoughts wander, she reminded herself that he was her guest—nothing else.

"Um…sure. No problem." In an effort to keep her thoughts from straying, she turned on the radio and switched stations until holiday music filled the air. As an afterthought, she said, "I hope you don't mind some music."

"Not at all. Back home my mother used to always have music filling the…house."

She noticed his use of the past tense and then the awkward pause. She wondered if he too was a member of the lost-a-parent-prematurely club. It was not something she'd wish on anyone—no matter the circumstances. But then again, maybe she was reading too much into his choice of words, as English was obviously his second language.

In an effort to change the topic of conversation to something more casual, she said, "That's right, I was supposed to guess where you're from. I'm not great with placing accents, but I'm thinking somewhere in the Mediterranean. Maybe Italy?"

"Very good guess. Maybe you are better at figuring out accents than you think."

English definitely had a different ring to it when Alex was speaking. It had a sort of soothing melody. She could listen to him talk for hours.

"If you don't mind me asking, what brought you to New York?"

"Business. Or should I say, I am between business negotiations. With people being out of the office for the holidays, I decided to stay in New York and experience a white Christmas."

"You hope."

"What?"

She could feel his gaze on her. "I meant you hope to see a white Christmas. Snow around these parts is hit or miss. The snow we're getting now might be all we get until after the New Year."

Was it possible he had no family to go home to? Why else would he rent out an inn for the holiday? Pity welled up in her. She couldn't blame him for not wanting to spend Christmas alone. She'd had a taste of that when her mother was having problems. It was lonely and sad, filled with nothing but memories.

Which led her to her next question: How did such a handsome, obviously successful man end up alone? Surely he wouldn't have a hard time finding a date or two. Oh, who was she kidding? He could probably have a different date for breakfast, lunch and dinner, seven days a week, and still have plenty leftover. Perhaps if her life were different she might have given him a chance.

Alex cleared his throat. "Are you sure we're going in the right direction? We're heading into the city."

She had been distracted by their conversation, but she couldn't imagine she'd turned the wrong way. Just to be sure, she glanced around at the landmarks. "This is the right way."

"But I thought you said we were going to cut down a Christmas tree."

"I said I was going to get one, but I never said anything about cutting it down." She glanced over at him as he slouched down in the seat and adjusted his ball cap. "I'm sorry to disappoint you. But this is really much faster and easier for me."

"Is it much further?"

"Not far at all. In fact, we're here."

She stared out the window at the familiar city lot that was cordoned off with fencing. Pine trees ranging in size from small chubby little guys to tall slender ones littered the lot. People from old to young meandered around, pointing at this tree and that tree. Smiles covered their faces and the years rolled away as each seemed to step back in time and remember the childhood fascination of choosing their very own tree for Santa to leave presents under. If only that feeling of wonderment stayed with everyone. Instead some learned the hard way that things weren't always as they appeared. Sometimes life was nothing more than an empty illusion.

Reese's jaw tightened at the grim thought. Anxious to get this over, she said, "I'll just go check out what's available that will fit in the foyer. Feel free to look around."

"What about a tree for yourself?" When she cast him a puzzled look, he added, "You know, for the apartment?"

"I don't want one. After what happened…oh, never mind. I just don't have the time to bother."

She threw open the truck door and hopped out. She'd already circled around to the sidewalk when Alex's door opened. She noticed that he had the collar on his jacket pulled up and his hat shielded a good portion of his face. He must be cold. If he was here long enough, he'd get used to the cold weather.

He stepped up to her. "Let me know if you need any help."

"I will. Thank you."

His gaze moved up and down the walk. If she knew him better, she'd say he looked stressed. But that couldn't be the case. Who got stressed going to the Christmas tree lot? Maybe a single mom of six active little kids. Now that could be stressful. But not a single grown man.

So what was the true story? Why was Alex all alone for the holidays?

What had he been thinking to agree to come to this very public place?

Alex glanced around to see if anyone had noticed him. It was far too early in his plan to have his true identity made known. Or worse, for someone to snap a picture of him and publish it on the internet. He pulled his ball cap a little lower. Sure, he had his disguise in place, but he knew that it would not hold up under the close scrutiny of the press's cameras.

He slouched a bit more and avoided making eye contact with anyone. Fortunately no one seemed to pay him the least bit of attention. The people meandering about seemed more interested in finding the perfect Christmas tree than the couple of dozen other shoppers.

Thousands of holiday lights were strung overhead. This town certainly had a thing for lights, from the little twinkle ones to big flashing signs. He gazed at the trees, wondering what it'd be like to be here with his own family choosing the perfect tree—not that he had any immediate plans for a family. He knew a proper marriage was expected of him, but the thought didn't appeal to him. His duty was to look after his father, the king.

After all, if it wasn't for him, his mother, the queen, wouldn't have been shot by a subversive. The poignant memory of his mother taking a bullet in the chest brought Alex up short. Because of one thoughtless act, he'd devastated lives, leaving his father brokenhearted and alone to shoulder the weight of Mirraccino's problems.

That long-ago day was still fresh in Alex's mind. He'd grown up overnight and learned the importance of rules and duty. He didn't have the luxury to wonder what his life might be like if he were an ordinary citizen. He was a prince and with that came duties that could not be shirked—the consequences were too much to bear.

Still, that didn't mean he should forgo his manners. And thanking Reese for her hospitality would be the proper thing to do. He stopped in front of a chubby little tree that would look perfect in the apartment. It'd certainly cheer the place up.

A young man with a Santa hat and red apron approached him. "Can I help you?"

"I'd like to buy the little tree in the corner."

The guy eyed him up as though wondering why he'd want something so tiny. The man rattled off a price and Alex handed over the money.

With the little tree stowed in the back of the pickup, Alex sought out his beautiful hostess, who was pointing out a tall, slender tree to an older man with a white beard.

His cheeks were chubby and when he laughed his round belly shook. Alex wondered how many times children had mistaken him for Santa. Even the man's eyes twinkled when he smiled.

The man glanced at Alex before turning back to Reese. "This must be your other half. You two make a fine-looking couple. Is this your first Christmas together?"

"We're not together." Reese's cheeks filled with color. "I mean, we're not a couple. We're…um—"

"Friends," Alex supplied.

Although on second thought, the man's observation did have some merit. In fact, the more he thought of it, the more he wondered if the man was on to something. Reese would make any man the perfect girlfriend.

She was certainly beautiful enough. When she smiled, she beamed. And in the short time he'd known her, he'd gotten a glimpse of her strength and determination.

She'd make the ideal fake girlfriend.

After all, he was supposed to be in the States because of a love interest. And with the speed with which he'd had to put this plan in motion, he hadn't had a chance to find someone to fill the role. But if the need arose, would Reese be willing to play along?

Something told him that with some gentle persuasion, she could be brought round to his way of thinking. Okay, maybe it was more a hope than a feeling. But for now none of that mattered. Hopefully his brother's rushed marriage would be resolved quickly and quietly so that involving Reese wouldn't be necessary. But it never hurt to be prepared. His father's motto was Hope for the Best, But Be Prepared for the Worst.

Perhaps Alex should do a little research and see what challenges he would be up against with Reese. He'd probe the subject with her when they were alone in the truck.

Alex leaned over to Reese. "You found a tree?"

"Yes, I did. I think it'll be perfect." She pointed to the tree the man inserted into a noisy machine. Alex watched as the tree's limbs were compressed and bound with rope.

"It'll make a great Christmas tree. You have good taste."

Reese turned to him and smiled. Such a simple gesture, and yet his breath hitched and he couldn't glance away. Big, fluffy snowflakes fluttered and fell all around them. And the twinkle lights reflected in her eyes, making them glitter like gemstones.

"As soon as they bundle it up we can go home." She moved as if to retrieve the tree, breaking the spell she'd cast over him.

Alex, at last gathering his wits, stepped forward. "I'll get it."

She frowned as though she were about to argue, but then she surprised him by saying, "Okay."

With the tree secured in the bed of the truck, Alex climbed in the heated cab. He rubbed his hands together. "I remembered everything for this outing except my gloves."

Reese's face creased with worry lines. "You should have said something. Here, let me crank up the heat."

"Not necessary. The sting from the pine needles is worse than the cold."

"Let me know if you need anything when we get back to the house. Antiseptic cream, maybe?"

"I will." This was his chance to broach the subject in the forefront of his mind. "What did you think of Santa back there mistaking us for a happy couple?"

"That he needs a new pair of glasses."

"Surely being my girlfriend wouldn't be so bad, would it?"

Once stopped at a red light, Reese gave him a long look.

He started to feel a bit paranoid, as though he had a piece of lettuce in his teeth or something. "What?"

"I'm just looking for some sign that you hit your head when you were swinging that tree around."

"Very funny." When she smiled, a funny sensation filled his chest. "You still haven't answered my question. Would I make good boyfriend material?"

She jerked her gaze forward just as the light changed. "You can't be serious. We—we don't even know each other. And I'm not looking for a relationship. Not with you. Not with anybody."

"Understood." He was at last breaking through her calm reserve. He couldn't push her too hard too fast. "I was just hoping your rejection of the idea of us being a couple wasn't a personal one. After all, I showered and shaved today. My clothes are clean," he teased. "And I carried that great big tree for you."

"That's the best you can come up with?" She smiled and his breathing did that funny little tickle thing at the back of his throat again.

"Pretty much. So if circumstances were different, would I stand a chance with you?"

"I'll give you this much, you are persistent."

"Or maybe I'm a glutton for punishment." He sent her a pleading look.

"And I'm sure those puppy eyes work on all of the ladies, don't they?"

He sat up a little straighter. "Is it working now?"

The chime of laughter filled the truck. "If you aren't a salesman, you certainly missed your calling."

Did that mean he'd sold her on the idea that he was worthy of a second or third look? He didn't know why her answer had suddenly become so important to him. It wasn't as though this part of his plan had to be implemented—yet.

Still, he found himself enjoying the smile on her face. It lit up the night. She should definitely do it more often.

Reese tramped the brakes a bit hard for a red light, jerking him against the seat belt. "I'm sure you'll make some lucky lady the perfect boyfriend."

It was his turn to smile. "Thanks for the ringing endorsement. What would it take to tempt you to play the part?"

"Of what? Your girlfriend?"

In for a penny, in for a pound. "Yes."

She laughed. "Fine. If you must know, if by chance I was looking—which I'm not, but if I were—you might have a chance. But I seriously don't have the time...if I was interested."

"Ouch."

"Is it your hands?"

"No. It was my ego. It just took a direct hit."

She shook her head and smiled. "I'm sure you'll survive."

He leaned back in the seat as she skillfully guided them homeward. With Reese behind the wheel, Alex relaxed enough to let his thoughts wander.

How was it that someone so beautiful and entertaining could be single? Surely she wouldn't be alone for long. The image of Reese in someone else's arms took shape in his mind and with a mental jerk, he dismissed the unsettling idea. Her future relationships were none of his business. Period.

CHAPTER FIVE

PEACE AND QUIET at last.

Reese smiled to herself. The wedding party was off for the rehearsal and dinner. They wouldn't be home until late. She'd even let the staff go early. After all, it was the holiday season and there was nothing here that she couldn't manage on her own. And her mother was upstairs watching her favorite crime drama.

"Reese?" Alex's deep voice echoed down the hallway.

"In here." She was kneeling on the floor, sorting strands of twinkle lights.

He stepped into the room. "What are you doing?"

"Trying to get these lights to work. I need to replace the lightbulbs—one by one. Someday I'll have to buy new strings, but not this year." They would light up—even if she had to sit here all night exchanging the little bulbs. "What do you need?"

"I finished with my work and wondered if I could lend you a hand."

"You spend a lot of time on your computer, don't you?"

"It's a portable office. It allows me to work from anywhere."

She pulled out another bulb and replaced it with one she was certain worked. Still the strand remained dark. "So this isn't a holiday for you?"

"I would rather keep busy. I am not good at sitting around doing nothing." He knelt down beside her. "Let me have a try."

She glanced at him, surprised anyone would voluntarily offer to fix Christmas lights. Before he had a chance to change his mind, she held out the strand to him. "Good luck."

He moved closer. His warm fingers brushed over hers. His touch lingered, sending an electrical current up her arm. The reaction frazzled her common sense. She stared into his eyes as her heart pounded in her ears. He was the first to turn away. A sense of disappointment plagued her.

Regaining her senses, she jumped to her feet. She took a step back, hoping to keep her wits about her. She'd been avoiding him since that awkward moment with Santa—er, that man at the tree lot. Why the man had assumed they were a couple was beyond her. It wasn't as if she looked at Alex with dreamy eyes. Okay, so maybe she just had. But it was just for a moment. And it wasn't as if she was truly interested in him.

But then Alex had continued the conversation in the truck. What was that all about? She still wasn't certain if he had just been joking around or if he'd been hitting on her. At least she'd set him straight—a relationship wasn't in her plans. She refused to be lied to by another man.

Alex pushed a small lightbulb into the socket. Nothing lit up. "I don't smell any food cooking. That's a first. This place always has the most delicious aromas."

In that moment, she realized in her exuberance to let everyone have the evening off that she hadn't thought about dinner. And she didn't have a good history with the stove. Anything she put near it burned—to a crisp.

"I'm afraid that I let the staff have the evening off. With the wedding party gone for the evening and the holidays approaching, I thought they would enjoy some time off. So I'm not sure what to do for dinner, as I'm an utter disaster in the kitchen."

"It doesn't have to be anything fancy. In fact, simple sounds good."

Against her better judgment, she was starting to like this guy. "How simple were you thinking? I can work the microwave, but that's about it."

His brow arched as amusement danced in his eyes.

"Hey, don't look at me like that. A person can't be good at everything. So how about a frozen dinner?"

His tanned nose curled up. "Or we could order a pizza?" He loosened a bulb from the strand. "They do deliver here, don't they?"

She nodded. "I'll check to see if my mother will join us. I'll be right back with the menus."

She rushed out of the room and up the stairs to the little apartment that she'd been sharing with her mother since her father's death two years ago, when her life had changed from that of a carefree college student with the whole world ahead of her to a college dropout, striving to keep a roof over her brokenhearted mother's head.

Not that she would have ever made any other choice. Her mother had always been there for her—she'd made her smile and wiped her tears. Now it was Reese's turn to pitch in and help. That's what families did—took care of each other.

"Hey, Mom," Reese called out, bursting through the door of their apartment. "How do you feel about—"

The words died in her throat as she noticed her mother sitting before a tiny Christmas tree on the coffee table. It was lit up and had a few ornaments on it. What in the world? Where had it come from?

Her mother was staring at it as if she were lost in her

thoughts. Was she thinking about the past? Was her mother remembering how Reese used to beg her father for her very own Christmas tree?

The memories Reese had been suppressing for so long came rushing back. The image of her father's joyful smile as he held a tiny pine tree in his hand had her chest tightening. Back then he'd call her his little princess, and she'd thought the sun rose and set around him. How very wrong she'd been.

"Mom?" Her voice croaked. She swallowed hard and stepped closer to her mother. "Are you okay?"

Her mother blinked and glanced up at her. "I'm fine. But I'm glad you're here. I just had a phone call and your aunt isn't doing well."

Relieved to find that her mother wasn't sinking back into that miserable black hole where she seemed virtually unreachable, Reese asked, "What's wrong with Aunt Min?"

"She's having a hard time adjusting since Uncle Roger passed on. That was her neighbor and she agreed to come pick me up. I know with the holiday approaching and the wedding this weekend that this is the wrong time to be leaving you alone, but no one knows your aunt as well as me."

Reese wasn't so sure about her mother leaving to comfort someone who was grieving. She knew for a fact it was not an easy position to be in. But her mother appeared to be determined, and she supposed there was nothing she could say to change her mind.

"What can I do for you?" Reese asked, ready to pitch in.

"Absolutely nothing. You already have your hands full here." Her mother gave her a hug. "I've got to pack before my ride gets here."

Her mother was headed for the bedroom when Reese called out, "Mom, where did the tree come from?"

"Alex. He thought you might like it."

Her mother disappeared into her bedroom and Reese turned. The long-forgotten handmade ornaments on the little tree caught her eye.

Well, if he was so interested in having a Christmas tree, he could have it in his room—er, her room. She unplugged the lights, carried the tree to the bedroom and pushed aside her collection of miniature teddy bears—some that were as old as she was and some that were antiques collected from her grandmother and yard sales.

She'd always planned to update the room, but once she'd formally withdrawn from college, she'd packed up her apartment and put everything in storage. There wasn't time to worry about knickknacks when there was an entire inn to run. And now she was just too tired after working and smiling at the guests all day to be worried about redecorating a room where she barely spent any time.

She glanced at the bed with its comforter haphazardly pulled up. She imagined Alex sleeping in it. There was something so intimate about knowing that the Mediterranean hunk was sprawled out in her bed. Just as quickly as the thought came to her, she vanquished it.

He was a man—not to be trusted. And he'd only gone and confirmed her thoughts when he went against her wishes with the little Christmas tree—even if it had been an effort to be considerate. Conflicting emotions churned in her stomach. Why couldn't he leave well enough alone?

Not needing or wanting the aggravation, she pulled the door closed on the room. And that's exactly what she needed to do with Alex—close the door on this thing that was bubbling just beneath the surface.

He'd put this off long enough.

Alex retrieved his phone from his pocket. It was time

to let the king know that he was safe. In return, hopefully he would have good news as well. Perhaps this mess with his brother, the crown prince, had been quietly resolved. Then Alex could pack his bags and catch the first flight home—away from his beautiful hostess, who muddled his thoughts and had him losing focus on his priorities.

He dialed the king's private line. The phone was answered on the first ring, as though his papa had been sitting there waiting for him to call.

"Papa, it's me, Alexandro."

"At last, you remember to call."

"I had to move quickly and quietly in order to elude the paparazzi."

"Tell me where you are so I can dispatch your security detail."

"No." Alex's body tensed as he envisioned the dark expression settling over his papa's distinct features. It wasn't often that someone said no to the king. In fact, this was the first time Alex had done it since he was an unruly child. "I have to do this. It's the only way to protect the family. If your enemies learn of Demetrius's rash actions, they'll make it a public scandal by painting him as unfit to rule. They'll gain more support for their planned takeover."

"That's not for you to worry about. The royal cabinet has that under control."

He wanted to believe his papa's comforting words, but Alex had his own sources and they all told him that these subversives meant business. He knew that no matter how old he got, his papa would still try to shield him from the harsh realities of life. But now wasn't the time for being protective. There'd already been one uprising that year. They couldn't risk another.

"I understand, Papa. But trust me when I say I have to do this. It's for the best. As long as the press is curious of my activities, they'll focus on me instead of sniffing around the palace for a piece of juicy gossip."

The king let out a long, weary sigh. "I'll admit that it has been helpful. So far only the necessary staff know of this debacle. The councillor seems to think we should be able to clear this up soon…if only your brother would come to his senses."

"You're still opposed to this marriage?"

"In these uncertain times, we need a strong liaison with one of our allies." There was a strained pause. "If only this girl had some important connections."

His papa sounded much older than he'd ever heard him before. Alex's gut knotted with frustration. When was his older twin ever going to learn that he had responsibilities to the crown, the kingdom and to their papa, who would never step down from the throne until he was secure in the fact that his successor was up to the challenge of safeguarding the kingdom. His father had never rebounded fully after the queen's death. And now his health was waning.

Alex recalled how he'd made it to her side as she drew in her last breaths. Pain arrowed through his chest. She'd told him to take care of his papa. He'd promised to do it. And that's what he'd been striving to do ever since. Not that anything he did could make up for his part in his mother's death.

"Don't worry, Papa. I know what I'm doing."

Alex's thoughts strayed back to their visit to the Christmas tree lot.

You two make a fine-looking couple.

The more he thought of Santa's words, the more he was certain he was right—Reese had the right beauty and poise to pull off the plan he had in mind. Perhaps it was time he started figuring out ways to fit Reese into his agenda.

"Papa, everything will work out. When the time is right, I'll call for my security detail."

There was another pause. He wondered if the king was debating whether or not to command he change his plans and return home immediately.

"Alex?" The sound of Reese's voice trailed down the hallway.

"Papa, I must go. I'll call again soon." And with that he disconnected the call and switched off his phone. "I'm coming." He reached for the cabinet next to the sink, searching for a glass.

"Oh, here you are. I thought maybe you changed your mind about dinner and decided to cook instead."

"I don't cook, either. I just got thirsty." And he truly was thirsty after tap-dancing around, trying to pacify his papa.

After he downed a glassful of water and set it aside, he turned to her. "What did you need?"

"I ran upstairs to get these." She held up an array of menus.

She'd been in the apartment and that meant she must have noticed the little Christmas tree that he'd decorated to cheer up the place. Her mother had supplied some old ornaments. So why hadn't Reese mentioned it?

"Here." She stepped closer with her hand outstretched. "Pick your favorite."

He waved her away. "You pick. Whatever you choose will be fine."

Her gaze didn't meet his. "Are you sure?"

He nodded. He'd made enough decisions for tonight. He didn't feel like making any more, even if it was something as simple as pizza. In some ways, he used to envy his brother for being the crown prince, with the way people looked up to him. But as Alex got older, he was relieved to have been delivered second. It was very stressful and tiring making decisions day in and day out that impacted so many people.

Sure, to the world being royalty was all glamour and five-star dinners and balls. But behind palace walls in the executive suite there were heated debates, and the newspapers were quite critical of the decisions made by the monarchy. There was no way to please everyone all of the time.

But in this one instance, Alex was needed to keep the Mirraccino Islands together and peaceful. He would do whatever it took to keep the paparazzi from finding out the truth. Because he knew all too well what happened when a royal forgot his allegiance to the kingdom—the price was much too dear.

He cleared the lump in his throat. "While you call in the order, I can set up the tree in the living room."

"Did you get the lights to work?"

"Yes, I did. It was one bulb that was burned out. I replaced it and at last, there was light."

"Thank you." Her tone held no warmth. "Um, about the tree...I usually set it up over there next to the staircase. But I can do that myself—"

"Consider it done."

"I thought maybe you'd be tired of decorating."

So she had noticed the little tree. And it didn't seem as though she was pleased. Sure, she'd told him not to bother, but he'd thought she was too busy to do it herself and would enjoy the surprise. Her cool demeanor told him that her reason for not wanting a tree went much deeper than that.

"Christmas is one of my favorite holidays." He wondered if maybe she'd open up a little.

"That's nice." Her frosty tone chilled him. "I put the boxes of decorations next to it."

"You'll need to show me. I don't know how you want it decorated."

"Oh, that's easy. I always start with the white twinkle lights. Then I add gold ribbon and red glass ornaments."

"Do you trim the tree by yourself?"

"Yes. I find it is easier. I know how it should look, so why bother explaining how I want it when I can just as easily do it myself? In fact, you don't need to bother with it. I'll just place this call and be right back."

Reese strode out of the room like a woman on a mission. He thought it was sad that she insisted on doing so much around this place by herself. It sounded very lonely. Well, this Christmas would be different. He walked over to the tree and moved it to a spot next to the steps.

This Christmas he'd help her find the joy of the holiday.

CHAPTER SIX

WHY DIDN'T HE listen to her?

Reese frowned when she returned to the foyer. Alex was busy stringing the lights. And he didn't have the tree in the right spot. She usually moved it a little closer to the stairs to keep it out of the way. She knew she was being picky. She'd known for a long time that it was one of her faults. But things must be in their proper place or it drove her to distraction.

Alex turned to her. "I went ahead and started."

She nodded, trying to not let it bother her that the tree was out of place. Or that the lights needed to be redone if they were going to make it the whole way to the top.

"You don't like it?"

She knew that he'd tried his best and she really did appreciate it. She shifted her weight from one foot to the other and continued holding her tongue. Why did it have to bother her so much? She was being silly.

"What is it?" His eyes beseeched her.

She let out a pent-up breath. "The tree needs to be moved back out of the way."

"I know. But it is easier to decorate it here."

"And the lights, they need to be spread out a little more or you'll run out before you get to the top."

He arched an eyebrow. "You can try to get me to quit, but I won't. I'm going to help you decorate this tree."

"You're stubborn."

"And you're picky."

"Something tells me we have that in common." She could give as good as she got.

He smiled. "Maybe I am. But I know what I like."

His gaze was directly on her as he stepped closer. Her heart shot into her throat, cutting off her breath. His gaze dipped to her mouth before returning to meet her curious stare.

"You're very beautiful." The backs of his fingers brushed her cheek.

She should move, but her feet wouldn't cooperate. Shivers of excitement raced down her neck and arms, leaving goose bumps in their wake. She stared into his mesmerizing blue eyes, drowning in their depths. It'd been so long since a man had been interested in her. And she hadn't realized until now how lonely she'd become. After Josh—

The memory of her ex jarred her to her senses. She stepped back. This couldn't happen. She'd promised herself that she'd keep men at a safe distance.

Alex's hand lowered to his side. If she didn't know better, she'd say there was a flicker of remorse in his eyes. What should she say to him? After all, he wasn't Josh. Her ex had been needy and demanding. Alex was thoughtful and understanding. They were opposites in almost everything. So why was she backing away? After all, he'd soon be moving on and returning to his home—far away.

Maybe she shouldn't have backed away. Maybe she should have satisfied her curiosity to see if his kisses were as passionate as she imagined them in her dreams.

But the moment had passed. There was no recapturing

it. She moved to the tree and knelt down to start adjusting the string of lights.

"Could you help me on the other side of the tree?" She tried to act as though the moment hadn't shaken her.

"Just tell me what you need me to do."

To Alex's credit, he let the awkward moment pass without question. By the time they moved the decorated tree into the correct position, Reese had to admit that she'd enjoyed her evening. Alex was actually quite entertaining with his various bits of trivia. Who would have guessed it?

It wasn't until after the wedding guests streamed through the front door that she was able to lock up the house. She climbed the steps to the tiny apartment, anxious to call it a night. She was just about to close the door when she heard footsteps bounding up the stairs. She didn't need two guesses to know that the heavy footsteps didn't belong to the anxious bride across the hall or one of her smiling attendants. No, it was the one man who got under her skin. She thought of rushing off to her mother's bedroom, but she felt the need to thank him for making a chore that normally came with some harsh, painful memories into a pleasant experience.

She turned to him. Her gaze settled on his lips. The memory of their almost kiss sent her stomach spiraling. "I—I'm heading to bed. I just wanted to thank you for the help tonight. If it wasn't for you, I would still be working at it."

"You're welcome. And it turned out well, even if it isn't exactly how you normally do it." His brows drew together as his gaze swept around the room. "What happened to the little Christmas tree?"

"I moved it to your room. I thought you could appreciate it better in there."

"But I did it for you."

"And I told you that I didn't want a tree."

"But the tree downstairs—"

"Is the price of doing business. Guests expect an inn to be decked out for the holidays, and it's my job to fulfill those expectations. But that doesn't mean I have to decorate my personal space."

"I was only trying to help."

"That's not the type of help I need." The words were out before she could stop them. Exhaustion and worry had combined, causing her thoughts to slip past her lips. "I'm sorry. I didn't mean to snap at you."

He shook his head. "You're right. I thought—ah, it doesn't matter what I thought."

The hurt look in his eyes had her scrambling for an explanation. "It's just that Christmas brings back bad memories for me and my mother. And I'm afraid that it'll upset her. I'll do anything to keep her from going back to that lonely dark place where she went after my father died."

He eyed her up as though he were privy to her most private thoughts. "Your mother seems like a strong lady. Perhaps she's stronger than you think."

Reese shook her head, recalling how her mother had crumbled after learning that her father had been on his way to his mistress when he'd died in a car accident on Christmas Eve. Loss and betrayal combined to create the perfect storm to level her mother—a woman she'd always admired for her strength. It had brought her mother to her knees and Reese never wanted to witness anything so traumatic again.

Reese pressed her hands to her hips. "You don't know her like I do."

"That's true. But sometimes an outsider can see things someone too close to the situation will miss."

She lifted her chin. "And what exactly have I missed?"

"Did you know it was your mother who got out the Christmas decorations for me to use on the little tree?"

"You must have pressured her. She wouldn't have voluntarily gotten those out. Those were…were our family ornaments, collected over the years."

"Actually, it was her idea. She insisted I decorate it for you. She thought it would make you happy."

No, that wasn't possible. Was it? Reese took a step back. When the back of her knee bumped into the couch, she sat down. What did this mean? Had she been so busy that she'd missed seeing that her mother truly was back to being herself?

"I had no idea it would upset you so much."

"It's just that…that my father always made Christmas such a big affair. It's hard to think of it and not think of him." But she failed to add the most painful part. She couldn't bring herself to admit that her father had left them on Christmas Eve for another woman. And he'd spent their money on that woman…buying her a house and leaving them in debt.

Alex stepped forward and took a seat beside her. "I didn't know."

"My mother didn't mention it?"

"She said that it has been awhile since you two celebrated Christmas, and she thought it was time you both had a good one."

Reese's heart filled with an unexpected joy. "She really said that?"

He nodded. "Otherwise I wouldn't have gone through with decorating the tree without your approval."

If this was okay with her mother, who was she to disapprove? Maybe it hadn't just been her mother who'd been deeply affected by her father's actions. In the past couple of years, Reese had been so busy worrying about keeping a roof over their heads that she hadn't realized how much her father's actions had hurt her. Or how she'd let her father steal the magic of the holiday from her.

Reese turned to Alex. "I'm sorry I was so grinchy about it."

"Grinchy?"

"Yeah, you know the story, *How the Grinch Stole Christmas?*"

"I'm not familiar with it."

"I didn't think there was anyone who didn't know that story. You must have lived a sheltered life."

"I had books, but they were educational."

"Like I said, you lived a sheltered life. Don't worry. I'm sure we can find you a copy somewhere and broaden your horizons."

"My horizons are plenty broad," he protested. "Would you mind if I brought the tree back out here?"

"Suit yourself." She most certainly wasn't the only one used to having her way.

As he strode away, she wondered why it had taken a total stranger from another land to open her eyes and help her see her life more clearly. It was as if she'd been living with tunnel vision these past couple of years, focusing on protecting her mother from further pain and keeping their home.

And though Alex was certainly a nice distraction, she couldn't let herself lose focus now. The Willows was far from being out of debt. In fact, even with Alex's generous fee she still might have to let go of Sandy, the maid and a single mom. The thought pinched at her heart.

With it being Christmas, surely there would be a miracle or something. It wasn't as though she was really a grinch, but if she had to eliminate Sandy's position at Christmastime, the comparison with that fictional character would hit far too close to home—heartless.

"Here we go." Alex strode back into the room.

She noticed how when he entered a room, his presence commanded attention. She wasn't sure what it was about him that gave her that impression. It could be his good looks or his six-foot-plus height. But no. It went beyond that. It was something much more significant, but she just couldn't put her finger on it. Maybe it was the way he carried himself, with a straight spine and level shoulders. Or the way he had that knowing look in his blue eyes. She sighed in frustration, unable to nail down exactly what was so different about him.

Alex paused. "Did you change your mind?"

"Oh, no. I guess I'm more tired than I'd originally thought."

"After I plug in this cord, would you mind turning out the lights? There's nothing like the glow of a Christmas tree."

She got to her feet and moved to the switch.

When the colored bulbs lit up the chubby little tree that to Reese resembled nothing more than a branch, she doused the overhead light. But it wasn't the tree that caught and held her attention. It was the look on Alex's face. For a second, it was the marvel of a little boy staring at a Christmas tree for the first time.

"Isn't your Christmas tree like this?" She was genuinely curious.

He shook his head. "It's quite tall and it's more formal, similar to the one you have downstairs."

"You mean it doesn't have candy canes and little bell and penguin ornaments?"

Again he shook his head. "No. Everything has to be picture-perfect. The way my mother would have wanted it."

A little voice in the back of her mind said to let the comment pass, but she couldn't. She wanted to know more about him. Maybe if she demystified him, he'd have less of a hold on her thoughts.

"Your mother…did you lose her?"

The words hung heavy in the air.

At last, Alex nodded. "She died when I was a teenager. Christmas was her favorite holiday. In fact, Papa still has the—the house decorated like she used to do. On Christmas Eve, for just a moment, it's like she's still there and going to step into the living room at any moment."

"It's good that you have such happy memories to hold on to."

"Enough about me. I'm sure you have special memories of the holidays."

She waved away his comment. "They aren't worth getting into."

She wished she could concentrate on the good times, but her father's betrayal had smeared and practically obliterated them. In her mind, that man was not worth remembering. Not after what he'd done to them. She stuffed the memories to the back of her mind.

This was why she no longer enjoyed the holidays—they dredged up unwanted memories. She wished she had nothing but good memories, like Alex. She envied him.

"I'm going to sleep." Not that she'd close her eyes any time soon. "Would you mind turning out the lights before you go to bed?"

"Not a problem." He smiled at her and her stomach fluttered. "But before you go, there's one other thing."

With nothing but the gentle glow of the little tree filling the room, it was far too romantic. Her gaze returned to his lips. They looked smooth and soft. She wondered what it'd be like to meet up with him under the mistletoe. Realizing she'd hung some downstairs for the bride and groom to indulge in, she wished she'd saved some for up here.

Alex cleared his throat. As her gaze rose to meet his, amusement danced in his eyes. Surely he didn't have a clue what she'd been thinking. Did he?

"What were you saying?" She struggled to do her best to sound normal and not let on that her heart was racing faster than the hooves of the horses who pulled the carriages around Central Park.

"I don't want to embarrass you, but did you know you have a leak in your roof?"

She nodded. "I had it fixed last week. I just haven't gotten around to getting the interior repaired."

"I could take a look at it. If you want."

She shook her head. "You're a paying guest. Not hired help."

"But I am volunteering."

Why did he always have to push? Well, this time he wasn't getting his way. "I don't need your help."

He stared at her long and hard as though trying to get her to change her mind. "Understood. I'll see you tomorrow."

At last she'd gotten through to him. "Good night."

She turned and headed back down the hall. She could sense his gaze following her, but she refused to glance back. He created a mixed-up ball of emotions in her that constantly kept her off kilter.

And what unsettled her the most was the fact that she liked him. No matter how much he pushed and prodded her, beneath it all he was genuinely a nice guy. Although he was awfully tight-lipped about his past and his family. She noticed how every time he started to mention a piece of his life, he clammed up. What was that all about?

Time passed quickly. In no time at all, Alex moved across the hall to the executive suite. He was amazed by how hard

Reese worked every single day, from the time she got up before the sun until she dropped into bed late at night. He soon found himself bored of the internet, even though his leaked letter to the paparazzi had worked as he'd hoped. Now the gossip sites were filled with all sorts of outlandish stories, but the most important part was that they were looking for him. He just had to keep his disguise in place a little longer.

He thought of Reese and how she'd react upon learning he was a prince. Somehow he couldn't imagine she'd treat him any different if she knew the truth. Or was it that he didn't want her to treat him different? He liked their budding friendship—in fact, he liked it very much.

Guilt plagued him for not being more open with her. She'd been kind and generous with him—he wanted to treat her with the same sort of respect. He considered telling her everything, but in the next thought he recalled how deviating from the plan had cost his mother her life.

Alex paced back and forth in his suite. It was best for everyone to keep up the pretense of being a businessman—which he truly was back in Mirraccino. What he needed now was something to keep him busy.

It was still early in the morning when he strode across the hall to Reese's apartment and rapped his knuckles firmly on the dark wood door. No answer. After having lived with her for the past few days, he didn't think anything of trying the doorknob. When it opened, he stepped inside.

"Reese, are you here?"

Again, no answer.

He glanced around, pleased to find that the little tree was still centered on the coffee table and a cottony white cloth with little sparkles had been placed around the base. Maybe at last Reese was starting to find her holiday spirit.

Though the place was clean, it was showing its age. It was very striking how different this apartment was from his polished, well-kept suite. He turned in a circle, taking in the details. The yellowing walls could use a fresh coat of paint. And the ceiling was missing plaster where the roof had leaked.

A thought started to take shape. He might be of royal blood, but that didn't mean he hadn't gotten his hands dirty. Thanks to a very patient maintenance worker who used to be put in charge of him whenever he got in trouble as a youth, he'd learned a lot. Probably a lot more than most people of his status. And it wasn't until now that he realized what a gift it was to have a practical skill set.

He set off to the downstairs in search of Reese. When he couldn't locate her anywhere, he ended up in the kitchen. The chef was there. He was a unique guy, tall and wiry and about Alex's age, maybe a little younger. But his worn face said that there was so much more to his life's story than cooking for pampered guests. Above all that, the guy seemed like an all-around fine fellow.

"Good morning, Bob. Have you seen Reese this morning?"

"Morning. What would you like for breakfast? I can whip you up something in no time. If you want to wait in the dining room, I'll bring it in to you."

"That won't be necessary. I can eat in here." Alex set about getting himself a cup of coffee before Bob could make the offer. "About Reese, have you seen her?"

"She passed through here awhile ago, mumbling something about business to take care of. She wasn't in a talkative mood. Come to think of it, I haven't seen her since. In fact, I'm not used to this place being so utterly quiet."

Bob's last comment stuck with Alex. He never really thought about Reese keeping her staff on duty just for him.

That certainly wasn't necessary. He could fend for himself. After all, he was supposed to be just an ordinary citizen— not royalty. He'd have a word with her later.

"Do you like working here?" Alex took his cup of black coffee and sat down at the marble counter.

"I'm lucky to have this job. Reese helped me out at a really bad time in my life." Bob turned back to the stove. "If it wasn't for Reese, who knows where I would have ended up."

"I take it she's a good boss?"

"The best." Bob turned from the omelet he was preparing and pointed his spatula at Alex. "And I won't stand by and let someone hurt her."

Alex held up his palms innocently. "You don't have to worry about me. I'll be moving on soon."

"Good."

"Now that we have that clear, I was wondering if you might help me with a special project."

Bob wiped his hands off on a towel. "Depends on what you have in mind."

"I have some extra time on my hands and I'd like to put it to good use."

"Well, if you're looking for things to do, you can sight-see or hit the clubs. They don't call it the city that never sleeps for no reason."

Alex shook his head. "I had something else in mind. But I'll need your help."

Bob sat an empty bowl in the sink. After a quick glance at the omelet, he stepped up to the counter. "What exactly do you have in mind?"

CHAPTER SEVEN

"WHAT ARE YOU DOING?"

Reese glared up at Alex, who was standing on a ladder in the corner of the living room. With a chisel in one hand and a hammer in the other, he turned. Was that guilt reflected in his blue eyes?

"I got bored." He lowered the hand tools to the top of the ladder.

She crossed her arms. "So you decided to make a mess of my apartment?"

Her gaze swept across the room, taking in the drop cloths covering everything. Cans and tools sat off to the side. And then her gaze settled back on the culprit. Alex was flashing her a guilty grin like some little boy caught with his hand in the cookie jar. But she refused to let his good looks and dopey grin get to her.

"Alex, explain this. What in the world are you doing?"

"Fixing the ceiling."

She frowned at him. What was this man thinking? Obviously he hadn't been when he made the hole in her ceiling. It would cost a small fortune to repair it—money she didn't have. She'd already made the rounds to the banks. No one was willing to help her refinance The Willows. She was officially tapped out.

In fact, she'd returned home determined to figure out a

way to meet next month's payroll. She really didn't want to let Sandy go before Christmas. Reese would do anything to keep that from happening, but sometimes the best of intentions just weren't enough.

"Alex, do you know what a mess you've created? There's no way that I'll be able to get someone in here to fix it."

"You don't need to hire anyone. I have this under control."

Her neck was getting sore staring up at him. "Would you get down off that ladder so I can talk to you without straining my neck?"

He did as she asked and approached her. He was so tall. So muscular. And as her gaze rose up over his broad chest and shoulders, she realized having him step off the ladder was a big miscalculation on her part.

His navy T-shirt was stretched across his firm chest. Her mouth grew dry. Did he have to look so good? Specks of crumbled plaster covered him, from his short dark hair to the jeans that hung low on his lean waist. She resisted the urge to brush him off—to see if his muscles were as firm as they appeared.

"If you'd give me a chance, I think you'll be impressed with what I can do."

She didn't doubt that she'd be very impressed, but her mind was no longer on the repairs. Her thoughts had tumbled into a far more dangerous territory.

Her gaze settled on his mouth. Was he an experienced kisser? With his sexy looks, he was definitely experienced in a lot more than kissing. The temperature in the room started to climb. When she realized that he was staring back at her, waiting for a response, she struggled to tamp down her raging hormones.

"You need to stop what you're doing. This—this is a

bad idea." She didn't know if the words were meant more for him or for herself.

"Really, I can do this. I used to help—" He glanced down at the carpet. "The guy who fixed up our house when I was a kid. I learned a lot."

She groaned. "When you were a kid? Are you serious?"

"Trust me."

She resisted the urge to roll her eyes and instead glanced back up at the looming hole in her ceiling. A cold draft brushed across her skin. A band of tension tightened across her forehead. She couldn't leave the ceiling in this condition; she'd go broke trying to keep the place warm.

"Seeing as you started this project without my permission, you can't possibly expect me to pay you to do the repairs."

His blue eyes lit up. "I agree. And truthfully, I did try to ask you before starting this, but when you were gone for the day, I thought I'd surprise you."

"Humph…you certainly achieved your goal." She eyed him. "You know I really should toss you to the curb. No one would blame me. Tell me, do you always go around vandalizing people's homes?"

His dark brows drew together. "That's not what I'm doing. And I've never done this for anyone else."

"What makes me so special?" She stared at him, looking for a sign of pity in his eyes. And if she found it, she didn't care what it cost her. She would show him to the door. She didn't do handouts.

His gaze was steady. "The truth is you'd be helping me."

"Helping you?" That wasn't the answer she'd been expecting. Before she could say more, the phone rang. "Don't move. I'll be right back."

She walked away, still trying to wrap her mind around what had gotten into him. She'd bet ten to one odds he didn't know what he was doing. She really ought to bounce him out on his very cute backside…but she needed the money he'd paid to stay here. Being hard up for money really did limit one's options—she hated learning things the hard way.

Of course when she answered the phone and found an impatient creditor at the other end, it did nothing to improve her mood. The man wanted to know why they hadn't received a payment for the past month. After she tap-danced her way into an extension, she walked back into the apartment. Alex was back up on the ladder, making the hole in her ceiling even bigger. She inwardly groaned.

"Do you ever listen to instructions?" She didn't even bother to mask the frustration in her voice.

He glanced down at her and shot her a sheepish grin. "I want to get as much done today as I can."

"And what if I tell you that I want you to stop?"

His gaze searched hers. "Is that what you really want?"

"It doesn't matter what I want. I don't have the money to hire a contractor. I've got creditors calling and wanting to know why they haven't been paid." She pressed her lips tightly together, realizing she'd spoken those words out loud.

"Are things really that bad?"

She shrugged, not meeting his gaze. "I'll turn things around. One way or the other."

"I'm sure you will." He glanced back at the work waiting for him. "In the meantime, I better get back to work, because I don't want to miss dinner."

She cast a hesitant look back at the hole in the ceiling before turning back to him. "You promise you know what you're doing?"

He smiled and crossed his heart. "I promise."

With effort, she resisted the urge to return the smile.

She wanted him to know that she was serious. Was it his sexy accent that made his promise so much easier to swallow? Or was it something more?

"Okay. I have a few things to do before dinner."

She reached the doorway when he said, "You know you don't have to keep Bob around on my account. I can fend for myself."

"This is his job and he's counting on a paycheck. The stubborn man doesn't accept anything that might be construed as charity."

Alex sent her a knowing smile. "Sounds like the pot calling the pot black."

"It's kettle. The pot calling the kettle black."

"So it is. And you, my dear, are the pot."

With a frustrated sigh, she turned her back on Alex and the crater-size hole in the ceiling. She had bigger problems to solve. Like finding a way out of this horrendous financial mess that she'd inherited. The thought of her father and how much trouble he'd brought to her and her mother renewed Reese's determination not to fall for Alex's charm. She needed to keep things simple where men were concerned—especially where Alex was concerned.

Not yet.

Alex groaned and hit the snooze setting on his phone, silencing the loud foghorn sound. He'd been having the most delightful dream and Reese was in it. He'd been holding her close with her generous curves pressing to him. A moan rose in his throat as he desperately tried to recreate the dream.

She'd been gazing up at him with those eyes that could bend him to her will with just a glance. He'd been about to kiss her when the blasted alarm interrupted.

Try as he might, there was no returning to Reese's arms.

He rolled over and stretched. Days had turned into two weeks and his body had adjusted to the time change. He wondered how much longer he'd be here.

For the first time, the thought of packing his bags and catching the first flight back to Mirraccino didn't sound appealing. This chance to be a regular citizen instead of a royal prince was far more appealing than he'd imagined— Reese's face and those luscious lips filled his mind.

The images from his dream followed him to the shower—a cold shower. After all, it was only a dream, a really hot dream, but a dream just the same.

He pulled a pair of jeans from the wicker laundry basket. Reese had generously offered to show him how to do his own laundry. He had much to learn, but he didn't mind. However, when he pulled a T-shirt out of the dryer to fold, he frowned. It was pink. Pink?

He balled it up and tossed it aside. His thoughts turned back to his beautiful hostess. Maybe if he were to tell her the truth about himself he could—what? Ask her to hook up with him? No. Reese wasn't the love 'em and leave 'em type.

He pushed the tormenting thoughts to the back of his mind as he finished up his laundry and sat down at his computer. He typed his name in the search engine. In no time at all, there were thousands of results. Good. He had their attention now. His gaze skimmed down over the top headlines: *With Rising Tensions in Mirraccino, Where Is Prince Alexandro? Is Prince Alexandro on a Secret Mission? The Mirraccino Palace Is Mum about Prince Alexandro's Absence.*

The headlines struck a chord with him. He should be at home, helping his papa. Instead he was here, repairing a hole in the ceiling for a woman whose image taunted him at night while her lush lips teased him by day. Still, he was doing an important function. As long as the press was sniffing out stories about him, his family could function under the radar.

A couple of older photos of him popped up on social networks with new tags. They were of him posing with beautiful women. All of them were strangers to him. He honestly couldn't even recall their names. Once the photos were taken, they'd gone their separate ways. *Then he saw one headline, proclaiming:*

Did the Prince Ditch Duty for Love?

His clenched hand struck the desktop, jarring his computer. No, he didn't. But no one outside of the family would ever know that he was doing his duty—no matter how much it cost him. No matter how much he hated keeping the truth from Reese.

His gaze roamed over the headlines again and he frowned. No one was going to win his heart. He didn't have time for foolish notions of Cupid and hearts. When it came time for him to marry, it would be because it was what was expected of him.

He wouldn't set himself up for the horrendous pain he'd seen his father live through after his mother's death. Or the years of loneliness. It had almost been too much to observe.

Yet Alex couldn't let the headlines get to him. They created the attention he wanted—even if they poked at some soft spots. He supposed under the circumstances he couldn't be choosy about how the swirl of curiosity happened as long as it worked.

Perhaps it was time to feed the press a few more bread crumbs. He wrote an anonymous email that because of his security precautions would be impossible for the paparazzi to trace.

To whom it concerns:
I have inside information about Prince Alexandro Castanavo's whereabouts. For a little extra money I have photos.
But this information will not come cheap. It'll be worth the
hefty price tag. Let's just say the prince is not off doing
diplomatic work. Time is ticking. This offer has gone out
to numerous outlets. First come, first served.

He smiled as he pressed send. That should spark some
interest.

Not about to waste any more time, he set aside his laptop
and headed straight to Reese's apartment to check on the
primer he'd applied to the walls and ceiling. All the while,
his thoughts centered on Reese. He desperately wanted to
be up front with her about everything.

But he knew people weren't always what they seemed
and that sometimes they were put in positions where they
were forced to make choices they might otherwise not
make. This financial crisis Reese was facing was one such
instance where she might do something desperate to bring
in money to keep this place afloat.

And what would be easier than selling the story of a
prince undercover while the crown prince eloped with a
woman he barely knew? But another voice, a much louder
voice inside him, said he was being overly cautious. Reese
was trustworthy. And the time had come to be honest with
her…about everything.

CHAPTER EIGHT

THIS WAS THE answer to her problems.

It had to be.

Reese stood in the inn's office, staring at the paintings she'd completed back before she'd dropped out of school. They'd been viewed by notable figures in the art world and generous offers had been made. Of course, in her infinite wisdom, she'd wanted to hold out, so she'd turned down the offers. She'd dreamed of one day having her own gallery showing. Of people requesting her work by name. But all of that had come to a crashing end one snowy night.

Now her only hope to hang on to the only life she'd ever known came down to selling these paintings. And if she didn't sell them, she'd have to let Sandy go just days before Christmas. The thought made her stomach roll.

Who ever said being the boss was a great thing?

Sometimes it just downright rotten.

And this was most definitely one of those times.

"What's put that frown on your face?"

She glanced up to find Alex leaning casually against the doorjamb. A black T-shirt stretched across his broad chest. The short sleeves strained around his bulging biceps as he crossed his arms. No one had a right to look that good.

When her gaze lifted to his mouth, he smiled. Her stomach did a somersault. What was it about him that had her thinking she should have taken more time with her makeup or at least flat ironed her hair into submission instead of throwing it haphazardly into a ponytail?

She swallowed hard and hoped her voice sounded nonchalant. "I was thinking."

"Must be something serious."

"I—I just figured out a solution to a problem." She moved away from the canvases, hoping Alex wouldn't be too curious.

"That's great—"

"Did you need something?" She shuffled some papers around on her desk to keep from looking at him. "Please don't tell me there's a problem with the apartment."

"Not like you're imagining. I'm almost finished."

"Really?" This good news was music to her ears.

"Yes. But I wanted to talk to you about something."

"Can it wait?" She sent him a pleading look. "I was on my way out the door."

He didn't say anything at first. "Of course it can wait until later."

"Good." She didn't need any more problems right now. "Do you need anything while I'm out?"

"Actually, I do." He stepped up to her desk. "And your offer keeps me from having to call a cab."

She laughed. "Come on. What was that cabbie's name? Freddy?" Alex nodded and she continued to tease him. "I'm sure Freddy would love to give you a ride."

Alex shook his head vehemently. "That is never going to happen. I think he had delusions of being a grand prix driver."

She patted Alex's arm, noticing the steely strength beneath her fingertips. As the zing of awareness arrowed into her chest, the breath caught in her throat. She raised her head and their gazes caught and held. Was he going to kiss her? They'd been doing this dance for so long now that it had become pure torture. The wondering. The imagining.

Her gaze connected with his. Definite interest reflected in them. Would it be so bad giving in this once and seeing if he could kiss as well as she imagined when she was alone in the dark of the night, tossing and turning?

Alex cleared his throat. "Do you have pen and paper?"

"What?" She blinked.

"I need to write you a list."

"Oh. Right."

Then, realizing she was still touching him, she pulled her hand away, immediately noticing how her fingers cooled off. He was definitely hot and in more than one way. And she'd just made a fool of herself. She'd only imagined he was interested in her. Her cheeks warmed as she handed over a pen and notepad.

His gaze was unwavering as he looked at her. "I appreciate you doing me this favor."

He wrote out the short list before reaching into his back pocket and pulling out some cash. He handed both over to her.

"I don't need money. After all, it's my ceiling that you're repairing. The least I can do is pay for the supplies."

"And you wouldn't be paying for those supplies right now if it weren't for my idea to surprise you and start the job without your permission."

She had a feeling that the money was being offered because he felt sorry for her. But he made a valid point. With that thought in mind, she folded the money and slipped it in her pocket.

"I should get going. I have to get the truck loaded up." It wasn't until the words were out of her mouth that she realized she'd said too much.

Alex glanced back at the canvases. "Are those what you need put in the truck?"

"Yes. But I've got it."

He strode over to her paintings. "What are you doing with these?"

How much should she tell him? She found herself eager to get his take on her plan. After all, it wasn't as though she could talk to any of the staff. She didn't want to worry them. And her mother, well, even if she was still at the house, she wouldn't understand. She'd beg Reese to keep the paintings—that they were too precious to part with.

But other lives were counting on her now.

Alex stepped over to the cases that held what she thought were her three best pieces of work. "Do you mind if I take a look?"

She did mind, but she found herself saying, "Go ahead. Just be careful. I can't let anything happen to those."

She had to admit that she really was curious about his reaction to her work. Would he like the pieces? Her stomach shivered in anticipation.

Alex took his time looking over each piece. He made some very observant comments that truly impressed her. If she didn't know better, she'd think that he too was an art student.

"Those are very impressive."

"Do you mean it?"

"Of course." He made direct eye contact with her. "You're quite talented."

Sure, she'd been told her work was good by experts, but there was just something about Alex seeing her work that made her feel exposed. Maybe it was that a stranger's opinions could be swept aside, but Alex's impression of her art would stay with her. For a moment, she wondered when his opinion had begun to mean so much to her.

"Do you still paint?"

She shook her head. "I don't have time for things like that these days."

"This place must keep you busy." He glanced back at the paintings. "Are you planning to sell these?"

"I'm going to speak with some gallery owners about showing them. I'm hoping that they'll fetch a good price. A couple of years ago, I had people interested in them. But back then I had bigger plans. I wanted to keep them and have a showing. But life took a sharp turn before any of that could happen...if it ever would have."

"I am sure it would have."

"Are you an artist?"

He shook his head. "I don't have an artistic bone in my body. I can only appreciate others' work. And you're very good."

"Thank you. At one point in my life I thought I'd have a future in art. I'd been dreaming about it since I was a little girl. But things change."

"You shouldn't give up on your dreams. No one should."

She shook her head, wanting to chase away the *what if*s and the *maybe*s. "That part of my life is over."

"You're young. You have lots of choices ahead of you."

"My mother needs me. I won't just abandon her like... erm...it doesn't matter. I don't even know why we're talking about it. I need to get these in the truck and soon I'll have the money to keep the doors to this place open."

What was taking her so long?

Alex paced the length of the living room. She'd been gone all day. How long did it take to talk to a couple of people? Surely they'd worked all of the details of the sale out by now. After all, he hadn't just been boosting her ego—she really was talented.

Now that he'd made up his mind to be honest with her about himself, he was anxious to get it over with. He doubted she would take the news well at first. She might not even believe him. But hopefully he'd be able to smooth things over. He couldn't imagine what it'd be like to have Reese turn her back on him—not speak to him again. His chest tightened. That couldn't happen.

He retrieved his laptop and settled down on an armchair, hoping to find a distraction. He logged on to his computer, anxious to see what the latest gossip consisted of. As long as it was about him and his fictitious romance and not his brother's real-life romantic disaster, he'd be satisfied.

The sound of a door closing caught his attention. He quickly closed his laptop and got to his feet. "Reese, is that you?"

She stepped into the living room. "Yes."

Her tone was flat and her gaze didn't quite reach his. He couldn't help himself—he had to know. "How did your day go?"

Her eyes were bloodshot and her face was pale. "It doesn't matter. I have some paperwork to do. Is there anything I can get for you?"

"Yes, there is." All thoughts of his need to tell her of his background vanished. Comforting her was his only priority. He attempted to reach out to her, to pull her close, but her cold gaze met his—freezing him out. His arms lowered. "You can talk to me. Tell me what happened."

Her eyes blazed with irritation. "Why do you always have to push? Why can't you leave things alone? First it's the Christmas tree. Then it's my apartment. You can't fix everything."

He took a step back, not expecting that outburst. "I am concerned. I'd like to help if I can."

"Well, you can't. This is my problem. I'll deal with it on my own."

No matter how much she wanted him to walk away, he couldn't. The raw pain in her brown eyes ate at him. Reese was the pillar of strength that everyone in this mansion leaned on. It was time that she had someone she could turn to for support.

"You don't have to do this alone."

"Why do you want to get involved?"

"I'd like to think that we're friends and that you can turn to me with your problems."

"You are my guest and I am the manager of this inn. That's all we are to each other." A coldness threaded through her words.

His voice lowered. "You don't believe that."

"I can't do this now." She turned away.

Acting against his better judgment, he reached out, wrapping his fingers around her forearm. "Don't push me away. Talk to me. Maybe there's something I can do to help."

She turned back, her gaze moving to his fingers. He immediately released her.

She sighed and lifted her chin to him. "I know you're trying to be nice, but don't you understand? You can't help. No one can."

"Something can always be done." He signaled for her to follow him to the couch. "Sit down and tell me what happened. If nothing else, you might feel better after you get it out in the open instead of keeping it bottled up inside."

She glanced around as though looking to see if anyone was close enough to overhear.

"Don't worry, Bob is at the market. And Sandy had to leave early because her little girl got sick and needed to be picked up from day care."

"Oh, no. Is it anything serious?"

"Not from what I could tell. Sandy said the girl hadn't felt well that morning, but she had hoped that whatever it was would pass. Apparently it didn't."

"So we're alone?"

He nodded. "Except for the groundskeeper. But I rarely ever see him inside the mansion. The only time I ever did see him inside was when I first arrived here and he'd dropped by to give your mother a pine cone wreath."

"Yes, Mr. Winston is very good to Mom."

It was good to know that there was someone around watching out for Reese and her mother. But that didn't mean Alex couldn't do his part, too.

"Sounds like Mr. Winston has more than one reason for keeping the grounds looking so nice."

Reese's fine brows drew together, forming a formidable line. And her eyes darkened. What in the world had he said wrong now?

CHAPTER NINE

"THAT'S IMPOSSIBLE."

Reese sat back, stunned by the thought of her mother liking Howard Winston. Her mother was still recovering from the mess after her father's death. Her mother would never let another man into her life, not after the way they'd been betrayed. It wasn't possible. Men weren't to be trusted.

"Are you so sure?" Alex persisted. "I mean, I only saw them together a couple of times, but there was definitely something going on there."

"They're just friends." Reese rushed on, unwilling to give his observation any credence. "Mom would never get involved with another man. Not after…after my father."

She'd almost let it slip that her father was a horrible, lying, conniving man, but she caught herself in time. Airing her family's dirty laundry to a stranger—well, Alex wasn't a stranger any longer. And the truth was she didn't know what he was to her.

Still, she didn't like to talk about her father—with anyone. The man wasn't worth the breath to speak his name. After all, he hadn't even loved them. His own family. He'd scraped off their savings and spent the money on his new woman—the woman he had left her mother for on Christmas Eve. And he'd been such a coward that he'd only left a note. He couldn't face them and admit what he'd done.

The backs of her eyes stung. Why did she still let the memory get her worked up? Two years had passed since her father's betrayal had come to light and her mother had crumbled.

Alex got to his feet. "I didn't mean to upset you. I thought you might be happy about your mother having someone in her life."

"I—I hadn't noticed." She choked the words out around the lump in her throat. "I've had a lot of other things on my mind. This place can take a lot of time and attention."

"Then maybe what you need to do is get out of here."

Her eyes widened. "You mean leave?"

He smiled, hoping to ease the horrified look on her face. "I am not talking about forever. I was thinking more along the lines of an early dinner."

"Oh." Heat flashed in her cheeks. She didn't know why she'd jumped to the wrong conclusion. Then again, maybe she did.

On the ride home, she'd been daydreaming about packing her bags and heading somewhere, anywhere but here. Not that she would ever do it. But sometimes the pressures got to be too much. Just like tomorrow, when she had to tell Sandy that she would have to lay her off. But she would hire Sandy back just as soon as possible—if there was still an inn to employ her.

Alex shifted his weight from one foot to the other. "If you want, we can leave a note for Bob letting him know he can have the evening off."

She shook her head. "I can't afford to splurge."

"Maybe you misunderstood. This is my treat. I think it's time for me to get out of here and check out a bit of

New York City. And who better to show me some of the finest cuisine?"

She arched a brow. "Are you serious?"

He nodded.

He was probably right about her getting out of the house. A little time away and a chance to unwind would have her thinking more clearly. Oh, who was she kidding? There was no way she'd unwind when she knew that she had the horrible task of laying off one of her valued employees, who was more a friend than a worker.

After her father's betrayal, she'd closed herself off, only letting those closest to her in. And the three people who worked for her had gained her trust and friendship. They were a family. They'd filled in when her mother wasn't capable of doing more than caring for herself. They'd been there to support her, to cheer her on, and she couldn't love them more.

Alex shot her a pleading stare. "Surely sharing dinner with me can't be that bad of an idea."

Reese worried her lower lip. She really had no desire to go out, but he was, after all, the paying guest—a guest who'd spent a lot of his time fixing up her private apartment. Giving him a brief tour of Rockefeller Center and dinner was the least she could do.

"I did hear Bob mention that he still needed to run out and buy his girlfriend a Christmas present. I'm sure he wouldn't mind leaving early. I'll give him a call."

"And I'll change out of these work clothes into something presentable."

When he turned away, she noticed how his dark jeans rode low on his trim waist and clung to him in all of the right places. The man was certainly built. She swallowed hard. Any woman would have to be out of her tree to turn his offer down.

She struggled to sound normal. "Um, sure. I'll meet you back here in ten minutes."

He nodded and headed for the steps.

If he was going to dress up, she supposed she should do the same thing. She mentally rummaged through her closet. She didn't own anything special. The best she could do was her little black dress. It was something she kept on hand for hosting weddings.

Some funny feeling inside her told her this dinner was going to be a game changer. They wouldn't be quite the same again. But in the next breath, she assured herself she was making too much of the dinner. After all, what could possibly happen?

What would it take to make her smile?

Alex sneaked a glance at Reese's drawn white face. The lights of the tall Christmas tree reflected in her eyes, but the excitement that had been there when they'd decorated the tree back at the inn was gone. He had to do something to make things better. But what?

She still hadn't opened up to him. Sure, he'd surmised that her plans to sell her paintings today hadn't worked out, but it went deeper than disappointment. He'd been hoping that when he took her out on the town, she'd loosen up and temporarily forget her problems. So far it wasn't working.

"Maybe stopping here was a bad idea." Alex raked his fingers through his short hair.

"No, it wasn't." She reached out and squeezed his hand. She smiled up at him, but the gesture didn't quite reach her eyes. "It's just that I used to come to Rockefeller Center every Christmas with my father. Back then the tree looked ginormous to me."

"I am sorry that it now makes you sad."

She shook her head. "It's not that. It's just that back then things weren't so messed up. At least, I don't think they were. I'd like to think that part of my life was genuine and not riddled with lies."

"What lies?" Had he missed something she said? Impossible. He was captivated by her every word.

She shook her head and turned back to the tree. "It's nothing. Just me rambling on about things that aren't important."

He stepped in front of her. "It sure sounded important to me. And I'd like to understand if you'll tell me."

"Why do you care? I am just your host."

"And my friend," he added quickly. Then he stopped himself before he could say more—things that he, the prince of a far-off land, had no right saying to anyone. His feelings were irrelevant. His duty was to the crown of Mirraccino. That was what he'd been telling himself for years.

She smiled up at him. "You're very sweet. It's surprising that you're not taken yet."

He pressed a hand to his chest. "Who would want to kidnap me?"

She laughed. "Your English is very good, but I'm quickly learning that you aren't as familiar with some of our sayings. What I meant was I'm surprised that you're not in a committed relationship."

His thoughts briefly went to the king and his insistence that Alex formalize the plans to announce his engagement to Catherine, an heiress to a shipping empire. The entire reason for the match was political positioning. Combining her family's ships with the ports of Mirraccino would truly make for a powerful resource and secure Mirraccino's economic future. It didn't matter that he and Catherine didn't have feelings for each other. An advantageous marriage was what was expected of him—his wants and desires did not count.

As dedicated as Alex was to the crown, he'd never been able to visualize a future with Catherine. In fact, they planned to get together after Christmas and discuss their options. His gut told him to end things—to let her get on with her life. He didn't like the thought of her waiting around for him to develop feelings for her that obviously weren't going to appear. And marrying her out of pure duty seemed so cold. But it was what his family wanted— what they expected.

Catherine was beautiful and he did enjoy her company, but there just wasn't an attraction. That spark. Nothing close to what he felt around Reese. Now where had that come from? It wasn't as though he was planning to start anything with Reese. The last thing his family needed was another complication.

He didn't want to think about himself. It was Reese who concerned him. "Who put that sadness in your eyes?"

She swiped at her eyes. "It's no one. I—I mean it's the problems with the inn. I just need a quick influx of cash."

"What can I do to make it better?" He would do anything within his power—aside from risking his nation.

A watery smile lit up her face as she shook her head. "You've already done enough."

"But how?" He was once again confused. "You mean my reservation?"

"No, by being a caring friend."

Before he had a chance to digest her words, she was on tiptoes and leaning forward. Her warm lips pressed to his. The breath caught in his lungs. Sure, he'd fantasized about this—heck, he'd dreamed of this—but he never imagined it could be this amazing.

She was about to pull back when he snaked his arms around her waist and pulled her closer. Her hands became pinned against his chest. The problems of the Mirraccino nation and the crown's expectations of him slipped away as the kiss deepened. When she met him lip to lip and tongue to tongue, no other thoughts registered except one—he was the luckiest man alive. Nothing had ever felt this right.

She worked her hands up over his shoulders. Her fingers raked through his hair, causing the low rumble of a moan to form in the back of his throat. Her body snuggled closer but with their bulky winter garb he was barred from enjoying her voluptuous curves pressed to his.

He nibbled on her full bottom lip, reveling in the swift intake of her breath. She wanted him as much as he wanted her. The only problem was they were standing in the middle of Rockefeller Center—and in front of the Christmas tree, no less. Not exactly the place to get carried away.

Still, he couldn't let her go...not quite yet. He'd been with his share of women, but they'd never touched a part of him deep inside. It was more than physical—not that the physical wasn't great. But there was something more about Reese, and in that moment his brain turned to mush and he couldn't put his finger on exactly why she was different.

A bright flash startled him out of the moment. His eyes sprang open and with great regret he pulled away from her. Immediately the cold air settled in, but his blood was too hot for him to be bothered by the crisp air.

"What's the matter?" Reese asked.

"I—I thought I saw something. I am certain it's nothing."

His gaze scanned the area, searching for the person with the camera. Had the paparazzi tracked him down? Had they snapped a picture of him holding Reese close?

He studied the other couples and families with small children. It could have been any of them. He was making too much of the situation. If it was the paparazzi, he couldn't imagine they'd worry about hiding. He was just being paranoid without his security detail.

When he turned his attention back to Reese, she glanced up at him. Her cheeks had bright pink splotches. He couldn't decide if it was the dipping temperatures or embarrassment. And now that the cold air was filling with white fluffy flakes, his brain was starting to make connections again. He owed her an apology.

Years of being a prince had taught him that there was a time and a place for everything. This was not the time to ravish her luscious lips—he needed to keep things low-key between them. He still had yet to reveal his true identity to her. But he would fix that this evening—no more secrets.

He gave her hand a squeeze. "My apologies. I shouldn't have taken advantage of the moment."

"You didn't." Her gaze lowered. "I'm the one who should be apologizing. I started it."

She had, but he was the one who'd taken it to the next level. When she started walking, he fell in step next to her. Hand in hand, they moved as though they'd been together for years.

She glanced over at him. "Are you still up for going to dinner like we planned?"

"Do you still want to go?"

She nodded.

He was hungry, there was no doubt about that. But food wasn't what he craved. He swallowed hard, trying to keep his thoughts focused on his mission tonight—being honest with Reese without chasing her away.

Big snowflakes drifted lazily to the ground. They quickly covered her hair, reminding him of a snow angel. He'd never seen anyone so beautiful. It was going to be hard to stay focused on his priorities when all he wanted to do was get closer to Reese. If only his life were different....

In that moment, he heard the king's clear, distinct voice in his head. *Your life is one of honor—of duty. You must always think of the kingdom first.*

And that's what he was doing, but each day it was getting harder and harder to live by those rules. He glanced at Reese. Definitely much harder than he'd ever imagined.

CHAPTER TEN

REESE WAS SURPRISED by how much she was enjoying the evening. The trendy restaurant had been mentioned by a few of her guests and she now understood why. It was cozy with soft lighting and a few holiday decorations scattered about. And the tapas menu was simply divine. She loved trying a bit of this and a bit of that.

And thanks to the deteriorating weather, the restaurant was quiet enough to make conversation. Everything was going fine until Alex turned the conversation back to her. After the waiter delivered the coffee and a slice of triple-chocolate cake, Alex studied her over the rim of his cup.

He took a sip of the steamy brew before returning it to the saucer. "Tell me about him?"

Reese's heart clenched. "Who?"

Please don't let him be asking about her father. She never spoke of him…with anyone, including her mother. And she certainly wasn't about to sit here in public and reveal how that man had lied to their faces before betraying her and her mother in the worst way.

Alex leaned forward, propping his elbows on the edge of the table. "I want to know about your ex-boyfriend. The man who broke your heart."

She let out a pent-up breath. Josh was someone she could talk about. It'd taken her time to sort through the pain he'd caused, but in the end, she'd realized his lies were what had hurt her the most—not his absence from her life.

"Josh was someone I met in college. He was a smart dresser with expensive tastes. I was surprised when he offered me a ride home from a party one night. When he dropped me off, he was impressed by my family's mansion—if only I'd known then what I know now. Anyway, he insisted I give him my phone number."

Sympathy reflected in Alex's blue gaze. "He was after your money?"

"Yes. But I was too naive to know it then. I let myself get so caught up in the thought of being in love that I let it slide when things always had to be his way. And when he'd criticize my outfits, I thought it was my fault for being so naive about fashion."

"What a jerk." Alex's jaw flexed.

"When my father died, things changed. Josh transformed into the perfect gentleman. He said all of the right things and even talked of us getting married. He made me feel secure."

The memories washed over her, bringing with them the forgotten embarrassment and pain. She blinked repeatedly. She'd been wrong—recalling her past with Josh hurt more than she'd been willing to admit.

Alex reached across the table and squeezed her hand. In his touch she found reassurance and a strength within herself that she hadn't known was there.

She swallowed down the jagged lump in her throat. "Everything was fine until he learned I wasn't an heiress. In fact, I was in debt. Poorer than a church mouse. I don't know if I'll ever get out of debt before I'm a little old lady."

"You're so much better off without him. He isn't worth your tears."

She ran her fingertips over her cheeks, only then realizing that they were damp. "Once Josh knew I couldn't support him, he stopped coming around and didn't return my calls. But by that point, I was so busy looking after my mother and keeping the bank from taking the house that Josh's absence got pushed to the back of my mind."

"I'm so sorry he hurt you like that—"

"Don't be. It's done and over with. I don't want to talk about him anymore." And she couldn't bear to think of that time in her life—it was truly her darkest hour.

"They say talking about things helps you heal."

"I tend to think that chocolate heals all." She took the last bite of chocolate cake and moaned at its rich taste. "Now it's your turn. Tell me more about yourself."

"Me?" His eyes widened. "I'm boring. Surely you want to talk about something more interesting."

She shook her head. "Fair is fair. I told you about my no-good ex. Now it's your turn to tell me something that I don't already know about you."

He leaned back in his chair as though contemplating what to tell her. Then he glanced around. She followed his gaze, finding the nearby tables empty. Her anticipation grew. He was obviously about to take her into his confidence—what could be so private?

"What if I told you I'm a prince?"

Disappointment popped her excitement. "I'd say you have delusions of grandeur. I thought you were going to be serious."

He leaned forward as though he were going to say more, but her phone chimed. She held up a finger for him to give her a moment as she fished the device out of her purse. "It's my mother. I have to get it."

She got to her feet, grabbed her coat and rushed to the exit, where she'd be able to hear better without the background music. She stepped out into the cold evening air when the chime stopped. Drat. It could be important. She better call back.

The snow was still falling, enveloping everything in a white blanket. Not many people were out in the wintry weather. Those who were had their hoods up and kept their heads low as they moved along the partially cleared sidewalk. Only one man was taking his time and gazing in the various restaurant and store windows. It seemed awfully cold to be strolling around. But to each his own.

The wind kicked up. She turned her back to the biting cold and pulled up the collar on her coat. She'd just retrieved her aunt's number when she heard a man's voice call out. She turned around.

"Hey!" The man who'd been window gazing was now staring at her. "Yeah, you."

Beneath the harsh glare of the street lamps decorated with tinsel, Reese spotted a camera in the man's hands. He lifted the camera and in the next instance a bright flash momentarily blinded her. She blinked repeatedly.

He stepped closer. "What's your name?"

She stepped back. "Excuse me."

Who was this guy? And why had he taken her photo? People on the sidewalk paused and stared at her as though trying to figure out if they should know her. Like a deer in headlights, she froze.

"Come on," the man coaxed. "Give me a pretty smile."

Reese put her hands up to block the man's shot. "I don't know who you are, but leave me alone!"

"How old are you, honey? Twenty? Twenty-two?"

She went to turn back toward the restaurant when she stepped on a patch of ice. Her arms flailed through the snowy air. Her feet slid. Clutching her phone in a death grip as though it could help her, she plunged face-first toward the pavement.

* * *

Alex smiled as he traced Reese's steps to the exit.

The evening had gone better than he'd ever imagined. The tip of his tongue traced over his lower lip as he recalled the sweetness of Reese's touch. She sure could turn a kiss into a full-fledged experience. He just hoped that once he convinced her he was telling her the truth she'd understand, because he wasn't ready to let her go—not yet.

He pushed open the glass door when he saw Reese sway and fall to the ground. The sound of her name caught in his throat. He moved into action as a flash lit up the night—the paparazzi. Right now, his only concern was making sure Reese was okay.

Alex knelt beside her sprawled body. His chest tightened as he waited for her to speak. "Reese, are you okay?"

"I…I don't know. The fall knocked the breath out of me." She turned over on her backside. "My arm hurts, and my knees."

"I'm so sorry." When she started to get up, he pressed a hand to her shoulder. "Sit still for a second and take a couple of breaths."

Alex glanced around, spotting a man with a camera farther down the sidewalk. His gut instinct was to go after the man, but he wouldn't leave Reese. She needed him.

The photographer took a moment to snap another picture before he escaped into the night. Alex was certain that it would end up in the gossip rags that night, but his only concern was Reese.

And this incident was all his fault. He'd gotten caught up in the moment—only thinking of his need to comfort Reese—to be with her. He'd failed to follow any of the safety protocols drilled into him as a kid. He'd gotten so comfortable in his anonymous role that he'd forgotten just how easily things could unravel. Now once again, his rash decision had hurt someone he cared about.

That thought struck him.

He cared about Reese. It was true. But he didn't have time right now to figure out exactly what that meant. Right now he had to determine if she was all right to move. He needed to get them both off this city street. Luckily, with the inclement weather, not that many people were out and about.

"This is my fault." Alex held his hands out to her. "The least I can do is help you up."

"I've got it."

"You need help. You're sitting on a patch of ice." He continued to reach out to her. "Take my hands."

When she went to reach out to him, she gasped.

"What is it?"

"My right arm. I had my phone in my hand and came down on my elbow."

"How about your left arm? Is it all right?"

"I think so."

He gripped her good arm while she held the injured arm to her chest. An urge came over him to scoop her up into his arms and hold her tight, promising that everything would be better, but he knew that could never happen. He'd waited too long. Too much had happened. Things had gotten too out of control.

And now when Reese found out the truth—the whole truth—she'd look at him with an accusing stare. She was hurt because of him. And he couldn't blame her. None of this would have happened if only he had stayed back at the inn. He'd had a plan. A good plan. And he'd abandoned it.

He noticed the grim line of her lips as she cradled the injured arm and he felt lower than a sea urchin. "I am taking you to a hospital."

"I don't need to go. It's just a sprain."

He sent her a disapproving stare. "I insist the doctors have a look at you."

Deciding that her black heels were definitely not to be trusted on the slick sidewalk, he wrapped his arm around her waist. Even though most of the walkway had been cleared, there were still patches of snow and ice. His arm fit nicely around her curves. The heat of her body permeated her clothes and warmed his hand.

At the truck, he paused by the passenger door and opened it for her.

She cast him a hesitant look. "You're going to drive?"

He nodded. "You can't drive with your arm injured. How far to the hospital?"

"It's just a few blocks from here."

"Good." He helped her into the truck and then set out to get her some help.

"I don't understand what that man wanted."

"What did he say to you?"

"He wanted my name and I think my age. If this is some sort of human interest story for the local paper, they have a strange way of conducting themselves."

"Did he mention which paper he works for?"

"I don't even know if he works for a paper. That's just my best guess. When I first spotted him, he was staring in windows. I didn't know what he was up to."

Mentally Alex kicked himself for letting this happen. He was certain that photographer had known who he was and had most likely tracked him from Rockefeller Center to where they'd had dinner. Well, it wouldn't happen again. When he got back to the inn, he would be placing a call to Mirraccino to update the king on the recent turn of events and would request that his security detail be dispatched immediately.

Worry and guilt settled heavily on his shoulders. There was no excuse for his poor behavior. How would he keep Reese from hating him?

In one evening, he'd broken his promise to himself to follow the rules and keep those closest to him safe. He glanced at Reese, who was still holding her arm. He'd failed her in more than one way.

He should have trusted her with the truth about himself before now. But at first he'd worried that she'd sell the information. And then he'd enjoyed his role as plain Alex and selfishly didn't want her treating him differently. Now he'd waited too long.

CHAPTER ELEVEN

WHY WAS HE acting so strangely?

Reese sat on the edge of the emergency-room exam table and studied the drawn lines on Alex's handsome face. She recalled him apologizing and blaming himself for her injury. What was up with that? He hadn't even been outside when she'd slipped.

Why did she have this feeling she was missing something? She was about to ask him when the doctor entered the room.

The gray-haired man in a white coat had a serious expression on his face as he introduced himself and shook her good hand. "The films show you didn't break any bones. However, you have some minor cuts and abrasions. The worst injury is a contusion to your elbow."

Alex's hands clenched as he stood next to her. "How bad is it?"

His worry and anxiety were palpable. Had he never seen anyone get hurt before? If this was how he reacted to scrapes and bruises, she was really glad there was no blood.

The doctor's brow arched as he took in Alex's presence.

Reese spoke up. "It's okay. He's my friend."

"All in all, she's lucky. We'll clean her up and give her some anti-inflammatories to help with the swelling. She'll be sore for a day or two, but she'll feel better soon."

Reese detected the whoosh of breath from Alex. She'd swear he was more relieved than she was over the diagnosis. Although the thought of a cast was not one she would have relished when she had to take over the maid duties. How exactly would she have changed linens one-handed? Or managed any of the other tasks?

It seemed to take an eternity until she was released from the hospital. She tried to talk to Alex, but his moodiness wasn't of any comfort. When he did speak, it was only in one-syllable answers. You'd think he was the one who'd been hurt, not her.

It was all his fault.

Reese had been put in harm's way. She'd been hurt. And it was all because he hadn't taken the proper precautions. It wouldn't happen again.

With her snug in bed, Alex moved into action. He had some explaining to do. His papa would not be pleased— not that he could make Alex feel any guiltier than he already did.

While he spoke with the king, Alex scanned the internet trying to locate the photo from this evening, but no matter what he typed in the search engine, nothing popped up. He was certain the man with the camera had been part of the media and not just some fan. So where was the picture?

Alex braced himself for some fictitious story to accompany the photo. He just hoped that it wasn't too scandalous. His family had been through enough with his brother's overnight marriage to a practical stranger.

"You should have listened to me!" The king's voice vibrated the phone. "How badly is the girl injured?"

"She's going to be sore for a while, but there's nothing serious."

"You know that you must make this right. Her injuries

are the result of your poor judgment. You shouldn't have been out in public without your security detail."

"I'll do my best to make it up to her."

"Make sure you do. We don't need her turning to the media with a sob story or worse. We're already dealing with enough here."

He would take care of it. But first he had to be honest with her. He just hoped that with her being so loyal to her mother and her need to hang on to this mansion that had been in her family for generations that she'd be able to understand his loyalty to his family and the crown.

"How are things with Demetrius? Have the issues been resolved?"

"Almost. We need another day or two. Can you make that happen considering everything that just occurred?"

"Yes." That was his duty, no matter what.

Alex raked his fingers through his hair and blew out a long slow breath. "I'll make sure our plan does not unravel because of tonight's incident. I already have a backup plan in motion. I will step things up and take care of Reese at the same time."

"I don't like the sound of this. The last time you had an idea, you snuck out of the palace and took too many risks with your safety. This time I insist you tell me about this backup plan."

Alex rolled out his plan for his papa. He also took into consideration the king's suggestions and made a few adjustments until they were both satisfied.

"What about Catherine?"

The muscles in Alex's neck tightened. "I'll speak with her when I get home."

The logical thing would be to go to Catherine and formalize the marriage that their families were so eager to see take place. But how was he supposed to make a commitment to a woman he didn't love?

His priority now was speaking with Reese. He'd do that first thing in the morning. Somehow he had to make her understand his choices were for the best—for all concerned.

She was, after all, understanding and generous with her employees. These were just two of the qualities that he admired about her. He just hoped she'd extend him the same courtesy.

CHAPTER TWELVE

BEEEEP! BEEEEP!

Who in the world had their finger stuck on the front-door buzzer?

Reese groaned. She rolled over and opened one eye. It was still dark out. What in the world? Her hazy gaze settled on the green numbers on the clock. It wasn't even 6 a.m. She still had another half hour to sleep. Maybe they'd go away.

Beep. Beep. Beep.

Another groan formed deep in her dry throat. She wasn't expecting anyone. Maybe one of the employees had forgotten their pass card. Wait. No one came in this early.

Well, she wouldn't know what was going on until she answered the door.

She clambered out of bed and grabbed her old blue robe. Her elbow throbbed. There was no way the wrap on her arm would fit easily through the sleeve. Instead she draped the robe over her shoulder while holding her arm to her chest.

Her bare feet padded quietly across the floor. The door to Alex's suite was just down the hall from hers. There were no sounds or light coming from his rooms. Lucky him. He was probably still enjoying a peaceful night's sleep. Whatever had her out of bed at this hour had better be important.

She glanced through the window that ran down each

side of the front door, finding Mr. Winston standing there. What in the world?

"Please come inside." She held the door open for him. "What are you doing here at this hour?"

"I was up early, reading the paper while drinking my coffee, when I stumbled across something you need to see."

"Couldn't this have waited a few more hours?"

"No. In fact, I got here just in time."

"In time for what?" She was thoroughly confused. She really needed a piping-hot cup of coffee to wash away the cobwebs in her mind.

"Read the headline." He held the morning paper out to her. "It'll explain everything."

She accepted the paper and unfolded it. Her eyes immediately met a black-and-white photo of Alex. Her gaze skimmed the headline: Royal Prince Finds Love.

The breath caught in her throat as she read the words once more. Below the headline was a picture of her on the sidewalk with Alex next to her. Her mouth gaped. The photo had been taken last night.

She struggled to make sense of her rambling thoughts. This is why the man on the sidewalk had been questioning her? Alex was a prince?

How could that be true? Alex was royalty? Impossible.

Then their conversation at the restaurant came rushing back to her. She read the headline again. He had been telling her the truth. Alex was an honest-to-goodness prince.

"It's true," she said in astonishment.

"You know about this?" Mr. Winston's gaze searched her face.

She hadn't meant to say the words aloud. "He mentioned something about this last night."

"Do you understand the trouble we're going to have here?" The groundskeeper wrung his hands together. "I already had to escort two reporters off the property and close the gate. Thank goodness your mother isn't here."

It wasn't just her mother who would not approve of the three-ring circus going on in front of the property. Ever since Reese's father had died, the snooty neighbors had stuck their collective noses up in the air. They didn't approve of the inn. They'd even gone out of their way with the local government and business associations to try to block her from opening The Willows. They didn't want their exclusive neighborhood blemished with a bunch of riffraff.

This latest scandal of sorts would only add fuel to a fire that had finally died down to small smoldering embers. And it was all Alex's fault—correction, it was all Prince Alexandro Castanavo's fault.

She glanced toward the window. "Do we need to call the police?"

Mr. Winston rubbed his gloved hands together. "I don't think it'll be necessary at this point. But if that fella you've got staying here decides to stay on, you might have a real problem on your hands. Do you want me toss him out?"

"Um…no. I'll take care of him." She worried her bottom lip as she figured out what to do next. "Until he leaves, can you keep the press off the property?"

"I can try. But they could sneak around back without me knowing."

She tapped the folded newspaper against her thigh. "I'll call Bob and ask if he can come help you. Surely they'll get bored and go away soon."

"I wouldn't count on that. They seem to be rapidly growing in numbers."

"Please do your best. And thank you for helping."

Mr. Winston's face softened. "No need to thank me. I'm just glad I was up early and saw the paper."

She marched up the steps, coming to a stop in front

of Alex's room. She lifted her hand to knock on his door when her robe slipped from her shoulder. The cool early-morning air sent goose bumps rushing down her skin.

What should she say? Why had he kept his identity a secret? What was he doing here at The Willows? The unending questions whirled round in her mind.

Maybe it'd be best if she got dressed before confronting him. It'd also give her a moment to figure out exactly what she was going to say to him. Most importantly, she wondered if he was truly going to come clean about last night.

Reese called Bob and then rushed through the shower. The more she thought about how Alex had duped her, the angrier she got. And to think she'd started to trust him—to open up to him.

Minutes later, she returned to his door. With her good hand, she knocked.

There was no answer.

She added more force to her rapid knock. "Alex, I know you're in there. Wake up!"

There was a crash. A curse.

The door swung open. Alex stood there in a pair of boxers. His short hair was scattered in all directions. "What's wrong? Is it your arm?"

"No." She drew her gaze from his bare chest to meet his confused look.

"Reese, what is it?"

"This. This is what's wrong." She pressed the paper to his bare chest. When the backs of her fingers made contact with his heated skin, a tingling sensation shot up her arm and settled in her chest. She immediately pulled away. Now wasn't the time for her hormones to take control. She had to think clearly.

He grabbed the paper and without even unfolding it to read the headline said, "I can explain this."

"So you know what's in it?"

He nodded. "I planned to explain everything in the morning. Speaking of morning, what are you doing up so early? The sun isn't even up yet."

"The sun may not be up, but that didn't stop the reporters from blocking the sidewalk and spilling out into the road. My neighbors are going to have a royal hissy fit over this one."

It wasn't until the words were out of her mouth that she realized her poor choice of words. She looked at him as he moved to the window facing the road and peered out. He was a royal prince. It was taking a bit for her to wrap her mind around that image. To her he was still Alex, who'd stood on the ladder plastering her ceiling. The same Alex who'd kicked back in her living room enjoying a pizza. And the Alex who'd kissed her last night.

She stared at him. His muscled shoulders were pulled back. His tanned back was straight and his head was held tall. And when he turned to her, his faraway gaze said he was deep in thought. His nose was straight and his jawline squared. He definitely looked like a very sexy Prince Charming.

In that moment, it struck her that she was speaking to an honest-to-goodness prince. Royalty. The accusations and heated words knotted up in her throat.

As though he remembered she was still in the room, his gaze met hers. "Do you mind if I throw on some clothes before we get into this?"

Realizing that she was staring at his very bare, very tempting chest, she nodded and turned away. "I'll meet you downstairs."

She headed for the door without waiting for his answer. She needed to talk to him, but not like this. Once he was dressed, she'd be able to have a serious conversation with him.

When she reached the ground floor, she glanced out the front window, finding Mr. Winston strolling along the perimeter of the property. He was such a good guy. She couldn't imagine letting him and the others go. How could she let them down?

She gave herself a mental shake. She would deal with that problem later. Right now she needed to deal with her guest—the man she'd begun to think of as a friend—the man she'd shared a kiss with the night before. She paced the length of the living room. How long did it take to throw on some clothes?

She walked to the foyer and glanced up the staircase. There was no sign of him. With each passing moment, her irritation rose. Why hadn't he been honest with her? Why all of the dodging and evasiveness?

When he finally stepped into the room, she stopped and met his unwavering gaze. His hair was still damp and a bit unruly. He'd put on a blue sweater and jeans. His feet were still bare. She drew her gaze upward, refusing to be swayed by his good looks and his royal breeding. There was something different about him.

"Your hair, it's lighter."

"I started washing out the temporary hair dye."

She openly stared at him. "There's something else."

"I didn't put in the colored contacts."

Instead of a vibrant blue, his eyes were a blue-gray.

"Is there more?" He'd really thought through his charade. Her gaze skimmed over him, looking for any other changes.

"That's all."

She tilted her chin up. "You owe me an explanation. And it better be good. Real good."

"I meant to tell you—"

"When? After you got me under your spell? After we—" She pressed her fingers to her lips.

She hadn't meant to go down that path. In fact, she hadn't meant to mention the kiss, but she just couldn't forget it. Nor could she dismiss the way his touch filled her stomach with a sense of fluttering butterflies.

"It's not what you're thinking. I'm staying at The Willows because I needed someplace quiet to stay."

"Someplace where you could hide from the press?"

He nodded. "This place is private enough while still being close to the city."

"And this explains why you could afford to rent out the whole place. But why weren't you up front with me?"

"I didn't have a choice—"

"Everyone has a choice. When we started getting closer, I started opening up to you about my past, but you still remained quiet."

"You don't know how many times I wanted to open up to you." He stepped up to her, but she backed away. His gaze pleaded with her. "I really do have a legitimate reason for not telling you the truth. Will you sit down and hear me out?"

She moved to the armchair while he took a seat on the end of the couch. "I'm listening."

Frustration creased Alex's face. "You must believe me when I say the kiss last night was real. And if you deny it, you'll only be lying to yourself."

The memory of his breath tickling her cheek. The gentle scent of his spicy cologne teasing her nose. And then his warm lips had been there, pressing against hers. Alex was right. The kiss had been out of this world.

"You mentioned something about a duty. A duty to do what?" she prompted, trying to keep not only him but also her own thoughts on target.

"To protect my country at all costs."

Reese rubbed the shoulder of her injured arm, trying to ease the dull ache. "Go on."

"I'm sorry about last night with that reporter. You were injured because I didn't follow protocol—again."

"Again?"

He paused as though searching for where to begin. "I was rebellious when I was younger. I hated all of the rules and protocols. I didn't understand their importance. When I was fifteen, I got in an argument with the king before a public outing."

"I'm guessing that was a no-no."

Alex nodded. "I ignored the mandated protocol of staying with the bodyguards at the event and took off into the crowd. With the guards chasing after me, the king and queen were not fully protected. A gunshot by a subversive meant for the king struck—struck my mother."

Reese sat back, stunned by the traumatic event in Alex's childhood. She reached out and squeezed his hand. Sympathy welled up in her for the guilt a fifteen-year-old should never have to experience.

"Before my mother died, she had me make a promise—to take care of Papa. I've kept that promise ever since. It's the very least I could do after what I did."

"Your mother must have loved your father dearly."

"Not always. Theirs was an arranged marriage."

Reese had heard of them existing in some cultures, but she found it startling that people would marry for something other than love. "How did they meet?"

"My grandfather wanted Mirraccino's wine industry to flourish beyond our nation's boundaries. He'd determined the best way to do that was to join forces with one of Italy's major wine producers and distributors. And during one of those meetings, my grandfather was introduced to my mother. It was then and there that my grandfathers came to agreement to merge the families through marriage."

"I can't imagine having to marry someone that you don't love."

"As a royal, one must always do their duty. It's an expectation that starts at birth." Alex shrugged.

"Lucky for your parents it all worked out—"

"Not quite. If only I'd have followed the rules, she… she might still be here."

"You can't blame yourself. You were young and kids don't think before they act."

"I grew up fast that day. I swore I would toe the line and protect my family at all costs—even at the risk of my own safety. I couldn't bear the thought of losing them both."

"And that's why you kept your identity from me—you were protecting your family?"

"I'm here on a most important mission for my country."

"A mission?" Alarm bells rang in her mind. What sort of situation had he gotten her mixed up in?

"If I tell you, do you promise that it'll go no further than you and me?"

She worried her bottom lip. She wanted to know. She needed to know. But what if it was something bad? She eyed up the man she knew as Alex. Her gut told her that he was a good guy, even if he had misled her.

"It'll stay between us."

The lines in his face eased. "My country is a small group of islands in the Mediterranean. It has a strong hold in the shipping industry and wines."

She listened as Alex revealed some of the history of his islands. She was amazed that his small country could have an uprising. When she thought of a sunny island, she thought of peaceful beaches and lazy afternoons. It just showed that she spent too much time wrapped up in her own little part of the world.

After he explained about his brother's impulsive marriage, Alex looked her directly in the eyes. "So you see how my brother's impulsive behavior would be disastrous for our nation."

She wasn't so sure she saw the situation the same as him. "So what you're saying is that you don't believe in love at first sight?"

He shook his head. "No, I don't. I believe in lust and need. But love...well, it grows over time. Like my parents' marriage."

Reese got his message loud and clear. The kiss last night meant nothing. A pain pinged in her chest. She sucked down the feelings of rejection. After all, it was only a kiss. Right now, she needed to hear the rest of Alex's explanation.

"So you think your brother married this girl just so he could have his way with her?" Reese didn't even know his brother, but she wasn't buying that story.

"I didn't say that."

"Sure you did. But something tells me if he looks anything like you that he could have almost any woman he wanted. So why would he offer marriage if he didn't love her?"

Alex paused and stared off into the distance as though he were truly considering her argument. "Maybe you do have a point. Perhaps he was genuinely infatuated with her."

She laughed in frustration and shook her head. "You just won't give in to the fact that your brother might truly love this woman and that your family is trying to tear them apart."

She was about to ask him what he would do if his family tried to come between them, but she stopped herself in time. After all, there wasn't anything for his family to disrupt.

Alex frowned. "It doesn't matter if he loves her or not. He's the crown prince. A wife will be chosen for him. Just as was done for my father and his father."

She wasn't going to argue his brother's case. It was none of her affair. But the pack of reporters outside was a different matter. "Now that you have the press off of your brother's trail, what are you going to do? The press can't camp out on my sidewalk. The neighbors are probably on the phone with the police right now."

"I have a plan, but I need your help."

The little hairs on the back of her neck lifted. "What do you want me to do?"

He held up the paper. "I need you to play the part of my girlfriend."

CHAPTER THIRTEEN

"I COULDN'T BE more serious."

Alex sent her a pleading look that had a way of melting through her resistance. He wanted her to be his pretend girlfriend? Her, Reese Harding, the girlfriend of an honest-to-goodness prince?

The phone started to ring. This was the perfect excuse for her to escape his intense stare. His eyes on her made her heart race and short-circuited her thoughts.

"You've got the wrong woman." She started for the hallway.

"Reese, please wait. Hear me out." There was a weary tone in his voice that stirred her sympathy.

She stopped but didn't turn around. She knew that if she did she'd cave. And she just wasn't ready to give in to him just yet. "I need to get the phone."

"Let the answering machine pick it up. This is important." He cleared his throat. "I know I made a mess of this. I'm truly sorry."

She nodded, letting him know that she'd heard him.

"Will you at least look at me?"

Reese drew in a deep breath. Part of her wanted to keep going out the door and let him know that what he'd done couldn't be forgiven with two little words of apology. But another part of her understood where he was coming from.

He'd been doing what he thought was right and necessary to protect his family. How could she fault him for that?

"I wouldn't ask you to do this if it were not a matter of national security."

Her gaze narrowed in on him, trying to decide if this was the truth or not. "National security? Shouldn't you be talking to some government agency?"

"Not the United States." He got to his feet and moved to stand in front of her. "My country is in trouble."

That's right. He was a prince. Not Alex the repair guy. Not Alex who helped her decorate the Christmas tree. And certainly not Alex the laid-back guy who enjoyed an extra-cheese pizza.

"I don't think I can help you. I run an inn. I'm not an actress. I could never pretend to be a rich debutante or some ritzy character."

"But you have something better than money and a well-known name."

"And what's that?"

"You are a woman of mystery. A woman who has the press waiting to eat out of your hand."

She was really getting confused. "What exactly is it you want me to do? Pose for the cameras?"

"In a way, yes."

She shook her head. "I'm not a model. The black dress that I wore last night and ripped on the pavement was my best dress. You'll have to find someone else."

"That isn't possible."

"Sure you can. This is New York City. The place is crawling with single women. And I'm sure a lot would clamor to be seen on your arm."

"But they're not you—the mystery woman in the photo." He glanced away as though he hadn't meant to blurt that part out. "We could make this a full-fledged business deal."

"A business deal?" She pressed her good hand to her hip. "It's really that important?"

He nodded. "If you were to continue our charade, I would pay off the debt on The Willows."

She stared at him. "You can't be serious. Nothing could be that important."

"Trust me. It's of the utmost importance." He leaned back in the ladder-back chair. "When this situation is behind us, you will own The Willows outright. Maybe then you can go back to art school and follow your dreams."

Reese placed a hand on the archway leading to the foyer to steady herself. Had she truly heard him correctly? Impossible. No one could toss around that much money…except maybe a prince. But what struck her even more was the desperation reflected in his eyes. How could she turn him down with so much at stake?

But did he know what he was asking of her? Did he know that her heart was still bruised by the way he took her feelings so lightly? Did he know that kiss was the most amazing thing to happen to her in a very long time?

Pretending to be his girlfriend would only stir up more unwanted emotions. She shouldn't even consider the idea. It spelled trouble with a capital *T*.

"If I agree, how long will this charade go on for?"

"Not long. Once my brother and the king have the situation settled, the press will find another story to interest them. The paparazzi's attention span is quite short."

"So we're talking a few days?"

"Perhaps longer."

"A week? Or two?"

"Maybe longer." When her mouth gaped open, he added, "No more than a month. At most."

Her gut told her to back out of this agreement as fast as possible—to save herself. But another part of her fancied the idea of dating a prince—even if it was all a show. Above all, she wasn't ready to say goodbye to Alex.

Before she could change her mind, she uttered, "Fine. You have yourself a fake girlfriend."

"There's one more thing you should know."

Her stomach tightened into a knot. "There's more?"

"We need to return to Mirraccino first thing in the morning."

"What?" He couldn't possibly be serious. This was just too much. "But I can't leave. It's Christmastime. I—I don't even have any presents bought for anyone."

He sent her a weary smile, as though relieved. "You can buy your gifts in Mirraccino and I'll make sure they're shipped in time for Christmas."

She frowned at him. "You seem to have an answer for everything."

"This is a once-in-a-lifetime proposition. How can you pass it up?" When she didn't say anything, he added, "If I didn't truly need your help, I wouldn't have asked."

"But what about The Willows? I can't just turn my back on it. And thanks to you, the place will most likely be booked solid through the New Year."

He smiled. "See, I told you things would turn around."

"Don't smile. This isn't good. I don't know how to do everything."

"How about your mother? She could run the inn while you're away."

"My mother? I don't think so."

"Why not? She seems fully capable to me. In fact, she seems to feel a bit left out. She almost glowed when your aunt needed her. Sometimes people need to be needed."

"And you think that she could run this place on her own?" Reese shook her head. "If you'd seen her after my dad died. She was a mess. No, it'd be too much for her."

"I don't think you give her enough credit. Maybe you've been caring for her for so long that you don't even see that she's recovered and ready to take on life if you would just let her."

"And what if something goes wrong and I'm out of the country?"

"Mr. Winston can help her."

Reese's mind replayed how Mr. Winston had always been there, trying to cheer up her mother. And over the past year, he'd made it his mission to bring her a bouquet each day from the flower gardens. She realized that her mother had seemed to spring back to life during that period. Was it possible it had something to do with Mr. Winston?

Her hands balled at her sides as she considered that maybe her mother didn't need her hovering anymore. Maybe it was time her mother stood on her own again.

She tilted her chin up and met Alex's steady gaze. "Tell me what you expect from me in exchange for this all-expenses-paid vacation to some Mediterranean island."

He reached into his pants pocket and pulled out a small black velvet box. "You'll need to wear this."

Reese's heart thumped. She'd always dreamed of the day a man would present her with a diamond ring and ask her to be his wife. What girl didn't at some point in her life? But not like this. She didn't want a fake engagement.

"I can't pretend to be your fiancée."

He gestured to the box in her hand. "Open it before deciding."

She had to admit she was curious to see the contents. The lid creaked open. Inside sat a ring with a large pink teardrop sapphire in the center with diamonds encircling it. The breath caught in Reese's throat. She'd never seen anything so beautiful. Ever.

"Is it real?"

"Most definitely."

"Where did you get it?"

"I had it shipped from Mirraccino. I hope you like it."

At a loss for words, she nodded and continued to stare at the stunning piece of jewelry. She was tempted to slip it on her finger...just to see how it'd look. After all, she'd probably never, ever hold something so precious in her hands again. Talk about your once-in-a-lifetime experiences.

Her gaze lifted to find Alex studying her reaction. She closed the lid and held it out to him. "I can't take this. It's too much. What if I lose it or something?"

"It's perfect for you. And you won't lose it. You're very responsible."

"But people will think that you and I...that we're something we're not."

"That's the point. I need people to talk about us instead of about my family."

As tempted as she was to place the magnificent ring on her finger, she returned the ring box to his hand and wrapped his fingers around it. "We'll be living a lie."

"Why does it have to be a lie? I am giving you this ring. That's a fact. You and I are friends. That's another fact. What stories people make up beyond that is out of our control."

"Still, it'll be a lie of omission."

"And sometimes a little white lie is more important than the truth. If your friend were to ask you if she looks like she put on weight and she has, would you tell her that she's fat?"

"Of course not." It wasn't until the words were out of her mouth that she realized she'd fallen into his trap.

"I just need a little diversion to keep my family safe and the country at peace. Please help me."

How could she turn away? And it wasn't just about

him. It was about the innocent people of his nation, who hadn't signed up for a scandal. Maybe she could help him. Maybe…

"I—I can't give you an answer now." No way was she jumping into this proposition without thinking it through—without the pressure of his pleading stare. "I'll have to think it over and talk to my mother. I'll let you know."

"By tonight."

"What?" He had to be kidding. This was a huge decision for her, to step into the spotlight with a prince and pull off some sort of charade. "I need more time than that. There are things to consider. Arrangements to be made."

"I'm sorry, but this has to happen before someone lets the bat out of the bag—"

"It's cat." When he sent her a puzzled look, she added, "Lets the cat out of the bag."

He sighed. "Someday I'll get all of your sayings straight."

Reese's mind had moved past Alex's loose grasp of idioms. She envisioned escaping the cold and snow to visit a far-off island. And what was even more tempting was being on the arm of the sexiest prince alive.

Some people would think she was crazy to even hesitate. But they hadn't lived the past two years of her life. If they had, they'd be cautious, too.

Still, the thought of jetting off to paradise with Alex made her heart flutter. It'd definitely be the experience of a lifetime. Could she honestly pass up a chance to spend more time with him?

She met his blue eyes. "If I agree to this, and I'm not saying that I will, I'm not lying to people. I won't tell them that you and I…that we're anything more than friends."

"And I wouldn't ask you to."

"Then I'll give you my answer tonight."

She turned and walked away before he could say anything else. She had enough things to consider. She didn't need him adding anything else. Once in the office, she turned off the ringer on the phone. She'd get to the messages shortly. She just needed a moment to breathe.

As she sat there and stared off into space, Alex's words came back to her—he was doing what he must to protect his family and heritage, much like she was trying to protect the patchwork of people whom she now considered her family. They weren't as different as she'd originally thought. The love for those they considered family came first. And this trip would help both of their families.

She really didn't have that much to consider after all. If her mother was able to handle the inn, she would be boarding a plane tomorrow. But when she thought of slipping on that ring and stepping in front of the cameras on Alex's arm, her insides quivered. Thankfully she'd have Alex to lean on. With his dream smile and charming ways, surely he'd be able to distract the paparazzi. He'd have them believing anything he told them.

But what about her? Would she be able to remember that this trip was nothing more than a fantasy and that they were each playing a part? How would she protect her heart from the charming prince?

The big moment had arrived.

A black limousine with diplomatic flags rolled to a stop by the airport entrance.

Alex took a deep breath, wondering if he'd been right to drag Reese into this game with the paparazzi. Still, he couldn't imagine anyone else playing the part of his girlfriend. He had absolutely no desire to hold anyone else's hand or to stare longingly into their eyes—for the media's sake, of course. Oh, who was he trying to bluff? Reese's kisses were as sweet as Mirraccino's juiciest grapes and held a promise of what was to come next.

He glanced over at Reese's now pale face. He hated that their departure had to be made such a public affair. She was wearing the newly repaired little black dress that had done him in the other night when they'd visited Rockefeller Center and he'd at last held her close.

He knew that any attempt to kiss her now would be rebuffed. Reese might have agreed to help him, but things had changed. She even looked at him differently, as though she didn't quite trust him. And he couldn't blame her.

None of this had worked out the way he'd wanted. His gaze slipped to her arm. "How's the arm feeling?"

"What?" She glanced at him with a questioning look.

"The arm—how is it today?"

"Don't start coddling me. My mother did enough of that when she got home yesterday from my aunt's."

He knew to tread lightly around the subject of her mother. Even though all of the staff at The Willows had offered to pitch in extra to help her mother run the place while they were in Mirraccino, Reese was still uncomfortable with the decision. He couldn't tell if it was leaving her mother or if it was letting go of the control she had over the inn, but either way this trip would do her some good. A well-deserved vacation.

"Make sure and tell me if the pain gets worse. We have some of the finest doctors in Mirraccino. They'll see that you're healing properly."

"Did you see all of those reporters and fans out there? Some are even holding signs."

"Don't worry. We have security. Those people won't be able to get to you."

"Is it always like this when you travel?"

"Not this bad. But I had to swirl up sufficient gossip

about my love life to gain the paparazzi's attention." With each passing moment it was getting more difficult to remember what was real and what was fake.

"I'd say it's working." She fidgeted with the hem of her dress. "So do you like all of this fuss?"

"Gaining positive press coverage is part of my duty as prince. A large part of Mirraccino's revenue comes from the tourism industry."

She inhaled a deep breath and lifted her chin to him. "Then let's get this over with."

"But first you will need this." He removed the black velvet box from his pocket and opened it.

She glanced at the ring and then back at his face. There was something in her expression, a tenderness—a question—and in a blink it was gone. Perhaps he'd just imagined it.

She held out her hand for the ring. He could just place it in her palm, but he wanted an excuse to touch her—to recover some of that closeness they'd shared before reality had pulled up the blind on their relationship and left all of the flaws visible under the bright light.

He took her hand in his, noticing how cold her skin was compared to his. Was she truly cold? Or was it a bad case of nerves? Did she also find this moment a little too real?

He slipped the ring on her finger and pushed it over her knuckle. It fit perfectly. And more than that, it looked perfect. He'd picked it out especially for her when this idea had started to take shape. Of course, working with his jeweler back in Mirraccino over the internet had been a bit of a risk, but the ring had turned out better than he'd hoped.

"Perfect."

"What?"

"The ring. It fits perfectly."

She glanced down at her hand, and he wanted to ask

what she was thinking, but he refrained. Was she having second thoughts? With them about to face the press, it was best just to let her be. He didn't want to say anything to upset her further.

When she lifted her gaze to meet his, there was such turmoil in her eyes—such agony. His resolve crumbled, spreading like snowflakes in a blizzard. He couldn't just sit by and not at least try to comfort her. He reached out and pulled her close. Her head willingly came to rest on his shoulder. Her silky hair brushed against his neck and the delicate scent of her floral shampoo teased his senses.

"You don't have to worry. I'll protect you." He meant it with every fiber of his being.

She lifted her head and looked at him. "You'll be my Prince Charming and ride to my rescue?"

"Yes." His gaze dipped to her lips. They were full and berry-red. Like a magnet, they drew him in and his head dipped. His mouth brushed her trembling lips.

It took him every bit of willpower to keep from devouring her lips. She tasted sweet and smelled divine. When she didn't back away, he continued his exploration. He'd never known a kiss could be so intoxicating. She tasted sweeter than the finest Mirraccino light pink Zinfandel.

This act of being a devoted couple was becoming more and more desirable with each fleeting second he held her close. He couldn't imagine ever letting her go. He wanted this kiss to go on and on. And if they hadn't been in the back of a hired car with the paparazzi just a few steps away, he'd have liked to find out where this heated moment would lead.

As it was, he was grateful for the tinted windows. There were certain things he must share with the world. This wasn't one of them. This was a very private moment that had nothing to do with providing cover for his family.

His hand slid up her arm and cradled her neck. Her pulse thumped against his palm, causing his heart to beat out a similar staccato pounding. This moment was something he would never forget. Everything about Reese was unforgettable. How in the world was he going to let her walk away when the time came?

A tap on the car door signaled that everyone was in place for them to make their grand entrance into the airport. Reese jerked back, her eyes wide and round.

"It's okay." Alex gave her arm a reassuring squeeze. "They won't open the door until I signal them."

Her fingers pressed to her now bare lips. They were slightly swollen. And her cheeks had taken on a rosy hue. He smiled, enjoying that he'd been the one to make her look ravished.

"I can't go out there now. I must look a mess."

"You look beautiful."

She reached for her purse. "I need to fix my makeup."

His hand covered hers. "Leave it. You can't improve on perfection."

Her questioning gaze met his and he pulled her hand away from her purse.

"Shall we go?"

"Wait! I—I've never done something like this. What if I make a mistake? What if I say or do the wrong thing?"

"Is that all you are worried about?" His face lifted into a smile. Relief flooded his body.

She nodded and stared at him as though not understanding his reaction.

"You'll do a wonderful job. The paparazzi are already enthralled with you."

"But I don't know how to be a prince's girlfriend."

"You're doing an excellent job." He sent her a certain look, hoping to steady her nerves. "And I don't plan to let you close enough to the press to speak to them. This is more about teasing them and letting them wonder about you and me."

Her shoulders straightened and she blinked away the uncertainty in her eyes. "You really think I can help you do this?"

He nodded. "I wouldn't have asked you otherwise."

She reached for his hand, lacing his fingers with hers.

He gave her a reassuring squeeze. "Ready?"

She nodded.

"Don't forget these." He handed her a pair of dark shades and a big black hat with a wide brim to shield her face from the cameras. "Make the paparazzi work for a close-up of you."

"Part of the cat-and-mouse strategy?"

"Exactly."

She settled the glasses on her face, hiding her expressive eyes. Next he handed over the hat, which she angled off to the side. And last, he helped her turn up the collar of her black wool coat.

"There. All set." Alex signaled the driver.

In seconds, the back car door swung open. For the first time, a natural smile pulled at his lips as he faced the cameras. He was proud to have Reese on his arm.

Alex knew it was dangerous to get too comfortable with this arrangement. Soon the final curtain would fall on their show. The thought niggled at him. Was this all just a show? Or was he more invested in this situation than he was willing to admit?

CHAPTER FOURTEEN

SO THIS WAS PARADISE?

Reese stared out the window as the private jet flew over Mirraccino, headed for the private landing strip used by the royal family. Alex's family. She couldn't believe that they'd gone from a gray, snowy day to clear blue skies. The sandy beaches captured her attention. She tried to restrain her awe over the islands' beauty, but she couldn't help herself. As the plane dipped lower, she had an even better view. Never had she seen such picturesque land—from the tropical gardens to the white beaches.

"This place is amazing."

"I'm glad you think so. Just wait until you see it all up close and personal."

She tore her gaze from the window to look at him as panic set in. "But I forgot my camera. My mother is never going to believe this place."

"I have a camera at the palace you can use." He leaned back in his seat. "Now you see part of the reason I want to protect it. The subversives have in mind to rip up the protected land surrounding the beaches and turn it all into exclusive resorts and condos. They can't see that they'll be destroying a national treasure."

"And that's what the revolt is over?"

"No. There's much more to it, but it boils down to a very

unhappy man who has an ax to grind with my papa about something from their childhood. I have never been privy to the details, as the king says that it is not worth repeating. Either way, I've met the man and he's hard, cold and revels in controversy."

"So if this man learns about your brother's marriage, he'll have more ammunition to use against your family."

"Yes. And over the years he has gained a following of troublemakers who think that they can manage the country better than the king and the governing body. But don't worry yourself about it. You have other things to think about. Like enjoying yourself and smiling—a lot."

She should know more about what was expected of her while she was here. "What exactly will I have to do while I'm here?"

"What would you like to do?"

"I'd like to tour the islands, especially the beaches. They look amazing. Maybe go swimming, except I forgot to pack my swimsuit."

"There's something you should know—"

Her body stiffened. "Not more bad news."

"No, nothing like that. I only wanted to warn you that though it is sunny out, the temperature is cool. So swimming in the sea wouldn't be advisable. However, there's a private pool within the palace walls that you're free to use at your leisure. As for clothes, you don't have to worry. I'll have someone stop by with an assortment for you to choose from."

"But I couldn't. I don't have the money."

"It's a perk of the job. You have to look the part of a prince's…um, girlfriend."

She didn't like the thought of taking handouts. But he was right. Her wardrobe was either supercasual, jeans and T-shirts, or business suits for hosting weddings and events.

With her recent lack of a social life, she hadn't needed anything else.

But ever since Alex had dropped into her world, things had changed drastically. In fact, it was just settling into her mind that she would be staying in a palace. An honest-to-goodness palace. This trip had some truly amazing perks—besides the devastatingly handsome guy beside her, who could make her insides melt when his lips pressed to hers.

Her gaze settled on Alex. He leaned back in the leather seat and attached his seat belt as the pilot came over the intercom to instruct them to prepare for landing. This was it. She was about to step into a fairy tale. This would be a story she could tell her children one day—if she ever found that one man she could trust.

Things moved quickly after the plane's wheels touched down. The Mirraccino palace with its enormity and beauty left her speechless, and that didn't happen often. The palace's warm tan, coral and turquoise tones glistened in the sunlight. It reminded her of fine jewelry. Its graceful curves and stunning turrets were regal while reflecting an island flair.

She pointed a finger at the magnificent structure as she struggled to find her voice. "You…you live here?"

His eyes lit up and his lips lifted at the corners. "Yes. I was born here. The whole royal family lives here. In fact, I need to check in on my papa and brother as soon as we get inside. I hope you don't mind."

"Not at all. I know you've been worried about them. It's really nice how close you are with your family."

Alex cleared his throat. "We're just your average family."

She couldn't help but laugh. "Not quite."

Nothing about Alex was average. Not the Learjet they

flew in on or the magnificent palace he called home. But there was more than just the physical elements of Alex's life that stood out. There was his need to look after her when she got hurt. And his need to fix her apartment.

But then there was the other side of this man—the side that withheld the truth about himself. How did she get past that? And should she even want to? After all, this whole game of charades was temporary. She had to be careful not to forget that this whole trip was nothing more than to benefit the paparazzi.

A man in a dark suit stepped out of the palace. He didn't smile or give any indication that he even saw her. The man's focus was on Alex. Something told her that he wasn't there to retrieve their luggage—not that she had much. She turned a questioning look to Alex.

His demeanor turned stiff and unreadable. "I need to deal with something. If you want to wait inside, I'll be right in."

"No problem." She didn't have to be asked twice. She was eager to see the interior of this amazing palace.

This all has to be a dream.

Reese resisted the urge to pinch herself.

She entered the grand entryway. Her high heels clicked over the marble floor. She craned her neck, taking in the splendor of the walls and high ceiling. She was in awe of the spaciousness and the sheer elegance of the interior, which included a crystal chandelier. And if that wasn't enough to make a girl swoon, standing before her was a man almost as handsome as Alex—in fact, they looked a lot alike. The man filled out a navy suit with the top two buttons of his blue dress shirt undone.

His hair was a deeper shade than Alex's. But it was the man's eyes that held her attention. They were blue, but there was something more—something she couldn't quite define. Perhaps it was loneliness or pain. Whatever it was her heart went out to him.

He spoke in a foreign language.

She held up her hands to stop him. "I'm sorry. I don't understand what you're trying to say."

"No, it is I who am sorry. I forgot that you're American. Welcome to Mirraccino." His voice was deep like Alex's. "I'm Demetrius. You must be Alexandro's friend."

"Ah, yes, I…I'm Reese." She clutched her purse strap tighter. "Alex is talking with someone outside. He'll be right in."

As if on cue, Alex stepped up behind her and placed his hands possessively on her shoulders, as though they belonged together. "Sorry about that. There's a problem down at the port. But nothing that can't be dealt with later. I see I am too late to make the introductions."

Demetrius stepped forward. "This will give me a chance to say this once. Thank you both for everything you've done to keep the paparazzi from making this difficult situation even worse."

Reese wasn't sure what to say to the crown prince. Should she just say *you're welcome?* Or offer her condolences on the dissolution of his marriage?

Alex rode to her rescue when he stepped around her. "Is everything resolved?"

Demetrius's shoulders slumped. "She's gone."

"It's for the best." Alex's matter-of-fact voice startled Reese. "You have a duty to Papa. To the nation. That must always come first."

Demetrius's pained stare met his brother's unflinching gaze. How could Alex be so emotionless? Reese obviously didn't know him as well as she'd thought. She struggled to keep the frown of disapproval from her face.

As it was, the room practically vibrated with emotion.

With bated breath she waited to see if the brothers would come to blows.

Demetrius's hands clenched at his sides. "That's the difference between us, little brother. I don't believe that duty is the be-all and end-all of life."

"And look what that thinking cost you. You look terrible and this whole episode was taxing on Papa."

"Just because you can live without love doesn't mean that I can." Demetrius's eyes narrowed. "And don't think I'm the only one who has his future drawn out for them. You have no more freedom than I do. And we all know that you're the good son who'll marry whoever they choose for you—"

"Enough." Alex's voice held a hard edge. "I know this is a hard time for you, but we have a guest."

Demetrius's gaze moved to Reese. "I'm sorry you had to witness that. Just be glad that you're here doing a job and you didn't actually fall for my brother. He can be heartless at times."

Before she could even think of a response, Demetrius stormed out of the room.

She turned a startled look at Alex. "How could you say that to him? Couldn't you see the pain he's in?"

"He has to remember what's at stake. Living here—" he waved his hands around "—comes with responsibilities others don't think of. My brother can't afford to forget that his decisions affect far more than just himself. He'll get over that woman."

Reese's mouth gaped open. "I was wrong. I'm not the grinch around here. You are."

"What's that supposed to mean?"

"Read the book, you'll find out. And maybe you'll learn a lesson, too."

His forehead wrinkled. "I don't need a child's book to

tell me that there's no room for romance when it comes to the future of this nation."

"And you had to remind your brother of that right now when you can plainly see that he's brokenhearted?"

Alex raked his fingers through his hair. "You're right. I didn't handle it very well."

"That's an understatement." There was one more thing that she had to know. "Is he right? Will a wife be chosen for you?"

Alex's gaze met hers. "My family has plans for me to make an advantageous marriage to a woman from an influential family. We are a small nation and in these uncertain times we can't have enough allies."

Reese's heart sank. "Will you go through with it? Will you marry who they choose?"

He sighed and raked his fingers through his dark hair, scattering the strands. "I don't know. I have more to consider than my happiness. If my marriage can benefit Mirraccino, I must take that into consideration."

All of a sudden this scenario was beginning to sound all too familiar. What was it about men putting everything ahead of love? Did they really think you could sustain a meaningful relationship without it?

She glared at Alex, letting her anger mask her disappointment. "You're just like Josh—"

"What?" Hurt reflected in Alex's eyes. In a blink it was replaced with a hard wall that locked her out. "I can't believe you'd compare me to him."

"Both of you are out to have relationships with women you think can help you. It doesn't matter if you care about them or not. All that matters is what you can get from them."

"That's not true. I'd never lead a woman on."

"True." He definitely wouldn't do that. "You'd tell them up front what you wanted."

Alex reached out to her, but she backed away. "You're tired after our long trip and you're letting my brother get you worked up. We can talk about this later."

He was right. She was getting worked up. But she refused to let another man hurt her—betray her. And the thought of Alex belonging to another woman hurt more than she wanted to admit—even to herself.

"Go after your brother and make things right."

Alex's eyes widened as though he wasn't used to being ordered around. "You're serious?"

"Yes. Go."

"I'll send someone to show you to your room. Later, I'll give you the grand tour."

She nodded her approval. "I need to call my mother and check on things."

Armed with the knowledge that Alex would have a bride chosen for him, she'd have to be careful going forward. She didn't want to get swept up in paradise with a sexy prince and lose her heart. Because in the end, she'd be going back to New York.

Alone.

CHAPTER FIFTEEN

IT WAS JUST the two of them, at last.

Alex stopped next to Reese in front of the glass doors leading to the garden. He hoped a good night's sleep had put her in a better frame of mind. She had to be overcome with exhaustion to accuse him of being anything like her ex-boyfriend. He was nothing like that jerk. He'd never intentionally use a woman. She just didn't understand how things worked when you were born into royalty.

"How are things between you and your brother?" Reese asked, drawing him from his thoughts.

"Getting better. You were right. He really cared about that woman."

They stepped onto the patio and Reese glanced up at him with those big brown eyes. "Does this mean you now believe in love at first sight?"

Alex smiled, amazed by her persistence. "I'll take it under advisement. Perhaps there's more to this love thing than I understand."

She smiled, too, and he had to resist the urge to plant a kiss on her upturned lips. He didn't want to press his luck. At least today she was speaking to him and not glaring at him as though he was the enemy.

They descended the sweeping steps to the edge of the sculpted garden. The sun was high overhead. He enjoyed the fact that she had on a teal dress that he'd personally picked out. When he'd first laid his eyes on it, he'd known it would look spectacular with Reese's long auburn hair.

"You look beautiful."

"Thank you. I don't even want to think how much this dress must have cost you. Did you know that it has a designer label?"

He smiled, enjoying the enthusiasm in her voice. "All that matters is that you like it and you look beautiful in it."

She ducked her head. "I considered not wearing it. It has to be so expensive. I didn't want to do anything to ruin it. But then I realized that I don't own anything suitable to wear here. And I didn't want to embarrass you."

"You could never do that." And he meant every word. He was proud to be seen with a woman who was just as beautiful on the inside as out.

She stopped in front of him and turned. Her shoulders straightened and her chin tilted up. "Tell me about her."

"Who?"

"The woman your family wants you to marry."

He resisted the urge to roll his eyes. "You don't want to hear about Catherine."

"Catherine. That's her name?"

"Yes." He didn't like where this conversation was headed. "There are some flowers over here that I think you'll like."

Reese didn't move. "This Catherine. What does she think of you being in the papers with me?"

"I—I don't know." He hadn't thought about it. Perhaps he should have let her in on the plan, but they'd never made a point of being a part of each other's lives. "We don't talk very often."

"But you're supposed to marry her."

"It's what our families have arranged. It's what is expected of us."

"But neither of you has agreed to the arrangement?"

Was that a glimmer of hope in Reese's eyes? Was she hoping there was room in his life for her?

"Catherine and I have never talked about marriage. We're friends and we spend time together when our families visit."

"Do you love her?"

At last, the question he'd been certain would come up. "Catherine is a wonderful friend. And a very sweet person. But no, I'm not in love with her."

Reese's mouth settled into a firm line as she glanced away, leaving him to wonder about the direction of her thoughts. He'd rather she get it all out in the open, but instead of prodding her, he remained silent. She was at least still here with him. He shouldn't push his luck.

Reese set off down one of the many meandering paths in the sprawling garden. It amazed him how fast she could move while wearing those silver high heels—but boy, was it a sight worth beholding. As she turned a corner, he realized she was getting away. He set off after her.

He'd just caught up to her when she came to an abrupt halt. It was all he could do to keep from running into her. His hands came to rest on her shoulders as he regained his balance. He was just about to ask what she thought she was doing when his gaze settled on the king.

His papa had stopped in front of them. "I didn't know anyone ever took the time to stroll through the gardens."

Alex glanced at Reese's wide-eyed stare and immediately knew that she was intimidated by not only his papa's title but also his booming voice. "I was just showing Reese around."

"There's lots to see. Your mama firmly believed that

it was necessary to pause every day and smell the roses. Your mama knew what was important in life. Sometimes I wonder if she'd approve of my choices, especially with you boys."

Alex was rendered silent, unused to seeing his papa in this state of contemplation concerning his family.

Reese cleared her throat. "I think you've done a great job with Alex. He's kind and thoughtful. You should be proud of him."

"I am." The king's tired face lit up. For a moment, he studied Reese. "Perhaps I am worried for no reason. Now, make sure my son shows you the yellow roses. They were his mama's favorites. If you'll excuse me, I've got to get back to work."

As his papa walked away, Alex was struck by how much his papa still vividly loved his mama. Alex wondered what it must be like to experience such a profound love. But was it worth the risk of ending up alone like his papa—

"Did you hear me?" Reese sent him a puzzled look.

"I'm sorry. What were you saying?"

"I wanted to know which direction led to the roses."

He led her along the wide meandering path edged with low-cut hedges that formed various geometric planting spaces. Each section was planted with just one type of flower, fruit or vegetable. Even though he'd lived here his whole life, he still found the vibrant colors beautiful, but today he only had eyes for Reese.

"With all of these gorgeous flowers, it's like paradise here. You're so lucky."

He looked around the vast garden. He definitely saw it in a different light after living in Reese's world for a few weeks. And though he was blessed financially, Reese was much better off. Her life contained priceless things such as the wonderful relationship she had with her mother, who obviously loved her very much. And even the people who worked for Reese were totally devoted to her.

His guards were devoted to him to the point of laying down their lives to protect him, but it wasn't out of love. It was a duty—an allegiance to a greater good. He wondered what it would be like to have a warm relationship with those around him like Reese had with her staff.

She glanced at him. "You seem to have a lot on your mind."

"I was thinking that until now I've never considered myself lucky. Sure, I appreciate the fact that I lead a privileged life, but sometimes I wake up and wish I had a normal life."

"You can't be serious. You'd really want to give all of this up?"

He shrugged. "Sometimes. When the rules and duties dictate my entire life."

Her forehead wrinkled. "You mean like now, when you had to drop everything and fly to New York?"

"Actually, that's something I'll always be grateful for." He stopped walking and turned to her. "It gave me the opportunity to meet you."

"Are you flirting with me?"

"I don't know. Is it working?"

A hint of a smile pulled at her rosy lips. "What do you think?"

His heart thumped against his ribs. The sun glistened off her auburn hair and her eyes sparkled. He was drawn to her as he was drawn to none other. His fingers stroked her cheek and she leaned ever so slightly into his touch.

His royal duties and the knowledge that Reese would never fit into the king's idea of the proper wife fled his mind. In this moment, the only thing that mattered was the

woman standing before him with longing in her eyes—
such beautiful eyes.

His head dipped down and her soft lips were there meeting his. He moved slowly at first. Like a bird to nectar, he didn't want to startle her. But when she matched him move for move, his heart pounded harder. Faster.

An overwhelming need grew in him for more of this—more of Reese. His arms encircled her waist, pulling her flush to him. He'd never experienced a kiss so tantalizing, so sweet. And he'd never wanted someone so much in his life. Not just physically. Her very presence in his life was like a smoothing balm, easing away the rough edges. It was as if he'd donned a pair of glasses and could see things so much more clearly.

A gentle moan swelled in his throat as her fingers threaded through his hair. He wanted more, oh, so much more. He needed to move them out of the garden. Someplace where they wouldn't be under constant supervision of the security detail—someplace where they could see where this would lead.

There was the sound of hurried footsteps followed by someone loudly clearing his throat. Alex knew the sound—it was time to get back to work. Damn. Why did duty call at the least inopportune times?

With great reluctance he released Reese. "I must go. I've been waiting on an important call."

It was as though he could see the walls rising between them in Reese's eyes. He couldn't blame her for wanting to come first in someone's life. The men in her life had relegated her to an afterthought and collateral damage. She deserved so much better. Not that he was the man to give her all the love she deserved.

As he walked away, he inwardly groaned. His common

sense and emotions warred with each other. When it came to Reese, she had him reconsidering everything in his life.

Reese was in dangerous territory.

And though she knew that Alex could never have a future with her, she couldn't resist his sultry kisses. Or keep her heart from pounding when his fingers touched hers.

She needed some space—a chance to clear her mind and remember that this was just a show for the press. But there was no time for getting away. There was no chance for her to be alone except at night in her room. They had a job to do—keep the press concentrating on them while his brother pulled himself together and the last of the legal negotiations were handled.

And this morning, Reese and Prince Alexandro were about to have their first press-covered outing. Alex's long, lean fingers threaded through hers as they strolled along the palace drive on their way to tour the nearby village of Portolina. His grip was strong and she drew comfort from it as she was about to be paraded before the cameras.

This public appearance didn't require big sunglasses or hats to hide behind. Instead Reese had selected a pair of dark jeans, a navy blazer and a white blouse. Alex had advised she dress casually. She hoped her choice in clothes would suffice.

Reese gripped Alex's hand tighter. When he glanced her way, her stomach quivered. But it had nothing to do with the reporters waiting for them on the other side of the palace gates. No, the fluttering feeling had everything to do with the man who had her mind utterly confused between her want to continue the kiss from yesterday and her need to protect herself from being hurt when this fairy tale ended.

Alex leaned over and whispered in her ear, "Trust me. You'll be fine."

She let out a pent-up breath and nodded. They approached the gate as it swung wide open. She faced the paparazzi's flashing cameras and smiled brightly.

"When will the formal engagement announcement be released?" shouted a reporter.

"Is there a ball planned to celebrate the impending nuptials?"

"When's the wedding?" chorused a number of voices.

"The palace has no comment." A spokesman stepped forward as planned to field the questions. "Prince Alexandro and Ms. Harding are out for a stroll about the village. If there are any announcements to be made in the future, my office will notify you."

Security cleared the drive for them. Reese wasn't sure her legs would support her—her knees felt like gelatin. As though Alex understood, he moved her hand to the crook of his arm for additional support and then covered it with his other hand.

As they made their way toward the small village, he leaned over and whispered in her ear, "You're doing great. Now they'll never guess your deep dark secret."

She turned to him and arched a questioning brow.

He leaned in again. His minty-fresh breath tickled her neck, sending delicious sensations racing to her core. His voice was low but clear. "That you're a bit grinchy. And that beneath that makeup you're really green."

She laughed and the tension in her body eased. "You looked up the story I told you about."

He nodded and returned her smile. So he really did hear what she said. Her lips parted as her smile intensified.

With the paparazzi trailing behind, Alex gave her a walking tour of Portolina—a small village near the palace. If not for the festive red-and-green decorations, it would not seem like Christmas—at least not the cold, snowy Christmas that Reese was accustomed to in New York.

The stroke of Alex's thumb against the back of her hand sent her pulse racing as she tried to keep her attention focused on this fascinating town. It was teeming with history, from the old structures with their stone-and-mortar walls to the stone walkways. She even found the doorways fascinating, as some were rectangular and others were arched. Beautiful old brass knockers adorned the heavy wood doors. This place definitely had a unique old-world feel to it. She could see why Alex and his family weren't eager to bulldoze this place and modernize it with condos.

Some people rode scooters but most villagers walked. Many of them smiled and waved. Some even came up to Alex—their prince—and greeted him like some returning hero. But most of all, she could feel their gazes on her. Of course, Reese couldn't tell if they were curious about her or the caravan of reporters. She noticed how Alex barely gave the paparazzi much notice. He merely went about his day and she tried following his lead, enjoying the sights and sounds.

The paths he led her on ebbed and flowed through the village, sometimes between buildings and sometimes under passageways. It was so different from her life in New York City. With the camera Alex had lent her, she took dozens of photos—eager to remember every moment of this amazing trip.

They sat down in a coffeehouse that had been closed to the public. Alex lifted her hand and kissed it. "What's bothering you, *bella?*"

Her heart stuttered as she stopped and stared at him. His reference to her with such an endearing term caught her off guard. But before she let herself get caught up in the moment, she reminded herself that this was all an illusion. She pulled her hand away. He was playing his part—acting like the ardent lover. Nothing more.

But if that was the case, why was he doing it when there was no one within hearing distance? Reese could feel her last bit of resolve giving way. And as he once again reached across the café table to her, she didn't shy away. His warm hand engulfed hers reassuringly. She could feel her resistance to his charms crumble even further.

"You can tell me anything." His voice was soft and encouraging.

Glancing around just to make sure they were in fact alone, she lowered her voice and said, "They expect us to get married. This is what I was worried about. They've jumped to the wrong conclusion. I'll have to call my mother and warn her not to believe anything she reads in the paper."

Reese glanced down at the ring causing all of the ruckus. She wiggled her finger, enjoying the way the light danced over the jewels. It truly was the most beautiful ring she'd ever seen.

Alex waved away her worries. "Don't worry about it. Just enjoy yourself." There was a pause and then he added, "You are enjoying yourself, aren't you?"

"Yes. But when this illusion ends, everyone will think it's my fault."

"*Bella,* you worry too much. After all, you are forgetting that I control what information is fed to the press. On my honor, I promise your good name will remain intact."

She wanted to smile and take comfort in his words, but she couldn't. They weren't the words she was longing to hear. She wanted him to say that she mattered to him. That this illusion was real to him. That it wasn't going to end.

After their extensive lunch was served, the waiter brought them espresso to wash it down. Reese, not used to such a large meal, wasn't sure she had room for it.

Alex took a sip of the steaming brew. "I have some meetings this afternoon that I must attend, but feel free to finish touring the village."

"I think I'll do that. I still have my Christmas shopping to do."

"I promise to return as soon as I can."

"Don't rush on my account. I know that you have important issues to attend to."

"Nothing is more important than you." His warm gaze met hers and her insides melted. "You're my guest and I want you to be happy here. I hope the paparazzi's attention has not been too much for you."

"Actually, your staff has done a great job of keeping them at a distance. And I think the people of Portolina are amazingly kind. You're lucky to live here. I'll never forget my visit."

Her heart pinched at the thought of one day waking up and no longer bumping into Alex. She didn't know how someone she'd only met recently could become such an important part of her life.

She brought her thoughts up short. This was ridiculous. She was falling for her own PR scam. They weren't a couple. And he wasn't someone that she should trust, but with each passing day she was finding her mistrust of him sliding away.

Maybe like the Grinch, Alex's heart was starting to grow. Which gave her a great idea for a Christmas present. There was a small bookstore just back a little ways. She would get him a copy of *How the Grinch Stole Christmas*. Perhaps it wasn't too late for him to see life differently.

CHAPTER SIXTEEN

How could it be more than a week since they'd arrived in Mirraccino?

Alex's body tensed as he realized there was no longer a need for Reese to stay—except for the fact that he wasn't ready to let her go yet. He'd spent every available moment with her, and he still hadn't gotten his fill of her. He'd never had this sort of experience with anyone before.

They'd toured Mirraccino's finest vineyards and taken a trip to the bustling port on the other side of the island. The outings allowed her to rest her arm and the bruises time to begin to fade. And best of all, her frosty demeanor had melted beneath the bright sunshine.

He knew as Prince Alexandro, he should end things here and now. But the plain, ordinary Alex didn't want to let go. He couldn't imagine Reese being gone from his life. How did one return to a dull and repetitive life after being shown a bright, sparkling world full of hope?

Alex had made his decision. No matter what the king said, it was simply too soon for Reese to leave. His brother, the crown prince, was simply not in good enough spirits yet to deal with the press. It wouldn't take much for them to notice the crown prince's melancholy expression. He wore it like an old war wound, reminding his whole family of what he'd lost in order to uphold his royal duty.

Thanks to Reese, Alex was starting to believe his brother's feelings for the woman had run much deeper than he'd originally thought. The price of being royal could cut quite deep at times. He was about to pay his own dues when Reese left for the States. He wasn't relishing that impending day. In fact, he refused to think of it today.

Christmas Day had at last arrived and the paparazzi had fled for their own homes, leaving everyone at the palace in peace—at least for one day. And now that the official photos had been taken, the gifts opened and the extravagant lunch served, he had a very special surprise in mind for Reese. He'd been working on it all week and now he was anxious to surprise her.

"I can't believe the size of your Christmas tree." Reese's voice was full of awe as they strolled back to their rooms, which were in two different wings. "It's a good thing I remembered to have you take my picture next to it. My mother never would have believed it was, what— twenty feet tall?"

"I don't know." He smiled over the things that impressed her. "If you want I can inquire."

"No. That's okay. The picture will say it all. You did get the whole tree in the picture, didn't you?"

"Yes. Now I have a question for you." He sensed her expectant look. "After we change clothes, would you join me for a stroll along the beach?"

"I don't know." Her gaze didn't meet his. "I'm kind of tired. It's been a really long day."

He wasn't going to give up that easily. This was far too important—he had a very special surprise for her. "Or is it that you stayed awake all night waiting for Santa?"

There was no hint of a smile on her face. "Something like that."

"I was only teasing you."

"I know." She continued staring at the floor.

His finger lifted her chin. Sadness reflected in her eyes. "Reese, talk to me. I'll make it better."

She shook her head. "You can't. No one can."

His voice softened. "Sometimes talking things over can make a person feel better."

She leaned her back against the closed door and pulled at the short sleeves of her midnight-blue dress. "Do you really care?"

His fingers moved some loose strands of silky hair from her face and tucked them behind her ear. "You know I do. I care very much."

Reese glanced up and down the hall as though to confirm that they truly were alone. This must be more serious than he'd originally thought.

"Why don't we step into your room?" he suggested.

She nodded and turned to open the door. Inside, she approached the bed, where she perched on the edge. With the door closed, no one would bother them. Alex's mind spiraled with all of the intimate possibilities awaiting them. Perhaps this hadn't been such a good idea for a serious talk.

Reese lifted her face. Her shiny eyes and pale face stopped his wayward thoughts in their tracks. He sat down beside her and took her hand in his.

Her voice came out very soft. "I was up last night thinking about how my life has changed since my father died at Christmas two years ago."

The news smacked into Alex, stunning him for a moment. "I had no idea."

"I didn't want to make a big deal of it. It was Christmas Eve, to be exact. He was leaving…leaving me and my mother to meet his longtime lover." She swiped at her eyes. "He didn't even have the nerve to tell us to our faces. He wrote a note. A note! Who writes a note to tell the people that he is supposed to love that their lives were a lie and he doesn't love them and he wants out?"

Alex didn't have a clue what to say. Her rigid back and level shoulders sent keep-away vibes. So he sat there quietly waiting for her to get it all out.

"He hit a patch of black ice and went over an embankment. They say he died on impact. He didn't even have the decency to stick around to say goodbye. There was no time for questions—and no answer to why he'd destroyed our family. It was all over in a heartbeat."

"I'm so sorry he did that to you and your mother."

Reese swiped at her eyes. "At the time, I thought I had Josh to lean on. He was there for the funeral. He was the perfect gentleman, sympathizing with me and my mother." A hollow laugh echoed from her chest. "He had the nerve to condemn my father for his actions. And yet when it came to light that the savings had been drained off and the mansion had been mortgaged to pay for my father's new life, Josh couldn't get out the door fast enough."

Her shoulders drooped as she got the last of the sad story out. It was as though without all of the anger and pain, she deflated.

Instead of words, he turned, drawing her into his arms. She didn't resist. In fact, she leaned into his embrace. Maybe his plan for today wasn't such a good idea after all.

Reese inhaled a shaky breath. "Now you know why I've been so hesitant to trust you—to trust anyone."

Alex lifted her chin with his thumb. When her brown gaze met his, he said, "You can trust me. I promise I won't abandon you and I won't betray you."

He leaned forward, pressing his lips gently against hers in a reassuring kiss. Her bottom lip trembled beneath his. He didn't know how anyone could take her for granted. Reese was everything he'd ever wanted in a woman and more.

She pulled back and gave him a watery smile. "Thank you. I didn't mean to put a damper on the day."

"And if I had known what a tough day this would be for you, I wouldn't have tried to talk you into an outing."

"The truth is, I'll never be able to relax now."

"Are you saying you want to go?" He didn't want her to do anything that she wasn't up for.

She nodded and wiped away the moisture on her cheeks. "Just let me get changed."

"I'll meet you back here in ten minutes."

"Sounds good. Thank you for listening and understanding." The smile that touched her lips this time was genuine, and it warmed a spot in his chest.

On second thought, maybe his plan was just what she needed to push away her not-so-happy past and replace it with new, happy memories. Yes, he liked that idea. Reese deserved to be happy after the way she went out of her way for the people in her life—he wanted to be the one who went out of his way for her.

In that moment, he realized something that he'd been avoiding for a while now. He had feelings for Reese—deep feelings. He knew it was a big risk with his heart. Thoughts of his heartbroken father flashed through his mind. But in the next breath, he envisioned Reese's face.

He didn't have a choice.

Somehow, someway, she'd sneaked past his defenses. He cared for her more than anyone else in his life. But he didn't know what to do with these feelings. He was a prince. There were expectations he must fulfill for the good of the kingdom.

As he headed for his suite, he realized it was time he called Catherine. They needed to meet after the holidays were over. In light of his genuine feelings for Reese, he couldn't let the lingering questions surrounding the anticipated royal engagement drag on.

Although with all that hinged on the engagement, breaking the news to Catherine would have to be handled face-to-face and very carefully.

Reese's mouth gaped.

Gripping the red beach bag hanging over her shoulder and with Alex holding her other hand, she stood on the sand utterly speechless. Her gaze searched his smiling face before she turned back to the towering palm tree all decked out with white twinkle lights. The scene belonged on a postcard. It was picture-perfect…just like Alex in his khaki pants and white shirt with the sleeves rolled up and the collar unbuttoned.

Alex gave her hand a squeeze. "Do you like your surprise?"

"I love it." She nodded and smiled. Her gaze roamed around, trying to take it all in. "Is this all for me?"

His eyes lit up as he gazed at her. "It's my Christmas present to you."

The wall around her heart that had been eroding all week completely crumbled in that moment. She was totally vulnerable to him and she didn't care. "But you've already given me so much that I can never repay."

"That was all about our deal. This, well, this is because I wanted to do something special for you." He shifted his weight from one foot to the other. "And I know how much you enjoy the little lights, so I ordered enough to decorate the bungalow inside and out. Do you like it?"

She nodded vigorously. "No one has ever done anything so thoughtful for me. Thank you."

She lifted up on her tiptoes and without thinking of how

their diverse lives would never mesh, leaned into him and pressed her lips to his. She heard the swift intake of his breath. They'd been building toward this moment since their first kiss at Rockefeller Center. With each touch, look, kiss, she felt a heady need growing within her. The electricity between them had crackled and arced ever since they met. And now beneath the darkening Mediterranean sky, it had the strength of a lightning bolt. Her insides warmed with undeniable anticipation.

She swallowed hard, trying to regain her composure. "Are you going to show me the inside?"

He blinked as though he, too, had been thoroughly distracted by the kiss that promised more to follow. "Um... yes. Lead the way."

She easily made it up the stone steps that meandered up the embankment and led to a wide-open terrace with a white table and matching chairs. An arrangement of red poinsettias was placed in the center of the table, where a burning white candle flickered within a hurricane lamp. She wondered if his attention to details extended to all parts of his life.

She stopped on the terrace and turned to Alex. This night was so romantic, so perfect. Her heart thumped against her ribs. He'd done all of this for her. With every passing moment it was becoming increasingly difficult to remember that she was only playing a part for the sake of his nation's national security.

And then her chest tightened. Her palms grew damp. And she bit down on her lower lip. In that moment, she remembered how much it hurt when happy illusions shattered and reality ran up and smacked her in the face. She'd promised herself she wouldn't set herself up to be hurt like that again. It was just too painful.

Needing to add a dash of reality to this picture-perfect

evening, she asked, "Have you thought about how we're going to end all of this?"

Alex's brow creased. "Why would I think about something like that when we're having such a wonderful time?"

He had a good point, but fear overrode his words. "But eventually you're going to have to tell the press something when I go back to the States without you."

His fingers caressed her cheek. "Just for tonight, forget about the future and enjoy the moment."

She wanted to, more than he knew. But this just wasn't right. They'd gotten caught up in the show they were putting on for the public. In reality, there was another woman in Alex's life.

The sobering reality propelled her away from him— needing a little space to resign herself to the fact that this evening, as beautiful as it was, couldn't happen. If they made love—if she laid her heart on the line—she couldn't bear to walk away from him. As it was, stepping on the plane now would be torture, but to know exactly what she'd be missing would be unbearable.

She stepped up to the rail to gaze out over the ocean as the sun was setting. Pink and purple stretched across the horizon as a big ball of orange sank beneath the sea. The breeze tickled over her skin while the scent of salt filled her nose.

When she heard his footsteps approaching her, she tried to act normal—whatever that amounted to these days. "I've never seen anything so beautiful."

"I have." Alex's hands wrapped around her waist. "And I am holding her."

His compliment made her heart go tap-tap in her chest. She turned in his arms. "I'm sure you've been with much prettier women. What about Catherine? Shouldn't she be the one who is here with you?"

His brows gathered. "No, she shouldn't."

"But you're supposed to marry her."

"Is that what's bothering you?" When she nodded, he added, "Then stop worrying. I've called Catherine."

He did? Her heart took flight. "You told her about me?"

"Yes—"

Reese launched herself at him, smothering his words with a passionate kiss. Excitement and relief pumped through her veins. Her arms wrapped around his neck, pulling him close. There was nothing more she needed to hear. He'd told Catherine that they were together now. How could she have ever doubted him?

Reese hadn't known she could ever be this happy. The rush of feelings inside her was intense and they were fighting to get out. The time had come to quit holding back and trust him with her heart. Because if anyone was a good guy, it was Alex.

She pulled back and looked up at him. "Sometimes fantasies really do come true."

"Yes, they do."

He drew her back to him, the heat of his body permeating her dress. His lips pressed to hers. This time there was no hesitation in his touch. There was a deep need and a passionate desire in the way his mouth moved over hers. It lit a fire within her that mounted in intensity with each passing second.

Someone cleared his throat.

Reese jumped, pulling away from Alex's hold. She didn't know why she'd automatically assumed that they were alone. And that Alex had planned this as a romantic getaway for two.

Heat scorched her cheeks as she turned to face their visitor.

The butler stood at attention. "Sir, we need to know if you would like us to set up the meal inside or out."

Alex glanced at her. "It's your choice. Where would you like to dine?"

"Without the sun, the temps are dipping." She rubbed her arms, which were growing cold without his warmth next to them. "Would you mind if we eat inside?"

"Not at all. Would you like a fire lit?"

She glanced through the glass doors at the stone fireplace. The idea of sitting next to a crackling fire with Alex sounded perfectly romantic. "Yes, please."

Once the butler and small staff set about laying out the meal, Alex approached the fireplace mantel and retrieved a red plush Santa hat. "I think this will help set the mood."

She let him place the hat upon her head. "I guess it depends on what sort of mood you're creating."

"I'll let you wonder about that for now."

She spied another Santa hat on the mantel and decided that the prince needed to have some fun with her. She tossed her beach bag on the couch and raced over to the mantel. With the other Santa hat in hand, she turned to Alex.

A smile lit up his face as he started shaking his head. "No way. I am not wearing that."

"This evening is all your creation. I think that you're more Santa today than I am. I'll be Santa's elf."

He stopped shaking his head as his eyes lit up with definite interest. "My elf, huh? I guess that means that you have to listen to me."

"I don't think so." She backed up but he followed her with a devilish look in his eyes. "Don't go getting any wild ideas."

He grabbed her by the sides and started tickling her. His fingers easily found her sensitive spots. She could barely breathe from all of the laughter. Though his magical fingers had stopped moving, he continued to hold her close. It felt so natural to be in his arms. Her arms draped over his shoulders as she leaned into him, trying to catch her breath.

His gaze met hers. "You know Santa left some packages over there under the tree for you."

She leaned her head to the side to see around his hulking form. "I can't believe I didn't see those before." She glanced back at him. "Are you sure they're for me?"

"I don't know. Were you a good girl this year?"

She nodded.

"Are you sure?"

She nodded again. "Can I open them now?"

"Not quite yet." When she stuck out her bottom lip, he added, "Surely you can wait until after dinner."

"But that's not what I'm pouting about. I only have one gift for you." She pulled away from him to move to the couch and reached in her beach bag. She removed a package all neatly wrapped in white tissue paper with a shiny red bow.

"You didn't have to get me anything."

"That's what makes it special. I wanted to. But I must warn you that it's nothing expensive or impressive."

"Anything you give me will be a thousand times more special than the most expensive wines or sports car."

"A sports car? So that's what you wanted Santa to bring you?"

He reached out for her hand and drew her to him, pulling her down on his lap. "Everything I want is here. You didn't have to get me a gift."

"I would have given it to you this morning at the gift exchange with your family, but I knew your family wouldn't understand the meaning behind it. And I didn't want to do anything that might be misconstrued by your father."

"That you don't have to worry about. Did you notice how well he's taken to you?"

"I know. What was up with that?"

"I told you that you had nothing to worry about by coming here. He really likes you—they all do. Most especially me."

By the glow of the firelight, they enjoyed soup and antipasto. Neither of them was that hungry after the large Christmas luncheon. This light fare was just perfect. And Alex was the perfect date as he kept her smiling and laughing with stories of adventures from his childhood.

"You were quite the daredevil back in the day," Reese surmised as she settled down on the rug and pillows in front of the fireplace. "Something tells me that the adventurous part of you is still lurking in there behind the prim and proper prince."

"You think so." He popped a bottle of Mirraccino's finest sparkling wine and the cork flew across the room. The contents bubbled over the top and he sucked up the overflow before it could make a mess.

"My point is proven." She laughed.

He poured them each a flute of the bubbly golden fluid and then held one out to her. She accepted it with a smile. This whole trip had been amazing and she had no doubt where the evening was headed.

"To the most beautiful woman I have ever known. May all of your wishes come true."

Their glasses clinked and before Reese even held the crystal stemware to her lips, a fluttery feeling filled her stomach. Her gaze met his hungry one. She took a sip of the sweet wine, but she barely noticed it as the cold liquid slid down her dry throat.

"You do know that we're all alone now?" He set aside his glass.

She set her wine next to his. Her gaze slipped down to his lips. They looked quite inviting. "Does this mean that I get my Christmas present now?"

His voice came out unusually deep and gravelly. "That depends on what present you want to unwrap first."

She leaned toward him. "I think I'll start right here."

In the next breath her lips were covering his. When his arms wrapped around her, pulling her close, she could no longer deny that she had fallen for her very own Prince Charming. She loved Alex with every fiber of her being.

His hands encompassed her waist, pulling her to him. She willingly leaned into him. The sudden shift of her weight sent them falling back against the stack of pillows. She met him kiss for kiss, touch for touch. The fire crackled as Alex nuzzled her neck, causing her to laugh. She couldn't remember ever feeling so alive—so in love.

CHAPTER SEVENTEEN

A KNOCK SOUNDED.

Alex woke with a start. He squinted as the bright morning sun peeked in through the windows, catching him in the eyes. He glanced over finding Reese still breathing evenly as she lay snuggled beneath the pile of blankets. His thoughts filled with visions of her being in his arms. It had been the most amazing night of his life.

One kiss had led to another. One touch had led to another. And at last they'd ended up curled in front of the fireplace. He recalled how Reese's face had lit up with happiness. The sparkle in her big brown eyes had been his undoing. Her joy had filled a spot in him that he hadn't even known was empty.

He turned away from her sleeping figure and ran a hand over his hair, trying to will away the fogginess of sleep. This wasn't supposed to have happened. He hadn't meant for them to get in so deeply. Not yet. He still had so much to set straight with his family. And yet he couldn't deny that he cared deeply for Reese.

Another knock had him jumping to his feet. The fire had died out hours ago and a distinct chill hung in the air. He rushed to throw on his discarded and now wrinkled clothes. He moved silently across the hardwood floor to the front door.

His personal assistant stood at the door. The older man's face was creased with lines, but nothing in his very proper demeanor gave way to his thoughts of finding Alex in an awkward moment.

"Good morning, Guido." Alex kept his voice low so as not to wake Reese, since they'd gotten very little sleep. "What can I do for you?"

"I'm sorry to interrupt, sir." He also kept his voice to a whisper. "There's an urgent matter you must deal with at the palace."

Alex's chest tightened. He didn't like the sound of that. Thoughts of his papa's health and his brother's latest fiasco raced through his mind. "What is it?"

"There's another problem with a shipment at the port. I don't know the details. Only that you are requested to come immediately. I have a car waiting for you."

"Thank you. I'll be along soon."

"Yes, sir."

Alex closed the door gently. One of the problems with being a small nation was that the government was much more hands-on. He didn't understand why all of a sudden they were having endless problems at the port. And it didn't help matters that the problems seemed to concern a fleet of cargo ships owned by Catherine's father, who had been less than pleased with the last problem, involving a falsified manifest and a very greedy captain.

Alex didn't even want to guess what the harbormaster had uncovered this time. Dread coursed through his body. Still, there was no way around it. The only thing he could hope was that it was another shipping company.

"Who was at the door?" Reese's sleepy voice was deeper than normal and very sexy.

If only Alex didn't have important matters to tend to, he'd spend a leisurely morning with her. But duty came first.

"It was a message from the palace that my attendance is needed."

Reese's eyes widened. "Is something wrong?"

"Nothing for you to worry about. Just a problem at the port." He slipped on his loafers and collected his things. "Take your time. There is food in the kitchen."

"But our presents. We didn't open them—"

"I'm sorry. There's no time now." He glanced at the fanciful packages beneath the tree. "It'll give us something to look forward to later."

"Unless we get distracted again." Her voice was still deep from sleep.

The sultry sound made him groan with frustration. "We'll get to them…eventually."

Her cheeks beamed a crimson hue, but that didn't stop her from teasing him. "I can't promise you that it'll be any time soon. I have plans for you."

"I'll hold you to your word." He leaned down and gave her a lingering kiss that made it almost painful to tear himself away from her. "I'll send the car back for you, but I have no idea how long I'll be."

How could someone be so unhappy when surrounded by such beauty?

Reese paced back and forth. It wasn't so much that she was unhappy…more like bored. Frustrated. Agitated. There was a whole dictionary full of words to describe her mood.

Sure, her palace suite was beautiful, from the high ceiling with its white, blue and gold polychrome tiles to the huge canopied bed. It was like sleeping in a very elegant museum—in fact, the entire palace was like something people only viewed in glossy magazines. It made her hesitant to touch anything for fear of breaking something.

She strolled over to the large window overlooking the sea. The sun was shining and the water was tranquil, unlike her mind, which could not rest. Her thoughts continually drifted back to Alex, as they had done so often since their very special evening together. Her cheeks warmed at the memory of how sweet and loving he'd been with her. It had been a perfect evening. So then why had Alex been gone the past twenty-four hours?

The only message she'd received from him had come the prior evening, when he'd extended his apologies for missing dinner, claiming he had work to do. The note only made her even more curious about his whereabouts. What was so important? And why couldn't he deliver the message in person?

Unable to spend another lonely moment in her opulent suite, she threw on some old comfy jeans and a pink hoodie with a navy-blue New York logo emblazed over it. The clothes certainly weren't anywhere close to the fancy ones she'd been wearing since she'd arrived in Mirraccino, but she didn't feel a need to put on a show today. Besides, where she was headed there wouldn't be any paparazzi. And if there were, she was in no mood to care.

She headed for the private beach, hoping to clear her head—to figure out where she and Alex went from here. The sun warmed her back and helped her to relax. As for Alex, things there were complicated. It wasn't like being in a relationship with the guy next door. But she couldn't just walk away, either. The other night had drastically changed things. She'd given her heart to him.

A smile tugged at her face as she thought of Alex and how far they'd come. When she'd met him, she hadn't wanted a man in her life. She'd been unhappy, even though she hadn't realized it at the time. She'd had her eyes closed to her mother's progress, but Alex had helped her see things that were right in front of her. She'd learned to trust him and that she didn't have to be in control of everything all of the time. In fact, her daily calls to her mother revealed that The Willows was prospering without Reese's presence.

Her steps were light. It was as if she were tiptoeing along the fluffy white clouds dotting the sky. She was humming a little ditty to herself as she strolled down the beach, and then she spotted Alex. He was dressed in blue slacks and a blue button-up shirt with the sleeves rolled up. The breeze off the sea rustled his dark hair, scattering the strands. She was just about to call out to him when she got close enough to notice someone at his side. A woman. She was much shorter, with long dark hair that shimmered in the sun. They leaned toward each other as they laughed about something.

A sick feeling settled in the pit of Reese's stomach. She took a step backward. So this was why he'd been too busy to see her?

No. Alex wouldn't do something like this to her. He'd promised that she could trust him. And she'd given him her heart.

She dragged in a deep breath, hoping to calm her rising heart rate. She was jumping to conclusions. After all, he wasn't her father. He'd never leave her bed to go to another woman. *Have faith. Alex will make this right.*

Reese leveled her shoulders and forced her feet to move in the direction of the man she loved. She refused to be childish and jealous. There was a simple explanation to this. One that would make her feel foolish for jumping to conclusions. Maybe she was his cousin. Or the woman his brother had married. That must be it. He was comforting the woman and passing along a message from his brother.

"Good morning." Reese forced a smile on her face.

They both turned to her. Alex's brows lifted and the woman's eyes lit up as her gaze moved from Alex to Reese and back again. The woman's painted lips lifted into a smile.

Reese's radar was going off loud and clear, but she insisted on giving Alex a chance. "Beautiful morning, isn't it?"

Alex nodded. "Um…yes, it is." The surprise on his face slid behind a blank wall. "Reese, I would like you to meet Catherine."

"It is good to meet you." The woman's voice was warm and friendly. "You are the one helping, no?"

Catherine's English was tough to understand behind a heavy accent. "Yes…yes, I am."

But there was so much more to their relationship. Why did the woman seem a bit confused? Alex had said he'd told Catherine about her. An uneasy feeling settled in her stomach. She'd once again let her naivety get her into trouble. She should have asked him exactly what he'd told the woman. Because it obviously wasn't that he loved Reese. That much was clear.

Catherine smiled and held out her hand. "I would like us to be friends, no?"

Reese didn't have much choice but to force a smile and extend her hand. The sunshine gleamed off the pink sapphire, reminding her of the heated kiss she'd shared with Alex when he'd given it to her. What would Catherine make of the ring?

She searched the woman's face for some hint of hostility or jealousy, but she didn't detect any. The woman truly appeared to be kind and outgoing. What was Reese missing? Had Alex duped them both?

Not understanding any of this, she turned a questioning look to Alex. But his gaze didn't meet hers. Except for the slight tic in his cheek, there was nothing in his outward appearance to let her know that he was uncomfortable with this meeting.

Oblivious to the undercurrents running between Alex and Reese, Catherine said, "You help Alex with paparazzi, no?" The woman's voice was soft and gentle. When Reese nodded, the woman continued to speak. "You are a good woman. He is lucky to have you."

What could she say to that? Though it killed her to exchange pleasantries when all she wanted to do was confront Alex, she uttered, "Thank you."

Alex cleared his throat. "Catherine and I were headed back inside. I have a meeting to attend. Would you care to join us?"

There was no warmth in his voice. No acknowledgement that they were anything more than casual acquaintances. Just the cool politeness of a politician.

"Yes, join us. I want to know about you and New York." Catherine's eyes reflected her sincerity.

With determined reserve, Reese maintained a cool outward appearance. "I think I'll stay out here. I'd like to stretch my legs. One can only be cooped up for so long."

Reese turned to Alex and bit back an impolite comment. There was no way she could be rude to Alex in front of this woman. As much as she wanted to dislike Catherine, she couldn't; she appeared to be a genuinely nice person. In another universe, Reese could imagine being fast friends with Catherine. But not here—not today.

Reese could only presume that the woman didn't know what had transpired between her and Alex the other night. And there was no way she would be the one to tell her. That was Alex's problem.

What she had to say to him—and there was a lot— would have to wait. She didn't need this woman knowing what a fool she'd made of herself, falling for a prince far outside her league.

A look of relief crossed Alex's face. "Then we'll leave you to enjoy the day."

He extended his arm to Catherine, who turned to Reese. "Nice to meet you. We talk later."

"Nice to meet you, too." Reese couldn't believe how hard it was to say those words without choking on her own tongue.

She stood there watching the departing couple. Catherine's head momentarily leaned against Alex's arm, as though she knew him well—very well. The thought slashed into Reese's heart. She was the odd man out.

It wasn't until they turned the corner and headed up the steps toward the palace that Reese realized she'd been holding her breath. She was afraid to breathe out—afraid the balled-up emotions inside her would come tumbling out. She blinked repeatedly, clearing her blurring vision. She wanted to believe that this was some sort of nightmare and she'd wake up soon. Because it just couldn't be possible that she'd been duped into being the other woman.

Her stomach lurched. Her hands wrapped around her midsection as she willed away the waves of nausea. After all of the days and nights of wondering how her father's lover could have carried on an affair—now Reese was in those very uncomfortable shoes. And she hated it.

She started walking down the beach with no destination in mind. Her only thought was to get away. Her steps came faster. Throughout the whole drama with her father's death and finding out that he'd siphoned off their savings, she'd had a hard time believing her mother hadn't known anything about it. How could she not?

Looking back on it, there had been so many clues—so many things that didn't add up. She'd ended up harboring angry feelings toward her mother for allowing all of that to happen to them by turning a blind eye to her father's activities. But now Reese had more compassion for the situation her mother had been in. When you love someone, you trust them.

Reese stopped walking, drawing one quick breath after the other. She glanced around, realizing she'd ended up back at the bungalow. She hadn't realized she'd wandered so far down the beach.

Her legs were tired and her face was warm from the sun, but it was the aching loss in her chest that had the backs of her eyes stinging. She refused to dissolve into a puddle of tears. She wouldn't stop living just because she'd once again let herself be duped by a man. The memory of Alex and Catherine arm in arm and with their heads together, laughing, was emblazoned on her memory. How could she have trusted him?

With renewed anger, she started off for the palace. This fairy tale had come to an end. And like Cinderella, it was time to trade in her gowns for a vacuum and a day planner.

She'd reached the bottom of the steps up the cliff when she spotted Alex sitting there. He didn't notice her at first and she paused, not sure she was up for this confrontation. Still, it was best to meet it head-on and get it over with. She didn't want any lingering *what if*s or *should have*s. This would end things cleanly.

Leveling her shoulders, she headed straight for him. When he saw her, he got to his feet and met her halfway. Lines bracketed his eyes and his face looked as though he'd aged a few years. Was he that worried that she'd blow things for him with Catherine? She took a bit of satisfaction in knowing that he was stressed. It was the least he could feel after he'd used her without any thought to her feelings.

"Reese, you had me worried. You didn't tell anyone where you were going."

She crossed her arms and narrowed her gaze on him. "I'm sure you were too busy to be worried about me."

"That's not fair. You know I care."

"Was Catherine the reason you took off after we spent the night together?" *Right after I'd given you my heart. When I'd at last trusted you.*

"No. I told you there was a problem at the port."

Reese crossed her arms and hitched up a hip. "So what's she doing here?"

"She knew I wanted to speak with her, and since a problem had arisen with one of the ships her father owns, she flew in. I knew nothing of her arrival until last evening."

Reese wasn't about to assume anything this time around. "Does Catherine know how you spent the other night?"

V-shaped lines etched between his brows. "Of course she doesn't know. What kind of man do you think I am? I don't go around discussing personal things."

"The kind who likes to keep a woman on the side like a spare suit or an extra pair of shoes." Her voice quavered with anger. "Is that what I am to you?"

"No, of course not." His blue eyes pleaded with her to believe him, but she was too worked up to be swayed so easily. "But you don't understand. I can't just blurt out to Catherine that I have feelings for you."

"Why?"

He glanced down and rubbed the back of his neck. "Because I won't hurt her like that. She deserves better."

Reese heard the words he hadn't spoken, louder and clearer than anything else. He cared about Catherine. Those powerful words blindsided Reese. They knocked into her full force, stealing the breath from her lungs. She stumbled back.

He had real feelings for Catherine.

Reese's teeth sank into her lower lip, holding in a backlash of anger and a truckload of pain. How stupid could she have been? Catherine oozed money and culture. The woman was a perfect match for a prince. Reese glanced down at her faded jeans and worn sweatshirt. She'd laugh at the comparison, but she was afraid that it'd come out in sobs. She swallowed down her emotions.

"We don't have anything left to say to each other. You should go to her—to your future fiancée."

"You're spinning this out of control. Catherine has nothing to do with you and me."

"Yes, she does. She has everything to do with this. You care about her."

Not me!

A sob caught in the back of her throat. A piercing pain struck her heart, causing a burning sensation at the backs of her eyes. She loved him, but he didn't feel the same way. She clenched her hands, fighting to keep her pain bottled up. She refused to let him see just how deeply he'd hurt her.

"Let me explain. We can work this out—"

"No, we can't." Her nails dug into her palms as she struggled to maintain her composure. "Do you know how much this hurts? It's killing me to stand here. To be so close to you and yet so far away."

He lifted his head and stared up at the blue sky for a moment, as though coming up with a rebuttal. "You don't understand. I do care about her. But I don't love her."

Reese heard the sincerity in his voice and saw the pleading look in his eyes. Maybe he hadn't set out to make her the other woman, but that didn't change the fact that three was a crowd. And she wasn't going to stick around to make a further fool of herself.

"I'm leaving."

Alex reached out, grabbing her arm. "Don't leave like this."

She spun around so fast his eyes widened in surprise. "Why not? What reason do I have to stay?" Her throat burned as the raw words came tumbling out. "Did you end things with Catherine? Did you tell your family the marriage is off?"

He held her gaze. "It's not that easy. Her father is very influential. If he pulls his business from Mirraccino, it'll have a devastating ripple effect on the country's economy. But you must know that I have never made any promises to her. It's all a business arrangement—my duty."

"You're forgetting I saw you two together. You aren't strangers."

"You're right. Catherine and I have been friends since we were kids. But I swear it has never gone further than that—"

"Stop." She wasn't going to let his smooth tongue and convincing words confuse her. "The fact is you can't have us both. It's time you choose between your duty and your desires."

She stood there pleading with her eyes for him to choose her—to choose love. But as the strained silence stretched on, her hopes were dashed. She had no choice but to accept that his duty to the crown would always come first. She might have fallen in love with him, but obviously it was a one-way street.

A tear dripped onto her cheek and she quickly dashed it away. "I—I have some packing to do."

She pulled her shoulders back and moved past him with determined steps. It was time to make a hasty exit before she dissolved into a disgusting puddle of self-pity. And she couldn't let that happen. Her heart was already in tattered ruins. The only thing she had left was her pride.

Alex jogged over to stand in front of her. "Give me time to sort things out."

"You can have all of the time in the world. I'm leaving." Then as an afterthought, she slipped off the pink sapphire and tossed it at him. "And I won't be needing this any longer."

She turned and strode up the beach...alone.

CHAPTER EIGHTEEN

ALEX PLACED THE STORYBOOK Reese had given him for Christmas next to his suitcase.

He probably shouldn't have opened it without her. But after she'd left he'd been so lonely without her that he needed a tangible connection.

He stared down at the hardback copy of *How the Grinch Stole Christmas.* Was she sending him a message? Did she really think his heart was three sizes too small? Probably. And he couldn't blame her for thinking so. He'd made a total mess of things.

Since the day she'd left him standing on the beach, he'd barely slept. He couldn't wipe the devastated look on her face from his mind. For all of his trying to stay aloof and objective, he'd fallen head over heels in love with her.

It wasn't until he'd tried explaining his relationship with Catherine and his family's expectations for him to Reese that he realized he'd spent his entire life being the perfect prince and honor bound to the crown. And he just couldn't do it any longer—not at the expense of his love for the one woman who made him want more than his position within the monarchy, the woman who made him believe that without love, he had nothing.

Now the time had come for him to make his needs a priority, even if they didn't coincide with the family's view of an acceptable life for a prince. At last, he fully understood what his brother had gone through with his brief marriage. And from the look of Demetrius, he really did love that woman. Now Alex wondered if his brother would ever have a chance at true happiness.

However, Alex wasn't the crown prince. He wasn't held to such high standards. He'd made his decision and now he didn't have time to waste. After a few phone calls to make the necessary arrangements, Alex went to meet with the king.

Papa was having breakfast with his brother and Catherine. Alex came to a stop at the end of the formal dining table, more certain than ever that he was doing the right thing.

"You're late." The king pointed at a chair. "Join us."

"I don't have time. I have something urgent I must do."

"I would think Catherine's presence would be your priority."

Alex glanced at Catherine. He'd spoken to her last night and explained how he had planned to do his duty, no matter what was asked of him, but somewhere along the way, he'd lost his heart to a beautiful firecracker from New York. And he just couldn't pass up his one chance to be truly happy. Catherine was happy for him. She had a secret of her own. She was in love with someone, too, but she had been reluctant to do anything about it. Now both Catherine and he could be happy.

She nodded at him, as though giving him encouragement to keep going. He hoped someday he, Reese and Catherine could all be friends. But he had to win back Reese's heart first.

"Catherine and I have spoken and we're not getting engaged. Not now. Not ever."

The king's gaze narrowed. "Alexandro, we've discussed

this and it has been decided that you'll marry Catherine. And it's high time that you do it."

Alex shook his head. "From now on, I'll be making my own decisions about who I marry." He made direct eye contact with the king. "I'll not let you bully me into giving up the woman that I love like you did with Demetrius."

The king's fork clattered against the plate. "I did no such thing. Your brother and that woman decided to part ways of their own accord."

Alex didn't believe it. Demetrius was too distraught to have dumped his wife. But when Alex turned to his twin, his brother nodded his head.

"It's true. Papa didn't split us up."

The king sat back and crossed his arms. Alex wasn't about to give up. This was far too important—Reese was far too important.

Alex continued to stand at attention the way he used to do when he was young and in a world of trouble. "You should also know that I'm not going to drop everything in my life to cover for the latest scandal to strike the family. I have my own life to lead. And my priority is seeking the forgiveness of the woman I love. I've put my duty ahead of her since the day I met her. Now it's time that she comes first."

His brother's mouth gaped. Too bad he hadn't been able to make such a bold move. But the crown prince didn't have as many options.

Everyone grew quiet, waiting for the king's reaction. What would he say? Alex didn't honestly know. The breath caught in his throat as he waited, hoping the king wouldn't disown him.

His papa made direct eye contact with him. "I've done a lot of thinking these past few weeks. Though there are legitimate reasons for a strategic marriage, perhaps there's another way to strike up the necessary allegiances. Who am I to deny my sons a chance to know love like your mother and I shared?"

Alex had to be certain he'd heard the king correctly. "You approve of Reese."

The king's silver head nodded. "When you are in New York, make sure you invite your new princess to the palace for the winter ball. It will be the perfect place to properly introduce her to everyone."

Alex truly liked the idea of escorting Reese to the ball. He just hoped she would find it in her heart to forgive him. "I'll most definitely invite her."

Alex didn't spare any time making his way to the private airstrip. With the king's blessing, he knew that he could now have his family and the woman he loved—if she would forgive him.

CHAPTER NINETEEN

THIS HAS TO WORK.

Alex stared blindly out the car window. Large, fluffy snowflakes fell, limiting visibility. Aside from the snow, his return to New York City was so different than his last visit. This time he was surrounded by his security detail and instead of a wild taxi ride he was settled in the comfortable backseat of a black town car with diplomatic tags. There was no looking over his shoulder. This time it didn't matter who knew he was in town.

His only goal for being here was to win back Reese's trust—her love.

The car tires crunched over the snow. He glanced out the window at the passing houses. They were getting close. His gut tightened. Normally when he had an important speech, he'd make notes and settle most of what he'd say ahead of time. This time, he didn't know what he'd say. He didn't even know if he'd get past the front door.

The car tires spun a bit as the car eased into the driveway. Alex pulled on his leather gloves. Before the car pulled to a full stop, Alex had the back door open. He took the porch steps two at a time.

His foot had just touched the porch when the door swung open. It was Reese. Her long hair was swept back in a smooth ponytail. Her bangs fell smoothly over her forehead.

Her eyes widened as she took in his appearance. "What are you doing here?"

He might have been prepared for the winter weather, but he wasn't prepared for the hard edge in her voice.

"Hello, Reese. You forgot your Christmas presents."

Her eyes grew round. "You flew all the way here to give me some presents?"

"And I thought we should talk—"

"No. Take your presents and go away. We said everything that needed to be said." She waved him away. When he didn't move, she added, "We were a publicity stunt. Nothing more. Now go home to Catherine."

He refused to be deterred. One way or another, she'd hear him out. "I am here on a matter of great importance."

"That's too bad. I'm on my way out. I don't have time to talk."

"Then let me give you a ride." He moved aside so she could see his hired car. Other women he'd met would swoon at this opportunity. But Reese wasn't other women. She wouldn't be easily swayed. But she was most definitely worth the effort.

When he sensed she was about to turn him down, he added, "Either let me take you or expect to see me waiting here when you return."

"You wouldn't."

He arched a brow. There was hardly a thing he wouldn't do to win her back.

She sighed and rolled her eyes. "Fine. If this is what it takes to get rid of you, let's get it over with."

Her pointed words stabbed at his chest. He knew he'd hurt her, but he'd been hoping with time that she would have become more reasonable—more understanding. So much for that wishful thinking. He would have to do a lot of pleading if he was ever going to get her to forgive him.

And he wasn't well versed in apologies. Good thing he was a quick learner.

He waved away the driver, getting the door for her himself. Reese was one of the strongest people he knew. She'd held together her family after her father's betrayal. Not everyone could do that. Now he had to hope that she had enough compassion in her heart for him—to realize that he'd learned from his mistakes.

Reese gave the driver a Manhattan address before turning to Alex. "I hope you really do have something important on your mind. Otherwise you're wasting both our time."

"Trust me. This is very important." She arched a disbelieving brow at him, but he didn't let that deter him. "Do you mind me asking where we're headed?"

"An art school. I've enrolled and this is the first class of the semester. I'm working on my graphic art."

"But what about The Willows? How do you have time to do everything?"

She leaned her head back against the black leather upholstery and stared up at the ceiling. "When I got back from Mirraccino, I found that you were right." Her face contorted into a frown as she made the admission. "I'd been hovering over my mother too much. While I was gone, she handled this place. She regained her footing."

"That's great news. And now you can follow your dreams."

Reese nodded. "It seems my mother and Mr.—erm, Howard are officially dating, too."

"And how does that make you feel?"

She shrugged. "Happy, I guess. After all, it isn't like she owed anything to the memory of my father. So if Howard makes her happy, I'm good with that. Now what brings you here?"

He removed an official invitation with the royal seal from the inner pocket of his black wool coat. He held it out to her. When their fingers brushed, a jolt rushed up his arm and settled in his chest. She quickly pulled back.

He cleared his throat. "Before you open that, I have a few things to say."

She glanced out the window into the snowy afternoon. "Make it quick. We're almost there."

"Reese, I want you to know how sorry I am for not being more up front about my situation with Catherine. I had mentioned you to her on the phone, but I didn't bring up that we were intimately involved. I wasn't sure of Catherine's feelings and didn't want to announce that I wasn't going through with the engagement over the phone."

Reese nailed him with an astonished stare. "So it was better to keep your fiancée in the dark?"

"She was never my fiancée. Not like you're thinking. I never proposed to her. I never loved her. We are friends. Nothing more. In fact, when I told her that you and I were involved, she told me that she was happy to be released from the arrangement because she had fallen in love with someone."

Reese's brows rose. "You're serious."

"Yes. Catherine was as relieved as I was to call off the marriage."

"I bet your family didn't take it well."

"The king respected my decision."

Reese twisted around to look at him face-to-face. "You're really serious? You stood up and told everyone about us?"

"Yes, I did. I realized that I'd let my sense of duty take over my life. I told them that I wouldn't be on call twenty-four-seven to cover up any scandals. You had to come first."

Her eyes opened wide. "You really said that?"

He nodded, reaching out to take her hands in his. "Please believe me. I know I messed up in the past, but I won't let that happen again. No more secrets."

His gaze probed hers, looking for some sign that he was getting through to her. But in a blink her surprise slid behind a solid wall of indifference. Was he wrong about her? Didn't she feel the same as him?

Before he could think of something else to say to convince her to give him another chance, the car pulled to a stop in front of a building.

She grabbed her backpack from the seat. "This is where I get out."

"Can I wait for you? We can talk some more. I know we can work this out."

"No. You've said what you've come here to say. Now please go."

She got out of the car and closed the door with a resounding thud. His chest ached as he watched her walk away. He raked his fingers through his hair and pulled on the short strands as he fought off the urge to go after her.

What had she just done?

Panic clutched Reese's chest. She rushed over to the building, heedless of the coating of snow on the sidewalk. She yanked open the door of the arts building and hustled inside with no real destination in mind. It wasn't until she was away from the wall of windows and out of sight of the car that she stopped and leaned against the wall. It was then that she let out a pent-up breath.

Had she lost her mind?

Had she really just turned down an honest-to-goodness prince?

But it wasn't a royal prince that she loved. It was plain Alex—a living, breathing, imperfect human—the same person who'd hurt her. Alex just happened to come with an impressive title and hung his coat in an amazing palace. But those physical things weren't enough to sway her decision.

The backs of her eyes stung and she blinked, refusing to give in to tears. He'd said all of the right things. Why couldn't she let down her guard? Why couldn't she give him another chance?

She glanced at the large metal clock on the far wall. She had five minutes until her class started. She'd been hoping that going back to school would fill the empty spot in her life—help her forget—but nothing could wipe away the memories of Alex.

Part of her wanted to run back out the door and into his arms. The other part of her said it just wasn't right. Something was missing.

She glanced down at the envelope he'd handed her in the car. Her name was scrolled over the front of the heavy parchment. The royal seal of Mirraccino was stamped onto the back. Curiosity poked at her.

Her finger slipped into the opening in the flap and she ripped along the fold. Inside was an invitation that read:

King Ferdinando of Mirraccino formally invites you to the Royal Winter Ball. The grand fete will take place at the royal palace on Saturday, the seventh of March at six o'clock. The honor of your presence is requested.

Reese stared at the invitation for a moment, stunned that she was holding an invitation to a royal ball. A deep, weary sigh passed her lips. When she went to put the invitation in her purse, it slipped from her fingers and fluttered to the floor.

She bent over to snatch it up when she noticed some handwriting on the back of the invite. She pulled it closer.

Reese, I love you with every fiber of my being. Please be my princess at the ball.
Alex

He loved her!

Those were the words she'd been waiting to hear.

Her lips lifted and her heart pounded. In that moment, the pieces all fell into place. She loved him and he loved her.

In the next breath, the smile slipped from her lips. She'd sent him away. Was it too late? Was he gone for good?

She took off running for the door. He had to be there. He couldn't have left yet.

Please let him still be here.

Practically knocking over a couple of young guys coming through the door, she yelled an apology over her shoulder and kept moving. She stepped onto the sidewalk and stopped.

The black town car was gone. For the first time ever, Alex had finally done as she'd asked. Why now? Tears pricked her eyes.

And then she saw it. The black town car. That had to be the one. It was approaching the end of the block and had on its turn signal.

She had to stop him. Not worrying about the ice or snow, she set off running after the car. She couldn't give up. She was so close to having the man she loved.

The car came to a stop at the intersection. She called out to Alex, not that he would hear her. Then the brake lights went out and the car surged forward. Reese's chest burned as she called out one last time to him.

Then the bright brake lights flashed on and Alex emerged from the back. He sent her a questioning look before he set off toward her with open arms. She rushed toward him with the intention of never leaving his embrace.

After he held her for a moment, he took a step back so they could make eye contact. "I don't understand. What changed your mind?"

"You did."

"But how? When you got out of the car, you were so certain."

She held up the invitation. "What you wrote here said everything I needed to know."

His eyes closed as he sighed. "I was so worried about apologizing that I totally forgot to tell you the most important part. Reese, since I've known you my heart has grown three sizes because it's so full of love for you. I promise I'll tell you every day for the rest of our lives."

She smiled up at him. "Why don't you start now?"

"I love you."

"I love you, too."

EPILOGUE

Two months later...

PRINCE ALEXANDRO CASTANAVO stared across the hallway at Reese. He'd never seen anyone so beautiful. She stole his breath away. And the best part was she was beautiful inside and out. After they'd spent the past couple of weeks at the palace, no one in Mirraccino could deny that Reese would make a generous and kind princess.

Tonight's ball was for the residents of Mirraccino. With it being between growing seasons, this was the nation's chance to celebrate the past year and the royal family's chance to mingle with the citizens—to bring the island together.

And it was Alex's chance to introduce them to the queen of his heart. They were going to love her as much as he did—well, maybe not that much, but pretty close.

He approached and offered his arm to her. She smiled up at him and his heart thumped. How had he ended up being the luckiest man alive?

"May I escort you into the ballroom?"

Reese grabbed the skirt of her royal-blue-and-silver gown and curtsied. Her eyes sparkled with mischief.

"Why yes, Your Highness."

"You know, I like the sound of that." He couldn't help but

tease her back and he put on a serious expression. "Perhaps I'll have you address me as Your Highness all the time."

Reese's mouth gaped. "You wouldn't."

He smiled. "I'm teasing you. I love you the way you are, strong and feisty. I'd never try to change that about you."

Before he could say more, they were summoned inside the ballroom to be announced.

"His Royal Highness, Prince Alexandro Castanavo, and Her Ladyship, Miss Reese Harding."

Before they could be ushered into the crowd, Alex held up his hand, pausing the procession. "If you all will allow me a moment, I have something very special to share."

A hush fell over the crowded room. He fished a black velvet box from his pocket. He was surprised the box had any material left after he'd looked inside at least a couple hundred times trying to decide if it was the right ring for Reese. In the end, he couldn't imagine her with any other ring.

He dropped to one knee and heard Reese's swift intake of breath. He lifted his head and smiled at her, hoping to reassure her. Still, she sent him a wide-eyed gaze.

He took her now trembling hand in his and he realized that perhaps his idea to share this very special moment with everyone he cared about had been a miscalculation. But he was on bended knee now and the room was so quiet that he could hear the beating of his own heart.

"Reese, would you do me the honor of being my princess today and for all of the days of my life?"

Her eyes sparkled with tears of joy as she vigorously nodded. "Yes, I will."

He stood tall and removed the ring from the box. His hands weren't too steady as he slipped the five-carat pink sapphire surrounded by sixty-four diamond side stones onto her finger.

"You kept it." She held up her hand to look at it.

"I thought the ring had a special meaning for us. You aren't disappointed, are you?"

She held up her hand to admire the engagement ring. "I love it!" Her warm gaze moved to him. "But not as much as I love you."

* * * * *

Join Britain's BIGGEST Romance Book Club

50% OFF your first parcel

- EXCLUSIVE offers every month

- FREE delivery direct to your door

- NEVER MISS a title

- EARN Bonus Book points

Call Customer Services
0844 844 1358*

or visit
millsandboon.co.uk/subscriptions

* This call will cost you 7 pence per minute plus your phone company's price per minute access charge.

Wed

1) (7 . 8 . 30 pm)

St Margaret Chapel
House

21 Old Ford Rd
Entrance via Gallery
Café
£ 6.50